PENGUIN (Ⓟ) CLASSICS

THE PENGUIN BOOK OF DRAGONS

SCOTT G. BRUCE is a professor of history at Fordham University. He is the editor of *The Penguin Book of the Undead* and *The Penguin Book of Hell*, and the author of three books about the abbey of Cluny: *Silence and Sign Language in Medieval Monasticism: The Cluniac Tradition, c. 900–1200* (2007); *Cluny and the Muslims of La Garde-Freinet: Hagiography and the Problem of Islam in Medieval Europe* (2015); and, with Christopher A. Jones, *The Relatio metrica de duobus ducibus: A Twelfth-Century Cluniac Poem on Prayer for the Dead* (2016). He has lectured throughout the United States, Canada, and Europe and has held visiting research appointments at the Technische Universität Dresden, in Germany; the Universiteit Gent, in Belgium; and Emmanuel College, University of Cambridge, in the United Kingdom. He worked his way through college as a grave digger.

The Penguin Book
of Dragons

Edited by
SCOTT G. BRUCE

PENGUIN BOOKS

PENGUIN BOOKS

An imprint of Penguin Random House LLC
penguinrandomhouse.com

LIBRARY OF CONGRESS CATALOGING-IN-PUBLICATION DATA
Names: Bruce, Scott G. (Scott Gordon), 1967– editor.
Title: The Penguin book of dragons / edited by Scott G. Bruce.
Description: [New York, New York] : Penguin Books, [2021] |
Includes bibliographical references and index.
Identifiers: LCCN 2021012200 (print) | LCCN 2021012201 (ebook) |
ISBN 9780143135043 (paperback) | ISBN 9780525506690 (ebook)
Subjects: LCSH: Dragons—Folklore. | Dragons—Fiction. |
Dragons in literature.
Classification: LCC GR830.D7 P454 2021 (print) | LCC GR830.D7 (ebook) |
DDC 398.24/54—dc23
LC record available at https://lccn.loc.gov/2021012200
LC ebook record available at https://lccn.loc.gov/2021012201

Printed in the United States of America
5th Printing

Set in Sabon LT Pro

For Gary Gygax (1938–2008),
emperor of the imagination

A dragon is no idle fancy. Whatever may be his origins, in fact or invention, the dragon in legend is a potent creation of men's imagination, richer in significance than his barrow is in gold.

—J. R. R. Tolkien

People who deny the existence of dragons are often eaten by dragons. From within.

—Ursula K. Le Guin

Contents

GUARDIANS OF THE HOARD: THE WYRMS OF NORTHERN LITERATURE

BOOKS OF MONSTERS: DRAGON LORE IN MEDIEVAL EUROPE

DRACONIC DEMONS AND OGRES: DRAGONS IN BYZANTIUM

DRAGONS AND THEIR SLAYERS IN THE LATER MIDDLE AGES

ANTICHRIST ASCENDANT:
DRAGONS IN EARLY MODERN LITERATURE

GODS AND MONSTERS: DRAGONS OF THE EAST

HERE BE DRAGONS:
MONSTROUS HABITATS IN EARLY
MODERN THOUGHT

TERROR TAMED:
DOMESTICATED DRAKES IN CHILDREN'S
LITERATURE

Introduction

We live in the golden age of dragons. The twentieth century witnessed the rapid ascent of these reptilian monsters in popular media and their momentum shows no sign of slowing down. In recent decades, readers have thrilled to the stories of heroes who sparred with weapons and words against dragons in the novels of J. R. R. Tolkien, Ursula K. Le Guin, George R. R. Martin, and J. K. Rowling. Through the magic of special effects, feature films like *The 7th Voyage of Sinbad* (1958) and *Dragonslayer* (1981) have allowed the viewer to experience wonder and awe at the might and majesty of these legendary creatures. Since the 1970s, tabletop role-playing games like Dungeons & Dragons (D&D) have introduced generations of aspiring adventurers to the perils and promises of doing battle with fire-breathing red dragons, poison-spewing black dragons, and lightning-shooting blue dragons. Building on the foundation of D&D, modern video games have gone one step further, allowing players to step into the role of fantasy heroes in imaginary worlds rendered in exquisite digital detail. Since the launch of *World of Warcraft* in 2004, millions of gamers have fought cooperatively against dragons, whether venturing into the dark lairs of Onyxia and Nefarian or launching their assault against the undead frost wyrm Sapphiron in the floating necropolis known as Naxxramas. In the past decade, dragons have featured prominently as "bosses" in many popular video game franchises, including *Dark Souls*, *Elder Scrolls V: Skyrim*, and *Minecraft*, the highest-selling video game in history. Most recently, the HBO series *Game of Thrones* captivated television audiences worldwide and made one of its lead characters Daenerys Targaryen, "Mother of Dragons," a household name.

By any measure, dragons are currently the most popular mythological creature in the human imagination, but our infatuation with these creatures is deeply rooted in the distant past. From classical antiquity to the dawn of the modern age, stories about the menace and mystery of dragons have been told and retold in the heroic and historical literature of Europe and Asia. Ranging from ancient Greece and India to medieval Europe and China to the badlands of modern America, this anthology collects legends and lore about dragons and explores the meaning of these monsters in religious myths and popular folklore. While dragons are ubiquitous around the globe, their character and habitat differ considerably from place to place, from author to author. Modern storytellers have so successfully distilled the essence of the great wyrms of northern European literature sung in mead-halls a millennium ago that it is easy to lose perspective on the rich diversity of dragons in world literature. From the dark halls of the Lonely Mountain to the blue skies of Westeros to the hidden vaults of Gringotts Wizarding Bank, we expect dragons to be gigantic, reptilian predators with massive, batlike wings, who wreak havoc and ruin by breathing fire to defend the gold and other treasures they have hoarded in the deep places of the earth. But dragons are full of surprises. Indeed, many of the stories collected here defy these expectations about the appearance and character of these creatures, their habitat and diet, and their relationship to human beings. As we will see, every culture shaped its dragons according to its needs and fears.

Dragons have a long and storied history that dates back to the earliest human civilizations in the eastern Mediterranean and the Near East. In the ancient world, they took the form of enormous serpents ready to crush with their coils and kill with their venomous breath. They stood guard over sacred groves and springs, their watchfulness implicit in their name in ancient Greek (*drakon*), which derived from the verb

derkomai, "to see." Roman encyclopedists like Pliny classified dragons as exotic fauna inhabiting distant lands, a tradition that persisted among medieval authors. The currency of
dragons did not diminish with the arrival of Christianity,
which transformed these winged giants from living perils
into agents of an older evil and amplified their importance on
a cosmic scale by depicting them as harbingers of the last
days. Northern pagan cultures of medieval Europe nurtured
their own traditions about the meaning of these great reptiles, from the Midgard serpent Jörmungandr of Norse mythology to the fire-breathing dragon of *Beowulf*, the earliest
extant poem in English literature.

Christian authors in premodern Europe were keenly interested in the natural history of dragons and ruminated at length
on their diet and habitats. Borrowing from ancient authorities,
medieval monks classified dragons as the largest of serpents,
recounted their relationship with other animals (especially
their enmity toward elephants), and recorded sightings of them
as portents of evil tidings. Time and again, however, these
natural explanations gave way to allegorical interpretations:
dragons almost always represented the Devil in the medieval
worldview. This interpretation was dominant in medieval
Byzantium as well, but with some surprising differences. Like
their western counterparts, medieval Greek authors were fas-
cinated with dragons, but in contrast to the Latin tradition,
they sometimes presented them as monstrous ogres rather than
giant serpents. By the later Middle Ages, dragons featured
prominently as the adversaries of Christian heroes in Arthurian legend, story cycles related to the crusades, and the lives
of holy champions like Saint George and Saint Margaret.

Far from the world of medieval Europe, the literature of
premodern Arabia, South Asia, China, and Japan presented
an altogether different image of dragons. To be sure, eastern
tales often depicted these creatures as fearful enemies to
highlight the martial prowess of noble heroes, but in the
Asian imagination dragons could also be vulnerable victims
who recruited human allies to fight for them against even

greater foes. In these stories, eastern dragons shared remarkable affinities with human beings by assuming the form of beautiful men and women and living in sumptuous dwellings with all the accoutrements of aristocratic life. Their attraction to humans could even lead to romantic relationships. Unlike the tales about their western cousins, legends about Asian dragons featured water rather than fire as a prominent motif. These eastern dragons controlled the flow of rivers, sometimes to the detriment of humankind; and they were often aquatic creatures themselves, who lived at the bottom of lakes and oceans. Moreover, as Chinese medical texts show, the body parts of dragons, particularly their bones, were highly prized for their curative properties, an aspect of dragon lore that held little interest for most European authors.

By the early modern period, dragons were on the wane in the western tradition. In literature, they retreated to the realm of allegory, like the serpentine adversaries in Edmund Spenser's poem *The Faerie Queene*, which were metaphors for vices in opposition to the virtues of the knights who vanquished them. Drawing on the work of ancient and medieval authors, Renaissance polymaths treated dragons as living creatures, but they pushed their habitats to the unexplored places of the earth, like distant oceans or deep underground. By the late nineteenth century, the march of human progress had all but eroded the last refuges of the premodern dragon. It was at this moment, however, that a remarkable inversion occurred. In contrast to ancient and medieval literary traditions, for the first time European authors began to domesticate dragons in stories that depicted these creatures as friends to humankind rather than enemies, with children playing a leading role in these narratives.

Stories about dragons have endured in cultures around the globe for over two millennia, their appeal tenacious for several reasons. Rippling with power and snorting flames, dragons are the test against which we measure the limits of the heroes we venerate. Inhabiting the fringes of the world, first in distant countries and then in places deep below the earth, dragons mark the boundary between the known and the unknown. Providing a malleable template for mythmakers and storytellers, dragons persist in our imagination both as flesh-and-blood monsters and as powerful metaphors for sin and other destructive forces. By the dawn of modernity, dragons were already in full retreat before the advance of human knowledge, but the domestication of these monsters in children's literature gave them a new lease on life, ensuring their survival as friends and as foes for generations to come.

SCOTT G. BRUCE

Suggestions for Further Reading

Arnold, Martin. *The Dragon: Fear and Power*. London: Reaktion Books, 2018.

Good Dragons Are Rare: An Inquiry into Literary Dragons East and West. Ed. Fanfan Chen and Thomas Honegger. Frankfurt: Peter Lang, 2009.

Honegger, Thomas. *Introducing the Medieval Dragon*. Cardiff: University of Wales Press, 2019.

Jones, David E. *An Instinct for Dragons*. New York and London: Routledge, 2002.

Lionarons, Joyce Tally. *The Medieval Dragon: The Nature of the Beast in Germanic Literature*. Enfield Lock, Middlesex: Hisarlik Press, 1998.

Ogden, Daniel. *Drakōn: Dragon Myth and Serpent Cult in the Greek and Roman Worlds*. Oxford: Oxford University Press, 2013.

Rauer, Christine. *Beowulf and the Dragon: Parallels and Analogues*. Rochester, NY: D. S. Brewer, 2000.

Acknowledgments

This book completes a trilogy of historical anthologies about the frontiers of the premodern imagination begun with *The Penguin Book of the Undead* (Penguin Classics, 2016) and continued with *The Penguin Book of Hell* (Penguin Classics, 2018). The scope and contents of each of these books developed in conversation with my editor John Siciliano, whose guidance and encouragement have been essential. I am also deeply indebted to numerous collaborators, colleagues, and students, who contributed to this book in meaningful ways. Professor Paul Acker (Saint Louis University) and Professor Anthony Kaldellis (Ohio State University) skillfully rendered the translations in chapters 3 and 5, respectively. Dr. Darius M. Klein kindly allowed me to adapt his translation of Athanasius Kircher's discussion of dragons for inclusion in chapter 9. Three PhD candidates in the Department of History at Fordham University lent their linguistic expertise and enthusiasm as well: Benjamin Bertrand, Douglass Hamilton, and W. Tanner Smoot. I am grateful to Professor Carla Nappi (University of Pittsburgh) and Professor Timothy Brook (University of British Columbia) for their assistance with Asian dragons. Professor Nick Paul (Fordham University) directed me to Herman of Tournai's dragon story in chapter 4, while Shannon Chakraborty recommended that I read *The Book of Kings* by Abolqasem Ferdowsi for chapter 8. I am also indebted to the undergraduate students who read and discussed many of these texts with me in History 3213 (Monsters, Magic, and the Undead: Stranger Things in Medieval Europe), which I taught at Fordham University in the fall semester of 2019. I completed this book with the support of a Faculty Fellowship from Fordham University, which relieved me from the burdens of teaching in the fall of 2020. Professor Christopher A. Jones (Ohio State University) and Dr. Julie Barrau (University of Cambridge) provided last-minute bibliographical assistance at a moment's notice, as good friends do. My thanks to Benjamin Bertrand, Amanda Racine, and W. Tanner Smoot for checking the page proofs of the manuscript. I owe my greatest thanks, as always, to Anne, Mira, and Vivienne, who love stories about dragons just as much as I do.

The Penguin Book
of Dragons

ANCIENT ENEMIES

Monstrous Snakes in the Greco-Roman World

The prominence of giant serpents in the imagination of the ancient Greeks and Romans was inscribed in the heavens. The undulating chain of stars in the northern sky known as Draco *(Latin for "dragon") was among the dozens of constellations described by the Roman astronomer Ptolemy in the second century CE. Greek and Latin authors identified this celestial dragon with the serpentine monsters vanquished by their mythological heroes, especially Hercules, whose constellation stands in close proximity to Draco. The dragons of Greco-Roman mythology shared a number of attributes that remained remarkably consistent over centuries of storytelling. They were usually depicted as massive snakes inhabiting sacred groves in remote places, where they guarded treasure and promised a quick death to trespassers with their lethal venom and crushing coils. Their monstrous menace amplified the courage and strength of the heroes who vanquished them. But dragons were not confined to the realm of legend in ancient literature. Classical authors also wrote about them as natural creatures. Roman poets provided breathless accounts of encounters between Roman legions and deadly monsters in far-flung theaters of war, while naturalists collected information about their habitats and diet. Dragons were living and breathing monsters in Greco-Roman literature and history, but they were always a distant threat, their menace mitigated by time and space.*

THE HYDRA OF LERNA[1]

As a child, the demigod Hercules strangled with his bare hands two serpents sent by the goddess Hera to slay him in his crib, thus foreshadowing not only his heroic power but also his confrontation with the Hydra of Lerna, a reptilian monster with nine serpentine heads. As an adult, Hercules performed twelve difficult tasks in the service of King Eurystheus. The second of these labors was the slaying of the Lernaean hydra that ravaged the countryside in the western Peloponnese in Greece. The longest version of the story appears in The Library, *a compendium of ancient Greek legends compiled in the second century CE and attributed to Apollodorus of Athens. According to Apollodorus, this task was especially difficult because the hydra sprouted two heads for each one that Hercules smashed with his club. With the help of his nephew Iolaus, however, the hero managed to cauterize the hydra's severed heads with torches to prevent them from growing back again and eventually killed the beast. Later commentators complained that Hercules deserved no credit for this labor, because he enlisted his nephew's aid rather than defeating the hydra by himself.*

As a second labor, Eurystheus ordered Hercules to kill the Lernaean hydra. That creature, bred in the swamp of Lerna, used to go forth into the plain and ravage both the cattle and the countryside.[2] Now the hydra had a huge body with nine heads, eight mortal, but the middle one immortal. So, mounting a chariot driven by Iolaus, Hercules came to Lerna, and having halted his horses, he discovered the hydra on a hill beside the springs of the Amymone, where its den was located.[3]

By pelting it with fiery arrows, he forced it to come out, and in the act of doing so he seized and held it fast. But the hydra wound itself around one of his feet and clung to him. Nor could he accomplish anything by smashing its heads with his club, for as fast as one head was smashed there grew up two more. A huge crab also came to the help of the hydra by biting Hercules' foot, so he killed it, and in his turn called to Iolaus for help, who set fire to a piece of wood and burned the roots of the hydra's heads with the brands, thus preventing them from sprouting. Having thus got the better of the sprouting heads, Hercules chopped off the immortal head and buried it and put a heavy rock on it, beside the road that leads through Lerna to Elaeus. But the body of the hydra he cut up and dipped his arrows in the gall. But Eurystheus said that this labor should not be reckoned among the ten because Hercules had not defeated the hydra by himself, but with the help of Iolaus.

MEDUSA,
MOTHER OF MONSTERS[1]

A century after the fall of the Roman Republic, Lucan (39–65 CE) composed the Pharsalia, *an epic poem about the civil war between Julius Caesar and Pompey. The ninth book of the poem was set in Africa, where the Roman forces loyal to Caesar regrouped after the death of Pompey at the hands of the ruling pharaoh of Egypt, Ptolemy XIII. Here the poet digressed to tell the story of the dreaded Medusa, a monstrous woman with snakes for hair, who lurked in the desert wastes of Libya. This fearful aberration, whose gaze turned people to stone, was defeated by the hero Perseus, who cut off her head with a magical sword. According to Lucan, the gore dripping from the Gorgon's severed head seeded the landscape of Libya with venomous serpents and winged dragons large enough to hunt elephants. This story was no idle distraction. Lucan's readers would have immediately recognized the parallels between Perseus's defeat of the Medusa and Rome's final conquest of the northern coast of Africa. In both cases, the heroes of reason and order triumphed over the forces of frenzy and chaos.*

Why the air of Libya abounds in so many plagues and is fruitful of death, or what secretive Nature has mixed in its harmful soil, our study and toil to know has been to no avail, besides the story that has spread throughout the world beguiling it for centuries, in place of the true cause. At Libya's farthest edges, where burning earth meets the Ocean heated by the sinking sun, sprawl the wastelands of Medusa, daughter of Phorcys. No forest canopy covers them, no sap softens them. A harsh land, rough with the rocks of those who beheld the gaze of its mistress, in whose body Nature, being cruel, first gave birth to nasty pests. From her throat snakes poured their piercing hisses with trembling tongues, and flowing down her back like a woman's hair, they lashed Medusa's neck, which gave her pleasure. The serpents rose up straight above her brow, and viper venom streamed down when she combed her locks.

Poor Medusa, these are what she had that everyone was free to gaze at with impunity. For whoever feared that monster's face and gaping jaws? Whoever looked Medusa straight in the face did she allow to die? She snatched fates while they wavered, preventing fear. Limbs perished with breath still in them, shades did not escape but froze deep down in the bones. The Eumenides' hair would only stir up fury, Cerberos calmed his hissing when Orpheus sang, Amphitryon's son saw the Hydra he was beating. *This* monster was feared by her own father, Phorcys, the waters' second power, and her mother, Ceto, and her sister Gorgons. She could threaten heaven and sea with uncommon sluggishness and cover the world with earth. Suddenly birds grew heavy and fell from the sky, beasts clung fast to rocks, whole tribes of Ethiopians living nearby were hardened into marble. No animal could endure the sight of her, and even her own serpents recoiled to avoid the face of the Gorgon. She turned Atlas, the Titan who holds up the Western Pillars, into rocky crags, and long ago when heaven feared the Giants rearing up on serpent tails in Phlegra, she turned them into mountains, and so the Gorgon on the breastplate of Pallas brought an end to that monstrous war of gods.

Here came Perseus, after his birth from Danae and the shower of gold, carried on the Parrhasian wings he got from Arcadia's god (inventor of the kithara and wrestling oil), swift and sudden he flew, carrying the Cyllenian saber—a saber already bloody from another monster, for it had killed the guardian of the cow that Jove had loved—and maiden Pallas helped her flying brother, getting from the bargain the monster's head. She instructed Perseus to turn round toward the sunrise once he reached the border of Libya, and to fly backward across the Gorgon's realms. For his left hand she gave him a gleaming shield of burnished bronze, in which she ordered him to watch out for Medusa, who turns things to stone.

The deep sleep that would drag her down into the eternal rest of death had not completely overwhelmed her. Much of her hair is awake and watching, snakes stretch out from her locks and defend her head, while some lie sleeping down over her face, shadowing her eyes. Pallas herself guides Perseus's trembling hand, and as he turns away she aims the shaky saber that Hermes gave him, breaking the broad neck that bore all those snakes.

What did the Gorgon's face look like then, with her head cut off and the wound from that hooked blade? I would imagine her mouth exhaled a mass of poison, and how much death poured out of her eyes! Not even Pallas could look, and they would have frozen the averted gaze of Perseus, if Tritonia had not shaken that thick hair and covered the face with snakes. So he grabbed the Gorgon and fled on wings to the sky.

He was about to change course and cut a shorter path through the air by plowing straight through the middle of Europe's cities, but Pallas told him not to harm those lands and to spare their peoples. For who would not gaze up in the sky at such a marvelous flight? He bends his wings into the west wind, heading over Libya, which sows and tends no crops and lies empty, exposed to stars and Phoebus: the beaten path of the sun furrows into it, burning out its soil. Nor does night fall deeper over the heavens of any land, obstructing the course of the moon if she forgets the slant of her wandering and runs straight across the zodiac signs, instead of fleeing north or south to avoid the shadow. Although that land is barren and its fields grow nothing good, it draws in the poison of Medusa's dripping gore, the dreadful dewdrops of that savage blood which heat gave strength, cooking it down into the stinking sand.

Here the gore first stirred a head out of the dust and raised up the neck of the asp, swollen with the sleep it gives. More blood fell there with a thick drop of poison, and so no serpent contains more of it. Needing heat, she doesn't pass into chilly regions and by her own will ranges the sands as far as the Nile. Nevertheless (when will our greed for profit give us shame?) Libyan forms of death are sought out here and we have made a commodity of the asp.

But the bizarre *haemorrhois* unrolls its scaly coils and stops its victims' blood from clotting at all. And the *chersydros* was born, it dwells among the Syrtes' pools and shoals, and the *chelydros*, which draws a smoking trail, and the *cenchris*, which always glides along in a straight line. The many markings on its belly are finer grained than the flecks of color in Theban serpentine. The *ammodytes* look exactly like burned sand, and the *cerastes* roves with curving spine. The *scytale* is unique in shedding its skin even when there's frost; the *dipsas* is hot and dry; the *amphisbaena* is burdened with two heads, each trying to turn it. The *natrix* pollutes its waters, the *iaculus* has wings; the *parias* is content to furrow a path with its tail, and the *prester* opens wide his ravenous fuming mouth; the *seps* corrupts the body, even dissolving bones. And raining hisses that terrify all other pests, harming without venom, the basilisk clears out all the rabble far and wide and reigns over desolate sands.

You dragons, too, who creep along in every land and are regarded as harmless spirits, gleaming bright as gold, scorching Africa makes you deadly. High in the air you mount on wings and hunt entire herds, winding your tails around enormous bulls, you lash them into submission. Not even elephants are big enough to be safe. You deal death to everything without resort to venom.

CADMUS AND THE DRAGON OF ARES[1]

A colossal reptile played a pivotal role in the legend of the foundation of the city of Thebes in Boeotia (central Greece). As told by Ovid (43 BCE–17 CE) in his epic poem of mythological stories called The Metamorphoses, *a Phoenician hero named Cadmus arrived in Greece in search of his sister Europa, who had been abducted by Zeus. There Cadmus consulted the oracle at Delphi, who instructed him to follow a wild cow to the place where he would establish a new city. Unfortunately, the heifer halted near a spring sacred to the god Ares (Mars) that was guarded by a gigantic serpent. After vanquishing the monster with his iron javelin, Cadmus was instructed by the goddess Athena to sow the dragon's teeth into the earth "as the seeds from which his people would spring." Much to his amazement, dozens of warriors sprang up from the furrows and fought a pitched battle against each other until only five remained. These survivors made a truce and founded the city of Thebes with Cadmus. Tracing their descent from these mythical warriors, members of the Theban nobility allegedly bore a birthmark shaped like a spearhead. For his part, Cadmus was not so fortunate. Ares later transformed him and his wife into snakes in revenge for slaying the guardian of his sacred spring. This legend gave rise to the phrase "sowing the dragon's teeth," an expression that still refers to any action that leads to a troubled outcome.*

Cadmus wandered over the whole world; for who can lay hands on what Jove has stolen away? Driven to avoid his native country and his father's wrath, he made a pilgrimage to Apollo's oracle, and begged him to say what land he should dwell in. This was Phoebus's reply: "In solitary pastures you will come upon a heifer, which has never felt the yoke, nor drawn the crooked plough. Go on your way with her to guide you, and when she lies down in the grass, there build your city walls, and call the place Boeotia."

Cadmus went down from the Castalian grotto: almost at once he saw a heifer walking slowly along with none to guard her. There was no trace of harness upon her neck. He followed her, keeping close behind, and offered a silent prayer of thanksgiving to Phoebus, who had directed his way.

They passed by the shallow pools of Cephisus and through the lands of Panope. When they had gone so far, the heifer stopped, lifted up her head, graced with lofty horns, and raising it towards the sky filled the air with her lowings. She looked back at the friends who were following her; then, sinking to her knees, lay down on her side in the tender grass. Cadmus gave thanks, kissed the foreign soil, and greeted fields and mountains to which he was as yet a stranger. Then, intending to offer sacrifice to Jove, he ordered his attendants to go in search of fresh spring water, for a libation.

There was an ancient forest which no axe had ever touched, and in the heart of it a cave, overgrown with branches and osiers, forming a low arch with its rocky walls, rich in bubbling springs. Hidden in this cave dwelt the serpent of Mars, a creature with a wonderful golden crest; fire flashed from its eyes, its body was all puffed up with poison, and from its mouth, set with a triple row of teeth, flickered a three-forked tongue. The Phoenician travelers entered the grove on their ill-omened errand and dipped their pitchers in the waters. At the sound, the dark gleaming serpent put forth its head from the depths of the cave, hissing horribly. The blood drained from the men's limbs, the jugs fell from their grasp, and they shuddered with sudden dread. As for the snake, it coiled its scaly loops in writhing circles, then with a spring shot up in a huge arc, raising more than half its length into the insubstantial air, till it looked down upon the whole expanse of the forest. It was as huge as the Serpent that twines between the two Bears in the sky, if its full length were seen uncoiled. Without a moment's pause the monster seized upon the Phoenicians, while some of them were getting their weapons ready, and some were preparing to flee. Others were too terrified to do either. With its fangs, its constricting coils, and tainted poisonous breath, it slew them all.

The noonday sun had reduced the shadows to their shortest. Agenor's son, wondering what was detaining his friends, went out to look for them. His shield was a lion's skin, his weapon a lance with shining point. He had a javelin too, and courage that was of more avail than any weapon. When he entered the grove he saw the dead bodies, and their monstrous foe, towering triumphant above them, the blood dripping from its tongue as it licked their cruel wounds. "My faithful friends," cried Cadmus, "I shall avenge your death, or share it!" As he spoke he lifted a great boulder in his right hand and hurled this huge missile with tremendous force. Towering walls with lofty battlements would have been shaken by the impact: but the serpent was unharmed. Protected by its scales as by a breastplate, and by the toughness of its black skin, it repelled the stoutest blows. But that same toughness was not proof against the javelin, which struck home in a coil in the middle of the creature's sinuous back: the whole iron tip sank deep into its belly. Maddened with pain, the serpent twined its head round to look at its back, and seeing the wound, bit at the shaft of the spear that was lodged there. By violent efforts it loosened the shaft all round, and just managed to drag it out: but the iron remained fixed in its bones. Then indeed, when this fresh irritation increased its normal savagery, the veins of the snake's throat filled and swelled with poison and white foam flecked its venomous jaws. Its scales rasped along the ground and its breath, rank as that from Stygian caves, spread foulness through the air. Now it coiled itself into huge spirals, now shot up straighter than a tree, or again, like a river swollen by the rains, swept violently along, its breast brushing aside the woods which barred the way. Cadmus drew back a little, received the onslaught on his lion's shield and, using his spear point as a barrier, blocked the threatening jaws. The serpent, in a frenzy, bit uselessly at the hard iron, and fastened its teeth on the point of the spear. Now the blood began to flow from its poison-laden throat, spattering the green grass. But the wound was a slight one, for the snake retreated from the blow, drawing back its injured neck; by yielding ground, it prevented the weapon from striking home, or entering more deeply. Meanwhile the son of Agenor kept pressing close, driving in the iron he had fixed in its throat; until an oak tree blocked the backward movement, and its neck was pinned to the trunk. The tree bent beneath the serpent's weight and groaned as the end of the creature's tail thrashed against its bark.

While the victorious Cadmus stood, eyeing the huge bulk of his defeated foe, suddenly a voice was heard. It was not easy to tell where it came from, but heard it was. "Son of Agenor, why stare at the snake you have slain? You, too, will become a serpent, for men to gaze upon." The colour drained from Cadmus' cheeks, and for a long time he stood panic-stricken, frozen with fear, his hair on end, his senses reeling.

Then Pallas, the hero's patroness, suddenly appeared, gliding down through the upper air. She told him to plough up the earth, and to sow the serpent's teeth, as seeds from which his people would spring. He obeyed, and after opening up furrows with his deep-cutting plough, scattered the teeth on the ground as he had been bidden, seeds to produce men. What followed was beyond belief: the sods began to stir; then, first of all a crop of spearheads pushed up from the furrows, and after them came helmets with plumes nodding on their painted crests. Then shoulders and breasts and arms appeared, weighed down with weapons, and the crop of armoured heroes rose into the air. Even so, when the curtains are pulled up at the end of a show in the theatre, the figures embroidered on them rise into view, drawn smoothly upwards to reveal first their faces, and then the rest of their bodies, bit by bit, till finally they are seen complete, and stand with their feet resting on the bottom hem.

Cadmus was terrified at the sight of this new enemy and

was about to seize his weapons: but one of the warriors whom the earth had produced cried out to him: "Don't take to arms! Keep clear of this family conflict!" With these words he drove his unyielding sword into one of his earthborn brothers, who was standing close at hand; then fell himself, pierced by a javelin thrown from a distance. The man who had killed him lived no longer than he did himself; he, too, gasped out the breath he had so lately received. The whole host fought madly in the same way, dealing each other wounds in turn. In the struggle which they had themselves begun, these short-lived brothers perished; until, of all the young warriors granted so brief a span of life, only five remained—the rest lay writhing on the bosom of their mother earth, which was all warm with their blood. One of the five survivors, Echion, flung down his arms, at the bidding of Pallas, promising to fight no more, and asking the same promise from his brothers. These were the companions with whom the foreigner from Phoenicia undertook the task of founding his city, as instructed by Phoebus's oracles.

THE DEATH OF LAOCOÖN[1]

*The Greek gods employed enormous serpents not only as
the guardians of sacred places but also as the violent instruments of their will. Such was the case in the story of a
priest of Neptune named Laocoön, as told by the Roman
poet Virgil (70–19 BCE). During their decade-long war
with Troy, the Greeks sent a giant wooden horse to the
gates of the besieged city. Laocoön warned his compatriots
that they should not accept gifts from their enemies. He
had good reason to be suspicious because the Trojan horse
was, in fact, a clever ruse hatched by the cunning of Odys-
seus: dozens of Greek warriors hid inside with plans to
attack the unwary Trojans and open their city gates under
the cover of darkness. When Laocoön advised his people
to burn the giant horse, the goddess Athena (Minerva), a
staunch ally of the Greeks, sent two giant serpents to crush
him to death before he could unmask their plans. With Laocoön silenced by the coils and venom of these monsters,
the Trojans brought the giant horse into their city and thus
precipitated its downfall.*

"But a new portent strikes our doomed people
Now—a greater omen, far more terrible, fatal,
shakes our senses, blind to what was coming.
Laocoön, the priest of Neptune picked by lot,
was sacrificing a massive bull at the holy altar
when—I cringe to recall it now—look there!
Over the calm deep straits off Tenedos swim
twin, giant serpents, rearing in coils, breasting
the sea-swell side by side, plunging toward the shore,
their heads, their blood-red crests surging over the waves,
their bodies thrashing, backs rolling in coil on mammoth coil

and the wake behind them churns in a roar of foaming spray,
and now, their eyes glittering, shot with blood and fire,
flickering tongues licking their hissing maws, yes, now
they're about to land. We blanch at the sight, we scatter.
Like troops on attack they're heading straight for Laocoön—
first each serpent seizes one of his small young sons,
constricting, twisting around him, sinks its fangs
in the tortured limbs, and gorges. Next Laocoön
rushing quick to the rescue, clutching his sword—
they trap him, bind him in huge muscular whorls,
their scaly backs lashing around his midriff twice
and twice around his throat—their heads, their flaring necks
mounting over their victim writhing still, his hands
frantic to wrench apart their knotted trunks,
his priestly bands splattered in filth, black venom
and all the while his horrible screaming fills the skies,
bellowing like some wounded bull struggling to shrug
loose from his neck an axe that's already struck awry,
to lumber clear of the altar . . .
Only the twin snakes escape, sliding off and away
to the heights of Troy where the ruthless goddess
holds her shrine, and there at her feet they hide,
vanishing under Minerva's great round shield."

THE DRAGON OF
BAGRADA RIVER[1]

The forbidding and inhospitable terrain of northern Africa was the cradle of giant reptiles in the Roman imagination (see pp. 7–10). During the First Punic War against the Carthaginians (256–241 BCE), Roman soldiers learned firsthand the hazards of campaigning in the African wilderness. At the outset of the war, the statesman and general Marcus Atilius Regulus led the initial assault on the city of Carthage. As his troops crossed the Bagrada River (the modern Medjerda River in Tunisia), they encountered a creature born of nightmares, a serpent of unrivaled size and strength that fell upon the Roman troops with lethal intent. In an act of exemplary heroism, Regulus rallied his soldiers to fight the monster and brought it low with a shower of spears and heavy blows from their catapults. In the sixth book of his epic poem about the Punic Wars (Punica), the Roman author Silius Italicus (ca. 28–ca. 102 CE) captivated readers with his thrilling account of the battle told from the point of view of an eyewitness. While this poem was almost unknown in medieval Europe, the story of the dragon of Bagrada River was frequently retold by naturalists and historians in late antiquity, who claimed that the surviving soldiers brought the remains of this creature back to Rome, where they displayed in public both its jawbone and its skin, which allegedly measured 120 feet in length.

"The turbid stream of Bagrada furrows the sandy desert with sluggish course; and no river in the land of Libya can boast that it spreads its muddy waters further or covers the wide plains with greater floods. Here, in that savage land, we were glad to encamp upon its banks; for we needed water, which is scarce in that country. Hard by stood a grove whose trees were ever motionless and sunless, with shade dark as Erebus; and from it burst thick fumes that spread a noisome stench through the air. Within it was a dreadful dwelling, a vast subterranean hollow in a winding cavern, where the dismal darkness let in no light. I shudder still to think of it. A deadly monster lived there, spawned by Earth in her wrath, whose like scarce any generation of men can see again; a serpent, a hundred ells in length, haunted that fatal bank and the Avernian grove. He filled his vast maw and poison-breeding belly with lions caught when they came for water, or with cattle driven to the river when the sun was hot, and with birds brought down from the sky by the foul stench and corruption of the atmosphere. On the floor lay half-eaten bones, which he had belched up in the darkness of his cave after filling his maw with a hideous meal of the flocks he had laid low. And, when he was fain to bathe in the foaming waters of the running stream and cool the heat engendered by his fiery food, before he had plunged his whole body in the river, his head was already resting on the opposite bank. Unwitting of such a danger I went forth; and with me went Aquinus, a native of the Apennines, and Avens, an Umbrian. We sought to examine the grove and find out whether the place was friendly. But as we drew near, an unspoken dread came over us, and a mysterious chill paralyzed our limbs. Yet we went on and prayed to the Nymphs and the deity of the unknown river, and then ventured, though anxious and full of fears, to trust our feet to the secret grove. Suddenly from the threshold and outer entrance of the cave there burst forth a hellish whirlwind and a blast fiercer than the frantic East-wind; and a storm poured forth from the vast hollow, a hurricane in which the baying of Cerberus was heard. Horror-struck we gazed at one another. A noise came from the ground, the earth was shaken, the cave fell in ruins, and the dead seemed to come forth. Huge as the snakes that armed the Giants when they stormed heaven, or as the hydra that wearied Hercules by the waters of Lerna, or as Juno's snake that guarded the boughs with golden foliage—even so huge he rose up from the cloven earth and raised his glittering head to heaven, and first scattered his slaver into the clouds and marred the face of heaven with his open jaws. Hither and thither we fled and tried to raise a feeble shout, though breathless with terror; but in vain; for the sound of his hissing filled all the grove. Then Avens, blind with sudden fear—blameworthy was his act, but Fate had him in the toils—hid in the huge trunk of an ancient oak, hoping that the horrible monster might not see him. I can scarce believe it myself; but the serpent, clinging with its huge coils, removed the great tree bodily, tearing it up from the ground, and wrenching it up from the roots. Then, as the trembling wretch called on his companions with his last utterance, the serpent seized him and swallowed him down with a gulp of its black throat—I looked back and saw it—and buried him in its beastly maw. Unhappy Aquinus had entrusted himself to the running stream of the river and was swimming fast away. But the serpent attacked him in midstream, carried his body to the bank, and there devoured it—a dreadful form of death!

"Thus I alone was suffered to escape from the monster so terrible and deadly. I ran as fast as grief would let me and told all to the general. He groaned aloud, in pity for the cruel fate of his men. Then, eager as he ever was for war and battle and conflict with the foe, and burning with a passion for great achievements, he ordered his men to arm instantly, and his cavalry, well tried in many a fight, to take the field. He galloped forward himself, spurring his flying steed; and at his command there followed a body of shieldsmen, bringing the heavy catapults used in sieges and the weapon whose huge point can batter down high towers. And now, when the horses speeding over the grassy plain surrounded the fatal spot with the thunder of their hoofs, the serpent, aroused by the neighing, glided forth from his cave and hissed forth a hellish blast from his reeking jaws. Both his eyes flashed horrible fire; his erected crest towered over the tall tree tops; and his three-forked tongue darted and flickered through the air and rose up till it licked the sky. But, when the trumpets sounded, he was startled and reared aloft his huge bulk; then, couching on his rear, he gathered the rest of his body beneath his front in circling coils. Then he began a fearsome conflict, quickly unwinding his coils and stretching his body out to its full length, till he reached in a moment the faces of men far away. All the horses snorted, in their terror of the serpent, refusing to obey the rein and breathing frequent fire from their nostrils. The monster, towering above the frightened men with swollen neck, waved his high head to right and left and, in his rage, now hoisted them on high, and now delighted in crushing them beneath his huge weight. Then he breaks their bones and gulps down the black gore; with his open jaws wet with blood, he leaves the half-eaten body and seeks a fresh foe. The soldiers fell back, and the victorious serpent attacked the squadrons from a distance with his pestilential breath. But then Regulus speedily recalled the troops to battle and encouraged them thus: 'Shall we, the men of Italy, retreat before a serpent, and admit that Rome is no match for the snakes of Libya? If his breath has conquered your feeble strength, and your courage has oozed away at sight of his open mouth, then I will go boldly forward and cope with the monster single-handed.' Thus he shouted and undismayed hurled his flying spear through the air with lightning speed. The weapon rushed on and did its work: it struck the serpent fairly on the head, gaining not a little force from the fierceness of the creature's charge, and stuck there quivering. A shout of triumph rose, and the sudden noise of it went up to Heaven. At once the earth-born monster went mad with rage: he spurned defeat and was a stranger to pain; for never before in his long life had he felt the steel. Nor would the swift charge, prompted by his pain, have failed, had not Regulus, skilled horseman that he was, eluded the onset with wheeling speed, and then, when the serpent, with a bend of its supple back, once again followed the turning horse, pulled the rein with his left hand and soon got out of reach.

"But Marus did not merely look on at such a scene and take no part: my spear was the second to transfix the great body of the monster. His three-forked tongue was now licking the rump of the general's tired horse; I threw my weapon and quickly turned on myself the serpent's fierce assault. The men followed my example and hurled their darts together with a will, making the creature shift its rage from one foe to another; and at length he was restrained by a blow from a catapult that would level a wall. Then at last his strength was broken; for his injured spine could no longer stand up stiff for attack, and the head had no strength to rear up to the sky. We attacked more fiercely; and soon a huge missile was lodged deep in the monster's belly, and the sight of both his eyes was destroyed by flying arrows. Now the dark pit of the gaping wound sent forth a poisonous slaver from the open jaws; and now the end of the tail was held fast to the ground by showers of darts and heavy poles; and still he threatened feebly with open mouth. At last a beam, discharged from an engine with a loud hissing sound, shattered his head; and the body lay at last relaxed far along the raised bank, and discharged into the air a dark vapor of poison that escaped from its mouth. Then a cry of sorrow burst from the river, and the sound spread through the depths; and suddenly both grove and cave sent forth a noise of wailing, and the banks replied to the trees. Alas, how great were our losses, and how dearly we paid in the end for our battle!"

DRAGONS AGAINST ELEPHANTS[1]

The sprawling encyclopedia of natural phenomena com-
piled by the Roman statesman Pliny the Elder (ca. 23–79
CE) was an astonishing feat of diligence and energy. A
keen observer of the world around him, Pliny's interest
in contemporary knowledge about animals, plants, min-
erals, and natural history in general stemmed from his
boundless curiosity. While writing a chapter on elephants,
his thoughts turned to dragons, for these two giants of the
natural world were mortal enemies. Pliny identified India
as the habitat of the dragon and described how, in the jun-
gles of that remote country, these writhing reptiles battled
to the death with their colossal rivals. Pliny's encyclope-
dia was widely read long after his death during the erup-
tion of Mount Vesuvius in 79 CE. Centuries later, in
medieval Europe, Christian thinkers pondered the sym-
bolic meaning of this combat between dragons and ele-
phants and interpreted it as an allegory for the Devil's
corruption of Adam and Eve.

Africa produces elephants, but it is India that produces the
largest, as well as the dragon, which is perpetually at war
with the elephant, and is itself so enormous in size, as easily
to envelop the elephant with its folds and encircle them in its
coils. The contest is equally fatal to both; the elephant, vanquished, falls to the earth, and by its weight crushes the dragon
which is entwined around it.

The cunning that every animal exhibits on its own behalf

is wonderful, but in these it is remarkably so. The dragon has much difficulty in climbing up to so great a height, and therefore, watching the road, which bears the marks of the elephant's footsteps, when going to feed, it darts down upon it from a lofty tree. The elephant knows that it is quite unable to struggle against the coils of the serpent, and so seeks for trees or rocks against which to rub itself.

The dragon is on guard against this, and tries to prevent it, first of all by confining the legs of the elephant with the coils of its tail; while the elephant, on the other hand, tries to disengage itself with its trunk. The dragon, however, thrusts its head into the elephant's nostrils and thus, at the same moment, stops its breath and wounds its most tender parts. When it is met unexpectedly, the dragon raises itself up, faces its opponent, and flies more especially at the eyes; this is the reason why elephants are so often found blind, and worn to a skeleton with hunger and misery.

———

There is another story, too, told in relation to these combats. The blood of the elephant, it is said, is remarkably cold; for this reason, in the parching heats of summer, the dragon seeks it with great eagerness. It lies, therefore, coiled up and concealed in the river, in wait for the elephants when they come to drink, upon which it darts out, fastens itself around the trunk, and then fixes its teeth behind the ear, that being the only place which the elephant cannot protect with its trunk. The dragons, it is said, are of such vast size that they can swallow all of an elephant's blood. Consequently, the elephant, being drained of its blood, falls to the earth exhausted, while the dragon, intoxicated with the blood, is crushed beneath it, and so shares its fate.

———

It is a well-known fact that during the Punic war, at the river Bagrada, a serpent 120 feet in length was taken by the Roman army under Regulus, being besieged, like a fortress, by means of ballistae and other engines of war. Its skin and jaws were

preserved in a temple at Rome down to the time of the Nu-
mantine war.

―――――――――

Draconitis or *dracontia* is a stone produced from the brain of
the dragon; but unless the head of the animal is cut off while
it is alive, the stone will not assume the form of a gem,
through spite on the part of the serpent, when finding itself
on the point of death. Hence it is that, for this purpose, the
head is cut off when it is asleep. Sotacus, who tells us that he
once saw a stone of this kind in the possession of a king, says
that persons go in search of it in a chariot drawn by two
horses and that, the moment they see the serpent, they strew
narcotic drugs in its way and then cut off its head when
asleep. According to him, this stone is white and clear, and
admits no polishing or engraving.

SATANIC SERPENTS

Dragons and Saints in
Early Christianity

Since the dawn of literature, the gods have waged war against gigantic serpents in epic stories that articulated the triumph of divine order over primordial chaos. Accounts of these ancient conflicts anchored many of the foundation myths of Near Eastern and Asian cultures. In Egypt, the sun god Ra battled Apep, the enemy of light, who took the form of a giant snake or crocodile. In Mesopotamia, the storm god Marduk fought against the goddess Tiamat, a sea dragon who gave birth to a host of serpentine offspring, whose bodies she filled with venom instead of blood. In South Asia, the celestial deity Indra wielded a thunderbolt to free the rivers of the world from the dragon Vrtra, who held them captive in a mountain (see pp. 203–205). While these stories speak to the important role of dragons in many ancient cultures, none of them could rival the impact and influence of the Hebrew scriptures and the New Testament on the depiction and understanding of dragons in the western tradition. Ancient Jewish and early Christian renderings of monstrous reptiles typically underscored their role in the exile of human beings from the Garden of Eden, their affinity with the Devil and their activity as agents of his will, and their adversarial role in the cosmic conflicts that herald the end of time. As servants of Satan, dragons were the natural adversaries of holy men and women in early Christian literature, with the result that late antique and early medieval accounts of the virtues and miracles of the saints often featured the conquest or taming of dragons as proof of their God-given power. From the northern coast of Africa to the highlands of Scotland, in the visions of martyrs and the deeds of missionaries, dragons were a menacing obstacle to the advancement of the Christian faith.

BIBLICAL BEASTS

The translation of the Pentateuch and writings of the Jewish prophets from Hebrew into Greek (in the third and second centuries BCE) and from Greek into Latin (before the fourth century CE) introduced the Greco-Roman world to the beguiling serpent of the Garden of Eden, the colossal sea monster known as Leviathan, and the dragon worshipped by the ancient Babylonians in the time of Daniel. These sacred tales also informed the depiction of the "great red dragon" of the Book of Revelation, an apocalyptic Christian text written around 95 CE. Taken together, the dragons of the Hebrew scriptures and the New Testament offered a powerful, multivalent image for later readers: as a monster of imposing size and unmatched strength, the dragon evoked fear; as an agent of the Devil, it represented the lure of false religion and the enticement of sin; and as an enemy of God, it made war against the forces of righteousness until the archangel Michael cast it into the pit of fire to suffer for all eternity.

(A) THE SERPENT IN THE GARDEN[1]

But the serpent was more subtle than all the other animals of the earth, which the Lord God had made. To the woman it said, "Why has God commanded you not to eat from every tree in Paradise?" To him the woman responded, "We can eat from the fruit of the trees which are in Paradise, but God has commanded us not to eat from the fruit of the tree in the middle of Paradise nor to even touch it lest perhaps we die." And the serpent said to the woman, "No, you will not die. For God knows that on whatever day you will eat from it, your eyes will be opened and you will be just like gods, knowing good and evils." And the woman saw that the tree was good to eat and beautiful to her eyes and a delight to see and she took some of its fruit and ate it and gave some to her man, who also ate it. And the eyes of both of them were opened and when they realized that they were naked, they sewed together the leaves of figs and made for themselves loincloths. And when they heard the voice of the Lord God walking in Paradise in the afternoon air, Adam and his wife hid themselves from the face of the Lord God in the midst of the tree of Paradise. The Lord God called for Adam and said to him, "Where are you?" And Adam replied, "I heard your voice in Paradise and I was afraid because I was naked and I hid myself." And the Lord said to him, "And who has told you that you are naked, unless you have eaten from the tree from which I commanded you that you should not eat." And Adam said, "The woman whom you have given to me as a companion gave to me fruit from the tree and I ate it." And the Lord God said to the woman, "Why have you done this?" She answered, "The serpent deceived me and I ate." And the Lord God said to the serpent, "Because you have done this, you are cursed among all animals and beasts of the earth. You will go upon your chest and you will eat earth for all the days of your life. I will put hostilities between you and the woman, between your seed and hers. She will crush your head and you will lie in wait for her heel."

(B) THE LEVIATHAN OF THE DEEP[2]

Can you reel in Leviathan with a hook or bind his tongue with a cord? Can you put a ring through his nostrils or pierce his jaw with a band of metal? . . . Will you fill trawling nets with his hide and fishing huts with his head? Place your hand upon him with battle in mind and you will speak no more. Behold, his adversary's hope will deceive him and for all to see, he will be cast down . . . Who has discovered the surface of his hide and who will enter into his mouth? Who can open the gates of his face through the circuit of his teeth, a horror? His body is like molten shields and enclosed with overlapping scales, one joined to another and not a breath of air passes through them. They will adhere, one to another, and holding fast, they will never be separated. His snuffling is like the brightness of fire and his eyes like the eyelids of dawn. From his mouth proceed lamps like torches of burning flame. From his nostrils proceeds smoke like a pot heated and on the boil. His breath sets coals on fire and a flame emits from his mouth. In his neck strength abides and want precedes his face. The folds of his flesh cleave together. He will send lightning against him and they will not be carried off to another place. His heart will be as hard as stone and as unyielding as a smith's anvil. When he has risen up, the angels will be afraid and, terrified, they will be purged. When a sword reaches him, it will have no effect, nor a spear nor a coat of mail. For he will treat iron like straw and brass like rotten wood. The archer cannot make him flee. For him sling stones are turned into stubble. Likewise will he esteem the hammer and he will deride the one shaking his spear. The rays of the sun will be beneath him and he will scatter gold like dirt. He will cause the deep sea to seethe like a pot and will make it just like when ointments boil. After him his wake will shine. He will consider the deep as though it grows old. There is no power upon the earth compared to him, who was made to fear no one. He will see everything that is high. He is the king over all the children of pride.

(C) THE DRAGON OF BABYLON[3]

And there was a great dragon in that place and the Babylonians worshipped it. And the king said to Daniel, "Behold, now you cannot say that this creature is not a living god, so worship it." And Daniel said, "I worship the Lord, my God because he is the living God. But give me your permission, O king, and I will slay the dragon without sword or staff." And the king said, "I give you leave." Therefore, Daniel took pitch and fat and hair and cooked them together and formed them into loaves and put them into the monster's mouth and the dragon burst apart. And Daniel said, "Behold what you worship." And when the Babylonians heard this, they became very angry.

(D) THE SEVEN-HEADED HORROR OF THE END TIMES[4]

And a great sign appeared in heaven: a woman cloaked with the sun and the moon under her feet and on her head a crown of twelve stars. And she was pregnant and cried out as she gave birth, for she was in pain to deliver the baby. And a second sign was seen in heaven: behold, there was a great red dragon with seven heads and ten horns and on its heads were seven diadems. And his tail swept down a third part of the stars of heaven and cast them to the earth and the dragon stood before the woman who was about to deliver her child so that, when she gave birth, he might devour her son. And she gave birth to a male child, who was destined to rule all nations with an iron rod and her son was taken up to God and to his throne. And the woman fled into the wilderness where she had a place prepared by God so that there they would feed her for one thousand two hundred and sixty days.

And a war broke out in heaven. Michael and his angels fought with the dragon and the dragon fought his angels. And they did not prevail and there was no longer any place for them in heaven. And the great dragon was cast forth, that great old serpent, who is called the Devil and Satan, who seduced the whole world. And he was cast forth to the earth and his angels were sent away with him. And I heard a great voice in heaven, saying, "Now let there be salvation and strength and the kingdom of our God and the power of his Christ because the accuser of our brothers has been cast forth, who accused them before the sight of our God day and night. And they conquered him by the blood of the Lamb and by the word of his testimony, for they did not love their lives even unto death. Therefore, rejoice, O heavens, and you who dwell in them! Woe to the earth and to the sea because the Devil descends to you, harboring a great wrath, knowing that his time is short." And when the dragon saw that he was cast forth to the earth, he persecuted the woman who gave birth to the male child. And to the woman were given two wings of a great eagle so that she might fly into the desert, to her place where she is nourished for a time and times and half a time, away from the face of the serpent. And the serpent sent forth from its mouth after the woman a rush of water like a river to cause her to be carried away by the flood. But the earth came to her aid, opening its mouth and swallowing the river that the dragon had sent forth from its mouth. And the dragon was angry at the woman and went out to make war with the rest of her offspring, who keep the commandments of God and have the testimony of Jesus.

———————————

And I saw an angel descending from heaven, holding the key to the abyss and a great chain in his hand. And he captured the dragon, that old serpent, who is the Devil and Satan, and bound him for a thousand years. And he cast him into the abyss and closed it and put his seal upon it so that he could not seduce the nations any more until one thousand years had passed. After that, it is necessary for him to be released for a little while.

THE GUARDIAN OF
HEAVEN'S LADDER [1]

The voices of early Christian women are vanishingly rare in the historical record, so the survival of a prison diary written by a Roman Christian named Perpetua is nothing short of miraculous. Imprisoned by the Roman government in 203 CE for her subversive faith and doomed to die in the colosseum in Carthage, Perpetua recorded in her diary the final days of her life in captivity, including the visions she received directly from God. Among them was a dream about a ladder to Heaven guarded by a dragon who lay in wait to attack anyone who dared to ascend it. Perpetua's taming of this monster provides us with the earliest example of a saint subduing the Devil in the guise of an ancient serpent as proof of God's power over evil and favor to the faithful.

What a difficult time that was! Stiflingly hot because of the huge crowds; soldiers extorting money; and during the whole time I was there I was tormented by worries about my baby. Then Tertius and Pomponius, those kind deacons who were looking after us, bribed someone to allow us to be moved to a better part of the prison for a few hours so that we could recover a bit. Everyone then left the prison cell and we had a rest. I fed my baby who was weak with hunger. In my anxiety about him I spoke to my mother, tried to comfort my brother, and entrusted my son to them, but I suffered because I saw them suffering on my account.

Such were the worries that tormented me for many days. Then I managed to get permission for my baby to stay with me in prison and as a result I immediately felt better, relieved as I was of my discomfort and of worry for the child. Suddenly the prison had become a palace, and I preferred to be there rather than anywhere else.

Then my brother said to me, "My dear sister, you are already greatly privileged—so much so that you can surely ask for a vision to find out whether you will be condemned or set free?" I faithfully promised that I would, for I knew I could talk with the Lord, whose great blessings I had experienced. I told my brother I would give him an answer the following day. I then asked for a vision and this is what I saw. I saw an amazingly tall ladder, made of bronze, reaching right up to Heaven. It was so narrow that only one person could climb it at a time. All kinds of metal objects had been fixed into the sides of the ladder: there were swords, spears, hooks, daggers, and spikes, so that if the person climbing up were not careful or if he failed to look where he was going, he would be gashed and his flesh would stick to the metal spikes. Under the ladder lay an enormous dragon, waiting to attack those who climbed it and to frighten off any attempt to climb. Saturus was the first to climb up—he who later surrendered voluntarily out of consideration for us (for it was he who had been our spiritual teacher), and so he had not been with us when we were arrested. When he got to the top of the ladder, he turned round and said to me, "Perpetua, I will help you up. But be careful that the dragon does not bite you." I replied, "He will not hurt me, in the name of Jesus Christ." Then hesitantly, as if it were afraid of me, the dragon stuck its head out from under the ladder and I trod on its head as if it were the first rung and began to climb up.

DESCENDANTS OF DARKNESS

On the eve of the Ascension, Jesus commanded his apostles to go forth and "make disciples of all nations" (Matthew 28:19). Throughout late antiquity, stories circulated about the missionary adventures of the apostles, as they preached the Christian faith in hostile environments throughout the Mediterranean world and as far afield as Armenia and India. While their authenticity has been called into doubt by modern scholars, these stories proved to be immensely popular with Christian readers throughout the Middle Ages. As recounted in the fourth-century Acts of Philip, *the mission of the apostle Philip and his companions to the Greek city of Ophiorhyme (ancient Hierapolis, near modern Pamukkale in Turkey) brought them into conflict with the giant reptiles worshipped by the local pagans. During Philip's confrontation with his serpentine adversaries, their leader—a great dragon covered with soot and spewing fire—revealed that he and his kin were the demonic descendants of the serpents conjured by the magicians of Pharaoh when they sparred unsuccessfully with Moses and Aaron (Exodus 7:8–13). Like those great patriarchs, Philip overcame his enemies with miraculous manifestations of God's power.*

(A) AGAINST THE SNAKE CULT[1]

It came to pass when the Savior divided the apostles and each went forth according to his lot, that it fell to Philip to go to the country of the Greeks; and he thought it hard, and wept. And Mariamne his sister (it was she who made ready the bread and salt at the breaking of the bread, but Martha was she who ministered to the multitudes and labored much) seeing it, went to Jesus and said, "Lord, do you not see how my brother is troubled?" And he said, "I know, you chosen among women, but go with him and encourage him, for I know that he is a wrathful and rash man, and if we let him go alone he will bring many retributions on men. But lo, I will send Bartholomew and John to suffer hardships in the same city [Ophiorhyme] because of the great wickedness of those who dwell there, for they worship the Viper, the mother of snakes." . . . They journeyed for five days, and one morning after the midnight prayers a sudden wind arose, great and dark, and out of it ran a great smoky dragon, with a black back, and a belly like coals of brass in sparkles of fire, and a body over one hundred cubits long, and a multitude of snakes and their young followed it, and the desert quaked for a long distance.[2] And Philip said, "Now is the time to remember the Lord's words: 'Fear nothing, neither persecution, nor the serpents of the land, nor the dark dragon.' Let us stand fast and his power will fail and pray and sprinkle the air from the cup and the smoke will scatter." So they took the cup and prayed, "You who spreads dew on all pyres and bridles darkness, putting a bit into the dragon's mouth, bringing to nothing his anger, turning back the wickedness of the enemy and plunging him into his own fire, shutting his doors and stopping the exits and buffeting his pride, come and be with us in this desert, for we run by your will and at your bidding." And he said, "Now stand and raise your hands, with the cup you hold, and sprinkle the air in the form of a cross." And there was as a flash of lightning that blinded the dragon and its brood, and they were withered up, and the rays of the sun entered their holes and broke their eggs. But the apostles closed their eyes, unable to face the lightning, and remained unhurt.

(B) THE NATURE OF THE DRAGON[3]

And while Philip and Bartholomew and Mariamne were rejoicing, suddenly an earthquake and a clamor and a seething sounded from the place close by where there happened to be a great amount of broken stones. And from there voices were emerging in confusion and saying: "Depart from here from this point on, servants of the ineffable God. Attend to your business as we also attend to ours. How long will you be against us, wishing to obliterate the entire demonic nature? No one has ever passed by this place whom we have not destroyed; against you alone we have become powerless. We are fifty demons of one nature who have obtained this small place as our portion. But you servants of Christ after passing through every place under heaven have come for our destruction, and this Jesus with you, who is the son of God, though he is only one, has obliterated countless kinds of demons. And now look, we are abandoning this cave, being cast out by force. We acknowledge from this point on that we have been brought to nothing, for the one who was crucified in opposition to us has destroyed our ancient nature."

The apostle said: "I call on you by the crucified one that you display what your ancient nature is." And the dragon who was among them answered: "My nature originates from the plotting in paradise, and there he cursed me, the one who now wishes to destroy me through you.[4] For at that time, after I withdrew from the lush garden, I found an opportunity to lurk in Cain because of Abel.[5] Then when I displayed feminine beauty for the angels, I threw them down from the heights. And the women gave birth to very large sons—they call all these the Watchers.[6] And when these increased in number, they were devouring human beings like locusts. And after the flood wiped them out, they engendered the demonic and serpent-like nature when the rod of Moses exposed the nature of the Egyptian sages and magicians. For we are the fifty serpents that Moses' large serpent devoured at that time.[7] Anyway, you, Philip, have seized victory over us."

Then the apostle, slave of God, looked toward heaven and said: "Holy Jesus, abode of unshaded light, glory of the Father, power of the powerless, timeless Word in the Father who also appeared on earth as a human being, come now and grant me strength, because a multitude of demons is inflicting indignities on your creatures in this wilderness. Do not delay, Master, but make haste with your aid." And as he was praying in this manner he cried out loudly and said: "I adjure you by the glorified name of the Father, of the only-begotten Son, of the Most High, show yourselves, you demons, of what sort you are, both your number and your form." Immediately a very great screaming and disturbance came forth: "Take flight now, you descendants of darkness and bitterness, quickly on account of our inevitable and imminent destruction."

And when the demons, who had the appearance of reptiles, came out from the seething of the stone, fifty serpents having raised their heads ten feet high (for they were each more than sixty feet long), they were saying in one voice: "Approach, you who have commanded us to come out, for we are children of your nature." Then there was such a tremendous earthquake that Bartholomew and Mariamne would have lost courage had not Philip strengthened them, saying: "Whoever you are, the one being called by the serpents, which are evil demons, come forth, you on account of whom the earthquake has happened, since already you have been defeated and all your stock has dried up." Immediately, a great dragon stood in the midst of the serpents, about a hundred cubits long, covered with soot and spewing fire and pouring out much poison in a burning torrent. It had a twenty-foot-long beard and a head like the peak of a mound of iron, swaying backward and forward, and a body completely like fire.

He raised himself to a great height and said to Philip: "Philip, son of thunder, what is this great authority that you possess so as to pass through this place against us? Why have you worked so hard to destroy me also, like the dragon in the wilderness? I implore you by the one who has granted you this authority, do not destroy us or obliterate us in the thunder of your anger. Send us into the mountain of the Labyrinth that we might lurk there and transform ourselves. And by our demonic power, in the same way as we served our lord Solomon the Just in Jerusalem—for it was with our assistance that he built the sanctuary of God—so now also let us serve you. And in six days let us prepare for you in this place a building, and it shall be called the church of the living God. And I will even permit seven immortal springs because of the name of the crucified one, only do not destroy us."

The apostle replied: "How will you be able to build since you have a creeping nature and in fact are serpents, inasmuch as every building is fabricated by human skill? Now by the power of Jesus I command you, that both you and these fifty serpents change your creeping kind and display a human form." The dragon said: "Listen, Philip, our nature is shadowy and dark, and our father is called Darkness and our mother Blackness. And they have brought us into the world as dark and black, with small feet, crooked hair, without knees, legs like the wind, airborne, with sparkling eyes, pointed beards, pointed hair, odious beings, mad for women, a mix of male and female." Then after sighing very deeply, the dragon said: "Philip, since you have become so strong, look upon our form." And immediately when the dragon and the fifty serpents revealed themselves as they are, they flew up like winds and cried out: "Let us now produce the building!" There was an interval of not quite three hours and they conveyed through the air fifty high columns and said: "Establish this place, Philip, as you wish, and you will see the building and the seven springs and the consecration of the church on the sixth day."

After six days the church was completed and streams were flowing like rivers. And in a few more days men, three thousand in number, and many women and infants were gathering together and they were magnifying Christ. And the dragon, showing himself even darker than an Ethiopian, said: "We are departing, Philip, to a place where we will no longer be seen by you, lest even there you command us to build. It suffices for us; we have been defeated."

(C) THE CITY OF THE SERPENTS[8]

Now the apostles were traveling toward the city ... And when they reached the peak of the mountain, they looked down and saw lying on the slope the city to which the Lord had sent them. While they were looking down, they saw men before the city and said to one another: "Let us go to these men and ask the name of the city." And as they proceeded, the men saw them and moved to encounter them. Now everyone in that region had a serpent on his shoulders, and they would receive signs from them. And they were asking the serpents: "Who are these people coming toward us?" This was how the sign worked for them. They would release the serpents upon the strangers, and if they were not bitten by them, they were shown to them as participating in the same abomination. But if they were bitten by the serpents, they were seen as their enemies and they did not permit them to enter into the city.

When the apostles approached to speak to these men, who were seven in number, each of them let down his own serpent. And the serpents bowed their heads to the ground before the apostles and remained there, biting their own tongues. And the men concluded that they also worshipped the Viper. So Philip went on his way with the others ... When they reached the city limits, behold, there were two large dragons in front of the city gate, one on the right and one on the left, keeping watch lest any stranger enter this city. For by breathing upon them they would blind their eyes. As the apostles were entering, the dragons raised their heads, and when they saw them at the gate they were roaring to one another. But when Philip looked toward them, they saw the ray of the light of the Monad shining in his eyes, and in that moment they turned their heads aside and they died.[9]

THE DRAGON BECAME
HER TOMB[1]

The memory of Saint Marcellus, a fifth-century bishop of Paris, would have been lost to the ages were it not for the industry of Venantius Fortunatus (ca. 530–ca. 600), who wrote an account of his life in the 570s. Fortunatus organized his account of Marcellus's life by the saint's miracles, which increased exponentially in power as the holy man progressed from humble origins to hold a position of leadership in the Christian church. The saint's final miracle was a dramatic confrontation with a dragon that inhabited the tomb of an adulterous noblewoman, whose cadaver it slowly devoured to torment her in death for the sins she had committed while alive. In the presence of the assembled citizens of Paris, Marcellus rebuked the monster and drove it from the city. Owing to Fortunatus's lively narrative, the memory of this dragon battle endured for centuries. In the later Middle Ages, Parisians marched in procession before the Feast of the Ascension (celebrated forty days after Easter) holding aloft dragon puppets made of wicker, while bystanders threw fruit and small cakes into the gaping mouths of these tamed monsters.

We have now arrived at that triumphal miracle, which, even though it is the last in order, we place it first with respect to its power. A certain wife of an honorable man, who was noble in lineage but had a worthless reputation, dimmed with an evil crime the brightness that shone from her birthright. After she had finished the final days of her fleeting life in diminished light, she went forth to her tomb accompanied by a procession that did her no good. Once she was buried, I am loath to relate what happened after her funeral, because the dead woman's corpse experienced a twofold lamentation. For a serpent of immense size began to frequent her tomb to devour her corpse and, to be more precise, as the beast devoured the limbs of this woman, the dragon itself became her tomb. Thus, a reptilian pallbearer oversaw her ill-fated funeral with the result that her body could not rest after death. Life's end should have allowed her to lie in one place, but she was always on the move in her punishment. Oh, what a detestable and very frightening misfortune! The woman who had not preserved the integrity of her wedding bed in this world did not merit to lie untouched in her tomb, for the serpent who lured her into sin while she was alive even now ravaged her corpse in death. Then, members of her family who were nearby heard the sound and rushing up together they saw the giant monster leaving the tomb with its sinuous coils, its enormous body slithering along, its tail lashing back and forth. Terrified by what they had seen, they returned to their own homes. When this was made known, blessed Marcellus knew that he had to triumph over the bloodstained enemy. Having gathered together the people from the city, he proceeded to the tomb. With the citizens remaining at a distance but within sight, Marcellus advanced alone to the place with Christ as his guide. He was ready to fight. And when the dragon returned to the tomb from the forest, they approached each other. Blessed Marcellus offered a prayer, while the serpent asked for pardon with a bowed head and a fawning tail. Then blessed Marcellus struck its head three times with his staff, wrapped his stole around the neck of the serpent, and displayed his victory before the eyes of the citizens. Thus, in a spiritual arena he fought the dragon alone while the people watched. In relief, the citizens ran toward their bishop with the desire to see his enemy in captivity. Then, with the bishop leading the way, everyone—nearly three thousand people—marched in procession after the beast, rendering thanks to the Lord and abandoning any funerary pomp for their enemy.

Finally, blessed Marcellus rebuked the dragon, saying: "From this day forth, either stay in the desert or plunge into the sea." Soon after the beast was sent away, no trace of it was ever seen again. Behold, the defense of the fatherland amounted to a single priest, who vanquished his enemy more effectively with his fragile staff than if ballistae had struck the dragon, for an arrow could well have rebounded from it, if a miracle did not lay it low. O holiest of men, whose light staff displayed the weight of strength, whose soft fingers became the serpent's chains! Thus, private weapons overcame a public enemy and a general victory applauded the capture of a single foe. If the merits of holy men are compared by their deeds, Gaul marvels at Marcellus just as Rome marvels at Sylvester, but they stand apart in their accomplishments, because Sylvester only set his seal upon a serpent while Marcellus banished a dragon completely.[2]

COILED COURIERS
OF THE DAMNED[1]

In his widely read Dialogues on the Miracles of the Italian Fathers *(written ca. 593–94), Pope Gregory the Great valorized the virtues of the saints of Italy for the edification of his young interlocutor Peter. Among these exemplary tales were warnings about the otherworldly doom awaiting monks who did not follow the rules of conduct expected in their cloistered life. In three such stories, negligent brothers experienced visions of dragons coiling around their bodies in anticipation of snatching their souls at the moment of death and carrying them away to infernal punishment. While the offenses of restlessness, anger, and gluttony seem mild to modern sensibilities, Gregory's message to his monastic audience was clear: the life of a monk was strict and any misbehavior could have eternal consequences for the delinquent's soul. Widely read for centuries throughout medieval Europe, the* Dialogues *popularized the image of dragons as couriers of the damned to Hell and may have inspired the iconography of the Hellmouth as the gaping jaws of a gigantic beast.*

A certain monk of Benedict's community had made up his mind to leave, for he had no desire to stay in the monastery. Even though the man of God corrected him over and over and admonished him frequently, this monk would not agree to remain in the community and with inappropriate entreaties he longed to be released. One day the venerable father Benedict, overcome with weariness by the repetition of his complaint, lost his temper and ordered him to go. As soon as the monk left the monastery, he discovered that there was a dragon coming toward him on the road, its mouth opened wide. When the dragon who had appeared before him sought to devour him, trembling and shaking the monk began to shout in a loud voice, "Run! Run! This dragon wants to eat me!" Running to his aid, his brethren did not see the dragon at all, but they led the monk trembling and shaking back to the monastery. He immediately promised never to leave the community again and from that time onward he remained true to his promise. In fact, by the prayers of the holy man, the monk could now see the dragon that approached him, whom he had followed previously without being able to see him.

———————

During this plague, which had recently ravaged the majority of the people of Rome, a monk named Theodore, having been struck in the abdomen, was delivered to death's door. When he was about to give up the ghost, his brethren gathered around to protect the departure of his soul with prayer. His limbs were already dead; only in his chest did a life-giving warmth still allow him to draw breath. All of his brethren began to pray for him most fervently in pace with his rapid departure from the world, when suddenly he began to shout at the monks assisting him and interrupted their prayers, saying: "Retreat! Retreat! Behold, I have been given to a dragon to be eaten, but he cannot yet devour me because of your presence. My head has already been placed in its mouth! Give it room so that it may torture me no longer, but let it do what it is going to do. If I have been given to a dragon to be devoured, why should I suffer any more delay because of you?" Then the brothers began to speak to him: "What is this that you are saying, brother? Make the sign of the holy cross to help you." This man responded with loud shouts, saying: "I want to make the sign, but I cannot because I am weighed down by this dragon's scales." When the brethren heard this, they fell prostrate on the ground and began to pray vehemently with tears for his release. And behold, suddenly the sick man improved and began to cry out in a loud voice, saying: "Thank

God, behold the dragon who wanted to devour me has fled, for he could not withstand your prayers. Now intercede for the sake of my sins, because I am ready to be converted and to abandon completely my former worldly life."

———————

There now dwells among us a presbyter named Athanasius of Isauria, who told us about a terrible event that took place during his time in Iconium.[2] For, as he says, there was a certain monastery there called Ton Galaton, in which there lived a monk of great character. This monk was perceived to be someone with good habits and deliberate in all of his actions, but as it became clear in the end, he was not at all what he appeared to be. For when he made a show of fasting with the brethren, he was in the habit of eating secretly, a fault concerning which his brethren were entirely in the dark. But when his body was overcome by an illness, he came to the end of his life. When death approached, he made all of the brethren who were in the monastery gather by his side, leading those monks to believe, as they thought, that they would hear high-minded and agreeable words of wisdom while the man lay dying. On the contrary, sick and trembling, this man was compelled to relate to them that he would be handed over to the Devil upon his death. For he said: "When you thought that I was fasting with you, I was eating in secret, and behold, now I have been given to a dragon to be devoured. It has already coiled around my knees and feet with its tail. Indeed, its head is right next to my mouth and it gulps down my spirit." Once he had uttered these words, he immediately died, so it was not expected that he could be freed by penance from the dragon he had seen.

THE MONSTER OF
THE RIVER NESS[1]

The habitat of the early Christian dragon extended as far
north as the shrouded hills and chilly waterways of mod-
ern Scotland. Unconquered by the Romans, the lands of
Caledonia remained an untamed wilderness in the early
Middle Ages. According to the account of the life of the
Irish saint Columba (521–97) written in the late seventh
century by his disciple Adomnán of Iona, the holy man
preached the tenets of Christianity among the Picts in the
vicinity of Loch Ness. There he encountered an aggres-
sive aquatic creature of enormous size. Columba ban-
ished the monster of the river Ness with the sign of the
cross, thereby impressing the pagans who witnessed the
miracle and encouraging them to embrace the Christian
faith. Such was the potency of Columba's rebuke that the
monster of the river Ness was not observed again until
the nineteenth century.

Once, on another occasion, when the blessed man stayed for
some days in the land of the Picts, he had to cross the River
Ness. When he reached its bank, he saw some of the local
people burying a fellow. They said they had seen a water
beast snatch him and maul him savagely as he was swimming
not long before. Although some men had put out in a little
boat to rescue him, they were too late, but reaching out with
hooks, they had hauled in his wretched corpse. The blessed
man, having been told all this, astonished them by sending
one of his companions to swim across the river and sail back
to him in a dinghy that was on the further bank. At the com-

mand of the holy and praiseworthy man, Luigne moccu Min obeyed without hesitation. He took off his clothes except for a tunic and dived into the water. But the beast was lying low on the riverbed, its appetite not so much sated as whetted for prey. It could sense that the water above was stirred by the swimmer, and suddenly swam up to the surface, rushing open-mouthed with a great roar toward the man as he was swimming midstream. All the bystanders, both the heathen and the brethren, froze in terror, but the blessed man looking on raised his holy hand and made the sign of the cross in the air, and invoking the name of God, he commanded the fierce beast saying:

"Go no further. Do not touch this man. Go back at once."

At the sound of the saint's voice, the beast fled in terror so fast one might have thought it was pulled back with ropes. But it had got so close to Luigne swimming that there was no more than the length of a pole between man and beast. The brethren were amazed to see that the beast had gone and that their fellow soldier Luigne returned to them untouched and safe in the dinghy, and they glorified God in the blessed man. Even the heathen natives who were present at the time were so moved by the greatness of the miracle they had witnessed that they too magnified the God of the Christians.

GUARDIANS OF THE HOARD

The Wyrms of Northern Literature

When Jacob Grimm published the first edition of Teutonic Mythology (Deutsche Mythologie) *in 1835, he un-
wittingly heralded a modern renaissance for the dragons
of the medieval north. In the chapter "Trees and Animals," this sprawling encyclopedia of ancient Germanic
beliefs boasted a long digression on dragons in its treatment of snakes and other reptiles. For the first time, Grimm
gathered the numerous references and allusions to dragons scattered throughout Scandinavian literature and
made inferences about their common characteristics. In
Old Norse, there were two words for dragon: an* ormr
(similar to the Old English wyrm) *was a monstrously
large serpent, while a* dreki *(borrowed from the Old English* draca) *had wings and sometimes legs. In the northern imagination, dragons of different shapes and sizes
brooded in subterranean chambers atop mounds of gold
and prowled the wintry wastelands in search of prey. Like
the giants, they were ancient creatures, much older than
humankind. Their venomous or fiery breath was lethal.
It was the work of heroes like Sigurd and Beowulf to vanquish these monsters from the earth, just as the thunder
god Thor had defeated the world-serpent Jörmungandr.
Grimm's* Teutonic Mythology *did more than any other
work of scholarship to advance the image of dragons in
Norse mythology as the archetype of these monsters in the
modern imagination. Thanks to him, "[p]opular belief
still dreams of glittering treasures lying on lonesome heaths
and guarded by dragons."*[1]

THE TERROR OF NATIONS[1]

No dragon in premodern literature has informed the modern imagination as much as the nameless wyrm in the early medieval poem Beowulf. *Composed in Old English perhaps in the decades after 700, the* Beowulf *poem survived in a single manuscript created at the turn of the first millennium. This poem tells the story of the hero Beowulf, who sailed from Sweden to Denmark to help King Hrothgar, whose mead-hall was under siege by a murderous human-shaped monster called Grendel. Once Beowulf had defeated Grendel and its loathsome mother, he returned to his homeland, where he became king of the Geats and ruled in peace for fifty years. As Beowulf neared the end of his life, his kingdom was beset by another fell creature: a winged, gold-hoarding, fire-breathing dragon. While the destructive power of the dragon in the* Beowulf *poem made it a formidable adversary, its penchant for hoarding treasure was equally dangerous, because it threatened to erode bonds of loyalty and friendship in a warrior society that relied on the redistribution of wealth by leaders to cement their relationships with their followers. Although the* Beowulf *poem was not widely read in the Middle Ages, it has played an important role in shaping modern perceptions of dragons by providing the inspiration for the "most specially greedy, strong and wicked worm named Smaug" in J. R. R. Tolkien's famous fantasy novel* The Hobbit.[2]*

[In celebration of Beowulf's defeat of Grendel, a poet praises another monster-killer, the dragon-slayer Sigemund the Wælsing.][3]

He recited most all
He had heard before about the brave deeds
Of Sigemund, many a strange matter,
Strife of the Waelsing on wide-ranging ventures,
Things scarcely known to the sons of men,
Feuds and violence, except Fitela with him
When Sigemund would say such things,
Uncle to sister's son, for always they were
In each of combats comrades in need;
A great many of the giants' kin
They brought down with swords. From Sigemund sprang
After his death-day a great deal of glory
When battle-hardened he bested the *wyrm*,
Treasure-hoard's guardian. Beneath grey rock
The nobleman's son set out alone
On a dangerous deed; nor did Fitela go with him.
Yet it so happened his sword went straight through
The wondrous *wyrm*, stuck fast in the wall,
The splendid steel; it struck the dragon dead.
The dreaded attacker with daring achieved
That he could have the hoard of rings
All to himself. The ship was loaded,
Treasures stowed in the sea-boat's hold,
By this son of Wæls. The *wyrm* went up in flames.

[*Beowulf returns to Geatland and rules for fifty years. A thief
steals a cup from a treasure hoard and awakens a dragon.*]

He ruled well
For fifty winters, a wise old king,
Homeland's guardian, until one began
In the dark nights to hold sway: a dragon,
He who in high home his hoard watched over,
A steep barrow of stone; below was a trail
Unknown to all until therein crept
Some nameless man, came nigh unto
The heathen hoard, his hand grasping a cup

Encrusted with gems. It gained him nothing
Though he deceived the sleeping beast
With thievish craft. The creature was furious
As soon discovered those dwelling nearby.
Not by choice did he trample the *wyrm*-hoard
Nor by will alone, that one who wreaked harm,
But in dire distress, the slave of someone
Of the sons of men had fled the stinging whip
And in need of a home made his way herein.
Beset by sin he soon discovered
That there stood a terror, a horror;
And yet the wretch risked his own life,
With fear in heart of a frightful attack,
And sought the precious cup; for many such things
In that earth-hall there were, of ancient treasures.

[*The last survivor of some ancient clan had deposited the treasures there, lamenting his fate before he died. Then a dragon found and claimed the hoard.*]

The old dawn-terror
Found a splendid hoard standing open,
He who burning seeks out barrows,
Sleek dragon of spite, and soars by night
Ensheathed in flame; him the land-folk
Do sorely dread. He is driven to seek
A hoard in earth where heathen gold
He guards, grown old, though it does him no good.
Thus the terror of nations for three hundred years
Kept hold of the treasure-house under the earth,
A force supreme, until someone enraged him,
Befouled his mood, bore to his liegelord
The gilded cup, craved a pardon
From his lord and master. The massive hoard was plundered,
The ring-hoard robbed, and request was granted
To the wretched man. Upon works of ancients
His generous lord looked for the first time.

Then the *wyrm* awoke, his wrath was renewed,
He slithered along stone, stark-hearted he found
His enemy's footprints. Too far he had stepped
With craft and cunning near the dragon's head.
So may the undoomed one easily escape
Misery and woe, whom the all-wielding lord's
Good keeping protects. The hoard-guard searched
Eagerly along the ground, to find the one
Who while he slept had sore mistreated him.
Hot in mood he circled the barrow-mound
All around the outside but no one saw
In that wilderness, yet enjoyed his war-mood,
The work of battle; then turned back to the barrow
To seek the treasured cup. Straightaway he found
Signs that someone dared damage his gold,
Glorious treasure. The hoard-guard waited
With painful impatience for evening to come;
The barrow's keeper was bursting with rage,
The hateful beast would pay back with flames
The precious drinking-cup. Then the day departed
To the *wyrm*'s delight; no longer on wall
Intended to abide but went forth blazing
In a burst of flames. The beginning was hard
For that land's folk, just as later it ended
For their gift-giver with grievous pain.
     Then the ghastly beast began to spew flames,
To burn bright halls; the fire-glow gleamed
To men's terror. Nor there intended
The loathsome flier to leave anything alive.
The *wyrm*'s warfare was widely seen
Fiendish cruelty, far and near,
How the grim attacker the Geatish folk
Hated and harmed; he shot back to his hoard,
His secret dwelling, before daylight arrived,
He enfolded in flames the folk of that land,
In fire and burning, then trusted the barrow,
Its walls and his warfare, but that trust deceived him.
Then to Beowulf was the terror made known

At once in truth that his own home,
Best of houses, had burnt up in flames,
Gift-throne of Geats. To the good king that was
The greatest of griefs, anguish in heart.
The wise king wondered if he the All-wielder,
Eternal Lord, against the old laws
Had bitterly offended. His breast surged within
With dark thoughts; that was not his custom.

    The fiery dragon had the folk's fastness,
Stronghold of that land on the seashore's edge
Reduced to coals. The king of war,
Prince of Weder-Geats, plotted revenge.
The protector of men commanded be made,
The leader of warriors, a wondrous shield
All out of iron. Well enough he knew
That wood of the forest would fail to help him,
Linden against flame. His loan of days
Would end before long, life on earth
For the proven warrior, and for the *wyrm* as well
Though he long had held his hoarded wealth.
The prince of rings did then disdain
To face the wide-flier with a force of men,
Long ranks of troops. No attack he feared
Nor worried much about the *wyrm*'s warfare,
Its strength and valor, for he survived before
Many a battle, braving dire straits
And the crash of war, since he had cleansed
King Hrothgar's hall, triumphant hero,
Crushed in combat the kin of Grendel,
Loathsome clan.

[*Guided to the monster's lair by the thief, Beowulf prepares
to face the dragon.*]

    Thus he came through every kind of combat,
Severest of conflicts, son of Ecgtheow
With acts of courage, until that one day

When he had to wage war against the *wyrm*.
Enraged he set out, one among twelve,
The lord of Geats, to look upon the dragon.
He had found out whence the feud arose,
Dire malice to men; came into his keeping
The famous cup from the one who found it.
He was in that throng the thirteenth man,
The one who started all their troubles,
Sad-minded thrall, who wretched thence
Guided them back. Against his will he went
To where he alone knew that earth-hall to be,
Hoard under ground near the surging sea,
The warring of waves; within it was full
Of gems and spun gold. The monstrous guardian,
Ever greedy for battle, held gold treasures,
Ancient under earth. That was not an easy bargain
To obtain for any of those among men.
Sat down then on headland the strife-hard king,
Gold-friend of Geats, offered good health
To his hearth-companions. He was heavy in heart,
Restless but ready, the fate was nigh
That soon would assault the aging king,
Seek his soul's hoard, divide asunder
Life from body; not much longer would
The king's spirit be clothed in flesh.
Beowulf spoke, son of Ecgtheow,
"In youth I survived many storms of battle,
Times of hard strife; I still remember them all."

[*The battle commences, but Beowulf succumbs to the drag-*
on's flames as his comrades flee.]

          "Now must blade's edge,
Hard sword in hand fight for the hoard."
Beowulf spoke, boast-words uttered
For the last time. "I lived through many
Battles in my youth, yet still will I,

Old guardian of folk, face the feud,
Do a glorious deed, if the evil enemy
Emerges from his earth-hall to mount an attack!"
Then he addressed each of his men,
Valiant helm-bearers for the very last time,
Dear companions. "I would not carry my sword,
Weapon against *wyrm*, if I knew another way
Against the awesome foe with all due honor
To grapple, as I did with Grendel;
But here I expect hot and baleful fire,
Breath and poison; so upon me I wear
Shield and byrnie.[4] From barrow's guardian
I will not flee a footstep, but fate shall decree
For us both beside the barrow walls,
As God determines. My mood is fierce
So I make no boast against the battle-flier.
Wait here on the barrow, protected by byrnies,
My men in armor, to see who better endures
His wounds after warfare deadly,
Which of us two. It is not your test,
Nor measure of might, but mine alone,
To match my strength against the monstrous foe,
Do a noble deed. With daring will I
Win the gold, unless warfare takes me,
Your lord and friend, with life-denying evil."
Stood up then with shield the warrior strong,
Hardy under helmet, in war-gear walked
Along cliffs of stone, trusting the strength
Of one solitary man. Such is no coward's way!
He who with manly virtues a great many
Combats survived, crashes of battle
When men on foot faced each other,
Saw stone arches standing beside the wall,
A stream of fire surging from the barrow,
Deadly and hot; nor near the hoard
Could any survive an instant unburnt
By the dragon's flames deep within his lair.
Out from his breast then, bursting with rage,

The Weder-Geats' leader let loose a cry,
Roared, stark-hearted; his voice rang in,
Beneath grey stone, a clear call to battle.
Hate was aroused when the hoard-guard knew
The voice was a man's. No time remained
To sue for peace. First there shot forth
The fierce one's breath out from the stone,
Steaming hot, hostile, shaking the ground.
At base of barrow the warrior swung his shield,
Lord of the Geats, to face the ghastly foe;
Then the ring-coiling one was roused in his heart
To seek out strife. His sword he drew,
The worthy war-king, an ancient heirloom,
Its edges undulled. Each to the other was
A source of terror, intent on evil.
Stout-hearted stood with towering shield
The lord of warriors, while the *wyrm* coiled himself
Swiftly together; the warrior waited.
Came then burning, the coiled one slithering,
Hastening to its fate. The shield defended
His life and limb a lesser while
Than the famous leader might have liked,
If he for once upon that day
Despite his doom might still prevail,
Succeed in battle. He swung up his arm,
The lord of Geats, the grim and mottled beast
He struck with ancient sword, but its sharp edge failed,
Bright against bone, bit with less force
Than the nation's leader had need of then,
Hard pressed in battle. The barrow's guardian
Felt that sword-stroke, and fierce in mood
Spewed waves of fire; widely then shone
The light of battle. Boasted not of victory
The gold-friend of Geats; his war-sword failed,
Unsheathed in battle, as it never should have,
Iron good of old; that was no easy trek
When the illustrious son of Ecgtheow
Had to leave this level plain of earth,

Against his will go to dwell in
A place elsewhere, as each man must,
Relinquish his loan of days. It was not long until
The awesome enemies advanced again:
The hoard-guard took heart, his breast heaving,
Attacked a second time; he suffered harsh straits,
Wrapped in fire, who his folk had ruled.
Nor did his comrades crowd round their leader,
The sons of nobles, stand and support him
With warlike strength, but into the wood they fled
To save their own lives. In one of them welled
His heart with sorrows; still less may kinship
Be set aside for one seeking what is right.
He was called Wiglaf, Weohstan's son,
Beloved shield-warrior, of the Scylfing clan
And Ælfhere's lineage. He saw his liegelord
Under his helmet be hurt by heat.
His mind cast back on the benefits he got
When living in wealth among the Wægmundings,
Each of the folk-rights his father had given him.
He could not hold back; one hand grasped shield,
Of yellow linden, the other drew ancient sword.

[*Wiglaf alone comes to the aid of his stricken lord and together they slay the dragon.*]

He strode in helmet to help his lord
Through smoke of slaughter, then spoke these words:
"Beloved Beowulf, as best you can
Perform what in youth you promised long since
Never to allow while yet alive
Your glory to dim; famous for deeds,
A stern-minded prince, with might and main
Defend now your life; and I will fight with you."
After those words the angry *wyrm* came,
The malevolent beast launched an attack
A second time with surging fire

Against hated foes, flames coming in waves;
Shield burned to the boss, his byrnie was
Of little use to the young spear-warrior
So shelter he sought under kinsman's shield,
Sped forth eagerly since his own had been
All wrecked by flames. Then yet the war-king
Remembered past deeds, and struck so mightily
With his sword of battle that it stuck in the skull,
Driven by hate and need. *Naegling* burst apart,
Beowulf's old sword, streaked with silver-grey,
Failed in the fight.[5] Fate granted him not
That the iron's edge at all provided
Help in the battle; his hand was too strong
So every blade as I have heard tell
Could not withstand his strokes in battle,
A weapon wondrous hard; it was no whit the better.
Then for a third time the terrible fire-dragon,
Destroyer of nations, intent on vile deeds
Rushed at the man of glory when it got the chance,
Hot and battle-grim it bit the neck deeply
With sharp, bony tusks; he became all bloody,
His life-blood's essence welled up in waves.
I heard in time of need by the nation-king's side
His steadfast thane showed great courage,
Craft and keenness, as befit his kin.
He heeded not the dragon's head but the hand was burned
Of the brave man coming to his kinsman's aid.
He lunged at the enemy somewhat lower down,
The man in armor, so his ornamented sword
Sank in where he struck and suddenly the flames
Began to subside. The king himself
Regained his wits and drew his war-dagger
Keen and battle-sharp from beside his byrnie;
The Weders' king cut the *wyrm* wide open.
They felled the foe, forced out its life,
Cut it down with courage, the kindred nobles,
Both together. So should a man be,
A thane in time of need! That for the king was

The last moment of triumph made by his own deeds,
Works in the world. Then the wound began,
Which the earth-dragon earlier had given him,
To burn and swell; too soon he found
Welling up in his breast a baleful evil,
A poison within. The noble king walked
Along the wall of rock, wisely pondering,
Then sat and gazed upon the work of giants,
How the stone-arches supported by pillars
Within the age-old earth-hall were held.
The incomparable thane then cupped his hands,
Laved with water his lord and friend,
Glorious king all covered in blood
And battle-weary. He unbuckled his helmet.
Beowulf spoke, despite his pain,
His mortal wounds; full well he knew
His span of days had all departed,
His joys on earth, that all were gone
His numbered days, his death full nigh.
"I would have given my war-gear all
Unto my son, had it been so granted
That any heir would live on after me,
Child of my own. I ruled over my people
For fifty winters; there was no folk-king,
Not any of those from neighboring tribes,
Who dared wage war with allies against me,
Threaten with horror. In my homeland I waited
For my time to come, my kingdom ruled well,
I sought no feuds nor falsely swore
Oaths unjustly. For all this I may,
Though wracked with wounds, take rightful pleasure;
The Ruler of men may not therefore
Accuse me of kin-slaying, while courses away
The life from my body. Go look you now,
Make haste to the hoard under hoary stone,
Beloved Wiglaf, while the *wyrm* lies sore wounded,
Asleep in death, stripped of treasure.
Go swiftly so that I may see

The ancient wealth, heirlooms of gold,
Bright precious gems, so I may more gently
With wealth of treasure take my leave
Of life and nation, which I long held."
Then I heard swiftly the son of Weohstan
Obeyed the words of his wounded lord,
Sick from battle; wearing byrnie went,
Woven battle-coat, under barrow's roof.
The fierce young thane, flushed with victory,
Passed by the seat, saw many jewels
And gold glittering on ground where it lay,
Wonders on walls and throughout the *wyrm*'s den,
The old dawn-flier's, flagons standing,
Vessels of ancients with no one to burnish them,
And missing their gems. There was many a helmet
Old and rusty, many an arm-ring,
Torque finely twisted. (Treasure may easily,
Gold on the ground, get the better of
Every last human, hide it who will.)
He saw too a standard shining and gilded
Hang high over hoard, of hand-crafts the best,
Woven with fine skill, reflecting the light
So he could discern the surface of the barrow,
Scan all the works of art. Of the *wyrm* there was
No sign whatsoever, for sword had dispatched him.
Then I heard the hoard was plundered,
Old work of giants by one man alone,
Filled his arms up with flagons and platters,
All much as he wanted, as well as the standard,
Brightest of banners. The bold king's sword
With edges of iron had already harmed
The one who guarded the golden treasure
For so very long, flames of terror it brought
For the sake of the hoard, hot and surging
In the middle of nights, before meeting its death.
The herald urgently hastened his way back,
Bold in spirit, spurred on by treasure,
Sore wanting to know whether in that place

He would find alive, if losing strength,
The lord of Weders where he had left him.
While laden with treasure, his lord and friend,
The famous king, he found all bloody,
His life at an end. Again he began
To cast water on him, until word's point
Broke through his breast. The bold one spoke,
The old man in sorrow surveyed the gold:
"For these precious things I peer at now
I thank the Lord, eternal leader,
King of Glory, give thanks in words
That I am permitted for my people's sake
To gain such gold before I go to my death.
For all this heap of hoarded treasure
I have paid with the life allotted to me.
Take care of my people; I cannot remain.
Bid the war-famed men build up a mound
After flames consume me on a cape by the sea.
It shall stand in memory to all my folk
And tower high on Hronesnes
So that seafarers since will name the place
Beowulf's barrow, who pass by in ships
Driven from afar through the fog-covered sea."
Then unclasped from his throat a collar of gold,
The glory-minded king gave it to his thane,
The young spear-warrior, as well as gilded helm,
Arm-ring and byrnie, bid him use those well.
"You are the last remaining member of our clan
Of Wægmundings, swept away by destiny
Our bloodline all, earls of valor
To meet their fates, and I must follow them."
Those were the last words of the wise old man,
Innermost thoughts before mounting the pyre,
Hot and hostile flames; from his breast flew out
His soul, gone to seek judgment, just and true.
Then befell the one still young in years
Great sorrow when seeing spread out on the earth
His dearest liegelord, his life at an end,

Suffering pitiably. His slayer too lay dead,
Awesome earth-dragon, emptied of life,
Overcome in battle. It could no longer,
The crooked-coiling *wyrm*, control the ring-hoard,
Had been snatched away by edges of iron,
Hard, hammer-struck, sharpened in battle,
So the wide-flier was felled by wounds,
Crashed down from above near the barrow's hoard.
It no longer moved in the middle of the night
Through the air with pleasure, proud of its gold,
Displaying its form, but it fell to earth
Cut down by the handiwork of the warrior king.
Indeed, few men have managed it,
However hardy, as I have heard tell,
Though they were daring of deeds till then,
To rush against the ravager's venom
Or disturb with hands the hall of rings,
Encounter the earth-hall's guardian awake,
Dwelling in its barrow. Beowulf paid
The price of death for his portion of treasure.
Each of them brought the other to an end
Of this fleeting life. It was not long until
The laggards in battle came back from the wood . . .

[*A messenger announces the death of Beowulf and the dragon.*]

"Now the giver at will of gifts to the Weder-folk,
Lord of the Geats, lies still on his death-bed,
A bed of slaughter, because of the *wyrm*'s deeds;
Alongside him lies his loathsome foe
Stricken with dagger-wounds; for sword could not
In any way inflict a wound
On the warring creature. Now does Wiglaf,
Son of Weohstan, sit beside Beowulf,
One nobleman next to another unliving,
Weary in heart keeps watch at the head
Of both friend and foe. Our folk can expect

A time of attack when the truth is disclosed
To Franks and Frisians, the fall of our king
Made widely known."

[*As the warriors survey the scene of the battle, the messenger
predicts bad tidings for the Geats now that Beowulf is dead.*]

　　　Thus the man made his many predictions,
Hateful tidings; he told few lies
About words or deeds. The warriors arose,
Went unblithely under Eagles Nest
With welling tears the wonder to behold.
They saw on the sand, his soul departed,
On his bed of rest, he who rings gave them
In earlier times; the end of days
Had come for the good and glorious king,
The lord of Weders met a wondrous death.
So too they saw the strangest creature,
The loathsome *wyrm* lying across from him
On the fields of earth; the fire-dragon was
Grim and mottled, besmirched by flames.
It was fifty feet in measures
Of length where it lay; lustfully had it ruled
The sky by night, descending down
To seek its den; but death stopped it cold,
No longer to use the earth-caves below.
Beside it lay countless cups and flagons,
Golden platters and precious swords,
Eaten through by rust, as if resting there
For eons in the earth's embrace.
That old inheritance was huge and mighty,
Ancient men's gold gripped in a spell,
So that none could touch that treasure-hall's rings,
Not any of men, unless God himself,
The true king of glory, should grant to someone
As he thinks meet among men to go
And open the hoard, for he holds and shields us.

[*The dragon's treasure is cursed, so they burn it on Beowulf's funeral pyre.*]

>   Little did any grieve
> That they with haste should haul outside
> The dear treasures. The dragon they shoved,
> *Wyrm* over cliff-walls, let waves take him,
> The sea gather in the guardian of treasures.
> Then was wrought gold on wagons loaded,
> Countless bright things, and the king beside them,
> The veteran of battles borne to Hronesnes.
> Then the Geatish people prepared for him
> A pyre on earth, by no means paltry,
> Hung round with helmets and shields of battle,
> Bright byrnies, as he had bid them.
> The glorious leader was laid down amidst
> Thanes lamenting their beloved lord.
> They began to kindle the greatest of bale-fires,
> Warriors on the hilltop; the wood-smoke rose up,
> Black above the blaze, the bonfire roared
> Mixed with weeping; the winds subsided
> And flames broke through the body's bone-house
> Hot at its core. With heavy hearts
> They mourned their misery, their murdered lord.
> A Geatish woman began to keen,
> Her hair bound up, her heart aching,
> Sang in sorrow and said repeatedly
> That she invasions sorely dreaded,
> Terror of war-troops, woeful slaughter,
> Humiliation and thralldom. Heaven swallowed the smoke.
> A burial mound the men of the Weders
> Built up on the headland; it was high and broad,
> Widely seen by men sailing the waves,
> Piled together in just ten days,
> A beacon for the brave. The brands and ashes
> Were all walled up, in as worthy a way
> As men of wisdom could best devise.
> They set in barrow brooches and arm-rings,

Such trappings as men, intent on evil,
Had stolen from the well-stocked hoard,
Let earth retake the treasure of earls,
Gold under ground where yet it dwells
As useless to men as ever before.
Brave horsemen round the barrow rode,
Born of nobles, a band of twelve
Lamenting in sorrow and mourning their king,
Finding in words fit things to say
About their prince in praise of bold deeds,
Adjudging his glory. So it is just
That a man should laud his lord and friend,
Hold love in heart when hence he must
From bodily life be led away.
Thus the tribe of Geats their grief expressed,
His close companions, for their dear king's death,
Said he was of all the world's kings,
Of men the mildest and most gracious,
Kindest to his people and keenest for praise.

SIGURD, THE SLAYER OF FÁFNIR[1]

The most famous Old Norse dragon-slayer was the hero Sigurd (Sigurðr), who slew the dragon Fáfnir. The story of their battle was ubiquitous in Scandinavian literature and art. The version presented here was part of the Völsunga saga, a poetic story about the fortunes of the Völsung clan composed around 1275. As a boy, Sigurd was fostered by a dwarf named Reginn, who told him about a great treasure guarded by his brother, a giant named Fáfnir, who had turned into a dragon because of his excessive greed. To aid Sigurd in the battle, Reginn forged a formidable sword named Wrath (gramr in Old Norse). The Sigurd legend is unusual because it depicted a dragon that had once had the form of a man. Like the monster in the Beowulf poem, Fáfnir lusted after gold and other treasure, but he did not fly or breathe fire. Instead, reminiscent of the giant serpents of Roman antiquity, he slithered along the ground and emitted clouds of venom, while the weight of his vast coils caused the earth to tremble when he moved.

Now Sigurd and Reginn ride up onto the heath. They come to the path where Fáfnir was accustomed to slither when he went to get water. And it is said that the crag was thirty fathoms high where he lay near the water when he drank.

Then Sigurd said, "You told me, Reginn, that this dragon was no bigger than a heath-snake, but his tracks look very big to me."

Reginn said, "Dig a pit and sit in it. And when the *wyrm* slithers to the water, stab him in the heart and kill him dead. For that you will win great fame."

Sigurd said, "What happens if I am hit by the serpent's blood?"

Reginn replies, "I can't give you any advice if you are afraid of everything. You are unlike your kinsmen in courage."

Now Sigurd rides along the heath but Reginn turned and rode off in great fear. Sigurd dug a pit. And while he was doing this work, an old man with a long beard came up to him and asked what he was doing there. Sigurd told him.

Then the old man replied, "That is ill-advised. Dig more pits and let the blood run into them, but sit in one and stab the *wyrm* in the heart." Then the man turned away and vanished. Sigurd dug the pits as he had been told.

And when the *wyrm* slithered to the water, there was a big earthquake such that all the land nearby trembled and shook. He snorted forth poison all over the path in front of him, but Sigurd was not afraid nor frightened by the din. And when the *wyrm* slithered over the pit, Sigurd thrust with his sword under the left shoulder, all the way up to the hilts. Then Sigurd leapt up out of the pit and pulled the sword out and his whole arm was bloody up to the shoulder. And when the huge *wyrm* felt its death-wound, he lashed about with head and tail so that everything burst asunder that was in his way. And when Fáfnir received his death-wound, he asked,

"Who are you, and who is your father, and who is your kin, that you are so bold that you dare wield weapons against me?"

Sigurd answers, "My kin is unknown to men. I am called Noble Beast and I have no father nor mother, and I always go alone."

Fáfnir replies, "If you have no father nor mother, from what wondrous being were you born? And even though you do not tell me your name on my death-day, you know that you are lying."

He answers, "I am called Sigurd, and my father Sigmund."

Fáfnir asks, "Who urged you on to do this deed, and why

did you yield to his urging? Had you not heard, that all folk are afraid of me and of my Helm of Terror? Young man with flashing eyes, you had a brave father."

Sigurd answers, "A brave heart urged me to do it and I was helped to get it done by a strong arm and sharp sword that you have now felt. Few are strong in old age if they are weak in their youth."

Fáfnir says, "I know that if you grew up among your kinsmen, you would know how to fight when angry. But it is more surprising to me that a prisoner captured in war should have dared to fight me, since few captives are bold in battle."

Sigurd said, "Do you blame me for being far from my kinsmen? Even though I was taken captive, I was not bound, and you have found that I am free."

Fáfnir replied, "You take whatever I say as words of hatred. But the gold that I have owned will be your bane."

Sigurd said, "Everyone wants to keep all the gold until that one day, but everyone has to die sometime."

Fáfnir said, "In few things will you follow my judgment, but if you sail the sea unwarily, you will drown; it is better to wait on land until it's calm."

Sigurd said, "Tell me then, Fáfnir, if you are so very wise: who are those Norns who take sons from their mothers?"

Fáfnir answers, "They are many and various. Some are from the family of gods, some from the family of elves, and some are daughters of Dvalinn."

Sigurd said, "What is that holm called, where Surtr and the gods will shed each other's blood?"

Fáfnir answers, "It is called Uncreated." And Fáfnir said further, "Reginn, my brother, caused my death, and it pleases me that he will cause your death too, and it will go as he wanted." Fáfnir spoke again: "I wore the Helm of Terror before all men, ever since I lay down upon my brother's inheritance, and I snorted venom all around me so that no one dared come near me, and I feared no weapon. I never encountered so many men before me that I didn't think myself much stronger, and all were afraid of me."

Sigurd said, "That Helm of Terror that you spoke about

gives victory to few, because whoever comes among many will find out eventually that no one is bolder than everyone else."

Fáfnir replies, "I advise you to take your horse and ride away as quickly as possible, because it often happens that he who receives his death-wound takes his own revenge."

Sigurd said, "That is your advice, but I will do otherwise. I will ride to your lair and take that vast amount of gold which your kinsmen have possessed."

Fáfnir replies, "You will be riding to a place where you will find enough gold to last you all your days, but that same gold will be your bane and that of everyone else who owns it."

Sigurd stood up and said, "I would ride home without this great treasure if I knew that I would never die. But every brave man wants to control all his wealth until that one day. But you, Fáfnir, lie in your death-throes until Hel takes you."

And then Fáfnir dies.

WINGED DRAGONS
OF THE NORTH

Fáfnir was not the only dragon to haunt the northern wastelands. Despite J. R. R. Tolkien's claim that dragons were "as rare as they are dire" in Scandinavian literature, many Old Norse and Icelandic sagas composed in the later Middle Ages told of violent encounters between hardy warriors and winged dragons.[1] In the Saga of Ketil Trout *(Ketils saga hœngs), a Norwegian chieftain named Ketil Trout of Hrafnista squared off against a flying reptile that attacked him while he was traveling. Likewise, the* Saga of Þiðrekr of Bern *(Þiðreks saga af Bern), whose titular character was based on the Ostrogothic king of Italy Theodoric the Great (d. 526), related how Þiðrekr and his companion Fasold interrupted a dragon as it attempted to devour a hapless victim whole. In the ensuing battle, they slew the monster to set him free. In these legend-shrouded stories, the dragons were predatory beasts of nature. They did not speak or hoard treasure like Fáfnir. Instead, they were simply one of the many perils that confronted those who were brave or foolhardy enough to traverse the harsh wilderness of the northern world.*

(A) THE HUNTER BECOMES
THE HUNTED[2]

One evening after sunset Ketil took his ax in hand and went north toward an island. But he had not gotten very far away from the farm when he saw a dragon flying southward toward him from some rocky cliffs. It had a coil and tail like a *wyrm* but wings like a dragon. Fire seemed to burn forth from its eyes and maw. Ketil thought he had never seen such a fish or any other such evil creature, and he would rather have had to defend himself against a host of men. The dragon attacked him, but Ketil defended himself well and manfully with his ax. So it went for a long while until Ketil was able to strike the coil and cut the dragon in two. It fell down dead.

(B) RESCUED FROM
THE DRAGON'S MAW[3]

They [Þiðrekr and Fasold] see a huge flying dragon (*flugdreka*). It is both long and stout; it has thick legs and claws both sharp and long. Its head is huge and terrifying. It flies along close to the ground and everywhere its claws rake the earth, it was as if the sharpest iron blade had struck it. In its mouth it is carrying a man [Sistram] and had swallowed his legs and everything up to his arms. His head and shoulders were sticking out of its mouth. His arms were in the lower jaws, and the man was still alive . . . They leap from their horses and draw their swords and both strike the dragon at the same time. Þiðrekr's sword cut somewhat, but Fasold's not at all. Although the dragon was big and strong, it was beyond its power to carry the man along with the weapons, and it could not rise aloft to fly or to defend itself, as it would have done if it were free. Then the man in the dragon's mouth said to Fasold: "I see that your sword does not cut into him because he is so tough-skinned. Take the sword here in the dragon's jaws; it is more likely to cut most anything that comes under its blade, if a brave man wields it . . . Strike carefully. My legs have gone way down into the dragon's throat and you should take care because I do not want to be wounded by my own sword . . . Strike hard, good lads, because the evil dragon is squeezing me so hard with his jaws that blood is springing from my mouth and I do not know how all this is going to turn out." Now they both struck with mighty strokes until the dragon was dead. The man was now set free from the dragon's mouth.

BOOKS OF MONSTERS

Dragon Lore in
Medieval Europe

In the decades around the year 1000, the skies of northern Europe were alive with dragons. Writing in the 1040s, the monastic chronicler Rodulfus Glaber reported that a great dragon had appeared over the city of Auxerre on Christmas Eve in the year 997. Traveling from north to south and shimmering with a great brightness, this monster terrified onlookers. In medieval Europe, a dragon aroused fear not only because it was an apex predator with the potential to lay waste to human habitation with its fiery breath but also because its sudden manifestation was a portent of bad things to come. Like the appearance of comets and eclipses, the arrival of a dragon anticipated calamity in one form or another for those who witnessed it. In this case, it heralded a civil war that ravaged Burgundy the very next year at the cost of many lives. As chroniclers like Glaber attested, dragons had multivalent meanings for premodern audiences. Medieval authors were as indebted to the musings of Roman authorities like Pliny for information about the habitat and diet of these great winged serpents as they were to the writings of early Christian authors who stressed their diabolical origins. But they also freighted dragons with new meanings drawn from the currents of oral tradition, local folklore, and even firsthand experience to craft new stories about their nature and significance for generations of later readers.

A TREASURY OF ANCIENT
DRAGON LORE[1]

Bishop Isidore of Seville (ca. 560–636) was a Spanish church prelate with a voracious appetite for knowledge about the world and its inhabitants. Throughout his lifetime, he compiled a massive encyclopedia of ancient learning about subject matter as diverse as astronomy and animals, roads and rocks, buildings and birds. Known as the Etymologies, *this towering compendium distilled and preserved traditions of classical knowledge for future generations. Isidore approached this diverse range of topics with a common methodology. He believed that an understanding of the origin and definition of words was the key to unlocking information about the natural world and human societies. For this reason, every entry in the* Etymologies *began with a derivation of the root meaning of the terms related to the topic under discussion. While this may seem like a specious approach to modern readers, the* Etymologies *was a very popular resource in medieval abbeys because it served as a digest of ancient knowledge presented with the authority of a bishop. Isidore's treatment of dragons and the gems that allegedly grew on their heads was little more than a distillation of anecdotes found in Pliny's* Natural History *(see pp. 23–25), but it informed a much wider readership throughout Christian Europe who may not have had easy access to the Roman naturalist's work.*

The dragon is larger than all other serpents or even all other animals on the earth. The Greeks call this creature *draconta*, from which we derive the Latin word *draco*. Drawn forth from its caves, the dragon often takes flight and disturbs the air. It is plumed with a small mouth and narrow windpipes through which it draws breath and sticks out its tongue. Its strength lies not in its teeth, but in its tail and it kills by lashing rather than by biting. Moreover, the dragon is unharmed by venom, but it is not necessary for it to use venom to cause death because whatever it wraps itself around soon perishes. The elephant is not safe from it, even though its body is huge. For, lying in wait on the paths along which elephants habitually walk, the dragon grabs hold of their legs with knotted coils and kills them by suffocation. Dragons are born in Ethiopia and India in the very blaze of continual heat.

Dracontites is forcibly taken from the brain of a dragon, and unless it is cut from the living creature it does not have the quality of a gem. For this reason, magicians cut it out of dragons while they are sleeping. For bold men explore the cave of the dragons, and scatter medicated grains there to put them to sleep, and in this way cut off their heads while they are sunk in sleep and take out the gems.

DARK AGE CREATURE CATALOGUES[1]

While Bishop Isidore of Seville took his inspiration directly from the works of Pliny and other Roman authors, some early medieval storytellers drew from the deep well of oral traditions and folklore for their information about dragons. Compiled in pre-Conquest England before the turn of the first millennium, catalogues of fantastic creatures like the Wonders of the East *and the* Book of Monsters *described the habitat and character of monstrous races and mythological beasts that populated distant lands like Africa and India. The anonymous authors of these texts enticed their readers with stories about "the most dreadful kinds of dragons and serpents and vipers." True to their word, these inventories provided brief, yet evocative accounts of the reptilian monsters that posed a danger to human beings in the distant parts of the world (and in the underworld as well!).*

And there is another island to the south of Brixonte river on which are born men without heads who have their eyes and their mouth on their chests.[2] They are eight feet in height and likewise eight feet across. Dragons also abound there, one hundred and fifty feet long and as thick as columns. Because of the multitude of dragons, it is difficult for anyone to go across the river.

The legends of the Greeks speak of men with gigantic bodies and yet, despite their great size, they are very much like human beings, except that they have the tails of dragons, whence they are also called Dracontopodes in Greek.

And the pagans with their slanderous speech speak of the dark river Styx in the underworld as the largest serpent in the entire world, so huge that it wraps its black coils nine times around Tartarus through the dark fen of wailing souls in such a way as to invoke tears. And thus the river Styx with its serpentine barrier and the swamp with its fetid water, the terrifying edge of which no one would dare to touch, encloses the braying souls of the dead in everlasting lament.

YOU CRUSHED THEIR
HEADS UPON THE
WATERS[1]

Hrabanus Maurus (ca. 776–856) was a monastic school-master at the abbey of Fulda and later served as the archbishop of Mainz. Among the most learned intellectuals of the Carolingian period, Hrabanus produced voluminous commentaries on the Bible and an arresting series of illustrated poems in praise of the Holy Cross. He also penned a massive encyclopedia fittingly entitled About Everything (De universo). *This sprawling book explained the historical and allegorical meaning of thousands of Latin words with reference to their use in the Bible and the writings of the early church fathers. In his chapter on serpents, Hrabanus unpacked the mystical significance of the word "dragon." After rehearsing ancient traditions about their nature and habitat culled from the works of Pliny and Isidore of Seville, Hrabanus turned to the Hebrew scriptures to unveil the hidden meaning of the dragon as an allegory for unclean spirits purged by baptism and even for the Devil himself. This diabolical affinity, already present in early Christian writings, would inform literary depictions of the dragon for the rest of the Middle Ages.*

The dragon is larger than all other serpents or even all other animals on the earth. The Greeks call this creature *draconta*, from which we derive the Latin word *draco*. Drawn forth from its caves, the dragon often takes flight and disturbs the air. It is plumed with a small mouth and narrow windpipes through which it draws breath and sticks out its tongue. Its strength lies not in its teeth, but in its tail and it kills by lashing rather than by biting. Moreover, the dragon is unharmed by venom, but it is not necessary for it to use venom to cause death because whatever it wraps itself around soon perishes. The elephant is not safe from it, even though its body is huge. For, lying in wait on the paths along which elephants habitually walk, the dragon grabs hold of their legs with knotted coils and kills them by suffocation. Dragons are born in Ethiopia and India in the very blaze of continual heat.[2] Allegorically, the dragon signifies either the devil or his servants or indeed the persecutors of the church, impious men whose secrets are found in many places in scripture. For it was written concerning this in the Psalter, and in the Book of Job, and indeed in the Apocalypse of John. In fact, the psalmist says, "You made firm the sea in your might, you crushed the heads of dragons upon the waters."[3] Indeed, he made the aqueous depths of the Red Sea firm, when he parted the water on both sides and turned a sailing route into a walking path. "You crushed the heads of dragons upon the waters" explains properly the mystery of the preceding miracle, because that prefiguration of the crossing of the Red Sea pointed to the waters of holy baptism, where the heads of dragons, that is, the spirits of the unclean, are brought to nothing, when the saving water washes clean the souls, which they stain with the filth of sinners. Moreoever, the psalmist adds: "You have broken the head of the great dragon."[4] Although the psalmist put "heads of dragons" in the plural in his desire to signify spiritual depravities, he put "great dragon" in the singular to indicate Satan himself, who is so much stronger and so much more wicked. When put in the singular, he is unwilling to dwell among the malign spirits. For his head was crushed when his pride was cast out of heaven and he did not deserve to retain that brightness with which he was born, when he stained himself with a darkness of his own making.

REMEMBERING A
PANNONIAN DRAGON[1]

*Around the year 1030, a monk of the Bavarian abbey of
St. Emmeram in Regensburg named Arnold encountered
a dragon while he was on a mission to Pannonia for his
abbot. Years later, he recorded his memory of this encounter in a collection of miracles that he compiled to celebrate the virtues of Saint Emmeram. In emulation of
Gregory the Great's* Dialogues *(see pp. 47–49), Arnold
presented this work in the form of a discussion, in which
he played the role of the gatherer of information* (Collectitius) *in conversation with an interlocutor who urged
him to stay on topic* (Ammonicius). *Arnold's digression
about his dragon encounter was among the most vivid reports of its kind from the premodern period with details
unattested in other ancient and early medieval authorities. The Pannonian dragon was a giant aerial serpent,
but unlike the depictions of dragons that Arnold knew
from illuminated manuscripts at his abbey, this monster
had no wings or legs. Strangely, it also emanated a supernatural chill that caused fevers and killed cattle. The
monk recognized that this was not the dragon described
in the* Book of Revelation *(see pp. 34–35), because the
end times were not yet at hand. Rather, it had more in
common with the description of dragons provided by
Isidore of Seville in his* Etymologies *(see pp. 85–86),
which Arnold quoted at length at the end of his report.*

Ammonicius: What are the powers of the air, and how can
wicked spirits take a place in the heavens, when the heavens

permit no evil to dwell there? Some ask this and thus it should be explained.

Collectitius: This report concerning these things is not my own, but the words of the blessed Apostle Paul. Thus, those who do not know that the reaches of the air are called the heavens and do not know that the rebel angels dwell in them and moreover are accustomed to doubt the words of the apostles, I send them to the second letter of Peter, in which he teaches the faithful about the reaches of the air, which are called the heavens, lost in the first flood and soon to be lost again in the second, saying thus: "The scoffers deliberately forgot that the heavens came into being before all else and the earth was formed out of water and by water. By these waters the world was flooded and destroyed at that time. By the same word, the heavens and the earth of today are reserved for fire, being kept for the day of judgment and the destruction of impious men." [2] And a little further on: "The burning heavens will dissipate and the elements will melt in the heat of the flame. We await new heavens and a new earth in which justice will dwell in accordance with the Lord's promise."[3] Concerning the expelled angels, who wander in the heavens to be destroyed by fire, whom the apostle calls aerial powers and evil spirits, whose multitude is so great in the air, that is, in the lower heavens, that it was revealed to a certain holy man that if these angels had corporeal bodies like ours, they would block the light of the sun from mortals, the apostle Jude shared his opinion in this manner in a letter that is counted among the canonical books: "The Lord will reserve for judgment with eternal chains in darkness the angels who did not keep their own sovereignty but abandoned their habitation in the judgment of the great day." [4] Therefore, concerning the question proposed and resolved in accordance with the testimony of the apostles, I do not know if anyone will have cause to doubt it. I certainly do not doubt it. But I learned and I know that the Devil and his damned followers exist both in Hell and in the air. Indeed, I am even more certain because when I was in Pannonia a few years ago, on a certain day from the third hour to the sixth hour I saw the Devil or a dragon suspended in the air. Its size was unbelievable with such a great length that it seemed to be one thousand feet long. Its head was plumed and lifted up like a mountain and its body was just like what the Lord said to blessed Job concerning Leviathan: enclosed with horrible scales and protected as though with small shields.[5] A sooty blackness stained its sides and back. A pale hue of blue like that of a hellish ghost discolored the underside of its belly and also the part of its body on which it was accustomed to lie. Every aspect of the dragon—its twisting, drawn-out form with its huge coils and the undulation of its entire body, whether in part or as a whole—was harmful to mortals, inasmuch as God permitted, and even more so the closer one was to the creature. For, although it was summertime, namely on the sixth weekday of the second week after Pentecost, the air grew cold from the chill that is more natural to the dragon than to any other animals with the result that many people contracted fevers and the coldness killed no small part of the livestock.[6] Finally, the dragon did not have nor seem to have wings and legs or feet, which painters are accustomed to render; rather, its scales and ribs sufficed for moving it around. The thickness of its chest was equal to the thickness of its head. After this, its body diminished gradually in size down to the end of its tail, the tip of which was equal in size to giant fir trees. Refusing to terrify the faithful any longer, the Lord caused this giant enemy, either the Devil or a friend of the Devil, to be blown away suddenly by the north wind and to be lost in the density of clouds with great speed. We watched it pass over us in the swiftest flight and not without fear we heard its hiss along with the harsh sound of its windpipes. Suddenly the clouds, which were resting as though immobile from the morning until that very hour, were agitated and set in violent motion, with the result that for that entire day and night the thunder and lightning did not cease; indeed, the storms lasted until the evening on the following day.

Ammonicius: Is it possible that you recalled at that time something that the blessed John wrote about the dragon and beast in his Apocalypse?

Collectitius: Indeed, these things came to mind, the recollection of this same scripture urged me especially, in which it is written, "Woe to you, because the dragon comes to you with great wrath, knowing that he may have but a little time."[7] For although I knew that the Antichrist and the Devil are indicated by the beast and the dragon, and the day of universal judgment had hardly arrived at that time, nevertheless, disturbed by these unusual sights, I reflected on many things and, fearful, I sighed for my death and the death of the others, who were witnessing these terrible events with me. Then, having been restored in the hope of living through the respite of divine mercy, I first gave thanks to almighty God, who freed us from the power of the Devil. Then I began to turn over or consider in my mind whether I had ever found in reading or in scrutinizing the scriptures anything such as I had seen happen on that day. And among the things that had run through my mind, the words and writings of the blessed bishop Isidore returned to my memory, who in the book of *Etymologies* wrote concerning the nature of the dragon in this manner: "The dragon is larger than all other serpents or even all other animals on the earth. The Greeks call this creature *draconta*, from which we derive the Latin word *draco*. Drawn forth from its caves, the dragon often takes flight and disturbs the air. It is plumed with a small mouth and narrow windpipes through which it draws breath and sticks out its tongue. Its strength lies not in its teeth, but in its tail and it kills by lashing rather than by biting. Moreover, the dragon is unharmed by venom, but it is not necessary for it to use venom to cause death because whatever it wraps itself around soon perishes. The elephant is not safe from it, even though its body is huge. For, lying in wait on the paths along which elephants habitually walk, the dragon grabs hold of their legs with knotted coils and kills them by suffocation. Dragons are born in Ethiopia and India in the very blaze of continual heat."[8]

Ammonicius: I believe that these things either seen by you or written by others concerning the nature of the dragon or concerning the beast, that friend of the ancient enemy, will suffice. Therefore, it is now necessary for you to return to the topic from which you have digressed.

GOD'S FIERY VENGEANCE[1]

When the cathedral of Laon burned down during a local insurrection in the year 1112, the canons who served there took their precious relics of Mary, the mother of God, on a series of tours around southern England and northern France to raise money to rebuild their church. Their efforts were successful. A few decades later, Abbot Herman of Tournai (1095–1147) recorded the wonders that took place on these tours in a work called Concerning the Miracles of Blessed Mary of Laon. Among the supernatural events recorded by Herman was the appearance of a dragon. When the deacon of a church near Winchester did not receive the Virgin's entourage with due respect and cast the canons and their relics out into the rain, the family of a tradesman in town for the local market offered to shelter them from the storm. Angered at the offense to his mother, God sent a fire-breathing dragon to lay waste to the deacon's church and his belongings, while sparing the property of those who had helped the canons. This dragon was unusual in the Christian tradition not only because it had five heads but also because it was depicted as an instrument of divine vengeance meted out to a careless believer who failed to show proper respect to the relics of the Virgin.

After a meal on the same day of the Lord, once we had received permission from the residents of that place and had given thanks to them for their kindness, we set forth from the town. But the just judge did not put off avenging the injury done to his mother. Indeed, we had hardly gone as far as the length of half of a stade when behold, couriers on horseback came after us with a shout and implored us to come to the aid of the burning town.[2] Looking back, we saw that the entire town had been reduced to ashes. When we asked how this had happened, we heard from them that a dragon had emerged from the sea nearby. It had flown to the town just as we were departing and had burned down first the church and then several houses with flames that it sent forth from its nostrils. Hearing this and thirsting with a natural curiosity to see such a wonder, we left the litter well guarded and rushed back to the town quickly on horseback.[3] There we saw a dragon of incredible size with five heads emitting sulfurous flames through its nostrils and flying from place to place, burning down houses one by one. Returning to the church, we found that it was now burned to ashes, and to an unbelievable degree, so that not only the wood, but also the very walls, even the largest stones and the very altars, had been utterly reduced to spark and cinder, with the result that a strange sense of amazement was felt by everyone who observed it.

Indeed, when the deacon saw that his house and his church had been burned down, he gathered up his clothes and his belongings and loaded them on a boat, which had been moored on the shore of the nearby sea, and he set it adrift in the hope that his possessions might be saved from the flames. But immediately, as if he came for this reason alone, the dragon sought the vessel from on high and burned everything that was in it and finally—remarkable to say and incredible to hear!—he incinerated the boat as well. Coming to the house of our host and eager to know how he was faring, we found him rejoicing that his house and everything in it had been saved. He attributed the safekeeping of his good home to the queen of Heaven. Not only did his house, in which we received hospitality, remain unharmed, but so too did other buildings further away, in which he said that his livestock were kept, so that he lost absolutely nothing from all of his belongings. Divine grace comforted the tradesmen as well, who had shown great kindness to us, with the result that either nothing or only a small amount of their goods were lost.

For, because it was a custom there for the market to last for only one day, once the meal had been finished, they had gathered all of their loads and had stored them safe and sound before the dragon came. But the sight of the dragon struck them with the utmost terror, so that we saw them fleeing with great speed hither and thither. Indeed, the very deacon who had cast out the litter of our Lady from the church was moved by a tardy penance. He followed after the litter in bare feet and prostrated in its presence. Once the deacon had testified to the just judgments of God brought on because he had behaved so poorly, he begged to be forgiven.

BONE FIRES AND DRAGON
SPERM[1]

The vigil of Saint John the Baptist (June 24) was a solemn feast day in the medieval church, on which Christians marked the birthday of the forerunner of Christ with a special solemnity. One of the customs associated with this feast day was the lighting of fires. In the twelfth century, the French theologian John Beleth (fl. 1135–82) revealed the ancient origins of this custom in a treatise on liturgical practices called the Summa on Ecclesiastical Offices *(composed ca. 1162). According to Beleth, the custom arose from the need to ward off dragons with the smoke of fires made of animal bones. Our modern term "bonfire" finds its origin in this medieval practice. Despite the dubious intent of their original purpose, these "bonfires" were a fitting way to celebrate the feast day of the Baptist because he was the "burning light" who foretold the coming of Christ.*

At this time [on the feast day of Saint John the Baptist], they were in the habit of burning the bones of dead animals according to an ancient custom. The origin of this custom is as follows. There are animals, which we call dragons, as we know from the psalm: "Praise the Lord, you dragons of the earth!"[2] . . . These animals, I say, fly in the air, swim in the waters, and walk on the land. But when they are aroused with lust in the air (which usually happens), they often squirt their sperm either in wells or in river waters, as a result of which a lethal year follows. Therefore, to ward them off, a remedy of this kind was contrived, namely, that a pyre was constructed from bones, and in this way the smoke chased away these animals. And because this happened chiefly at that time of year, everyone observed it in this fashion. There is also another reason why the bones of animals were burned, namely, because the bones of Saint John were burned by the pagans in the city of Sebasta.[3] Likewise, it is customary on this vigil to carry small burning torches because John was the burning light, and he prepared the way of the Lord.

THE PROPHECIES OF
MERLIN[1]

Dragons also featured prominently in prophecies attributed to the wizard Merlin in story cycles related to the legends of King Arthur. The British historian Geoffrey of Monmouth (ca. 1095–ca. 1155) incorporated many of these tales in his chronicle, The History of the Kings of Britain (Historia regum Britanniae). *Written in 1136, Geoffrey's work provided a mythical history of Britain from the founding of the kingdom by Brutus, the great-grandson of the Trojan refugee Aeneas, who established the city of Rome, to the death of King Arthur around the seventh century. In one of his many prophecies, Merlin revealed to King Vortigern that the cause of a collapsing tower was two dragons—one red and one white—sleeping in a subterranean pool of water beneath the structure. When the pool had been drained, the dragons woke up and fought one another until the white dragon emerged victorious. When asked to elucidate the meaning of this dragon battle, Merlin explained to his king that it portended the end of his kingdom, for the red dragon represented the people of Britian, who would soon be overrun by Saxon invaders.*

In the end Vortigern summoned his magicians, asked them for their opinion, and ordered them to tell him what to do. They all gave him the same advice: that he should build for himself an immensely strong tower, into which he could retreat in safety if he should lose all his other fortresses. He surveyed a great number of places in an attempt to find a site suitable for this, and in the end he came to Mount Erith. There he assembled stonemasons from different parts of the country and ordered them to build a tower for him. The masons gathered and began to lay the foundations of their tower. However much they built one day the earth swallowed up the next, in such a way that they had no idea where their work had vanished to.

When this was announced to Vortigern, he consulted his magicians a second time, to give them a chance of explaining the reason for it. They told him that he should look for a lad without a father, and that, when he had found one, he should kill him, so that the mortar and the stones could be sprinkled with the lad's blood. According to them, the result of this would be that the foundations would hold firm.

Messengers were immediately sent out through the different parts of the country to find such a person if they could. They came to a town which was afterwards called Kaermerdin and there they saw some lads playing by the town gate. They went to look at the game. Tired by their journey, they sat down in a circle, still hoping to find what they were seeking. At last, when much of the day had passed, a sudden quarrel broke out between two of the lads, whose names were Merlin and Dinabutius. As they argued, Dinabutius said to Merlin: "Why do you try to compete with me, fathead? How can we two be equal in skill? I myself am of royal blood on both sides of my family. As for you, nobody knows who you are, for you never had a father!" At this word the messengers looked up. They examined Merlin closely and asked the standers-by who he was. They were told that no one knew who his father had been, but that his mother was daughter of a king of Demetia and that she lived in the same town, in St. Peter's Church, along with some nuns.

The messengers lost no time. They hurried off to the governor of the town and ordered him in the King's name to send Merlin and his mother to Vortigern. When the governor knew the object of their errand, he immediately sent Merlin and his mother to Vortigern, so that the King could do what he wanted with them. When they were brought into his presence, the King received the mother with due courtesy, for he knew that she came of a noble family. Then he began to ask her by what man she had conceived the lad. "By my living soul, Lord King," she said, "and by your living soul, too, I did not have relations with any man to make me bear this child. I know only this: that, when I was in our private apartments with my sister nuns, someone used to come to me in the form of a handsome young man. He would often hold me tightly in his arms and kiss me. When he had been some little time with me he would disappear, so that I could no longer see him. Many times, too, when I was sitting alone, he would talk with me, without becoming visible; and when he came to see me in this way he would often make love with me, as a man would do, and in that way he made me pregnant. You must decide in your wisdom, my Lord, who was the father of this lad, for apart from what I have told, I have never had relations with a man."

The King was amazed by what he heard. He ordered a certain Maugantius to be summoned to him, so that this man could tell whether or not what the woman said was possible. Maugantius was brought in and listened to the whole story, point by point. "In the books written by our sages," he said to Vortigern, "and in many historical narratives, I have discovered that quite a number of men have been born in this way. As Apuleius asserts in the *De deo Socratis*, between the moon and the earth live spirits which we call incubus demons.[2] These have partly the nature of men and partly that of angels, and when they wish they assume mortal shapes and have intercourse with women. It is possible that one of these appeared to this woman and begot the lad in her."

When he had listened to all this, Merlin went up to the King and asked: "Why have my mother and I been brought into your presence?" "My magicians have advised me," answered Vortigern, "that I should look for a fatherless man, so that my building can be sprinkled with his blood and thus stand firm." "Tell your magicians to appear in front of me," answered Merlin, "and I will prove that they have lied."

The King was amazed at what Merlin said. He ordered his

magicians to come immediately and sit down in front of Merlin. "Just because you do not know what is obstructing the foundations of the tower which men have begun," said Merlin to the magicians, "you have recommended that my blood should be sprinkled on the mortar to make the building stand firm. Tell me, then, what lies hidden under the foundation. There is certainly something there which is preventing it from holding firm."

The magicians, who were terrified, said nothing. Merlin, who was also called Ambrosius, then went on: "My Lord King, summon your workmen. Order them to dig in the earth, and, underneath, you will find a pool. That is what is preventing the tower from standing." This was done. A pool was duly found beneath the earth, and it was this which made the ground unsteady.

Ambrosius Merlin went up to the magicians a second time and said: "Tell me, now, you lying flatterers. What lies beneath the pool?" They remained silent, unable to utter a single sound. "Order the pool to be drained," said Merlin, "and at the bottom you will observe two hollow stones. Inside the stones you will see two Dragons which are sleeping."

The King believed what Merlin said, for he had told the truth about the pool. He ordered the pool to be drained. He was more astounded by Merlin than he had ever been by anything. All those present were equally amazed by his knowledge, and they realized that there was something supernatural about him.

While Vortigern, King of the Britons, was still sitting on the bank of the pool which had been drained of its water, there emerged two Dragons, one white, one red. As soon as they were near enough to each other, they fought bitterly, breathing out fire as they panted. The White Dragon began to have the upper hand and to force the Red One back to the edge of the pool. The Red Dragon bewailed the fact that it was being driven out and then turned upon the White One and forced it backward in its turn. As they struggled on in this way, the

King ordered Ambrosius Merlin to explain just what this battle of the Dragons meant. Merlin immediately burst into tears. He went into a prophetic trance and then spoke as follows:

"Alas for the Red Dragon, for its end is near. Its cavernous dens shall be occupied by the White Dragon, which stands for the Saxons whom you have invited over. The Red Dragon represents the people of Britain, who will be overrun by the White One: for Britain's mountains and valleys shall be leveled, and the streams in its valleys shall run with blood."

THE DEVIL IS THE LARGEST SERPENT[1]

Based on late antique models and reaching a height of popularity in the twelfth and thirteenth centuries, medieval bestiaries were collections of pithy stories about the nature of animals (and often plants and stones as well) that explained their symbolic meaning in a medieval Christian worldview. Some of these animals were common, like dogs and horses; others were exotic, like elephants and panthers; while others still were legendary, like unicorns and the hydra. Medieval bestiaries varied in content, containing anywhere between fifty and one hundred anecdotes, but they all served the same purpose: to educate and entertain medieval readers with stories about manifestations of Christian truth in God's creation. The dragon featured prominently in the medieval bestiary tradition as an avatar of the Devil, who entangled the unwary in the bonds of sin in the same way that the dragon snared the legs of the elephant in its dark coils and thereby brought about its death.

THE PANTHER

There is an animal called the panther, varied in color, but exceptionally beautiful and very docile. The naturalist says that it is the dragon's only enemy.[2] For when it has eaten and sated itself from all of its hunts, it returns to its cave and lying down, it sleeps for three days. Rising from sleep, it suddenly emits a roar on high and at the same time it emits an odor of exquisite sweetness with its roar, the smell of which surpasses all aromas and pigments. When all of the beasts hear the panther's voice, whether they are near or far, they assemble and follow its sweetness. But the dragon alone is struck with fear when he hears the panther's voice and hides in his subterranean caves. There, unable to bear the power of the odor, the dragon curls up, numb and stiff, and remains immobile and lifeless, as though dead. In contrast, the other animals follow the odor wherever it goes. Thus our Lord Jesus Christ, the true panther, rescued the entire human race that was held captive by the Devil and vulnerable to death, drawing them to him through his incarnation and, leading captivity as a captive, he gave gifts to men.[3]

THE DRAGON

The dragon is the largest of all the serpents and all the animals on earth. The Greeks call it *draconta*, the Latins *draco*.[4] Drawn forth from its caves, the dragon often takes flight. The air shines when the dragon disturbs it. The dragon is plumed with a small mouth and narrow windpipes, through which it draws breath and sticks out its tongue. Its strength lies not in its teeth, but in its tail and it kills by lashing rather than by biting. Moreover, the dragon is unharmed by venom, but it is not necessary for it to use venom to cause death because whatever it wraps itself around soon perishes. The elephant is not safe from it, even though its body is huge. For, lying in wait on the paths along which elephants habitually walk, the dragon grabs hold of their legs with knotted coils and kills them by suffocation. Dragons live in Ethiopia and in India where from the heat of the sun there is continual heat like summer. The Devil, who is the largest serpent, is similar to the dragon. He is often roused from his cave and takes to the air, which shines because of him, for from the beginning the Devil raised himself up and transfigured himself into an angel of light and deceived the foolish with the hope of false glory and human happiness. He is said to be plumed because he is the king of pride. He has venom not in his teeth, but in his tongue because, having lost all of his power, he deceives with lies those whom he has drawn to himself. He lurks on the paths, along which the elephants walk, because the Devil always follows mighty men. He binds their legs with the coils of his tail and ensnares them, if he can, because he will hinder their way to heaven with the coils of sin, and he slays by suffocating because whoever dies entangled in the bond of sins will without doubt be damned in Hell.

THE PERIDEXION TREE

There is a tree in India whose branches hang down. Moreover, the fruit of this tree is altogether sweet and very delicious. The doves delight in the fruits of this tree and they reside in it, eating its fruit. The dragon, however, is an enemy to the doves, and it fears the tree and its shadow where the doves linger, and it is able to approach neither the tree nor its shadow. For if the tree's shadow falls to the west, the dragon flees to the east, and vice versa. If, however, it should happen that a dove is found beyond the tree or its shadow, the dragon kills it. Consider that this tree is God the Father, the shadow is his son, just as Gabriel says to Mary: "The Holy Spirit will come over you, and the power of the Almighty will cast a shadow upon you." [5] The fruit is the heavenly wisdom of the Lord, namely, the Holy Spirit. See, therefore, O man, that after you have received the Holy Spirit, that is, the spiritual dove, perceivable and hovering above you, that you do not forsake immortality by becoming a stranger to the father, the son, and the Holy Spirit, lest the dragon destroy you, that is, the Devil. For if you have the Holy Spirit, the dragon cannot approach you. Harken, therefore, O man, and remain in the Catholic faith. Take care as much as you can lest you find yourself outside the house and the dragon, that ancient serpent, catches you outdoors and devours you like Judas, who as soon as he left the house with his apostolic brothers was immediately devoured by a demon and perished. [6]

HUNTING MONSTERS IN
KARA-JANG[1]

*Toward the end of the thirteenth century, the Venetian
merchant and explorer Marco Polo (1254–1324) visited
the court of Kublai Khan, the ruler of the Mongol Empire. Polo lived in China for seventeen years in the service
of the khan, traveling extensively throughout his vast territories on diplomatic missions to neighboring polities in
southern Asia. Upon his return to Europe in the 1290s,
Polo was imprisoned in Genoa, where he narrated the
stories of his travels to his cellmate Rustichello da Pisa.
Throughout his* Travels, *Polo provided eyewitness accounts of the cultures of many Asian peoples hitherto unknown to European readers. In the kingdom of Kara-jang
(modern Yunnan Province, China), he described enormous serpents that resembled dragons. These were most
likely Chinese alligators (the critically endangered* Alligator sinensis*), whose size and eating habits had been amplified in Polo's imagination by time and distance. Free
from the moralizing of the popular bestiary tradition (see
pp. 106–108), Polo described in detail the ways in which
local hunters killed these creatures not only for their meat
but for the medicinal properties of their gall.*

In this province live huge snakes and serpents of such a size
that no one could help being amazed even to hear of them.
They are loathsome creatures to behold. Let me tell you just
how big they are. You may take it for a fact that there are
some of them ten paces in length that are as thick as a stout
cask: for their girth runs to about ten palms. These are the

biggest. They have two squat legs in front near the head, which have no feet but simply three claws, two small and one bigger, like the claws of a falcon or a lion. They have enormous heads and eyes so bulging that they are bigger than loaves. Their mouth is big enough to swallow a man at one gulp. Their teeth are huge. All in all, the monsters are of such inordinate bulk and ferocity that there is neither man nor beast but goes in fear of them. There are also smaller ones, not exceeding eight paces in length, or six or it may be five.

Let me tell you how these monsters are trapped. You must know that by day they remain underground because of the great heat; at nightfall, they sally out to hunt and feed and seize whatever prey they can come by. They go down to drink at streams and lakes and springs. They are so bulky and heavy and of such a girth that when they pass through sand on their nightly search for food or drink they scoop out a furrow through the way sand that looks as if a butt full of wine had been rolled that way. Now the hunters who set out to catch them lay traps at various places in the trails that show which way the snakes are accustomed to go down the banks into the water. These are made by embedding in the earth a stout wooden stake to which is fixed a sharp steel tip like a razor-blade or lance-head, projecting about a palm's breadth beyond the stake and slanting in the direction from which the serpents approach. This is covered with sand, so that nothing of the stake is visible. Traps of this sort are laid in great numbers. When the snake, or rather the serpent, comes down the trail to drink, he runs full-tilt into the steel, so that it pierces his chest and rips his belly right to the navel and he dies on the spot. The hunter knows that the serpent is dead by the cry of the birds, and then he ventures to approach his prey. Otherwise he dare not draw near.

When the hunters have trapped a serpent by this means, they draw out the gall from the belly and sell it for a high price, for you must know that it makes a potent medicine. If a man is bitten by a mad dog, he is given a drop of it to drink—the weight of a halfpenny—and he is cured forthwith. And when a woman is in labor and cries aloud with the pangs of travail, she is given a drop of the serpent's gall and as soon as she has drunk it she is delivered of her child forthwith. Its third use is when someone is afflicted by any sort of growth: he puts a drop of this gall on it and is cured in a day or two. For these reasons the gall of this serpent is highly prized in these provinces. The flesh also commands a good price, because it is very good to eat and is esteemed as a delicacy.

Another thing about these serpents: they go to the dens where lions and bears and other beasts of prey have their cubs and gobble them up—parents as well as young—if they can get at them.

DRACONIC DEMONS AND OGRES

Dragons in Byzantium

Long after the collapse of the imperial administration in western Europe in the fifth century CE, the legacy of Rome thrived in the eastern Mediterranean for another millennium until the fall of Constantinople to the armies of Sultan Mehmed II in 1453. During this period, the inhabitants of the eastern Roman Empire (now commonly known as Byzantium) pondered the mysteries of dragons in theological works and scientific treatises, while portraying them as frightful adversaries in saints' lives and vernacular poetry. Situated between the cultures of western Europe and eastern Asia, Byzantine thinkers drew from ancient, Christian, and Islamic traditions for their information about dragons, but they also embroidered these traditions with new representations of these frightful creatures. While dragons appeared as giant reptiles in Byzantine literature, they were often demons in disguise. More surprisingly, they also took the form of humanoid monsters with a lust for women. The legacy of their depredations still resonates today, because these draconic ogres of the Middle Ages very likely informed the contemporary use of the word "dragon" in modern Greek (drakos) to describe violent serial rapists who stalk particular areas.

A THEOLOGIAN
CONTEMPLATES THE
NATURE OF DRAGONS[1]

John of Damascus (ca. 675–749) was one of the greatest theologians in the Byzantine Orthodox tradition and lived under Muslim Arab rule in Syria and Palestine. Among his voluminous works was preserved a short discussion of dragons followed by a shorter one on witches (succubae). Scholars have rejected the attribution of these works to John, so they are effectively anonymous. It was common for works to be attributed to famous authors so that they would be taken seriously. This discussion of dragons was recopied (with minor changes) by an eleventh-century author of practical maxims, Kekaumenos, and so we can date its composition to between the later eighth and the early eleventh century. It took the form of a response to those who tell fantastic tales about dragons and argued that they are, after all, only natural creatures.

People sometimes imagine that dragons take human form, or sometimes become small snakes while at other times they become very large snakes, gargantuan in bulk and bodily size. Sometimes, as mentioned, they become people and hold conversations with other people; they come along, seize women, and have sex with them.[2] So we ask people who imagine these things, "How many rational kinds of creature did God make?" And if they do not know, we tell them, "The answer is two: angels and human beings. The Devil is one of the angelic powers, and he voluntarily separated himself from the light and walks in darkness. These are the two rational entities that God made. But as for dragons, since they speak with human beings, change their own shape and have intercourse with women, and are sometimes snakes and sometimes people, becoming one among the many, it is clear that they are rational creatures, even above human beings in honor. But this was never the case, nor will it ever be true."

Suppose they say, "Who explains this?" We say, "We trust in the teachings of Moses, or rather of the Holy Spirit, who spoke through Moses. And this is what he says: 'God led every kind of animal before Adam, to see what he would call it. And whatever he called it, that was its name.'[3] Thus, the dragon must have been one of the animals. I am not saying to you that dragons do not exist. Dragons do exist, but they are snakes, born of other dragons. When they are newborns and young, they are small, but when they grow up, and then grow old, they become large and fat, surpassing other snakes in bulk and size. They say that dragons grow to more than thirty cubits and grow in girth like a large wooden beam. Dio the Roman, who wrote the history of the kings and Republic of Rome, recounted the famous Punic war. He says that when Regulus, the consul of Rome, was fighting against Carthage, a dragon suddenly slithered out and lay outside the Roman camp.[4] At his command, the Romans killed it and skinned it, and he sent the skin to the Roman Senate. It was an amazing sight. The Senate measured it, as Dio himself says, and it was found to be 120 feet long. Its girth was comparable to its length.

"There is also another species of dragon that has a broad head and golden eyes; some of them have horns on their tendon whereas others have beards under the chin.[5] This species is called the Agathodaemon, or Benevolent Spirit. It is said that these do not have venom. So a dragon is a natural species, just like the rest of the animals. It has a beard just like the goat, and a horn on its tendon. Its eyes are large and golden in color. Dragons come in both large and small sizes. All other species of snakes have venom, except the dragon alone, which does not.

"The fables also say that dragons are pursued by thunderstorms, for they are swept up by the air currents and killed. But when I heard this, I laughed. How can they sometimes give it a human shape and make it rational, and at other times a snake? Or sometimes an enemy of God, and other times hunted down by God? Truly, ignorance is a dangerous thing. We are greatly harmed by not reading the sacred books and conducting research in them, according to the Word of the Lord. Instead, the soldier says, 'I am a soldier and do not need to read.' As for the farmer, he cites farming as his excuse, and the other professions likewise, and so we all end up deficient. Thunderstorms do not hunt dragons but are caused by clouds, when the humidity fills them up with water and they acquire more volume and then are driven on by the air, namely, the wind. When the wind gets inside and ruptures the cloud, it causes the sound. This clap from above, then, is called thunder. And that which is driven forcibly by the wind down to earth is called a thunderbolt. Whether it falls upon a house or a tree, it ruptures and tears them apart. If it falls upon a person or some other animal, it kills it. Accordingly, we frequently see people and other animals killed by thunderstorms, but not dragons."

WHY DRAGONS FEAR
LIGHTNING[1]

Michael Psellos (1018–ca. 1075) was one of the most versatile Byzantine intellectuals. A politician intimately implicated in the events of his time, he wrote a fascinating history, the Chronographia. *He also sought to revive ancient philosophy and science, which, he believed, had fallen into decline among his contemporaries. He composed works in almost every genre of Byzantine literature and gave lectures at a school that he founded with imperial support. Some of these lectures are on scientific matters and largely summarize ancient theories, but that is apparently not true of the following presentation on dragons, which weighs the possible reasons why dragons fear lightning, a topic hitherto unaddressed in ancient or medieval dragon lore.*

You have asked me today for the first time about rainbows, but let us postpone that discussion for another day, for it is a large and complicated topic that requires a detailed investigation . . . Now, I will try to give a scientific explanation about the other matters that you have set forth, as far as I am able. They are the following: What manner of fire does lightning have and from where does it come when it flashes forth? Is every fire that rushes down from the clouds capable of burning? . . . Is it true what some people say, that the race of dragons fears lightning-fire, or even that this fire is actually waging a war against dragons and that it targets them with an irresistible momentum, propelled by almost voluntary powers? And what are we to make of the sights we observe in the blaze of lightning, which sometimes imitate one animal, and sometimes another? . . .

As for dragons, I have not yet, to this day, come across any treatise that explains, in the terms of natural science, why they fear lightning. So once the first person has done so [that is, Psellos himself]—and I too will refer it to my conception of nature—then perhaps another person will give a more exact interpretation of it.

I, then, say that the race of dragons is dry by nature and fiery in substance. Even their eyes blaze forth with fire and the venom that they vomit forth is smoky and it dissolves any bodies that it touches. Thus, dragons are vulnerable to fire on account of their dryness and they are liable to be burned up. Hence, they fear lightning and leap through the air looking for enclosed spaces under the earth, especially around lakes and cisterns, since, as I said, they are vulnerable to fire on account of their dryness and can be burned up by lightning-fire, even from a distance. That is why, wherever a dragon appears, hissing as it passes through, lightning strikes there, ravaging the adjacent areas. It is often the case that rattling, hissing, and grunting sounds are heard even without a dragon present . . . But if a malicious demon should take on the body of a dragon and, pursued by fire, should lead the beast to those places where the demon was already accustomed to spread its malice, this account is not to be rejected entirely out of hand. For this is the ancient agenda of that race, on account of which it formerly drove us out of Paradise and is now attempting, again through its ill-omened malice, to remove us from the earth as well.

A DEMON IN DISGUISE[1]

When Psellos said that demons sometimes take the form of dragons, he may have been thinking of the Martyrdom of Saint Marina, *a hagiographical romance written probably before the seventh century. It concerned a (legendary) virgin maiden from Pisidian Antioch (modern Turkey), who lived when the Roman Empire was still pagan. As happened often to her kind in these tales, she was persecuted by an imperial official who was captivated by her beauty. After torturing her, he placed her in a jail cell, where a demon named Rufus appeared in the form of a dragon to kill her. When Marina defeated the dragon, its demonic accomplice arrived to finish the job, but it too succumbed to the power of her prayers. Elements of this story later circulated in medieval Europe in legends associated with Saint Margaret (see pp. 158–60).*

When Marina finished her prayer, a great earthquake occurred in that place, and the jail was shaken. Suddenly, out from the corner a great dragon emerged, terrible to behold, and its skin varied in color. His hair and beard were like gold. His teeth gleamed and his eyes were like pearls. Fiery flame and a great quantity of smoke issued from his nostrils. His tongue was like blood and serpents were coiled about his neck. The corners of his eyes were like silver and he stood in the middle of the jail, roaring and hissing. Then he ran in a circle around Marina, holding a bared sword, and his hissing filled the jail with a horrendous stench. The holy virgin was terrified: her bones rattled and her face changed complexion. She forgot her prayer out of sheer fear. But the Lord complied with her request and revealed to her the Enemy and

Adversary of all people. Bending her knee, she began to pray and to say, "Invisible God, whose visage can dry up the deep sea, you are the one who places limits on Hades; who loosens the bonds of the earth, so that it does not waver; who humbles the power of the dragon, that enemy of the good; who bound Hades and freed those who were enclosed within it. Give me now the benefit of your watchfulness and take pity on me. Do not allow me to be treated unjustly by the evil demon. May it be your will, Lord, that I defeat his flame, whose identity I would not have recognized."

When she said these things, the dragon was provoked and hissed at her fiercely. But the holy servant of God made the sign of the cross on her forehead and over her entire body. In tears, she prayed, saying, "Lord, make this evil wolf and rabid dog be gone from my presence, along with his stench. And let the sweet goodness of your holy spirit come upon me." As she said these things, the dragon became mightily angry at her and took hold of her . . . With his feet planted on the ground, some of the snakes that were coiled upon him slithered off his neck and opened his maw so that it gaped. He then dragged the holy maiden toward himself and placed his mouth upon her neck, while sending his tongue down, underneath her heels. And in this way, like a stag, he raised her up and swallowed her into his belly. Her hands made the sign of holy Christ, and, as this sign went down ahead of the rest of her, they ruptured the dragon's innards. He fell from the square in a great crash; he was split asunder and died. The holy maiden emerged from his belly without having suffered any harm. Turning around, she said to him, "Truly, you have found that which you sought."

The dragon lay there, sprawled upon the ground. And suddenly again, from the other corner of the jail a great demon fell upon Saint Marina's knees. She saw him and began to pray, saying, "Praise your name and all glory be to you, Lord Jesus Christ. I rejoice in gladness and exalt you, Father of All, our most powerful Creator Christ . . ." And when she said that, the demon stood up with a howl, took her by the hand, and said to her, "Be quiet for a little while, Marina.

You have said enough. I will reveal great things to you. For I sent my relative Rufus, in the form of a dragon, to kill you. Yet you killed him with your prayers, and now you want to kill me too. But spare me, Marina, and do me no harm." But holy Marina sealed her entire body with the sign of the cross and she grabbed the demon by his hair and beard. He then dragged her toward himself and they wrestled. The demon said, "Ow, my beard really hurts!"

THE TREASURY DRAGON
OF CONSTANTINOPLE[1]

Hypatios, the bishop of Gangra, was believed to be among those who assembled at the Council of Nicaea in 325, which condemned the heretical teachings of Arius and decreed that the Father and the Son were of the same substance. Although Emperor Constantine (r. 306–37) had convened this council, his son Constantius (r. 337–61) stood by Arianizing beliefs that the Son of God was subordinate to the Father. This controversy about the nature of Christ resonated centuries later in miracles attributed to Hypatios. In one such legend, a dragon took up residence in the imperial treasury in Constantinople. The prayers of Constantius's heretical priests were unable to dislodge this monster, so Bishop Hypatios, a staunch supporter of Nicaean orthodoxy, was summoned to subdue it. Composed around the same time as the Beowulf *poem (see pp. 57–73), this story also concerned a serpentine dragon attracted to a treasure hoard, but the similarities end there. Unlike its northern European counterpart, this creature had been sent by God to demonstrate to Constantius the error of embracing heretical teachings about the nature of Jesus Christ.*

The bright glow of the saint's superlative and glorious miracles was visible everywhere, and even the emperor himself benefited from them. This was Constantius, the son of the most faithful and Cross-Bearing Constantine, who, through his naïveté, had converted to the impious heresy of Arius. For this reason, he was being set straight by God's corrective power, which sometimes took strange forms. State revenue flowed from every part of the inhabited world to the imperial treasury and from there the emperor's hand dispersed it to service the common needs of the republic. A great beast, known as a dragon, of such size as times past had never seen, entered into the treasury and, wrapping itself around the pile, prevented the emperor from accessing this wealth. He killed many people whether by depriving them of money or through his breath. For all who came near the money in order to carry out the emperor's commands, knowing nothing in advance about the dragon, would be desiccated by his breath alone and the sparks that flew from his eyes. And those who tried to ascertain how the others had met their end would also fall dead just like them. One could now see a pile of dead bodies adjacent to the pile of money and the public affairs of the republic were extremely imperiled. The emperor was reduced to continual groaning and lamenting, because of his fear and uncertainty how to handle this situation. He had only one hope, namely that the prayers of the priests who shared his beliefs and outlook could help him. He summoned them and bid them to end this disaster by pleading intensively with God. Well, his companions in Arian insanity readily obeyed his order. When they advanced to the treasury gates and ordered them to be opened, even those who stood farthest away were killed by the deadly breath of the beast. Many of these evil-thinking priests fell dead, for all that they had promised that they would slay the dragon with their prayers.

This failure of Arius's falsehood and deception disheartened and depressed the emperor, the magistrates, and that entire City of Great Name [Constantinople]. As the emperor was wallowing in his misery, someone brought him salvific news, saying "O most serene lord, if you summon Hypatios of the Church of Gangra, he will quickly turn your woes into joy." When the emperor received this most excellent piece of advice from one of the messengers, he sent envoys to the holy archpriest, including men honored with high rank at the court, and persuaded him to come swiftly to those afflicted

with danger and confusion . . . The vast multitudes of the
populace assembled and they all begged the servant of God
to help them. They led the great Hypatios to the dragon's
lair. That initiate of the truth and upholder of the teachings
of Saint Paul then imitated the divine Paul, in both thought
and deed, in taking on the dragon. For just as Paul shook off
the snake that bit him and decreed that it be burned by fire,
so too did the hierarch decide regarding the dragon.[2] Through
his communion with the faith of the Apostle and the similar-
ity between the miracles, he persuaded the emperor, the populace, and those who were ill with the Arian mental disorder
that even wild beasts and venomous serpents can be subdued
by confessing the Consubstantial Trinity. Straightaway, that
noble follower of Christ, Hypatios, opened the doors of the
treasury and entered into combat, alone among all. For everyone else left him and fled because of their heretical delusion . . .
Most of the city populace stood at a great distance from the
doors, in the circular open space where the column of the
most faithful Emperor Constantine stands, which the locals
call the "forum." The great Hypatios ordered a great fire to
be lit. As the furnace burned, he ventured toward the common destroyer of mankind, grasping his staff in his hand.
First, he terrified the dragon with the words of peace, wielding the sign of the cross as if it were a weapon, the greatest
guarantee of safety that the Lord bestowed upon his own disciples. For even though animals lack speech, they say, they
nevertheless have an implanted sensation of fear of the servants of their Creator. Thus, writhing and pain took hold of
the dragon; lifting his head to the holy man, he then lowered
it again, striking the money. Wrapping himself around his
face, he contrived a way to hide his own head. He forgot all
about killing people and even sensed his own demise. He was
ordered to crawl out through the doors and to part from his
pile of money. This he did, though he did not want to. The
old man rapidly struck the dragon with his staff and caused
him to hasten his departure. Thus, aggrieved by the continual
blows, the dragon quickly stood up at the insistence of the
rod, and thus a majestic miracle took place. The leviathan

could be seen standing up in one place and receiving multiple blows from the staff, unable to do any harm to his punisher.

As the contest took place, the day drew to a close. The crowd gathered outside was taking the delay hard. They imagined that God's champion had been devoured by the beast, in a like manner to those whom it had already killed. But the saint emerged slowly from the treasury, dragging his staff on the ground and pulling the dragon along, as if he had been tied to it by a hook. Even so, it instilled a sudden terror in the crowd. The hierarch ordered the dragon to mount the pyre with haste. He went to the place of the furnace, circled around it, and then threw himself onto it. Thus, before all the people, he was consumed by fire. And after that point, the emperor had free use of his treasury, just as before, and placed upon it, as a security seal and guard, the honorable visage of the hierarch, drawn in a picture. This has been preserved there until this day, without any alteration or decay, in commemoration of the miracle.

THE TERROR OF
TREBIZOND[1]

*Saint Eugenios was remembered as a martyr who died in
the persecution of the Christians launched by the emperor
Diocletian (r. 284–305). His cult was later prominent in
the city of Trebizond (modern Trabzon, in northeastern
Turkey) and he was honored as the chief patron-saint of
the independent Byzantine empire of Trebizond, which
lasted from ca. 1200 to 1461. In the fourteenth century,
the bishop of Trebizond Ioannes (Ioseph) Lazaropoulos
(r. 1364–67) collected centuries' worth of stories about
the saint's miracles, including a tale in which he inspired
an emperor to slay a dragon. The emperor in question was
probably meant to be Alexios II Grand Komnenos
(r. 1297–1330) of the (Roman) empire of Trebizond.*

How the saint helped to kill the dragon: Having reached this
point in our account, let us, in order to pay back our debt [to
the saint], take up the thread of our story and tell of the slaying
of the dragon that happened in our own days. There is a great
mountain to the east of the city of Trebizond, which was called
Mithros by the ancient Greeks, on account, I presume, of the
rituals of Mithras that took place there. Even today the place
is called Mithrion by all the locals. Just above this mountain,
near the adjacent lake and the spring that flows there, lurked
a large dragon, because of which the place is called Dragon's
Well by the locals down to this day. The dragon was terrible to
behold and fierce. Fire flashed from its eyes and venom dripped
from its lips. The beast was unapproachable and entirely evil,
invincible, and murderous. The harm that he brought to that

whole region made it utterly impassable. The city was hard pressed and extremely vexed, because the goods that it needed had to come from that road, and the city's suppliers were no longer able to use it out of fear of the dragon. Thus, seeing this state of affairs, that celebrated emperor was unable to endure the extent of the harm that was being caused or the harmful behavior of the dragon. He realized that he had to prepare himself for a showdown with the beast. And look now at the fight that he put up!

The emperor immediately set out for the monastery of the great martyr Eugenios, not only with an imperial retinue but also as a suppliant, with his soul eager to humble itself. For already from his adolescence he had been filled with a divine devotion to this saint. Each and every day he deemed this monastery worthy of much consideration, support, and care, which is why he always called upon Eugenios as his benefactor and steady champion in war, in disaster and grief, and in severe diseases, if any came upon him. He frequently visited the church, fell before the saint's holy relic that gushed with myrrh, embracing it with all his strength, kissing it, praising the saint, and singing hymns to celebrate his feats and victories, crowning him with speeches of thanksgiving. He did the same now too when he set out for the saint's monastery, pleading with the saint as before and calling on him to be his staunch ally in the fight against the venomous dragon. He asked for swift aid and a speedy dispatch of this enemy.

After praying, the emperor assembled his best officers and said this to them: "O men, for me the prospect of fighting the dragon induces no hesitation, lack of daring, or constriction of the heart. There is no other way for us to overcome the beast. God will provide and so will his saint, the powerful Eugenios, whose aid I have always requested from God in our wars. You too should pray, brothers, as is reasonable." Thus he spoke, and he donned armor and weapons, especially the cross of Christ, and, mounting his horse, he immediately rode off in pursuit of his quarry, riding around in those parts searching for him.

The dragon was now spotted, a huge thing breathing fire,

as it were. The emperor stood opposed to it with steely resolve, fully a warrior, fully as if he were breathing fire back
against it, brandishing his spear at it and his shining sword.
Quickly he dared the dragon to attack him, trusting in God
and the martyr. Seeing his opponent act like this, the beast
charged him even more eagerly. But in his rush to kill him, the
beast was mortally wounded by the emperor, and fell dead.
His carcass was a magnificent sight, which had only slightly
coiled in on itself. After this feat of valor, the emperor re-
joiced and returned to the monastery of Eugenios, to repay
his gratitude for victory, while his followers carried the dragon's head in their arms, which is still preserved in the palace
to this day. When news of this event spread, almost everyone,
both lordly and humble people, flocked to the saint's monastery and, seeing what had been done, they marveled, gave
thanks to God, and sung hymns for the holy martyr. They
celebrated the heroic emperor with speeches, praising him as
a new and powerful giant and a divine general.

THE OGRE-DRAGON'S
PITILESS HEART[1]

Kallimachos and Chrysorrhoe is a late Byzantine romance. This was a genre of literature in vernacular Greek strongly influenced by the traditions of the narrative French poetry popular in western Europe. Written between 1310 and 1340 by Andronikos Palaiologos, nephew of the emperor Michael VIII Palaiologos (r. 1259–81), it is a standard boy-meets-girl story: here the boy meets the girl when he rescues her from the clutches of a "dragon," who is more like a hulking ogre than a reptilian beast. The story begins with the dilemma of a rich barbarian king with three sons. He loved them all equally, so he did not know to which of them to leave his throne. He sent them out with an army and declared that his heir would be the one who performed the greatest feat. After a long march, they came to a steep mountain, which the third son, Kallimachos, persuaded them to climb. At the top they found a pleasant valley with a terrifying "dragon-fort," whose high walls were made of gold and whose gates were guarded by huge living serpents. Only Kallimachos was brave enough to leap over the walls (using a magic ring) and enter the verdant garden inside. The palace, as well as the "dragon's" bedchamber, was empty, except for a beautiful woman named Chrysorrhoe, who was suspended from the ceiling by her hair.

She said to him, "Oh man, who are you? Where are you from? Perhaps you are an apparition with human form? Are you brave, polite, a fool, or in despair? Who are you? Why are you silent? Why do you just stand there, staring? I hope that my evil fate has not brought you too to torment me. Have no fear, you could not bring me additional torment. My body, as you can see, has already been delivered over to torment. But if you see this and are pained at the sight of it, as you say, and if my evil fate has had its fill of the many tortures it has inflicted upon me for so many years, and has finally sent its deliverance today to set me free from my many afflictions, then I thank my fate: Butcher me! Kill me! ... Say something, why are you silent? Let me breathe, even if briefly. This is the house of a dragon, the dwelling of a man-eater. Do you not hear the thunder, do you not see the lightning? He comes. Why are you just standing there? He comes. Go now, hide. He has the power of a dragon, this man-eater's offspring. If you hide and guard yourself, you might just survive. Do you see that silver basin over there? If you get inside it and cover yourself up, it might just happen that you escape the dragon's irresistible power. Go, climb in there, hide, and be quiet. He's almost here."

He took her advice and trusted in the words of the maiden, who hung there suspended from her hair, and he quickly covered himself in the basin.

The dragon arrived, full of malicious intent. Who could describe the dragon's malicious rage with a cool mind and steely heart? Who could tell of his cold-hearted mind and pitiless heart? Who could put into words the dragon's stony guts? Taking up a slender branch that was there, he whipped the hanging maiden for some time, from her head down to her feet, to the very ends of her fingers. The painting of Eros that was there, Eros who sets men on fire and tames their cruel hearts, was unable to light a fire in the dragon's heart, was unable to soften the dragon's cruel mind; instead, the dragon's harshness escaped the fires of passion, for a dragon does not fear the fire or the bow of Eros. After that horrific lashing, he inhumanly brought up a golden stool beneath the maiden's golden feet. She stepped on the stool, in great pain, but even then her hair remained attached above. He brought a small amount of bread and gave it to her, and water as her only drink, nothing more than that, in a cup made of precious stone, an emerald. In truth, he was saving her for another torture session. She, swollen from the pain, drank the water, in pain, after the torture, hanging from her hair. The dragon immediately removed the stool from under her feet, and again the maiden was hanging from her hair. There was a small bed there, luxurious you might call it, in the dragon's wondrous chamber, which was also the maiden's room of ordeals and prison-cell. If you called it a chamber of torture, you would not be wrong.

There was a small bed there, close to the ground, low-lying, made of precious stones. The dragon sat upon it alone, gave a command, and immediately a table came, of its own accord, bearing delicious delicacies for his insatiable mouth. He ate most of them and, as soon as he was full, moved by no pity for the hanging maiden, he lay down to sleep, heavy with food.

Now, the maiden saw the dragon sleeping, satisfied as he was after his heavy drinking and gorged with food, snoring as he slept, stretched out from end to end—this was sleep brought on from great drinking and feasting—so, when Chrysorrhoe saw the dragon sleeping so deeply and altogether senseless, she said to the hidden man: "Oh man, are you in fear of your life? Have you died already? Have no fear! Now you should man-up. Come out of there. Don't be afraid, for you might still survive my many ordeals and the fear of the beast. Come out quickly and slay the beast even faster!"

When he heard her voice, he came out in great fear. The maiden said to him, "Show no hesitation at all. This is your chance, kill the beast while he slumbers. Thus, you will save both your body and soul. You carry a sword: pull it out and let the man-eater have it! Butcher him who has slain so many souls of men, and kill the one who had darkened my very heart." He stood up, drew a deep breath, and wielded his sword in good form, with a brave heart, and struck the sleeping one as hard as he could. But the dragon did not even wake up from the blow. The maiden groaned and said to Kallimachos, "Put down that wooden toy, lest we are both killed. Now, take the key from the headboard, and you see the dragon's wall-cupboard over there? Open the wall-cupboard, and you will find the dragon's sword inside. It has a fine hilt, a ruby stone. If you have the strength to draw it and are not trembling with fear, stand and have at him with that, you will slay the beast."

And so he took the key from the headboard, and opened the dragon's wall-cupboard. Taking the dragon's sword from inside, he struck him with it and immediately slew him. Then he untied the hanging maiden, and her tortured body was freed from its ordeal. Freed from captivity and those bitter afflictions, her body was fine, delightful, gorgeous, ripe.

[*Chrysorrhoe asks him who he is and, after telling her, Kallimachos asks her for her story.*]

Crying, she told him, speaking through her pain: "You see my humble body naked. Bring me first, so that I may cover myself, some of the clothes that are hanging inside, where they are kept, which he himself received from my parents. Also, take out the body of that voracious dragon, because I hate even the sight of its dead corpse. Light a fire, burn him all up, make him into fine dust, and then you will learn my family and homeland, my native country and where I come from."

Kallimachos immediately took up the dragon's body on his shoulders and hauled it outside. Then he ran like an eagle to the furnace, and, taking fire, he burned up the loathsome body. He returned to her and opened the chamber; taking a fine woven cloak, he brought it to her. She put it on and sat down again, and she began at the beginning, telling him everything, her family, her upbringing, land, and native country, and all the other bitter tales of her unjust fate.

"I was a noble and well-bred daughter, coming from money and an illustrious imperial parentage. This dragon fell in love with my beauty—where has that gone now, eh?—and he wanted to have me as his wife. He pressured and harassed my parents, the kings, to consent to this bitter transaction, this marriage against nature. They agreed out of fear of the beast. For he would not allow any water to flow down from the top of the mountain, water from that river, to the empire of my father, to his lands and castles. Such was my cruel fate. For in all the rest of the entire circuit of our empire, the land of my parents, there was no other water-source, except for this one river, which he, the dragon, controlled, in his furious rage. They said it, they agreed, but I would not consent, a terrible beast . . . or rather he became a dragon again, as he always was. He gulped down all the quadrupeds of my native land, as if they were but water through a straw, and again he wanted to have me and pressed his demand. My parents did not want to give me away and they fell into lamentation, which inflamed his draconian nature and made him rage. Threatening me, he forced the marriage through. As for myself, I refused to marry him, come what may. Not even in my dreams would I consent to live with a dragon. But then immediately he devoured everyone, the small and the large, men, women, the old and young together, he gulped them all down, leaving no one behind, stuffing them with his tongue into his gullet and stomach. And then he ate and swallowed my parents too, my lords, the emperors themselves, he utterly made them vanish. O what a calamity and sorrow, what a thing to endure! I am bereaved! How can I live, how might I endure? He caused me to be alone, without any hope. He did me only this one favor with respect to them, namely that he swallowed them separately, killed them apart from all the rest, from the commoners and the nobles. What a shame that he did not then split open, that the stinking stomach of the voracious dragon did not burst. So what happened next, after all the killing? He grabbed me and wanted to have me, for all that I was unwilling. I entirely refused, and so I have suffered all these torments, and yet through all these afflictions and so much pain I prevailed over the dragon's pitiless heart, and remain to this day an undefiled virgin."

DRAGONS AND THEIR SLAYERS IN THE LATER MIDDLE AGES

By the twelfth century, dragons held a privileged place in the literature of medieval Europe. For a millennium, they had prowled the Christian imagination as avatars of the Devil, who had once tempted Eve in the form of a serpent with dire results for all humankind. The ultimate adversary, the dragon reached its full potential in the later Middle Ages as the enemy of the faithful in legends and songs celebrating the virtues of saints and heroes. In these stories, brave knights and holy maidens vanquished the Devil in his draconic guise with the power of sword and cross. Much like early Christian authors, later medieval storytellers and songsmiths rendered dragons with little texture or depth. The attributes of these monsters—their reptilian appearance; their powerful jaws, wings, and tails; their fiery breath and venomous bite—were commonplace by this period and thus required little elaboration. The symbolic power of the dragon was far greater than its physical threat. To be sure, readers may have shuddered at the thought of serpentine creatures larger and more dangerous than any animal they had ever encountered in their daily lives, but the literary value of the dragon lay primarily in its allegorical potential. When saints and crusaders slew these monsters, not only did they rid the countryside of a predatory menace but they also vanquished false beliefs contrary to Christianity, doused the fires of human lust, and escaped the snares of the Devil himself.

THE DRAGON AND
THE LION[1]

*Chrétien de Troyes was a French poet of the late twelfth
century, whose Old French poems about King Arthur
and the knights of the Round Table earned him respect at
the court of Marie de France, the countess of Champagne
(1145–ca. 1198). Among his poems was* Yvain, the Knight
of the Lion *(composed ca. 1180). A companion of Arthur,
Yvain stood out among the knights of the Round Table
because he had a ferocious lion as his companion. He obtained this unusual pet when he happened upon a battle
between a lion and a dragon in a dark forest. Choosing to
take action, he sided with the lion because the dragon was
"so full of wickedness." Upon the defeat of the dragon,
the noble lion recognized Yvain as his friend and savior
and accompanied him faithfully on his chivalric adventures.*

Deep in thought, my lord Yvain rode through deep woods
until he heard from the thick of the forest a very loud and anguished cry. He headed immediately toward the place where
he had heard the cry, and when he arrived at the clearing, he
saw a dragon holding a lion by the tail and burning its flanks
with its flaming breath. My lord Yvain did not waste time
observing this marvel. He asked himself which of the two he
would help. Then he determined that he would take the lion's
part, since a venomous and wicked creature deserves only
harm: the dragon was venomous and fire leapt from its mouth
because it was so full of wickedness. Therefore my lord Yvain
determined that he would slay it first.

He drew his sword and came forward with his shield in front of his face, to avoid being harmed by the flame pouring from the dragon's mouth, which was larger than a cauldron. If the lion attacked him later, it would not lack for a fight, but with no thought of the consequences Yvain was determined to help it now, since Pity summoned and urged him to aid and succour the noble and honourable beast. He pursued the wicked dragon with his sharp sword: he cut it through to the ground and then cut the two parts in half again; he struck it repeatedly until it was hacked into tiny pieces. However, he was obliged to cut off a piece of the lion's tail, which the wicked dragon still held in its clenched teeth; he cut off only as much as he had to, and he could not have taken off less.

Once he had rescued the lion, he still thought that it would attack him and he would have to do battle with it; but the lion would never have done that. Listen to how nobly and splendidly the lion acted: it stood up upon its hind paws, bowed its head, joined its forepaws and extended them toward Yvain, in an act of total submission. Then it knelt down and its whole face was bathed in tears of humility. My lord Yvain recognized clearly that the lion was thanking him and submitting to him because, in slaying the dragon, he had delivered it from death; these actions pleased him greatly. He wiped the dragon's poisonous filth from his sword, replaced it in his scabbard, and set off again upon his way. Yet the lion stayed by his side and never left him; from that day on it would accompany him, for it intended to serve and protect him.

A DRAGON WITH THE
DEVIL INSIDE[1]

*Composed between 1180 and 1220, the Old French epic
poem* The Captives (Les Chétifs) *was a "chanson de
geste" (literally "song of deeds"), a common medieval
French literary medium for recounting historical events
in a mythic or legendary way.* Les Chétifs *was part of the
Old French Crusade Cycle, which comprised several chansons de geste that related the events of the First Crusade
(1095–1101). It purported to recount what happened to
certain crusaders taken prisoner after the disastrous Battle of Civetot (1096) and how those captives were eventually reunited with the main crusading army before the
sack of Jerusalem (1099).* Les Chétifs *included a lengthy
sequence in which a fictional crusader named Baldwin of
Beauvais battled with the dragon called Sathanas. Baldwin's brother, Ernoul of Beauvais, had set out first to slay
the dragon, but was quickly killed. Fueled by rage and
grief, Baldwin mounted a fearsome and vengeful attack
on the monster. But Sathanas was no common dragon,
for he was possessed by the Devil himself. Only with the
aid of God, the archangel Michael, and a litany of saints
could the holy knight defeat this demon-ridden drake in
combat.*

Upon Mount Tigris in a natural cave[2]
Dwelt a beast who was very cruel.
Thirty feet it had in length. It was great and strong,
With a hide so hard that no sword swung
Nor weapon so great or sharp could wound it in any way.

It was of such color that no man could say for certain:
It was indigo and violet and blue and green as well,
Black, scarlet, even yellow, with reddened skin.
Its head was quite large with hideous ears.
The ears were larger than an ornate shield,
With which the beast covers itself when pained.
The tail was large and long (don't think it absurd!),
It well had a measure of nine feet.
Anyone it struck could not survive.
[The dragon] had a devil inside, which made it cruel.
When angered it howled and cried so fiercely
That from two leagues out one heard it clearly.[3]
On its brow was a stone that glowed and shone,
By which one saw better at night than with a bright lantern.
A good two and a half leagues around the mountain
No man or woman could come there and not be doomed.

————————

Lords, now listen to this glorious song;
Never has any Christian man heard such.
There has not been one sung like this since the time of
  Solomon.
It is very good to hear (indeed it is more worthwhile than a
  sermon)
How Jesus of glory, by His salvation,
Saved the hero Baldwin on that day
When he did battle with the felonious Sathanas.[4]
By the virtue of God he took vengeance in such a manner[5]
As you will hear in the verses of this song.
But before he paid [Sathanas] back, I will not lie to you,
His renowned blood ran down to his spurs,
Bleeding all over his body and around it.
He searched the mountain along the cliff,
Climbed up onto a stone which was curved on top,
[And] cried out with a loud voice and rightly said:
"God, where is this dragon since I am unable to find it?
True God, pray show him to me through your most blessed
  name!"

The serpent was sleeping near a stone platform.

Just as God aided him through his blessing,

Envision Saint Michael, the angel, in the guise of dove![6]

On behalf of the Holy Spirit he said to [Baldwin] in a vision:

"Friend, do not be dismayed, you will not have it so bad.

He will come to aid you who forgave Longinus[7]

And [who] raised Lazarus from the dead to life.[8]

When you have faith in Him, you have a very good
companion.

Before you have gone to the Temple of Solomon,[9]

Seven thousand Franks who are in pagan hands and in harsh
captivity

Will be led from prison by you.

They were brought there from the army of master Peter.[10]

They have called upon God in good spirit so often

That now God wishes to reward them through you."

When Baldwin heard this, he raised his head

On account of the joy he had and sat down on the stone
landing.

Baldwin was seated and the angel [Michael] came to him.

He had great joy in his heart, I will not mislead you about
this now,

On account of the holy words that Jesus conveyed to him.

At that moment he well knew that God would certainly aid
him.

He stood up [and] signed himself four times.

Having commended his body to the great name of Jesus,

He came thither quickly whereupon he found the beast.

When the dragon sensed him, it roused itself immediately.

Swiftly and speedily it rose up on its feet.

When it then saw Baldwin it showed him utter contempt.

It advanced on him in a rage (such a face it showed him!);

Its hairs, long and sharp, all bristled.

It had a frightful appearance, so fiercely it stared at
[Baldwin].

It concealed itself with its ears and scratched its talons

Upon the dark rock such that sparks flew out.

This was the grand marvel that God displayed there:

It had wolfed down so much of Ernoul that it very nearly
   burst;
It had devoured his body but did not eat the head.
It laid the head down on the stone and strangled [Ernoul's]
   donkey.
When Baldwin saw this, his heart sank.
Willingly he picked [the head] up. The serpent rushed him,
Coming toward him with its monstrous maw agape.
Now, God, who formed the world, protect him!
If the Lord who made and created all does not think of him,
[Baldwin] cannot survive. But God will aid him!
Now you will be able to hear how [Baldwin] fought.
Baldwin was a very worthy and gallant knight.
He saw the serpent who was huge and strong approaching.
It attacked Baldwin with its large gaping mouth,
[But] the baron saw it coming. It did not frighten him at all.
He raised his hand [and] made a cross in the middle of his
   chest.
He grasped his arrow [and] began to shout.
He professed in a loud voice: "God the Father, Jesus Christ;
I summon you, beast, in the name of noble Saint Denis[11]
And through the Lord who was killed for us
On the Holy Cross when Longinus struck him.
Thus I conjure you in the name of all the blessed confessors:
Saint George of Ramleh, the lordly Saint Maurice,
Saint Peter the Apostle who safeguards Paradise,
The noble Saint Laurence who was roasted for God,
And Saint Leonard who frees the imprisoned,
And Saint Nicolas who is quite cherished by God,
And the noble Saint James who is venerated in Galicia,
And the valiant Saint Gilles whom I have visited in Provence,
And all the apostles by whom Jesus is served,
And the Holy Cross whereupon his body was left,
And the exalted Sepulcher where he lay both dead and living,
[And] Heaven and the Earth as was established,
That you shall not have power,
And you shall neither devour my body nor damage it
   severely."[12]

When Baldwin had summoned the serpent
In the name of Jesus in glory, the king of majesty,
He moved from it a little, hardly delaying at all,
As he shot his well-fletched arrow at it.
Listen to this great spectacle, noble and powerful Christians!
So hard were the skin and hide of this demon
That he unfortunately could no more do with his sharp
    missile
Than if he had struck it upon a stone.
It hit [the beast] so harshly that, know this in truth,
The iron tip and the wooden shaft broke and shattered into
    pieces.
It had a devil in its body which had protected it so well.
It gave to [the beast] power and severe cruelty,
But God cast it out in His great mercy.
When Sathanas realized that He had thus banished the devil,
Angrily it then produced such a cry
[That] the mountain resounded with it on all sides.

———————————

The serpent attacked [Baldwin] both rapidly and repeatedly.
If the Lord who is king of the East, He who was born
Of the blessed Virgin in Bethlehem, does not aid him,
He will surely have neither safety nor protection from death!
Sathanas stared at him full of rage.
It was a great marvel how he defended himself so well.
It never before found a man [who could] endure so long
Or who could escape from it.
Then, Baldwin rushed upon the [dragon] in his great fury.
It swiped its claws at him (they were exceptionally sharp!)
From the left such that they split his shield.
His hauberk was worth nothing to him in this case!
Whatever of the chainmail it hit, [the claws] rent and tore.
It swiftly slashed the flesh beneath his ribs,
Leaving none behind all the way down to his hips,
Such that the bone became visible, if history does not lie.
It is not at all surprising, by God the all-powerful,
That the knight faltered, and that fear seized him.

He loudly shouted out the great name of Jesus,

And took up one of his swords which was marked by a silver
        cross;

He well intended to smite [the dragon]. Sathanas took
        [the sword]

Horizontally in its mouth then swiftly snapped it.

Then, it thought to swallow it without any delay.

God, to whom the world belongs, made a great miracle there:

Baldwin's sword extended itself in [the beast's] throat

Such that its flank nearly split open.

Now be quiet and listen to the miracles

That Lord God did there, He and Saint Nicolas

And Saint Michael the angel and the noble Saint Gervais.

[Baldwin] thrust his sword point into the roof of [the
        dragon's] mouth

[And] blood flowed out abundantly from its maw.

Thus Baldwin of Beauvais could now defend himself

From the claws so sharp, since he is now untroubled by the
        teeth.

Now may the Lord who made both the clergy and laity aid
        him!

Baldwin stared down [the dragon]. He had never had such
        joy before,

He would not be so happy even for the honor of Rohais.[13]

The dragon rushed him and opened its mouth wide,

And Baldwin suddenly cried out the names of God.

As Baldwin recalled the names

And invoked the saints who have great power,

Jesus the king made there a great miracle for him:

The devil exited through [the dragon's] mouth,

[As] it had neither permission nor the power to stay any
        longer;

It was seen in the guise of a raven by the knight [Baldwin].[14]

Sathanas stumbled to the point that it nearly fell over

Because the devil had gone out from it.

The land had been ravaged and devastated by it,

Saracens both young and old had died.[15]

The enraged serpent came at Baldwin,

It sought to break him upon the sharp stones.
It slashed [Baldwin's] helm from above with its talons,
Knocking it from his head [and] breaking the lacing.
It gave him four wounds [such that] blood streamed out;
But the knight comported himself well, as Jesus availed him.
To my knowledge he would soon have been dead and beaten,
But God, who did not forget him, saved the day,
As well as Saint Michael and his virtue.
Baldwin held his sword which had been forged thrice
And [was] very refined, tempered, and sharp.
He fiercely attacked [the dragon], rushing upon it.
He gave it a mighty blow above the ears
With his forged blade, but the hide did not split
Because [the beast] had [skin] harder than forged steel.
The steel blade bent such that it nearly broke.
Baldwin stood fast, then drew himself back.
"Alas, God," said Baldwin, "how hard this devil is!
There has not been one made so since God was born."

Baldwin struck it often, front and back and on the side,
But the hide was so tough that he could not pierce it
   so much
That he could damage it a bezant's worth.[16]
The dragon bristled, with the sharp sword
Crosswise in its mouth by the order of Jesus,
Such that it could not defend itself at all with its teeth.
The dragon had a tail that was large and long and weighty,
And he struck [it] upon Baldwin's shield of resplendent gold.
Thrice it made Baldwin to spin around so that he nearly fell
   over.
Now it made the shield fly off from around his neck.

But the power of the redeeming Father of Heaven
And the Holy Spirit will not forget him,
And the angel came to him from Heaven, comforting.
Baldwin took up his shield from the hard stone,

Grasped his sword in his right hand and came running at the
    dragon.
So great was the battle before the setting of the sun
That no cleric could tell you and no *jongleur* [could] sing
    of it.[17]
Baldwin of Beauvais was a bold knight,
Since God, with whom he was friends, supported him.
Swiftly and with haste he took his shield up again;
The dragon had greatly weakened and damaged it.
He held his sword, whose edge was keen, in his right
    hand.
The angel comforted him [and] he was greatly emboldened
    for it.
With great anger he assailed the dragon.
Sathanas was very slow to move,
Having lost so much blood that it was quite enfeebled
And because the Devil had leapt from his body.
[The dragon] surged at Baldwin enraged and anguished,
Striking him upon his vaulted shield with its talons
Which pierced it ten times, sending it flying from his neck
[Because] it broke the strap, which was of fine gray cloth.
The claws followed up on [Baldwin's] white interlinked
    hauberk;
Whatever it caught with its claws was broken and undone.
Lord God made sure that it did not reach his flesh.
At this point the dragon had put him between its two feet.
He could no longer endure without being killed
If God and the Holy Spirit did not preserve him,
Along with the most blessed angel, who placed itself before
    [Baldwin].
The battle was great and fierce and long,
Do not doubt it at all, the truth was proven!
Never before was such a Christian seen.
Now listen to the power of God, which He demonstrated
    there:
Baldwin was fully upright, his sword grasped in his hand.
He ran upon the beast and it did not turn away from him.
Sathanas kept its great maw wide open

Since the sword, which was stuck in its neck, was making it
   do so,
Having penetrated both above and below [the beast's] palate.
Indeed, the dragon was distressed since it was so wounded
That it could not fully catch its breath,
And Baldwin rushed it because he feared it a great deal.
As such, Jesus and His renowned power aided him:
The beast fell unconscious from the blood it lost.
When Baldwin saw this, he raised his head.
Were someone to give him a valley's worth of gold,
He would not be so joyous as he was about how things
   turned out.
He then went forth; nothing there would make him stop.
He struck [the dragon's] throat with the blade of his sword.
He courageously smote it and thrust [his blade] in
Such that it went right through the middle of [the beast's]
   entrails and beyond.
The sword tip stopped at its heart which was very hard.
Before it could enter into [the heart], it passed into another
   part,
Cutting into [the beast's] liver alongside the spine.
The dragon fell prostrate and died on the spot
[And] commended its soul to the devils of Hell.
[Baldwin] removed his blood-covered sword from the beast,
Then withdrew back into a hollow in the rocks.
His vision clouded [and] he lowered his head,
His color faded on account of the blood that he had lost,
Then he collapsed unconscious on a wide stone.
He arose to his feet when he came to.
He took time to look around and all over
And saw the head of his brother lying on a mound
Upon a wide stone which was mossy on top.
[Baldwin] well recognized him by his face with its features,
With a beard that was long and a well-defined chin.
Then he lowered himself down and made a great lamentation:
"Alas, brother," he said, "how unfortunate that
Your son and wife await you in our homeland.
You will never see them, noble son of a baron."

FOUR SAINTLY
DRAGON-SLAYERS

The Golden Legend *(Legenda aurea) was an encyclopedic thirteenth-century compendium of stories about the life of Christ and the saints. Its popularity was unrivaled among lay and religious readers alike. Composed by the Dominican Jacobus de Voragine (ca. 1228–98), the* Golden Legend *became the most widely read text of the later Middle Ages and second only to the Bible in terms of the sheer number of surviving manuscripts (over one thousand copies), vernacular translations, and early printed editions. Jacobus organized his work according to the liturgical calendar, beginning with Advent (which begins on the fourth Sunday before Christmas Day) to emphasize the centrality of Christ's incarnation in salvation history. Several of the saints featured in the* Golden Legend *confronted dragons of one kind or another as a measure of their sanctity. The symbolism of these monsters would have been clear to medieval readers. In the story of Saint George, set in the third century, the dragon represented the paganism of the people of Libya and its defeat marked their conversion to Christianity. Likewise, Saint Sylvester liberated the people of Rome from the worship of false idols when he tamed a dragon lurking beneath the city. For Saint Margaret, the dragon was the Devil in disguise, who attempted to frighten her so that she would forsake her virginity and her faith. Her defeat of the monster by bursting forth from its stomach was clearly distasteful to Jacobus, who dismissed the anecdote as apocryphal, but the popularity of this tale played no small part in the designation of Margaret as the patron saint of women in labor. For Saint Martha, as for Saint George, the taming of the tarasque stood for the arrival of Christianity and the extirpation of pagan belief from the valley of the Rhône.*

(A) ST. GEORGE, DRAGON'S BANE[1]

George was a native of Cappadocia and a tribune in the Roman army. One day he came to Silena, a city in the province of Libya. Close by this city was a vast lake, as big as an inland sea, where a pestilential dragon had its lair. The people had often risen in arms against it, but the dragon always put them to flight, and would venture right up to the city walls and asphyxiate everyone with its noxious breath. So the citizens were compelled to feed it two sheep every day, in order to allay its fury, otherwise it would make straight for the city walls and poison the air, causing a great many deaths. But in time, since their flocks were not large, the supply of sheep began to run out, and the citizens decided to give the dragon one sheep and one human being. The names of the victims were drawn by lot, and no one of either sex was excluded. But in due course nearly all the young folk were eaten up, and one day the lot fell upon the only daughter of the king, and the people seized her to feed her to the dragon. The king was heartbroken. "Take my gold and silver," he cried. "Take half my realm, and let my daughter go, save her from this dreadful death!" But the people rounded on him in fury. "It was you who issued this decree, your majesty, and, now all our children are dead, you want to save your own daughter? If you do not sacrifice your daughter, and do what you forced all the rest of us to do, we will burn you alive, you and all your household!" At this, the king began to weep for his daughter. "Woe is me!" he cried. "My sweetest child, what am I to do about you. What can I say? Can I no more hope to see your wedding day?" Turning to the people, he said: "I beg you, grant me a week's grace in which to mourn my daughter." This the people agreed to, but at the end of the week they came back and demanded angrily: "How can you destroy your subjects just for your daughter's sake? We are all dying from the breath of the dragon!" Then the king, seeing that he could not save his daughter, dressed her in all her regal finery and, embracing her, said tearfully: "Alas, my sweetest daughter, I thought to see you rear royal children at your bosom, and now you are going to be devoured by the dragon! Alas, my sweetest child, I hoped to invite all the nobility to your wedding, to deck the palace with pearls, to hear the music of timbrels and trumpets, and now you are going to be devoured by the dragon!" He kissed her and let her go with a final word: "Oh, my daughter, would I had died before you, rather than lose you in this way!" She then fell at her father's feet, asking his blessing, and, when in a flood of tears he had blessed her, she set off towards the lake.

Now St. George happened to be passing that way, and when he saw her weeping, he asked her what was the matter. "Good youth," she replied, "mount your horse with all speed and flee, or you will share my fate and die as I must." "Do not be afraid, my child," George told her. "But tell me, what are you waiting here for, and why are all these people watching?" "Good youth," she replied, "I see you have a noble heart, but do you want to die with me? Make haste and flee!" George told her: "I shall not move from here until you tell me what is the matter." So then she told him the whole story, and George said: "My child, do not be afraid, for in the name of Christ I will help you." "You are a brave knight," she replied. "But do not perish with me. It is enough that I die, for you cannot save me, you would only die with me." While they were talking, the dragon suddenly lifted its head from the lake. Trembling, the young girl cried: "Flee, good lord, make haste and flee!" But George mounted his horse, armed himself with the sign of the cross, and bravely went to meet the dragon as it came toward him. Brandishing his lance and commending himself to God, he dealt the beast such a deadly wound that he threw it to the ground. He called to the princess: "Throw your girdle round the dragon's neck! Do not be afraid, child!" She did as he told her, and the dragon followed her as meekly as a puppy. She led it to the city, but when the people saw it, they began to run for the mountains and hills, crying: "Help! We are all done for!" But St. George waved at them to come back. "Do not be afraid," he told them. "The Lord has sent me to free you from the tyranny of the dragon. Only believe in Christ and be baptized, every one of you, and I will slay your dragon!"

So the king and all the people were baptized and St. George drew his sword and slew the dragon, and gave orders that it should be carried outside the city walls. Four pairs of oxen dragged the beast out of the city and left it on a broad open plain. That day twenty thousand were baptized, not counting women and children. The king built a large and splendid church there in honor of Blessed Mary and St. George, and from its altar there still issues a natural spring whose waters cure all illnesses. The king also offered St. George a vast sum of money, but the saint refused to accept it, and ordered it to be given to the poor. He then gave the king four brief rules of life: to cherish the Church of God; to honor priests; to be scrupulous in attending mass; and always to be mindful of the poor. With that he kissed the king farewell and left. We read in some sources, however, that when the dragon was rushing towards the girl to devour her, George actually armed himself with a cross, and then attacked and killed the dragon.

(B) ST. SYLVESTER MUZZLES
A MONSTER [2]

Some days later, the priests of the idols came to the emperor, saying "Most sacred emperor, since the time when you adopted the Christian faith, the dragon that lives in the cave slays more than three hundred people every day with its breath." Constantine consulted with Sylvester about this problem. The pope said: "Through the power of Christ, I can stop the dragon from harming anyone ever again." The priests promised that, if he accomplished this, they would believe in the Christian faith. While Sylvester was praying, the Holy Spirit appeared to him, saying "Go down safely to the dragon, you and two presbyters with you, and when you reach him, speak to him in this way: 'Our lord Jesus Christ, born from a virgin, crucified and buried, who rose again and sits at the right hand of the Father, this is the one who will come to judge the living and the dead. Therefore, you, Satan, must await him in this cave until he comes.' You will bind his mouth with a thread and you will seal it with a seal bearing the imprint of the cross. Thereafter, you will all come back to me safe and sound and you will eat the bread that I will have prepared for you." With the two presbyters, Sylvester descended into the cave carrying two lanterns down 150 steps. Then he spoke the aforesaid words to the dragon and bound the mouth of the rasping and hissing creature, as he had been instructed. As Sylvester went back up the stairs, he discovered two magicians, who had followed them to see if they had descended to the dragon, almost dead from the fetid smell of the monster. Indeed he led them out with him safe and sound and they immediately converted to the Christian faith with an innumerable multitude. And thus the people of Rome were freed from a double death, namely from the worship of the demon and from the venom of the dragon.

(C) ST. MARGARET, BREAKER OF DRAKES[3]

Margaret was a citizen of Antioch and daughter of Theodosius, patriarch of the pagans. As a child she was entrusted to a nurse, and when she reached the age of reason she was baptized, and so incurred the wrath of her father. One day, when she was fifteen years old, she and some other young girls were looking after her nurse's sheep, and the prefect Olybrius happened to pass by; as soon as he saw how beautiful she was, he fell madly in love with her, and at once sent his men after her. "Go and seize her," he told them, "and if she is freeborn, I shall make her my wife; if she is a slave girl, I shall

take her as my concubine." Margaret was then brought before him, and he asked her about her family and name and
religion. She replied that she was of noble birth, her name
was Margaret, and she was a Christian. The prefect said:
"'Noble' and 'Margaret' suit you perfectly; you are clearly
noble, and you are a pearl of beauty![4] But Christianity does
not! How can a girl so beautiful and noble worship a God
who was crucified?" "How do you know," Margaret asked,
"that Christ was crucified?" "From the Christians' books,"
he told her. "You have read, then, of Christ's suffering and
his glory," she said. "How can you believe in the one, but
deny the other?" Margaret went on to explain to him that
Christ had died on the cross willingly for our redemption,
but now lived on in eternity. But this angered the prefect, and
he had her thrown into gaol.

Next day he summoned her and said: "You foolish girl,
have pity on your beauty! Worship our gods and you have
nothing to fear." Margaret replied: "I worship him before
whom the earth trembles, the sea quakes in fear, and all creatures stand in awe!" "If you do not obey me," the prefect told
her, "I will have your body torn to pieces!" Margaret said:
"Christ gave himself up to death for me, so I want nothing
more than to die for Christ!"

The prefect had her put on the rack; then she was beaten
cruelly with rods, and her flesh was raked with iron combs
until the bones were laid bare and the blood gushed from her
body as if from the purest spring. All those who were present
wept as they watched. "O Margaret," they said, "we pity
you, truly! To see your body torn so cruelly! What beauty
you have lost because of your unbelief! But there is still time:
believe and you will live!" "You counselors of evil!" Margaret cried. "Be off, be gone! This torture of the flesh is the
soul's salvation!" And she said to the prefect: "You shameless
dog! Ravening lion! You may have power over the flesh, but
my soul is Christ's alone!" The prefect, unable to stand the
sight of so much blood, covered his face with his cloak. He
then had Margaret taken down and thrown back into her
cell, which was at once filled with a miraculous radiance.

While she lay there, Margaret prayed the Lord to show her, in visible form, the enemy who was fighting her. A monstrous dragon suddenly appeared before her and sprang at her to devour her, but she made the sign of the cross and it disappeared. According to another account, the dragon got its jaws over Margaret's head and its tongue round her feet and swallowed her; and it was while it was attempting to digest her that she armed herself with the sign of the cross, and this proved too much for the dragon, who burst apart, and the virgin emerged unhurt. But this story of the dragon devouring the virgin, then bursting apart, is considered apocryphal and of no historical value.

(D) ST. MARTHA TAMES THE TARASQUE[5]

Martha, who welcomed Christ to her home, was of royal descent. Her father was named Syrus and her mother Eucharia. Her father was governor of Syria and of many coastal territories. Martha inherited through her mother and possessed jointly with her sister three towns: Magdalum and the two Bethanies, and part of the city of Jerusalem. Nowhere do we read that she had a husband or ever lived with a man. This noble hostess attended upon the Lord and wanted her sister to do so, too, because, to her way of thinking, there were not enough people in the entire world to serve so great a guest as he deserved.

After the Lord's ascension, when the disciples went their separate ways, Martha, with her brother Lazarus, her sister Mary Magdalene, blessed Maximinus (who had baptized the two sisters and to whose care the Holy Spirit had entrusted them) and many others were put on boats by the infidels with no oars, sails, rudders, or provisions, and, with the Lord's guidance, landed at Marseilles. From there they made their way to Aix where they converted the people to the faith. St. Martha was a gifted speaker and universally popular.

There was at that time in the forest along the banks of the Rhône between Arles and Avignon a dragon, half-beast, half-fish, larger than an ox, longer than a horse, with sword-like teeth as sharp as horns and flanks as impenetrable as twin shields. This monster lurked in the river, killing everyone who tried to pass and sinking their boats. It had come by sea from Galatia in Asia, and was an offspring of Leviathan, an unbelievably savage aquatic serpent, and a beast called Onachus, a native of the region of Galatia, which lets fly its dung like an arrow at anyone who gives chase and can shoot it up to an acre away, scorching whatever it touches as if it were fire. The people begged Martha to help, so she set off with them, and when she found the dragon in the forest, it was in the act of devouring a man. Martha threw some blessed water over it and held up a cross. The beast was at once defeated and stood there as meek as a lamb while St. Martha tied it up with her girdle, and the people pelted it with stones and spears and killed it. The local people called this dragon "Tarasconus," and that is why, in commemoration of this miracle, the place is still called Tarascon (it had formerly been known as "Nerluc," i.e., the "black place," because the forest there was dark and shadowy). With the permission of her teacher Maximinus and her sister, Martha stayed on at this place and devoted herself unremittingly to prayer and fasting. Later she gathered a large community of sisters there, and built a great basilica in honor of Blessed Mary Ever Virgin. She led a life of great austerity, avoiding all meats and fats, eggs, cheese and wine, eating only once a day, and bending knee in prayer a hundred times each day, and the same number of times each night.

ANTICHRIST ASCENDANT

Dragons in Early Modern Literature

Medieval dragon lore persisted in the European imagination long after the Protestant Reformation fractured the millennium-old unity of Christian belief in the sixteenth century, but dragons found a new purpose in this age of religious contention. Catholics and Protestants alike employed the printing press to create polemical pamphlets adorned with images that vilified their opponents. For their part, Catholics condemned Martin Luther's challenge to traditional Christian values as a depraved heresy and depicted him as a seven-headed monster akin to the dragon in the Book of Revelation (see pp. 34–35), each head spouting a different falsehood. Protestants responded in turn with caricatures representing the pope and his advisors as a loathsome beast with seven heads sitting on an altar fashioned to look like a chest full of money collected by the Church of Rome through the sale of indulgences. While the belief in living dragons and inquiries about their habitats remained topics of scholarly rumination throughout the early modern period (see pp. 239–83), the sixteenth and seventeenth centuries witnessed the popular revival of the dragon as an avatar of the Antichrist in Christian polemics and poetry.

THE DRAGONS OF
FAIRYLAND[1]

The longest and most vivid dragon battles in premodern literature appeared in Edmund Spenser's towering allegorical poem, The Faerie Queene. *Published in stages during the last decade of the sixteenth century, these epic verses earned Spenser the esteem of Queen Elizabeth I (r. 1558–1603) and lasting renown as one of the most important poets of the Elizabethan age. Despite its poetic charms,* The Faerie Queene *was not solely a source of entertainment for the queen's court; it also served a polemical purpose. Spenser's virtuous heroes represented adherents to the Anglican Christianity of his royal patron and her supporters in their struggle against the papal see, depicted as the Antichrist and his monstrous accomplices. In the poem's first book, the Redcrosse Knight and his lady Una confronted two dragonic monsters in Fairyland. Their first adversary was a cave-dwelling creature called Errour. This hybrid horror—half-woman, half-serpent—was a thinly veiled allegory for the errant teachings of the Church of Rome. After she was slain by Redcrosse, the dragon's offspring swarmed her body to drink her blood, illustrating how difficult it was to stamp out the errors of false belief. Their second adversary was even more daunting: a fire-breathing monstrosity that laid siege to the castle of Una's parents, the king and queen of Eden. Redcrosse's epic battle with this dragon was an allegory for Christ's triumph over the Devil and the devout Christian's rejection of sin. Their contest lasted for three days, during which the knight was healed*

by the waters of the Well of Life (representing baptism)
and refreshed by the balm of the Tree of Life (representing
the eucharist). Just as Christ rose from his tomb three
days after his crucifixion, Redcrosse rose from apparent
death on the third day of the battle to triumph against his
ancient enemy.

CANTO I:

The patron of true Holinesse
  Foule Errour doth defeate;
Hypocrisie, him to entrappe,
  Doth to his home entreate.

———————

Redcrosse and Una Discover a Cave in a Forest[2]
  At last resolving forward still to fare,
  Till that some end they finde, or in or out,
  That path they take that beaten seemd most bare,
  And like to lead the labyrinth about;
  Which when by tract they hunted had throughout,
  At length it brought them to a hollowe cave
  Amid the thickest woods. The Champion stout
  Eftsoones dismounted from his courser brave,
And to the Dwarfe awhile his needlesse spere he gave.[3]

Una Warns Redcrosse to Be Wary
  "Be well aware," quoth then that Ladie milde,
  "Least suddaine mischief ye too rash provoke:
  The danger hid, the place unknowne and wilde,
  Breedes dreadful doubts. Oft fire is without smoke,
  And perill without show: therefore your stroke,
  Sir Knight, with-hold, till further tryall made."
  "Ah Ladie," (sayd he) "shame were to revoke
  The forward footing for an hidden shade:
Vertue gives herself light through darknesse for to wade."

Una Reveals That the Forest is Home to a Monster Called Errour

"Yea but" (quoth she) "the perill of this place
I better wot than you: though nowe too late
To wish you backe returne with foule disgrace,
Yet wisedome warnes, whilest foot is in the gate,
To stay the steppe, ere forced to retrate.
This is the wandring wood, this *Errours* den,
A monster vile, whome God and man does hate:
Therefore I read beware." "Fly, Fly!" (quoth then
The fearefull Dwarfe) "this is no place for living men."

Redcrosse Enters the Cave and Sees the Monster

But, full of fire and greedy hardiment,
The youthfull Knight could not for ought be staide;
But forth unto the darksom hole he went,
And looked in: his glistering armor made
A little glooming light, much like a shade;
By which he saw the ugly monster plaine,
Halfe like a serpent horribly displaide,
But th'other halfe did womans shape retaine,
Most loathsome, filthie, foule, and full of vile disdaine.

The Loathsome Prodigy of Errour Surround Her

And, as she lay upon the durtie ground,
Her huge long taile her den all overspred,
Yet was in knots and many boughtes upwound,
Pointed with mortall sting. Of her there bred
A thousand yong ones, which she dayly fed,
Sucking upon her poisnous dugs; each one
Of sundrie shape, yet all ill-favored:
Soone as that uncouth light upon them shone,
Into her mouth they crept, and suddain all were gone.

Errour Seeks to Flee the Approaching Knight

Their dam upstart out of her den affraide,
And rushed forth, hurling her hideous taile

About her cursed head; whose folds displaid
Were stretcht now forth at length without entraile.
She lookt about, and seeing one in mayle,
Armed to point, sought backe to turne againe;
For light she hated as the deadly bale,
Ay wont in desert darkness to remaine,
Where plain none might her see, nor she see any plaine.

Redcrosse Corners Errour and Strikes with His Sword
Which when the valient Elfe perceiv'ed, he lept[4]
As Lyon fierce upon the flying pray,
And with his trenchand blade her boldly kept
From turning backe, and forced her to stay:
Therewith enrag'd she loudly gan to bray,
And turning fierce her speckled taile advaunst,
Threatning her angrie sting, him to dismay;
Who, nought aghast, his mightie hand enhaunst:
The stroke down from her head unto her shoulder glaunst.

Errour Rears Up and Wraps Redcrosse in Her Coils
Much daunted with that dint her fence was dazd;
Yet kindling rage her selfe she gathered round,
And all attonce her beastly bodie raizd
With doubled forces high above the ground:
Tho, wrapping up her wrethed sterne arownd,
Lept fierce upon his shield, and her huge traine
All suddenly about his body wound,
That hand or foot to stir he strove in vaine.
God helpe the man so wrapt in Errours endlesse traine!

*At Una's Urging, Redcrosse Breaks Free and Grabs Errour
by the Neck*
His Lady, sad to see his sore constraint,
Cried out, "Now, now, Sir knight, shew what ye bee;
Add faith unto your force, and be not faint;
Strangle her, els she sure will strangle thee."
That when he heard, in great perplexitie,

His fall did grate for griefe and high disdaine;
And, knitting all his force, got one hand free,
Wherewith he grypt her gorge with so great paine,
That soon to loose her wicked bands did her constraine.

Errour's Vomit Forces Redcrosse to Retreat
Therewith she spewd out of her filthie maw
A floud of poison horrible and blacke
Full of great lumps of flesh and gobbets raw,
Which stunck so vildly, that it forst him slacke
His grasping hold, and from her turne him backe.
Her vomit full of bookes and papers was,[5]
With loathly frogs and toades, which eyes did lacke,
And creeping sought way in the weedy gras:
Her filthie parbreake all the place defiled has.

The River Nile Produces Strange Creatures
As when old father Nilus gins to swell
With timely pride above the Aegyptian vale,
His fattie waves doe fertile slime outwell,
And overflow each plaine and lowly dale:
But, when his later spring gins to avale,
Huge heapes of mudd he leaves, wherin there breed
Ten thousand kindes of creatures, partly male
And partly female, of his fruitful seed:
Such ugly monstrous shapes elswher may no man reed.

The Offspring of Errour Swarm Redcrosse
The same so sore annoyed has the knight,
That, welnigh choked with the deadly stinke,
His forces faile, ne can no lenger fight:
Whose corage when the feend perceivd to shrinke,
She poured forth out of her hellish sinke
Her fruitfull cursed spawne of serpents small,
Deformed monsters, fowle, and blacke as inke,
Which swarming all about his legs did crall,
And him encombred sore, but could not hurt at all.

Like Gnats, They Annoy Redcrosse but Cannot Harm Him
As gentle shepheard in sweet eventide,
When ruddy Phebus gins to welke in west,
High on a hill, his flocke to vewen wide,
Markes which doe byte their hasty supper best;
A cloud of cumbrous gnattes doe him molest,
All striving to infixe their feeble stinges,
That from their noyance he no where can rest;
But with his clownish hands their tender wings
He trusheth oft, and oft doth mar their murmurings.

Redcrosse Cuts Off the Head of Errour
Thus ill bestedd, and fearfull more of shame
Then of the certeine perill he stood in,
Halfe furious unto his foe he came,
Resolvd in minde all suddenly to win,
Or soone to lose, before he once would lin;
And stroke at her with more than manly force,
That from her body, full of filthie sin,
He raft her hatefull heade without remorse:
A streame of cole-black blood forth gushed from her corse.

Errour's Offspring Devour Her Body
Her scattred brood, soone as their Parent deare
They saw so rudely falling to the ground,
Groning full deadly, all with troublous feare
Gathred themselves about her body round,
Weening their wonted entrance to have found
At her wide mouth: but being there withstood,
They flocked all about her bleeding wound,
And sucked up their dying mother's blood:
Making her death their life, and eke her hurt their good.

Errour's Offspring Die from Drinking Her Blood
That detestable sight him much amazde,
To see th'unkindly Impes, of heaven accurst,
Devoure their dam; on whom while he so gazd,
Having all satisfide their bloudy thurst,

Their bellies swolne he saw with fulnesse burst,
And bowels gushing forth: well worthy end
Of such as drunke her life the which them nurst!
Now needeth him no lenger labour spend,
His foes of slaine themselves, with whom he should contend.

Una Congratulates Redcrosse on His First Victory
His Lady, seeing all that chaunst from farre,
Approcht in hast to greet his victorie;
And saide, "Faire knight, borne under happie starre,
Who see your vanquisht foes before you lye,
Well worthie be you of that Armory,
Wherein ye have great glory wonne this day,
And proov'd your strength on a strong enimie;
Your first adventure: many such I pray,
And henceforth ever wish that you succeed it may!"

CANTO II:

The knight with that old Dragon fights
two days incessantly:
The third him overthrows, and gains
most glorious victory.

Una and Redcrosse Approach the Castle of Eden
High time now gan it wex for Una fayre
To thinke of those her captive Parents deare,
And their forwasted kingdom to repayre:
Whereto whenas they now approched neare,
With hartie wordes her knight she gan to cheare,
And in her modest maner thus bespake:
"Deare knight, as deare as ever a knight was deare,
That all these sorrowes suffer for my sake,
High heven behold the tedious toyle, ye for me take!"

Una Warns Redcrosse That a Dragon Awaits
"Now are we come unto my native soyle,

And to the place where all our perilles dwell;
Here hauntes that feend, and does his dayly spoyle;
Therefore, henceforth, bee at your keeping well,
And ever ready for your foeman fell:
The sparke of noble corage now awake,
And strive your excellent selfe to excell:
That shall ye evermore renowmed make
Above all knights on earth, that batteill undertake."

They Spy the Castle of Una's Parents
And pointing forth: "Lo! yonder is," (said she)
"The brasen tower in which my parents deare
For dread of that huge feend emprisond be;
Whom I from far see on the walles appeare,
Whose sight my feeble soule doth greatly cheare:
And on the top of all I do espye
The watchman wayting tydings glad to heare;
That, (O my Parents!) might I happily
Unto you bring, to ease you of your misery!"

Enter the Dragon
With that they heard a roaring hideous sownd,
That all the ayre with terror filled wyde,
And seemd uneath to shake the stedfast ground.
Eftsoones that dreadful Dragon they espyde,
Where stretcht he lay upon the sunny side
Of a great hill, himselfe like a great hill.
But, all so soone as he from far descryde
Those glistring armes that heven with light did fill,
He rousd himselfe full blyth, and hastned them untill.

Redcrosse Asks Una to Withdraw to Safety Before the Battle
Then badd the knight his Lady yede aloof,
And to a hill herselfe withdraw asyde;
From whence she might behold that battailles proof,
And eke be safe from daunger far descryde.
She him obayd, and turned a little wyde.—

Now, O thou sacred Muse! most learned Dame,
Fayre ympe of Phoebus and his aged bryde,
The Nourse of time and everlasting fame,
That warlike handes ennoblest with immortall name;[6]

The Poet Evokes the Muse of History

O! gently come into my feeble brest;
Come gently, but not with that mightie rage,
Wherewith the martiall troupes thou doest infest,
And hartes of great Heroës doest enrage,
That nought their kindled corage may aswage:
Soone as your dreadfull trompe begins to sownd,
The God of warre with his fiers equipage
Thou doest awake, sleepe never he so sownd;
And scared nations doest with horror sterne astownd.

The Evocation of Clio Continues

Fayre Goddesse, lay that furious fitt asyde
Till I of warres and bloody Mars doe sing,
And Bryton fieldes with Sarazin blood be dyed,
Twixt that great faery Queene and Paynim king,
That with their horror heven and earth did ring;
A worke of labour long, and endless prayse:
But now a while lett downe that haughtie string,
And to my tunes thy second tenor rayse,
That I this man of God his godly armes may blaze.

The Dragon's Monstrous Body

By this, the dreadful Beast drew nigh to hand,
Halfe flying and halfe footing in his haste,
That with his largenesse measured much land,
And made wide shadow under his huge waste,
As mountaine doth the valley overcaste.
Approching nigh, he reared high afore
His body monstrous, horrible, and vaste;
Which, to increase his wondrous greatnes more,
Was swoln with wrath and poyson, and with bloody gore;

The Dragon's Scales

And over all with brasen scales was armd,
Like plated cote of steele, so couched neare,
That nought mote perce; ne might his corse bee harmed
With dint of swerd, nor push of pointed speare:
Which as an Eagle, seeing pray appeare,
His aery plumes doth rouze, full rudely dight,
So shaked he, that horror was to heare:
For as the clashing of an Armor bright,
Such noyse his rouzed scales did send unto the knight.

The Dragon's Wings

His flaggy winges, when forth he did display,
Were like two sayles, in which the hollow wynd
Is gathered full, and worketh speedy way:
And eke the pennes, that did his pineons bynd,
Were like mayne-yards, with flying canvas lynd;
With which whenas him list the ayre to beat,
And there by force unwonted passage fynd,
The cloudes before him fledd for terror great,
And all the hevens stood still amazed with his threat.

The Dragon's Stinging Tail

His huge long tayle, wownd up in hundred foldes,
Does overspred his long bras-scaly back,
Whose wreathed boughtes when ever he unfoldes
And thick entangled knots adown does slack,
Bespotted as with shieldes of red and blacke,
It sweepeth all the land behind him farre,
And of three furlongs does but litle lacke;[7]
And at the point two stinges in fixed arre,
Both deadly sharpe, that sharpest steele exceeden farre.

The Dragon's Claws and Jaws

But stinges and sharpest steele did far exceed
The sharpnesse of his cruel rending clawes:
Dead was it sure, as sure as death in deed,
What ever thing does touch his ravenous pawes,

Or what within his reach he ever drawes.
But his most hideous head my tongue to tell,
Does tremble; for his deepe devouring jawes
Wyde gaped, like the grisly mouth of hell,
Through which into his darke abysse all ravin fell.

The Dragon's Teeth

And, that more wondrous was, in either jaw
Three ranckes of yron teeth enraunged were,
In which yett trickling blood, and gobbets raw,
Of late devoured bodies did appeare,
That sight thereof bredd cold congealed feare;
Which to increase, and all atonce to kill,
A cloud of smoothering smoke, and sulphure seare,
Out of his stinking gorge forth steemed still,
That all the ayre about with smoke and stench did fill.

The Dragon's Eyes

His blazing eyes, like two bright shining shieldes,
Did burne with wrath, and sparkled living fyre:
As two broad Beacons, sett in open fieldes,
Send forth their flames far off to every shyre,
And warning give that enimies conspyre
With fire and sword the region to invade:
So flam'd his eyne with rage and rancorous yre;
But far within, as in a hollow glade,
Those glaring lampes were sett, that made a dreadfull shade.

The Dragon Advances

So dreadfully he towardes him did pas,
Forelifting up a-loft his speckled brest,
And often bounding on the brused gras,
As for great joyance of his newcome guest.
Eftsoones he gan advance his haughty crest,
As chauffed Bore his bristles doth upreare;
And shoke his scales to battaile ready drest,
That made the Redcrosse knight nigh quake for feare,
As bidding bold defyaunce to his foeman neare.

Redcrosse Strikes a Glancing Blow; the Dragon Knocks Him Down

> The knight gan fayrely couch his steady speare,
> And fiersely ran at him with rigorous might:
> The pointed steele, arriving rudely theare,
> His harder hyde would nether perce nor bight,
> But, glauncing by, foorth passed forward right.
> Yet sore amoved with so puissaunt push,
> The wrathfull beast about him turned light,
> And him so rudely, passing by, did brush
> With his long tayle, that horse and man to ground did rush.

Redcrosse Recovers and Strikes Again without Success; the Dragon Grows Angry

> Both horse and man up lightly rose againe,
> And fresh encounter towardes him addrest;
> But th'ydle stroke yet backe recoyld in vaine,
> And found no place his deadly point to rest.
> Exceeding rage enflam'd the furious Beast,
> To be avenged of so great despight;
> For never felt his imperceable brest
> So wondrous force from hand of living wight;
> Yet had he prov'd the powre of many a puissant knight.

The Dragon Takes Flight, Snatching Up Redcrosse and His Horse

> Then, with his waving wings displayed wyde,
> Himselfe up high he lifted from the ground,
> And with strong flight did forcibly divyde
> The yielding ayre, which nigh too feeble found
> Her flitting parts, and element unsound,
> To beare so great a weight: he, cutting way
> With his broad sayles, about him soared round;
> At last, low stouping with unweldy sway,
> Snatcht up both horse and man, to beare them quite away.

The Dragon Releases Redcrosse and His Horse

> Long he them bore above the subject plaine,

So far as Ewghen bow a shaft may send,[8]
Till struggling strong did him at last constraine,
To let them downe before his flightes end:
As haggard hauke, presuming to contend
With hardy fowle above his hable might,
His wearie pounces all in vaine doth spend
To trusse the pray too heavy for his flight;
Which, comming downe to ground, does free it selfe by fight.

Redcrosse Wounds the Dragon with a Mighty Thrust of His Spear

He so disseized of his gryping grosse,
The knight his thrillant speare againe assayd
In his bras-plated body to embosse,
And three mens strength unto the stroake he layd;
Wherewith the stiffe beame quaked as affrayd,
And glauncing from his scaly necke did glyde
Close under his left wing, then broad displayd:
The percing steele there wrought a wound full wyde,
That with the uncouth smart the Monster lowdly cryde.

The Dragon Roars in Pain

He cryde, as raging seas are wont to rore
When wintry storme his wrathful wreck does threat;
The rolling billowes beate the ragged shore,
As they the earth would shoulder from her seat;
And greedy gulfe does gape, as he would eat
His neighbour element in his revenge:
Then gin the blustring brethren boldly threat
To move the world from off his stedfast henge,
And boystrous battaile make, each other to avenge.

The Dragon Bleeds Profusely and Breathes Fire

The steely head stuck fast still in his flesh,
Till with his cruell clawes he snatcht the wood,
And quite a sunder broke. Forth flowed fresh
A gushing river of blacke gory blood,
That drowned all the land whereon he stood;

The streame thereof would drive a water-mill:
Trebly augmented was his furious mood
With bitter sence of his deepe rooted ill,
That flames of fire he threw forth from his large nosethril.

The Dragon Snares the Horse with Its Tail, Causing Redcrosse to Fall

His hideous tayle then hurled he about,
And therewith all enwrapt the nimble thyes
Of his froth-fomy steed, whose courage stout
Striving to loose the knott that fast him tyes,
Himselfe in streighter bandes too rash implyes,
That to the ground he is perforce constraynd
To throw his ryder; who can quickly ryse
From off the earth, with durty bloud distaynd,
For that reprochfull fall right fowly he disdaynd;

Redcrosse Strikes the Dragon with His Sword, but the Blow Recoils

And fercely tooke his trenchand blade in hand,
With which he stroke so furious and so fell,
That nothing seemd the puissaunce could withstand:
Upon his crest the hardned yron fell,
But his more hardned crest was armd so well,
That deeper dint therein it would not make;
Yet so extremely did the buffe him quell,
That from thenceforth he shund the like to take,
But when he saw them come, he did them still forsake.

Redcrosse Smites Again

The knight was wroth to see his stroke beguyld,
And smote againe with more outrageous might;
But backe againe the sparcling steele recoyld,
And left not any marke, where it did light,
As if in Adamant rocke it had beene pight.
The beast, impatient of his smarting wound
And of so fierce and forcible despight,
Thought with his winges to stye above the ground;
But his late wounded wing unserviceable found.

The Dragon Engulfs Redcrosse in Flames
    Then full of griefe and anguish vehement,
    He lowdly brayd, that like was never heard;
    And from his wide devouring oven sent
    A flake of fire, that flashing in his beard,
    Him all amazd, and almost made afeard:
    The scorching flame sore swinged all his face,
    And through his armour all his bodie seard,
    That he could not endure so cruell cace,
But thought his armes to leave, and helmet to unlace.

Redcrosse's Struggles Surpass the Labors of Hercules[9]
    Not that great Champion of the antique world,
    Whom famous Poetes verse so much doth vaunt,
    And hath for twelve huge labours high extold,
    So many furies and sharpe fits did haunt,
    When him the poysoned garment did enchaunt
    With Centaures blood, and bloody verses charmd;
    As did this knight twelve thousand dolours daunt,
    Whom fyrie steele now burnt, that earst him arm'd;
That erst him goodly arm'd, now most of all him harm'd.

Weary from the Battle, Redcrosse Falls
    Faint, wearie, sore, emboyled, grieved, brent,
    With heat, toyle, wounds, armes, smart, and inward fire,
    That never man such mischiefes did torment:
    Death better were; death did he oft desire,
    But death will never come when needes require.
    Whom so dismayd when that his foe beheld,
    He cast to suffer him no more respire,
    But gan his sturdie sterne about to weld,
And him so strongly stroke, that to the ground him feld.

Redcrosse Topples into the Well of Life
    It fortuned, (as faire it then befell)
    Behynd his backe, unweeting, where he stood,
    Of auncient time there was a springing well,
    From which fast trickled forth a silver flood,

Full of great vertues, and for med'cine good.
Whylome, before that cursed Dragon got
That happy land, and all with innocent blood
Defyld those sacred waves, it rightly hot
The well of life, ne yet his vertues had forgot:

The Miraculous Healing Properties of the Well of Life
For unto life the dead it could restore,
And guilt of sinfull crimes cleane wash away;
Those that with sicknesse were infected sore
It could recure; and aged long decay
Renew, as one were borne that very day.
Both Silo this, and Jordan, did excel,
And th'English Bath, and eke the German Spau;
Ne can Cephise, nor Hebrus, match this well:[10]
Into the same knight back overthrowen fell.

Night Falls; the Dragon Seems to Have Won the Battle
Now gan the golden Phoebus for to steepe
His fierie face in billowes of the west,
And his faint steedes watred in Ocean deepe,
Whiles from their journall labours they did rest;[11]
When that infernall Monster, having kest
His wearie foe into that living well,
Can high advance his broad discoloured brest
Above his wonted pitch, with countenance fell,
And clapt his yron wings as victor he did dwell.

Una Prays All Night for Her Knight
Which when his pensive Lady saw from farre,
Great woe and sorrow did her soule assay,
As weening that the sad end of the warre;
And gan to highest God entirely pray
That feared chaunce from her to turne away:
With folded hands, and knees full lowly bent,
All night shee watcht, ne once adowne would lay
Her dainty limbs in her sad dreriment,
But praying still did wake, and waking did lament.

The Second Day of the Battle Dawns

The morrow next gan early to appeare,
That Titan rose to runne his daily race;[12]
But earely, ere the morrow next gan reare
Out of the sea faire Titans deawy face,
Up rose the gentle virgin from her place,
And looked all about, if she might spy
Her loved knight to move his manly pace:
For she had great doubt of his safety,
Since late she saw him fall before his enimy.

Redcrosse Rises from the Well Refreshed

At last she saw where he upstarted brave
Out of the well, wherein he drenched lay:
As Eagle, fresh out of the ocean wave,
Where he hath lefte his plumes all hory grey,
And deckt himselfe with fethers youthly gay,
Like Eyas hauke up mounts unto the skies,
His newly-budded pineons to assay,
And marveiles at himselfe stil as he flies:[13]
So new this new-borne knight to battell new did rise.

Redcrosse Strikes the Dragon on the Head

Whom when the damned feend so fresh did spy,
No wonder if he wondred at the sight,
And doubted whether his late enimy
It were, or other new supplied knight.
He now, to prove his late-renewed might,
High brandishing his bright deaw-burning blade,
Upon his crested scalp so sore did smite,
That to the scull a yawning wound it made:
The deadly dint his dulled senses all dismaid.

The Well of Life Has Given Redcrosse New Strength

I wote not whether the revenging steele
Were hardned with that holy water dew
Wherein he fell, or sharper edge did feele,
Or his baptized hands now greater grew,

Or other secret vertue did ensew;
Else never could the force of fleshly arme,
Ne molten mettall, in his bloud embrew;
For till that stownd could never wight him harme,
By subtilty, nor slight, nor might, nor mighty charme.

The Wounded Dragon Roars and Rears

The cruell wound enraged him so sore,
That loud he yelled for exceeding paine;
As hundred ramping Lions seemd to rore,
Whom ravenous hunger did thereto constraine:
Then gan he tosse aloft his stretched traine,
And therewith scourge the buxome aire so sore,
That to his force to yielden it was faine;
Ne ought his sturdy strokes might stand afore,
That high trees overthrew, and rocks in peeces tore.

The Dragon Impales Redcrosse with Its Sharp Tail

The same advauncing high above his head,
With sharpe intended sting so rude him smott,
That to the earth him drove, as stricken dead;
Ne living wight would have him life behott:
The mortall sting his angry needle shott
Quite through his shield, and in his shoulder seasd,
Where fast it stucke, ne would thereout be gott:
The griefe thereof him wondrous sore diseasd,
Ne might his rancling paine with patience be appeasd.

Redcrosse Hews the Dragon's Tail

But yet, more mindfull of his honour deare,
Then of the grievous smart which him did wring,
From loathed soile he can him lightly reare,
And strove to loose the far infixed sting:
Which when in vaine he tryde with struggeling,
Inflam'd with wrath, his raging blade he hefte,
And strooke so strongly, that the knotty string
Of his huge taile he quite a sonder clefte;
Five joynts thereof he hewd, and but the stump him lefte.

The Dragon Attacks Again

Hart cannot thinke what outrage and what cries,
With fowle enfouldred smoake and flashing fire,
The hell-bred beast threw forth unto the skyes,
That all was covered with darknesse dire:
Then, fraught with rancour and engorged ire,
He cast at once him to avenge for all;
And, gathering up himselfe out of the mire,
With his uneven wings, did fiercely fall,
Upon his sunne-bright shield, and grypt it fast withall.

Redcrosse Struggles to Release the Dragon's Grip on His Shield

Much was the man encombred with his hold,
In feare to lose his weapon in his paw,
Ne wist yett how his talaunts to unfold;
Nor harder was from Cerberus greedy jaw
To plucke a bone, then from his cruell claw
To reave by strength the griped gage away:[14]
Thrise he assayd it from his foote to draw,
And thrise in vaine to draw it did assay;
It booted nought to thinke to robbe him of his pray.

Redcrosse Forces the Dragon to Release One Paw

Tho, when he saw no power might prevaile,
His trusty sword he cald to his last aid,
Wherewith he fiersly did his foe assaile,
And double blowes about him stoutly laid,
That glauncing fire out of the yron plaid,
As sparkles from the Andvile used to fly,
When heavy hammers on the wedge are swaid:
Therewith at last he forst him to unty
One of his grasping feete, him to defend thereby.

Redcrosse Severs the Dragon's Other Paw

The other foot, fast fixed on his shield,
Whenas no strength nor stroks mote him constraine
To loose, ne yet the warlike pledge to yield,

He smott thereat with all his might and maine,
That nought so wondrous puissance might sustaine;
Upon the joint the lucky steele did light,
And made such way that hewd it quite in twaine;
The paw yet missed not his minisht might,
But hong still on the shield, as it at first was pight.

The Dragon Spits Fire
For griefe thereof and divelish despight,
From his infernall fournace forth he threw
Huge flames that dimmed all the hevens light,
Enrold in duskish smoke and brimstone blew:
As burning Aetna from his boyling stew
Doth belch out flames, and rockes in peeces broke,
And ragged ribs of mountaines molten new,
Enwrapt in coleblacke clowds and filthy smoke,
That all the land with stench and heven with horror choke.[15]

Redcrosse Retreats from the Fire and Falls
The heate whereof, and harmefull pestilence,
So sore him noyd, that forst him to retire
A little backward for his best defence,
To save his body from the scorching fire,
Which he from hellish entrailes did expire.
It chaunst, (eternall God that chaunce did guide)
As he recoiled backward, in the mire
His nigh forewearied feeble feet did slide,
And downe he fell, with dread of shame sore terrifide.

Redcrosse Lands at the Foot of the Tree of Life
There grew a goodly tree him aire beside,
Loaden with fruit and apples rosie redd,
As they in pure vermilion had beene dide,
Whereof great vertues over-all were redd;
For happy life to all, which thereon fedd,
And life eke everlasting did befall:
Great God it planted in that blessed stedd
With his Almighty hand, and did it call
The tree of life, the crime of our first fathers fall.[16]

The Trees of Eden
In all the world like was not to be fownd,
Save in that soile, where all good things did grow,
And freely sprong out of the fruitfull grownd,
As incorrupted Nature did them sow,
Till that dredd Dragon all did overthrow.
Another like faire tree eke grew thereby,
Whereof whoso did eat, eftsoones did know
Both good and ill. O mournfull memory!
That tree through one mans fault hath doen us all to dy.

The Balm of the Tree of Life Saves Redcrosse
From that first tree forth flowd, as from a well,
A trickling streame of Balme, most soveraine
And dainty deare, which on the ground still fell,
And overflowed all the fertile plaine,
As it had deawed bene with timely raine:
Life and long health that gracious ointment gave,
And deadly wounds could heale, and reare again
The sencelesse corse appointed for the grave:
Into that same he fell, which did from death him save.

The Dragon Cannot Approach the Tree; Night Falls
For nigh thereto the ever damned Beast
Durst not approch, for he was deadly made,
And al that life preserved did detest;
Yet he it oft adventur'd to invade.
By this the drouping day-light gan to fade,
And yield his rowme to sad succeeding night,
Who with her sable mantle gan to shade,
The face of earth and wayes of living wight,
And high her burning torch set up in heaven bright.

Una Prays Throughout the Night for Redcrosse's Recovery
When gentle Una saw the second fall
Of her deare knight, who, wearie of long fight
And faint through losse of blood, moov'd not at all,
But lay, as in a dreame of deepe delight,

Besmeard with pretious Balme, whose vertuous might
Did heale his woundes, and scorching heat alay;
Againe she stricken was with sore affright,
And for his safetie gan devoutly pray,
And watch the noyous night, and wait for joyous day.

The Third Day of the Battle Dawns

The joyous day gan early to appeare;
And fayre Aurora from the deawy bed
Of aged Tithone gan herselfe to reare
With rosie cheekes, for shame as blushing red![17]
Her golden locks for hast were loosely shed
About her eares, when Una her did marke
Clymbe to her charet, all with flowers spred,
From heven high to chace the chearelesse darke;
With mery note her lowd salutes the mounting larke.

To the Dragon's Dismay, Redcrosse Rises Up Fully Restored

Then freshly up arose the doughty knight,
All healed of his hurts and woundes wide,
And did himselfe to battaile ready dight;
Whose early foe awaiting him beside
To have devourd, so soone as day he spyde,
When now he saw himselfe so freshly reare,
As if late fight had nought him damnifyde,
He woxe dismaid, and gan his fate to feare;
Nathlesse with wonted rage he him advaunced neare.

Redcrosse Thrusts His Sword into the Dragon's Mouth

And in his first encounter, gaping wyde,
He thought attonce him to have swallowd quight,
And rusht upon him with outragious pryde;
Who him rencountring fierce, as hauke in flight,
Perforce rebutted backe. The weapon bright
Taking advantage of his open jaw,
Ran through his mouth with so importune might,
That deepe emperst his darksom hollow maw,
And, back retyrd, his life blood forth with all did draw.

The Dragon Falls

So downe he fell, and forth his life did breath,
That vanisht into smoke and cloudes swift;
So downe he fell, that th'earth him underneath
Did grone, as feeble so great load to lift;
So downe he fell, as an huge rocky clift,
Whose false foundacion waves have washt away,
With dreadfull poyse is from the mayneland rift,
And rolling downe great Neptune doth dismay:
So downe he fell, and like a heaped mountaine lay.

Una Praises the Valor of Redcrosse

The knight him selfe even trembled at his fall,
So huge and horrible a masse it seemd;
And his deare Lady, that beheld it all,
Durst not approch for dread which she misdeemd;
But yet at last, when as the direfull feend
She saw not stirre, off-shaking vaine affright
She nigher drew, and saw that joyous end:
Then God she praysd, and thankt her faithful knight,
That had atchievde so great a conquest by his might.

A FARTING DRAGON
BURLESQUE[1]

The popularity of Spenser's lofty Christian verses invited parody in the form of humorous and raunchy songs like the anonymous "Dragon of Wantley." This burlesque first appeared in print in 1685 and remained popular for centuries, inspiring both a successful opera by Henry Carey (1737) and a widely read novel by Owen Wister (1892). The original lyrics made fun of traditional tales of dragon battles, subverting their religious symbolism while adorning them with absurd characters, like an arrogant knight whose spiky armor gave him the appearance of a "porcupig" and a farting dragon the size of the Trojan Horse. While heroes of old typically vanquished their foes with epic sword blows, "The Dragon of Wantley" depicted a rowdy warrior delivering a lethal kick to his flatulent enemy's "assgut." As revealed in the final stanza of the song, this dragon's Achilles's heel was his anus!

Old stories tell, how Hercules
   A dragon slew at Lerna,
With seven heads, and fourteen eyes,
   To see and well discern-a:
But he had a club, this dragon to drub,
   Or he ne'er had done it, I warrant ye:
But More of More-hall, with nothing at all,
   He slew the dragon of Wantley.[2]

This dragon had two furious wings,
   Each one upon each shoulder;

With a sting in his tayl, as long as a flayl,
  Which made him bolder and bolder.
He had long claws, and in his jaws
  Four and forty teeth of iron;
With a hide as tough, as any buff,
  Which did him round environ.[3]

Have you not heard how the Trojan horse
  Held seventy men in his belly?
This dragon was not quite so big,
  But very near, I'll tell ye.
Devoured he poor children three,
  That could not with him grapple;
And at one sup he eat them up,
  As one would eat an apple.

All sorts of cattle this dragon would eat,
  Some say he ate up trees,
And that the forests sure he would
  Devour up by degrees:
For houses and churches were to him geese and turkies;
  He ate all, and left none behind,
But some stones, dear Jack, that he could not crack,
  Which on the hills you will find.

In Yorkshire, near fair Rotherham,[4]
  The place I know it well;
Some two or three miles, or thereabouts,
  I vow I cannot tell;
But there is a hedge, just on the hill edge,
  And Matthew's house hard by it;
O there and then was this dragon's den,
  You could not chuse but spy it.

Some say, this dragon was a witch;
  Some say, he was a devil,
For from his nose a smoke arose,

And with it burning snivel;
Which he cast off, when he did cough,
    In a well that he did stand by;
Which made it look, just like a brook
    Running with burning brandy.

Hard by a furious knight there dwelt;
    Of whom all towns did ring;
For he could wrestle, play at quarter-staff, kick, cuff and
    huff,
    Call son of a whore, do any kind of thing:
By the tail and the main, with his hands twain
    He swung a horse till he was dead;
And that which is stranger, he for very anger
    Eat him all up but his head.

These children, as I told, being eat;
    Men, women, girls, and boys,
Sighing and sobbing, came to his lodging,
    And made a hideous noise:
O, save us all, More of More-Hall,
    Thou peerless knight of these woods;
Do but slay this dragon, who won't leave us a rag on,
    We'll give thee all our goods.

Tut, tut, quoth he, no goods I want;
    But I want, I want, in sooth,
A fair maid of sixteen, that's brisk, and keen,
    With smiles about the mouth;
Hair black as sloe, skin white as snow,
    With blushes her cheeks adorning;
To anoynt me o'er night, ere I go to fight,
    And to dress me in the morning.

This being done he did engage
    To hew the dragon down;
But first he went, new armour to
    Bespeak at Sheffield town;[5]

With spikes all about, not within but without,
    Of steel so sharp and strong;
Both behind and before, arms, legs, and all o'er,
    Some five or six inches long.

Had you but seen him in this dress,
    How fierce he look'd and how big,
You would have thought him for to be
    Some Egyptian porcupig:
He frighted all, cats, dogs, and all,
    Each cow, each horse, and each hog:
For fear they did flee, for they took him to be
    Some strange outlandish hedge-hog.

To see this fight, all people then
    Got up on trees and houses,
On churches some, and chimneys too;
    But these put on their trowses,
Not to spoil their hose. As soon as he rose,
    To make him strong and mighty,
He drank by the tale, six pots of ale
    And a quart of aqua-vitæ.

It is not strength that always wins,
    For wit doth strength excell;
Which made our cunning champion
    Creep down into a well;
Where he did think, this dragon would drink,
    And so he did in truth;
And as he stoop'd low, he rose up and cry'd, boh!
    And hit him in the mouth.[6]

Oh, quoth the dragon, pox take thee, come out,
    Thou disturb'st me in my drink:
And then he turn'd, and farted at him;
    Good lack how he did stink!
Beshrew thy soul, thy body's foul,
    Thy dung smells not like balsam;

Thou son of a whore, thou stink'st so sore,
  Sure thy diet is unwholesome.

Our politick knight, on the other side,
  Crept out upon the brink,
And gave the dragon such a douse,
  He knew not what to think:
By cock, quoth he, say you so: do you see?
  And then at him he let fly
With hand and with foot, and so they went to't;
  And the word it was, hey boys, hey!

Your words, quoth the dragon, I don't understand:
  Then to it they fell at all,
Like two wild boars so fierce, if I may,
  Compare great things with small.
Two days and a night, with this dragon did fight
  Our champion on the ground;
Tho' their strength it was great, this skill it was neat,
  They never had one wound.

At length the hard earth began to quake,
  The dragon gave him a knock,
Which made him to reel, and straitway he thought,
  To lift him as high as a rock,
And thence let him fall. But More of More-Hall,
  Like a valiant son of Mars,
As he came like a lout, so he turned him about,
  And hit him a kick on the arse.

Oh, quoth the dragon, with a deep sigh,
  And turn'd six times together,
Sobbing and tearing, cursing and swearing
  Out of his throat of leather;
More of More-hall! O thou rascàl!
  Would I had seen thee never;
With the thing at thy foot, thou hast pricked my assgut,
  And I'm quite undone forever.

Murder, murder, the dragon cry'd,
  Alack, alack, for grief;
Had you but missed that place, you could
  Have done me no mischief.
Then his head he shaked, trembled, and quaked,
  And down he laid and cry'd;
First on one knee, then on back tumbled he;
  So groan'd, kickt, farted, and died.

THE GREAT SERPENT
RETURNS[1]

No work of western literature treated the figure of Satan with as much depth as Paradise Lost, *a magisterial poem in twelve books published in 1674 by the English poet John Milton (1608–74). Milton's poem depicted the war waged by Lucifer and the rebel angels against God, their defeat and banishment to Hell, and the creation of the world and the first human beings, Adam and Eve. Eager to thwart God's plans, the Devil infiltrated this new world, where in serpentine form he tempted Eve with alluring words to eat the fruit of the Tree of the Knowledge of Good and Evil, thus dooming the human race to mortality (see pp. 31–32). Leaving Adam and Eve to their shame and guilt, Satan returned to Hell triumphant. There he relished his victory over humankind and the loss of Paradise before an audience of fallen angels. When he finished his speech, the Devil anticipated praise and applause, but instead he heard "a dismal universal hiss" as his followers transformed before his eyes into a host of hideous snakes. Then, as a punishment for his crime in Eden, God transformed Satan himself into a enormous serpent and deprived him of his ability to speak as punishment for bringing about the Fall of Man with his words.*

So having said, a while he stood, expecting
Thir universal shout and high applause
To fill his eare, when contrary he hears
On all sides, from innumerable tongues
A dismal universal hiss, the sound
Of public scorn; he wonderd, but not long

Had leasure, wondring at himself now more;
His Visage drawn he felt to sharp and spare,
His Armes clung to his Ribs, his Leggs entwining
Each other, till supplanted down he fell
A monstrous Serpent on his Belly prone,
Reluctant, but in vaine, a greater power
Now rul'd him, punisht in the shape he sin'd,
According to his doom: he would have spoke,
But hiss for hiss returnd with forked tongue
To forked tongue, for now were all transform'd
Alike, to Serpents all as accessories
To his bold Riot: dreadful was the din
Of hissing through the Hall, thick swarming now
With complicated monsters head and taile,
Scorpion and Asp, and *Amphibæna* dire,
Cerastes hornd, *Hydrus*, and *Ellops* drear,
And *Dipsas* (not so thick swarm'd once the Soil
Bedropt with blood of *Gorgon*, or the Isle
Ophiusa) but still greatest hee the midst,[2]
Now Dragon grown, larger then whom the Sun
Ingenderd in the *Pythian* Vale on slime,
Huge *Python*, and his Power no less he seem'd
Above the rest still to retain;[3] they all
Him follow'd issuing forth to th' open Field,
Where all yet left of that revolted Rout
Heav'n-fall'n, in station stood or just array,
Sublime with expectation when to see
In Triumph issuing forth thir glorious Chief;
They saw, but other sight instead, a crowd
Of ugly Serpents; horror on them fell,
And horrid sympathie; for what they saw,
They felt themselves now changing; down thir arms,
Down fell both Spear and Shield, down they as fast,
And the dire hiss renew'd, and the dire form
Catcht by Contagion, like in punishment,
As in thir crime. Thus was th' applause they meant,
Turnd to exploding hiss, triumph to shame
Cast on themselves from thir own mouths . . .

GODS AND MONSTERS

Dragons of the East

The civilizations of premodern Asia nurtured rich literary traditions about the nature of dragons far removed from the cultures of Greco-Roman antiquity and Christian Europe. Eastern dragons boasted many similarities to their western counterparts: they were sinuous, reptilian monsters often endowed with the power of flight; they featured in legends as the adversaries of great heroes; and their appearance was usually a portent that something calamitous was about to take place. Despite these parallels, the dragons of the east also had attributes that set them apart from their western cousins. They were able to change shape and often appeared in the form of a comely man or woman; they had the power of speech; and they sometimes asked human beings to help them against even more monstrous enemies. Moreover, unlike European dragons, they were known to give away treasures rather than hoarding them, and their bones had specific medicinal values, so eastern dragons featured prominently in works of Asian medical lore.

THE DRAGON OF DROUGHT[1]

Composed in South Asia between 1500 and 1200 BCE, the ancient collection of Sanskrit hymns known the Rig Veda *preserves the oldest account of a dragon battle in human history. Many of these hymns sing the praises of the storm deity Indra. His greatest achievement was the slaying of the dragon Vrtra, a monstrous manifestation of drought who held the waters of the world captive in a mountain. Fueled by a ritual drink called soma and wielding a thunderbolt, Indra brought ruin upon "the first-born of dragons" and released the rivers for the benefit of humankind. Vrtra's physical form is difficult to decipher from the elusive language of the* Rig Veda, *but the hymn's description of him as "shoulderless" suggests the form of a giant serpent. Predating the heroes of Greco-Roman mythology by a millennium, Indra was the world's first dragon-slayer.*

Let me now sing the heroic deeds of Indra, the first that the thunderbolt-wielder performed. He killed the dragon and pierced an opening for the waters; he split open the bellies of mountains.

He killed the dragon who lay upon the mountain; Tvastr fashioned the roaring thunderbolt for him. Like lowing cows, the flowing waters rushed straight down to the sea.

Wildly excited like a bull, he took the Soma for himself and drank the extract from the three bowls in the three-day Soma ceremony. Indra the Generous seized his thunderbolt to hurl as a weapon; he killed the first-born of dragons.

Indra, when you killed the first-born of dragons and overcame by your own magic the magic of the magicians, at that very moment you brought forth the sun, the sky, and dawn. Since then you have found no enemy to conquer you.

With his great weapon, the thunderbolt, Indra killed shoulderless Vrtra, his greatest enemy. Like the trunk of a tree whose branches have been lopped off by an axe, the dragon lies flat on the ground.

For, muddled by drunkenness like one who is no soldier, Vrtra challenged the great hero who had overcome the mighty and who drank Soma to the dregs. Unable to withstand the onslaught of his weapons, he found Indra an enemy to conquer him and was shattered, his nose crushed.

Without feet or hands he fought against Indra, who struck him on the nape of the neck with his thunderbolt. The steer who wished to become the equal of the bull bursting with seed, Vrtra lay broken in many places.

Over him as he lay there like a broken reed the swelling waters flowed for man. Those waters that Vrtra had enclosed with his power—the dragon now lay at their feet.

The vital energy of Vrtra's mother ebbed away, for Indra had hurled his deadly weapon at her. Above was the mother; below was the son; Dānu lay down like a cow with her calf. In the midst of the channels of the waters which never stood still or rested, the body was hidden. The waters flow over Vrtra's secret place; he who found Indra an enemy to conquer him sank into long darkness.

The waters who had the Dāsa for their husband, the dragon for their protector, were imprisoned like the cows imprisoned by the Panis. When he killed Vrtra he split open the outlet of the waters that had been closed.

Indra, you became a hair of a horse's tail when Vrtra struck you on the corner of the mouth. You, the one god, the brave one, you won the cows; you won the Soma; you released the seven streams so that they could flow.

No use was the lightning and thunder, fog and hail that he [Vrtra] had scattered about, when the dragon and Indra fought. Indra the Generous remained victorious for all time to come.

What avenger of the dragon did you see, Indra, that fear entered your heart when you had killed him? Then you crossed the ninety-nine streams like the frightened eagle crossing the realms of earth and air.

Indra, who wields the thunderbolt in his hand, is the king of that which moves and that which rests, of the tame and of the horned. He rules the people as their king, encircling all this as a rim encircles spokes.

A BLACK WIND FROM
THE SEA[1]

In the Muslim polities of the medieval Middle East, Arabic scholars compiled sprawling encyclopedias of historical knowledge that betrayed their curiosity about dragons and other mythical monsters. One of the earliest of these compendiums was known by a poetic name: Meadows of Gold and Mines of Gems. Its author, al-Masudi (ca. 896–956), was a tireless traveler. He explored Persia, Arabia, Syria, and Egypt; he ventured east as far as the Indus Valley in modern India and south as far as the coasts of East Africa; and he sailed on the Mediterranean Sea, the Indian Ocean, and many points in between. Like the ancient Greek historian Herodotus, al-Masudi gathered information about all manner of foreign peoples and places. During his travels, he compiled one of the earliest accounts in Arabic on the nature of dragons. Like other medieval authors, he situated the habitat of these creatures far from his homeland (in this case, the Atlantic Ocean), rehearsed many theories about their origins and character, and ultimately concluded that God alone knew the secret of their true nature.

The *Tinníns* (dragons) are quite unknown in the Abyssinian sea and its numerous estuaries and bays. They are most frequent in the Atlantic. Different opinions have been advanced as to what the dragon is: some believe that it is a black wind in the bottom of the sea, which rises into air, that is to say, the atmosphere, as high as the clouds, like a hurricane whirling dust aloft as it rises from the dragon, and destroying vegetation. The shape of the dragon becomes longer the higher it ascends in the air.

Some people believe that the dragon is a black serpent which rises into the air, the clouds are at the same time black, all is dark, and this is succeeded by a terrible wind.

Some are of the opinion that it is an animal which lives in the bottom of the sea, and that, when it is haughty and over-bearing, God sends an angel in a cloud, who draws it out. It has the shape of a black shining serpent. When it is carried through the air it goes so high that it does not touch anything with its tail, excepting, perhaps, very high buildings or trees; but it frequently damages many trees. It is carried in the clouds to Gog and Magog. The clouds kill the dragon through cold and rain and give it to Gog and Magog to devour. This is the opinion of Ibn 'Abbas. There are various other popular traditions respecting the dragon, which are recorded by biographers of Mohammad and other prophets, but we cannot insert them all here. They say, for instance, that the dragons are black serpents which live in the desert, whence they pass, by rivers swelled with rain, into the sea. They feed there on sea animals, grow to an immense size, and live a long time; but when one of them has reached an age of five hundred years, it becomes so oppressive to sea animals, that there happens something like what we have related, as being the account of Ibn 'Abbas. Some, they state, are white, and others black like serpents.

The Persians do not deny the existence of dragons. They believe that they have seven heads, they call them Gorgons, and allude frequently to them in their tales. God knows best what the dragons really are.

NO ONE EVER ESCAPES
MY CLAWS[1]

The indebtedness of medieval Persians to western conceptions of dragons was on full display in The Book of Kings (Shahnameh), *an epic poem about the heroic exploits of the kings of the Persian Empire from ancient times to the seventh century CE, when Muslim Arabs conquered Iran. Among the mightiest of these celebrated kings was the legendary Rostam. Like the Greek hero Hercules, Rostam was famous for completing a series of difficult trials that involved vanquishing mythological monsters. Accompanied only by his faithful steed Rakhsh, who plays no small part in the action, Rostam fought a dragon on a desolate plain. In Asian traditions, the banter between the hero and the monster was not unusual for depictions of dragons often had the ability to converse with human beings, but all the more distinctive when compared with western European stories, in which dragons roar and hiss, but only rarely have the power of speech.*

A dragon, from which no elephant had ever escaped, appeared on the plain. Its lair was nearby, and even demons were afraid to cross its path. As it approached it saw Rostam asleep and Rakhsh standing awake, alert as a lion. He wondered what had lain down here in his sleeping place, because nothing ever came this way, neither demons nor elephants nor lions; and if anything did come, it didn't escape this dragon's teeth and claws. It turned toward Rakhsh, who trotted over to Rostam and woke him. Rostam was immediately alert, ready to fight, but he gazed about him in the darkness, and the fearsome dragon disappeared. In his annoyance Rostam chided Rakhsh for waking him. He slept again, and again the dragon emerged from the darkness. Rakhsh stamped on Rostam's pillow and pawed at the ground, and once more Rostam woke. He sprang up, his face sallow with apprehension, and gazed about him, but he saw nothing except the darkness. He said to his kind, wise horse, "You should sleep in the night's darkness, but you keep waking me up; why are you in such a hurry for me to be awake? If you disturb me again like this, I'll cut your feet off with my sword. I'll go on foot, dragging my lance and heavy mace to Mazanderan." For a third time he lay his head down to sleep, using Rakhsh's barding as his mattress and bedcovers. The fearsome dragon roared, his breath seeming to flicker with flames, and Rakhsh galloped away, afraid to approach Rostam. His heart was split in two, fearing both Rostam and the dragon. But his agitation for Rostam urged him back to the hero's side; he neighed and reared up, and his hooves pawed violently at the ground. Rostam woke from a sweet sleep, furious with his horse, but this time God produced a light so that the dragon could not hide, and Rostam made him out in the darkness. He quickly drew his sword, and the ground flashed with the fire of combat. He called out to the dragon, "Tell me your name, because from now on you will not see the world to be as you wish. It's not right for me to kill you without learning your name." The fearsome dragon said, "No one ever escapes my claws; all of this plain is mine, like the sky and air above it. Eagles don't dare fly over this land, and even the stars don't look down on it." It paused, and then said, "What is your name, because your mother must weep for you?" The hero replied, "I am Rostam, the son of Zal, who was the son of Sam, of the family of Nariman." Then the dragon leaped at him, but in the end he could not escape from Rostam, because when Rakhsh saw the strength of his massive body bearing down on Rostam, he laid back his ears and sank his teeth into the dragon's shoulders. He tore at the dragon's flesh, and the lion-like Rostam was astonished at his ferocity. Rostam smote with his sword and lopped the dragon's head off, and poison flowed like a river from its trunk. The ground beneath its body disappeared beneath a stream of blood, and Rostam gave a great sigh when he looked at the dragon, and saw that all the dark desert flowed with blood and poison. He was afraid, and stared in horror, murmuring the name of God over and over again. He went into the stream and washed his body and head, acknowledging God's authority over the world. He said, "Great God, you have given me strength and intelligence and skills, so that before me demons, lions and elephants, waterless deserts and great rivers like the Nile, are as nothing in my eyes. But enemies are many and the years are few." When he had finished his prayer, he saddled Rakhsh, mounted, and went on his way through a land of sorcerers.

THE EIGHT-HEADED
SERPENT OF KOSHI[1]

The oldest surviving text from Japan is known as the Rec-
ords of Ancient Matters (Kojiki). The statesman Ō No
Yasumaro allegedly compiled this chronicle of ancient
stories about the Japanese past for the court of Empress
Genmei (r. 707–21), the forty-third monarch of Japan.
His purpose was both scholarly and political. Drawing
on folktales, old songs, and imperial genealogies, Ō No
Yasumaro constructed an elaborate myth of national ori-
gins that legitimated the rule of the royal family by trac-
ing their descent from celestial beings. Chief among these
heavenly heroes was Rushing Raging Man (literally His-
Swift-Impetuous-Male-Augustness), who vanquished an
enormous eight-headed serpent with a penchant for forti-
fied liquor. This deed earned for him the hand of his bride
Wondrous-Inada-Princess as well as a legendary great
sword, the Grass-Cutter, a symbol of valor that in time
became one of the three sacred treasures making up the
imperial regalia of Japan.

So having been expelled, Rushing Raging Man descended to
a place called Tori-kami at the head-waters of the River Hi in
the Land of Idzumo. At this time, some chopsticks came
floating down the stream. So Rushing Raging Man, thinking
that there must be people at the head-waters of the river,
went up to look for them. He came upon an old man and an
old woman, who had a young girl between them. They were
all weeping. Then he deigned to ask: "Who are you?" So the
old man replied, saying: "I am spirit of the land, a child of

the spirit Great Mountain Majesty. I am called by the name of Foot-Stroking Elder. My wife is called by the name of Hand-Stroking Elder. My daughter is called by the name of Wondrous-Inada-Princess." Again he asked: "Why are you crying?" The old man answered, saying: "I had originally eight young girls as daughters, but the eight-headed serpent of Koshi has come every year and devoured them one by one, and it is now its time to come again, and therefore we weep." Then he asked him: "What does it look like?" The old man answered, saying: "Its eyes are like winter cherries, it has one body with eight heads and eight tails. Moreover, on its body grows moss and also cypress trees. Its length extends over eight valleys and eight hills, and if one looks at its belly, it is always bloody and inflamed." Then Rushing Raging Man said to the old man: "If this is your daughter, will you offer her to me?" He replied saying: "With honor, but I do not know your name." Then he replied, saying: "I am the younger brother of the great and mighty spirit Heaven Shining. I have recently descended from Heaven." Then Foot-Stroking Elder and Hand-Stroking Elder said, "If that is so, then we offer her to you with reverence." So Rushing Raging Man took the young girl and changed her at once into a close-toothed comb which he stuck into his august hair-bunch and said to her parents: "Distill some liquor eight times to make it strong. Then build a fence round about. In that fence make eight gates. At each gate, tie together eight platforms. On each platform, put a liquor-vat and into each vat pour the fortified liquor, and wait." So as they waited after having thus prepared everything in accordance with his bidding, the eight-headed serpent came just as the old man had said, and immediately dipped a head into each vat and drank the liquor. Thereupon it became intoxicated with drinking and all the heads lay down and slept. Then Rushing Raging Man drew his holy long sword that was girded on him and cut the serpent in pieces, so that the River Hi transformed into a river of flowing blood. When he cut the middle tail, however, the edge of his holy sword broke. Then, thinking it strange, he thrust into the serpent's flesh with the broken point of his sword and looked and found a great sword within. So he took this great sword and, marveling, he respectfully informed the mighty spirit Heaven Shining. This is the Grass-Cutter Great Sword.

CHIEF OF THE SCALY
CREATURES[1]

*In premodern Chinese culture, dragons had a utility well
beyond their role as nefarious adversaries in ancient
stories about indomitable heroes. During the Ming dynasty (1368–1644), scholars wrote about the medicinal
properties of dragon bones (in all likelihood, dinosaur
bones), which the great rivers of China deposited on their
banks. The proper use of this precious natural resource
by medical practitioners required an understanding of the
character of the dragon as a quasi-divine creature, its affinities with particular animals, and its aversion to certain insects and objects. In his vast compilation of medical
lore (Bencao Gangmu), the famed herbologist Li Shizhen
(1518–93) gathered the insights of medieval Chinese authorities on the dragon to fashion a portrait of this mysterious beast far more vivid than any descriptions that
survive in the heroic literature of ancient Asia.*

Li Shizhen says: According to Luo Yuan in the *Erya yi*: The
dragon is the chief of the scaly creatures. Wang Fu described
how its shape contains nine similarities. To wit, the head of a
camel, the antlers of a deer, the eyes of a rabbit, the ears of an
ox, the neck of a snake, the belly of a clam, the scales of a
fish, the claws of an eagle, and the paws of a tiger. Its back
has eighty-one scales, which as nine nines is a yang number. Its sound is like tapping on a copper plate. The sides of
its mouth have whiskers. Beneath its chin is a bright pearl.
Under its throat are reversed scales. On top of its head is the
boshan, also called the *chimu*. Without its *chimu*, a dragon

cannot ascend to the heavens. Its exhalations of *qi* form clouds and can transform into both water and fire. Lu Dian in the *Piya* stated: The fire of a dragon will blaze in humidity and will burn in the presence of water. Attacking it with human fire will extinguish the dragon's fire . . . The dragon is born from an egg that it hatches and conscientiously protects. When the male calls upwind and the female calls downwind, through the wind a new dragon is conceived. According to *Shidian*: When dragons mate they change into two small snakes. Furthermore, according to some stories, the dragon's nature is coarse and violent, yet it loves beautiful jade and *kongqing* stones and enjoys eating the flesh of swallows. It is afraid of iron and *mangcao* herb, centipedes and *lianzhi* branches, and Five Colored [multicolored] silk. Therefore, those who have eaten swallows avoid crossing waters, those who pray for rain use swallows, those who want waters to subside use iron, those who want to provoke a dragon use *mangcao* herb, and those who sacrifice to Qu Yuan wrap dumplings in *lian* leaves and colored silk and throw them in the river. Medical practitioners use dragon bones, so they ought to understand the dragon's affinities and aversions as they are presented here.

MY LORD BAG OF RICE [1]

In stark contrast to the dragons in medieval European tra-
ditions, Asian dragons could change their shape to appear
as human beings and exhibited many characteristics of
aristocratic culture: they had the ability to speak elo-
quently and persuasively; they lived in opulent buildings
where servants tended to their needs; and they made alli-
ances when necessity dictated. These features are all evi-
dent in an anonymous Japanese short story composed in
the early Edo Period (1603–1868) known as "The Tale of
Tawara Tōda." In this tale, a serpent-dragon implored the
aid of a human hero named Fujiwara Hidesato to defeat
his archenemy: a colossal centipede. Hidesato readily
agreed. After being entertained in the dragon's under-
water palace, the hero used his cunning to slay the centi-
pede and thereby earned the boundless gratitude of his
serpentine host. Among the gifts Hidesato received for his
service to the dragon was a magical bag of rice that never
emptied, no matter how much rice was poured from it. In
a reversal of most traditional dragon stories, "The Tale of
Tawara Tōda" cast the Dragon King of the Lake as a vic-
tim with human characteristics, who required the aid of a
hero to save him from an inhuman predator.

Long, long ago there lived in Japan a brave warrior known
to all as Tawara Tōda, or "My Lord Bag of Rice." His true
name was Fujiwara Hidesato, and there is a very interesting
story of how he came to change his name.

One day he sallied forth in search of adventures, for he had
the nature of a warrior and could not bear to be idle. So, he
buckled on his two swords, took his huge bow—much taller

than himself—in his hand, and slinging his quiver on his back, he started out. He had not gone far when he came to the bridge of Seta-no-Karashi spanning one end of the beautiful Lake Biwa. No sooner had he set foot on the bridge than he saw lying right across his path a huge serpent-dragon. Its body was so big that it looked like the trunk of a large pine tree and it took up the whole width of the bridge. One of its huge claws rested on the parapet of one side of the bridge, while its tail lay right against the other. The monster seemed to be asleep, and as it breathed, fire and smoke came out of its nostrils.

At first Hidesato could not help feeling alarmed at the sight of this horrible reptile lying in his path, for he must either turn back or walk right over its body. He was a brave man, however, and putting aside all fear went forward dauntlessly. Crunch, crunch! he stepped now on the dragon's body, now between its coils, and without even one glance backward he went on his way.

He had only gone a few steps when he heard someone calling him from behind. Upon turning back, he was very surprised to see that the monster dragon had entirely disappeared and in its place was a strange-looking man, who was bowing most ceremoniously to the ground. His red hair streamed over his shoulders and was surmounted by a crown in the shape of a dragon's head, and his sea-green dress was patterned with shells. Hidesato knew at once that this was no ordinary mortal and he wondered much at the strange occurrence. Where had the dragon gone in such a short space of time? Or had it transformed itself into this man, and what did the whole thing mean? While these thoughts passed through his mind he had come up to the man on the bridge and now addressed him:

"Was it you that called me just now?"

"Yes, it was I," answered the man; "I have an earnest request to make to you. Do you think you can grant it to me?"

"If it is in my power to do so I will," answered Hidesato, "but first tell me who you are?"

"I am the Dragon King of the Lake, and my home is in these waters just under this bridge."

"And what is it you have to ask of me?" said Hidesato.

"I want you to kill my mortal enemy the centipede, who lives on the mountain beyond." And the Dragon King pointed to a high peak on the opposite shore of the lake.

"I have lived now for many years in this lake and I have a large family of children and grandchildren. For some time past, we have lived in terror, for a monster centipede has discovered our home, and night after night it comes and carries off one of my family. I am powerless to save them. If it goes on much longer like this, not only shall I lose all my children, but I myself must fall a victim to the monster. I am, therefore, very unhappy, and in my extremity, I determined to ask the help of a human being. For many days with this intention I have waited on the bridge in the shape of the horrible serpent-dragon that you saw, in the hope that some strong brave man would come along. But all who came this way, as soon as they saw me were terrified and ran away as fast as they could. You are the first man I have found able to look at me without fear, so I knew at once that you were a man of great courage. I beg you to have pity upon me. Will you not help me and kill my enemy the centipede?"

Hidesato felt very sorry for the Dragon King on hearing his story, and readily promised to do what he could to help him. The warrior asked where the centipede lived, so that he might attack the creature at once. The Dragon King replied that its home was on the mountain Mikami, but that as it came every night at a certain hour to the palace of the lake, it would be better to wait until then. So Hidesato was conducted to the palace of the Dragon King, under the bridge. Strange to say, as he followed his host downward the waters parted to let them pass, and his clothes did not even feel damp as he passed through the flood. Never had Hidesato seen anything so beautiful as this palace built of white marble beneath the lake. He had often heard of the Sea King's Palace at the bottom of the sea, where all the servants and retainers were saltwater fishes, but here was a magnificent building in the heart of Lake Biwa. The dainty goldfishes, red carp, and silvery trout waited upon the Dragon King and his guest.

Hidesato was astonished at the feast that was spread for him. The dishes were crystallized lotus leaves and flowers, and the chopsticks were of the rarest ebony. As soon as they sat down, the sliding doors opened and ten lovely goldfish dancers came out, and behind them followed ten red-carp musicians with the koto and the samisen. Thus, the hours flew by until midnight, and the beautiful music and dancing had banished all thoughts of the centipede. The Dragon King was about to pledge the warrior in a fresh cup of wine when the palace was suddenly shaken by a tramp, tramp! as if a mighty army had begun to march not far away.

Hidesato and his host both rose to their feet and rushed to the balcony, and the warrior saw on the opposite mountain two great balls of glowing fire coming nearer and nearer. The Dragon King stood by the warrior's side trembling with fear.

"The centipede! The centipede! Those two balls of fire are its eyes. It is coming for its prey! Now is the time to kill it."

Hidesato looked where his host pointed, and, in the dim light of the starlit evening, behind the two balls of fire he saw the long body of an enormous centipede winding round the mountains, and the light in its hundred feet glowed like so many distant lanterns moving slowly toward the shore.

Hidesato showed not the least sign of fear. He tried to calm the Dragon King.

"Don't be afraid. I shall surely kill the centipede. Just bring me my bow and arrows."

The Dragon King did as he was bid, and the warrior noticed that he had only three arrows left in his quiver. He took the bow, and fitting an arrow to the notch, took careful aim and let fly.

The arrow hit the centipede right in the middle of its head, but instead of penetrating, it glanced off harmless and fell to the ground.

Undaunted, Hidesato took another arrow, fitted it to the notch of the bow and let fly. Again, the arrow hit the mark; it struck the centipede right in the middle of its head, only to glance off and fall to the ground. The centipede was invulnerable to weapons! When the Dragon King saw that even this brave warrior's arrows were powerless to kill the centipede, he lost heart and began to tremble with fear.

The warrior saw that he had now only one arrow left in his quiver, and if this one failed, he could not kill the centipede. He looked across the waters. The huge insect had wound its horrid body seven times round the mountain and would soon come down to the lake. Nearer and nearer gleamed the fireballs of eyes, and the light of its hundred feet began to throw reflections in the still waters of the lake.

Then suddenly the warrior remembered that he had heard that human saliva was deadly to centipedes. But this was no ordinary centipede. This was so monstrous that even to think of such a creature made one creep with horror. Hidesato determined to try his last chance. So, taking his last arrow and first putting the end of it in his mouth, he fitted the notch to his bow, took careful aim once more and let fly.

This time the arrow again hit the centipede right in the middle of its head, but instead of glancing off harmlessly as before, it struck home to the creature's brain. Then with a convulsive shudder the serpentine body stopped moving, and the fiery light of its great eyes and hundred feet darkened to a dull glare like the sunset of a stormy day, and then went out in blackness. A great darkness now overspread the heavens, the thunder rolled, and the lightning flashed, and the wind roared in fury, and it seemed as if the world were coming to an end. The Dragon King and his children and retainers all crouched in different parts of the palace, frightened to death, for the building was shaken to its foundations. At last the dreadful night was over. Day dawned beautiful and clear. The centipede was gone from the mountain.

Then Hidesato called to the Dragon King to come out with him on the balcony, for the centipede was dead and he had nothing more to fear.

Then all the inhabitants of the palace came out with joy, and Hidesato pointed to the lake. There lay the body of the dead centipede floating on the water, which was dyed red with its blood.

The gratitude of the Dragon King knew no bounds. The

whole family came and bowed down before the warrior, calling him their preserver and the bravest warrior in all Japan.

Another feast was prepared, more sumptuous than the first. All kinds of fish, prepared in every imaginable way, raw, stewed, boiled, and roasted, served on coral trays and crystal dishes, were put before him, and the wine was the best that Hidesato had ever tasted in his life. To add to the beauty of everything the sun shone brightly, the lake glittered like a liquid diamond, and the palace was a thousand times more beautiful by day than by night.

His host tried to persuade the warrior to stay a few days, but Hidesato insisted on going home, saying that he had now finished what he had come to do, and must return. The Dragon King and his family were all very sorry to have him leave so soon, but since he would go, they begged him to accept a few small presents (so they said) in token of their gratitude to him for delivering them for ever from their horrible enemy, the centipede.

As the warrior stood in the porch taking leave, a train of fish was suddenly transformed into a retinue of men, all wearing ceremonial robes and dragon's crowns on their heads to show that they were servants of the great Dragon King. The presents that they carried were as follows:

First, a large bronze bell.
Second, a bag of rice.
Third, a roll of silk.
Fourth, a cooking pot.
Fifth, a bell.

Hidesato did not want to accept all these presents, but as the Dragon King insisted, he could not well refuse.

The Dragon King himself accompanied the warrior as far as the bridge, and then took leave of him with many bows and good wishes, leaving the procession of servants to accompany Hidesato to his house with the presents.

The warrior's household and servants had been very much concerned when they found that he did not return the night before, but they finally concluded that he had been kept by the violent storm and had taken shelter somewhere. When the servants on the watch for his return caught sight of him, they called to everyone that he was approaching, and the whole household turned out to meet him, wondering much what the retinue of men, bearing presents and banners, that followed him, could mean.

As soon as the Dragon King's retainers had put down the presents, they vanished, and Hidesato told all that had happened to him.

The presents which he had received from the grateful Dragon King were found to be of magic power. The bell only was ordinary, and as Hidesato had no use for it, he presented it to the temple nearby, where it was hung up, to boom out the hour of day over the surrounding neighborhood.

The single bag of rice, however much was taken from it day after day for the meals of the knight and his whole family, never grew less—the supply in the bag was inexhaustible.

The roll of silk, too, never grew shorter, though time after time long pieces were cut off to make the warrior a new suit of clothes to go to Court in at the New Year.

The cooking pot was wonderful, too. No matter what was put into it, it cooked deliciously whatever was wanted without any firing—truly a very economical saucepan.

The fame of Hidesato's fortune spread far and wide, and as there was no need for him to spend money on rice or silk or firing, he became very rich and prosperous, and was henceforth known as "My Lord Bag of Rice."

THE FISHERMAN AND THE
DRAGON PRINCESS[1]

While the hero Hidesato earned the gratitude of his dragon host by defeating its mortal enemy, other human visitors to the underwater palace of the Dragon King did not fare as well. In a Japanese folktale that may date back to the eighth century, a benevolent fisherman named Urashima Taro saved a tortoise from the cruelty of some children. For his kindness, the tortoise offered to take him to the Dragon King's palace far under the sea. When they arrived, the tortoise revealed its true identity as Otohime, the princess of the palace. Despite the wonderous surroundings and the unearthly beauty of Otohime, Urashima Taro refused her offer to stay with her forever beneath the waves because he feared for the safety of his elderly parents. Choosing his human family over his dragon bride, the fisherman abandoned the palace beneath the sea. When he returned to his village, however, he was shocked to discover that his three-day sojourn in the ocean realm had in fact lasted three centuries. Everyone he knew was long dead, and soon thereafter, filled with despair, he too met his fate.

Long, long ago in the province of Tango, there lived on the shore of Japan in the little fishing village of Mizu-no-ye a young fisherman named Urashima Taro. His father had been a fisherman before him, and his skill had more than doubly descended to his son, for Urashima was the most skillful fisher in all that countryside and could catch more *bonito* and *tai* in a day than his comrades could in a week.

But in the little fishing village, more than for being a clever fisher of the sea was he known for his kind heart. In his whole life he had never hurt anything, either great or small, and when he was a boy, his companions had always laughed at him, for he would never join with them in teasing animals, but always tried to keep them from this cruel sport.

One soft summer twilight he was going home at the end of a day's fishing when he came upon a group of children. They were all screaming and talking at the tops of their voices and seemed to be in a state of great excitement about something, and on his going up to them to see what was the matter, he saw that they were tormenting a tortoise. First, one boy pulled it this way, then another boy pulled it that way, while a third child beat it with a stick, and the fourth hammered its shell with a stone.

Now Urashima felt very sorry for the poor tortoise and made up his mind to rescue it. He spoke to the boys:

"Look here, boys, you are treating that poor tortoise so badly that it will soon die!"

The boys, who were all of an age when children seem to delight in being cruel to animals, took no notice of Urashima's gentle reproof, but went on teasing it as before. One of the older boys answered:

"Who cares whether it lives or dies? We do not. Here, boys, go on, go on!"

And they began to treat the poor tortoise more cruelly than ever. Urashima waited a moment, turning over in his mind what would be the best way to deal with the boys. He would try to persuade them to give the tortoise up to him, so he smiled at them and said:

"I am sure you are all good, kind boys! Now won't you give me the tortoise? I should like to have it so much!"

"No, we won't give you the tortoise," said one of the boys. "Why should we? We caught it ourselves."

"What you say is true," said Urashima, "but I do not ask you to give it to me for nothing. I will give you some money for it—in other words, the Ojisan (Uncle) will buy it from you. Won't that do for you, my boys?" He held up the money to them, strung on a piece of string through a hole in the center of each coin. "Look, boys, you can buy anything you like with this money. You can do much more with this money than you can with that poor tortoise. See what good boys you are to listen to me."

The boys were not bad boys at all, they were only mischievous, and as Urashima spoke they were won over by his kind smile and gentle words and began "to be of his spirit," as they say in Japan. Gradually they all came up to him, the ringleader of the little band holding out the tortoise to him.

"Very well, Ojisan, we will give you the tortoise if you will give us the money!" And Urashima took the tortoise and gave the money to the boys, who, calling to each other, scampered away and were soon out of sight.

Then Urashima stroked the tortoise's back, saying as he did so:

"Oh, you poor thing! Poor thing! There, there! You are safe now! They say that a stork lives for a thousand years, but the tortoise for ten thousand years. You have the longest life of any creature in this world, and you were in great danger of having that precious life cut short by those cruel boys. Luckily, I was passing by and saved you, and so life is still yours. Now I am going to take you back to your home, the sea, at once. Do not let yourself be caught again, for there might be no one to save you next time!"

All the time that the kind fisherman was speaking he was walking quickly to the shore and out upon the rocks; then putting the tortoise into the water he watched the animal disappear, and turned homewards himself, for he was tired and the sun had set.

The next morning Urashima went out as usual in his boat. The weather was fine and the sea and sky were both blue and soft in the tender haze of the summer morning. Urashima got into his boat and dreamily pushed out to sea, throwing his line as he did so. He soon passed the other fishing boats and left them behind him till they were lost to sight in the distance, and his boat drifted farther and farther out upon the blue waters. Somehow, he knew not why, he felt unusually happy that morning; and he could not help wishing that, like the tortoise he set free the day before, he had thousands of years to live instead of his own short span of human life.

He was suddenly startled from his reverie by hearing his own name called:

"Urashima, Urashima!"

Clear as a bell and soft as the summer wind the name floated over the sea.

He stood up and looked in every direction, thinking that one of the other boats had overtaken him, but gaze as he might over the wide expanse of water, near or far there was no sign of a boat, so the voice could not have come from any human being.

Startled, and wondering who or what it was that had called him so clearly, he looked in all directions round about him and saw that without his knowing it a tortoise had come to the side of the boat. Urashima saw with surprise that it was the very tortoise he had rescued the day before.

"Well, Mr. Tortoise," said Urashima, "was it you who called my name just now?"

The tortoise nodded its head several times, and said:

"Yes, it was I. Yesterday in your honorable shadow my life was saved, and I have come to offer you my thanks and to tell you how grateful I am for your kindness to me."

"Indeed," said Urashima, "that is very polite of you. Come up into the boat. I would offer you a smoke, but as you are a tortoise doubtless you do not smoke." And the fisherman laughed at the joke.

"He—he—he—he!" laughed the tortoise; "rice wine is my favorite refreshment, but I do not care for tobacco."

"Indeed," said Urashima, "I regret very much that I have no rice wine in my boat to offer you, but come up and dry your back in the sun—tortoises always love to do that."

So the tortoise climbed into the boat, the fisherman helping him, and after an exchange of complimentary speeches the tortoise said:

"Have you ever seen Rin Gin, the Palace of the Dragon King of the Sea, Urashima?" The fisherman shook his head and replied: "No; year after year the sea has been my home, but though I have often heard of the Dragon King's realm under the sea, I have never yet set eyes on that wonderful place. It must be very far away, if it exists at all!"

"Is that really so? You have never seen the Sea King's Palace? Then you have missed seeing one of the most wonderful sights in the whole universe. It is far away at the bottom of the sea, but if I take you there we shall soon reach the place. If you would like to see the Sea King's land I will be your guide."

"I should like to go there, certainly, and you are very kind to think of taking me, but you must remember that I am only a poor mortal and have not the power of swimming like a sea creature such as you are."

Before the fisherman could say more the tortoise stopped him, saying:

"What? You need not swim yourself. If you will ride on my back I will take you without any trouble on your part."

"But," said Urashima, "how is it possible for me to ride on your small back?"

"It may seem absurd to you, but I assure you that you can do so. Try at once! Just come and get on my back, and see if it is as impossible as you think!"

As the tortoise finished speaking, Urashima looked at its shell, and strange to say he saw that the creature had suddenly grown so big that a man could easily sit on its back.

"This is strange indeed!" said Urashima; "then, Mr. Tortoise, with your kind permission I will get on your back. Alright!" he exclaimed as he jumped on.

The tortoise, with an unmoved face, as if this strange proceeding were quite an ordinary event, said:

"Now we will set out at our leisure." And with these words he leapt into the sea with Urashima on his back. Down through the water the tortoise dived. For a long time these two strange companions rode through the sea. Urashima never grew tired, nor his clothes moist with the water. At last, far away in the distance a magnificent gate appeared, and behind the gate, the long, sloping roofs of a palace on the horizon.

"Ah," exclaimed Urashima, "that looks like the gate of some large palace just appearing! Mr. Tortoise, can you tell what that place is we can now see?"

"That is the great gate of the Rin Gin Palace. The large roof that you see behind the gate is the Sea King's Palace itself."

"Then we have at last come to the realm of the Sea King and to his Palace," said Urashima.

"Yes, indeed," answered the tortoise, "and don't you think we have come very quickly?" And while he was speaking the tortoise reached the side of the gate. "And here we are, and you must please walk from here."

The tortoise now went in front, and speaking to the gate-keeper said:

"This is Urashima Taro, from the country of Japan. I have had the honor of bringing him as a visitor to this kingdom. Please show him the way."

Then the gatekeeper, who was a fish, at once led the way through the gate before them.

The red bream, the flounder, the sole, the cuttlefish, and all the chief vassals of the Dragon King of the Sea now came out with courtly bows to welcome the stranger.

"Urashima Sama, Urashima Sama! Welcome to the Sea Palace, the home of the Dragon King of the Sea. Thrice welcome are you, having come from such a distant country. And you, Mr. Tortoise, we are greatly indebted to you for all your trouble in bringing Urashima here." Then, turning again to Urashima, they said, "Please follow us this way," and from here the whole band of fishes became his guides.

Urashima, being only a poor fisherman, did not know how to behave in a palace; but, strange though it all was to him, he did not feel ashamed or embarrassed, but followed his kind guides quite calmly where they led to the inner palace. When he reached the portals a beautiful Princess with her attendant maidens came out to welcome him. She was more beautiful than any human being, and was robed in flowing garments of red and soft green like the underside of a wave, and golden threads glimmered through the folds of her gown. Her lovely black hair streamed over her shoulders in the fashion of a king's daughter many hundreds of years ago, and when she spoke her voice sounded like music over the water. Urashima was lost in wonder while he looked upon her, and he could not speak. Then he remembered that he ought to bow, but before he could make a low obeisance the Princess took him by the hand and led him to a beautiful hall, and to the seat of honor at the upper end, and bade him be seated.

"Urashima Taro, it gives me the highest pleasure to welcome you to my father's kingdom," said the Princess. "Yesterday you set free a tortoise, and I have sent for you to thank you for saving my life, for I was that tortoise. Now if you like, you shall live here for ever in the land of eternal youth, where summer never dies and where sorrow never comes, and I will be your bride if you will, and we will live together happily for ever afterward!"

And as Urashima listened to her sweet words and gazed upon her lovely face, his heart was filled with a great wonder and joy, and he answered her, wondering if it was not all a dream:

"Thank you a thousand times for your kind speech. There is nothing I could wish for more than to be permitted to stay here with you in this beautiful land, of which I have often heard, but have never seen to this day. Beyond all words, this is the most wonderful place I have ever seen."

While he was speaking a train of fishes appeared, all dressed in ceremonial, trailing garments. One by one, silently and with stately steps, they entered the hall, bearing on coral trays delicacies of fish and seaweed, such as no one can dream of, and this wondrous feast was set before the bride and bridegroom. The wedding was celebrated with dazzling splendor, and in the Sea King's realm there was great rejoicing. As soon as the young pair had pledged themselves in the wedding cup of wine, three times three, music was played, and songs were sung, and fishes with silver scales and golden tails stepped in from the waves and danced. Urashima enjoyed himself with all his heart. Never in his whole life had he sat down to such a marvelous feast.

When the feast was over the Princess asked the bridegroom if he would like to walk through the palace and see all there was to be seen. Then the happy fisherman, following his bride, the Sea King's daughter, was shown all the wonders of that enchanted land where youth and joy go hand in hand and neither time nor age can touch them. The palace was built of coral and adorned with pearls, and the beauties and wonders of the place were so great that the tongue fails to describe them.

But, to Urashima, more wonderful than the palace was the garden that surrounded it. Here was to be seen at one time the scenery of the four different seasons; the beauties of summer and winter, spring and autumn, were displayed to the wondering visitor at once.

First, when he looked to the east, the plum and cherry trees were seen in full bloom, the nightingales sang in the pink avenues, and butterflies flitted from flower to flower.

Looking to the south all the trees were green in the fullness of summer, and the day cicada and the night cricket chirruped loudly.

Looking to the west the autumn maples were ablaze like a sunset sky, and the chrysanthemums were in perfection.

Looking to the north the change made Urashima start, for the ground was silver white with snow, and trees and bamboos were also covered with snow, and the pond was thick with ice.

And each day there were new joys and new wonders for Urashima, and so great was his happiness that he forgot everything, even the home he had left behind and his parents and his own country, and three days passed without his even thinking of all he had left behind. Then his mind came back to him and he remembered who he was, and that he did not belong to this wonderful land or the Sea King's palace, and he said to himself:

"O dear! I must not stay on here, for I have an old father and mother at home. What can have happened to them all this time? How anxious they must have been these days when I did not return as usual. I must go back at once without letting one more day pass." And he began to prepare for the journey in great haste.

Then he went to his beautiful wife, the Princess, and bowing low before her, he said:

"Indeed, I have been very happy with you for a long time, Otohime Sama" (for that was her name), "and you have been kinder to me than any words can tell. But now I must say good-bye. I must go back to my old parents."

Then Otohime Sama began to weep, and said softly and sadly:

"Is it not well with you here, Urashima, that you wish to leave me so soon? Where is the haste? Stay with me yet another day only!"

But Urashima had remembered his old parents, and in Japan the duty to parents is stronger than everything else, stronger even than pleasure or love, and he would not be persuaded, but answered:

"Indeed, I must go. Do not think that I wish to leave you. It is not that. I must go and see my old parents. Let me go for one day and I will come back to you."

"Then," said the Princess sorrowfully, "there is nothing to be done. I will send you back today to your father and mother, and instead of trying to keep you with me one more day, I shall give you this as a token of our love—please take it back with you"; and she brought him a beautiful lacquer box tied about with a silken cord and tassels of red silk.

Urashima had received so much from the Princess already that he felt some compunction in taking the gift, and said:

"It does not seem right for me to take yet another gift from you after all the many favours I have received at your hands, but because it is your wish I will do so," and then he added:

"Tell me what is this box?"

"That," answered the Princess, "is the Box of the Jeweled Hand, and it contains something very precious. You must not open this box, whatever happens! If you open it something dreadful will happen to you! Now promise me that you will never open this box!"

And Urashima promised that he would never, *ever* open the box whatever happened.

Then bidding good-bye to Otohime Sama he went down to the seashore, the Princess and her attendants following him, and there he found a large tortoise waiting for him.

He quickly mounted the creature's back and was carried away over the shining sea into the East. He looked back to wave his hand to Otohime Sama until at last he could see her no more, and the land of the Sea King and the roofs of the wonderful palace were lost in the far, far distance. Then, with his face turned eagerly towards his own land, he looked for the rising of the blue hills on the horizon before him.

At last the tortoise carried him into the bay he knew so well, and to the shore from whence he had set out. He stepped on to the shore and looked about him while the tortoise rode away back to the Sea King's realm.

But what is the strange fear that seizes Urashima as he stands and looks about him? Why does he gaze so fixedly at the people that pass him by, and why do they in turn stand and look at him? The shore is the same and the hills are the same, but the people that he sees walking past him have very different faces to those he had known so well before.

Wondering what it can mean he walks quickly towards his old home. Even that looks different, but a house stands on the spot, and he calls out:

"Father, I have just returned!" And he was about to enter, when he saw a strange man coming out.

"Perhaps my parents have moved while I have been away, and have gone somewhere else," was the fisherman's thought. Somehow he began to feel strangely anxious, he could not tell why.

"Excuse me," said he to the man who was staring at him, "but up until the last few days I have lived in this house. My name is Urashima Taro. Where have my parents gone whom I left here?"

A very bewildered expression came over the face of the man, and, still gazing intently on Urashima's face, he said:

"What? Are you Urashima Taro?"

"Yes," said the fisherman, "I am Urashima Taro!"

"Ha, ha!" laughed the man, "you must not make such jokes. It is true that once upon a time a man called Urashima Taro did live in this village, but that is a story three hundred years old. He could not possibly be alive now!"

When Urashima heard these strange words he was frightened, and said:

"Please, please, you must not joke with me, for I am greatly perplexed. I am really Urashima Taro, and I certainly have not lived three hundred years. Until four or five days ago I lived on this spot. Tell me what I want to know without more joking, please."

But the man's face grew more and more grave, and he answered:

"You may or may not be Urashima Taro, I don't know. But the Urashima Taro of whom I have heard is a man who lived three hundred years ago. Perhaps you are his spirit come to revisit your old home?"

"Why do you mock me?" said Urashima. "I am no spirit! I am a living man—do you not see my feet;" and he stamped on the ground, first with one foot and then with the other to show the man.[2]

"But Urashima Taro lived three hundred years ago, that is all I know; it is written in the village chronicles," persisted the man, who could not believe what the fisherman said.

Urashima was lost in bewilderment and trouble. He stood

looking all around him, terribly puzzled, and, indeed, something in the appearance of everything was different to what he remembered before he went away, and the awful feeling came over him that what the man said was perhaps true. He seemed to be in a strange dream. The few days he had spent in the Sea King's palace beyond the sea had not been days at all; they had been hundreds of years, and in that time his parents had died and all the people he had ever known, and the village had written down his story. There was no use in staying here any longer. He must get back to his beautiful wife beyond the sea.

He made his way back to the beach, carrying in his hand the box which the Princess had given him. But which was the way? He could not find it alone! Suddenly he remembered the box, the Box of the Jeweled Hand.

"The Princess told me when she gave me the box never to open it—that it contained a very precious thing. But now that I have no home, now that I have lost everything that was dear to me here, and my heart grows thin with sadness, at such a time, if I open the box, surely I shall find something that will help me, something that will show me the way back to my beautiful Princess over the sea. There is nothing else for me to do now. Yes, yes, I will open the box and look in!"

And so his heart consented to this act of disobedience, and he tried to persuade himself that he was doing the right thing in breaking his promise.

Slowly, very slowly, he untied the red silk cord, slowly and wonderingly he lifted the lid of the precious box. And what did he find? Strange to say only a beautiful little purple cloud rose out of the box in three soft wisps. For an instant it covered his face and wavered over him as if loath to go, and then it floated away like vapor over the sea.

Urashima, who had been until that moment like a strong and handsome youth of twenty-four, suddenly became very, very old. His back doubled up with age, his hair turned snowy white, his face wrinkled and he fell down dead on the beach.

Poor Urashima! Because of his disobedience he could never

return to the Sea King's realm or the lovely Princess beyond the sea.

Little children, never be disobedient to those who are wiser than you, for disobedience was the beginning of all the miseries and sorrows of life.

HERE BE DRAGONS

Monstrous Habitats in Early Modern Thought

Constructed in 1504, the Lenox Globe is one of the earliest known examples of a three-dimensional model of the earth. On the eastern coast of Asia, far from the European origins of the globe, the artist inscribed the phrase HERE BE DRAGONS (HIC SUNT DRACONES). Echoing ancient and medieval authorities who had situated their habitat in remote places like Africa and India, this fanciful inscription banished the dragon to the farthest reaches of Asia. In the early modern period (ca. 1500–1800), global systems of exploration and commerce signaled the retreat of these reptilian monsters from the relentless march of human societies. At the same time, however, the fascination with dragons increased in step with their growing rarity. Naturalists were eager to report encounters with them in remote swamps and desolate mountainsides, while antiquarians collected and published voluminous works of dragon lore culled from the annals of ancient and medieval authors and peppered with rumors of contemporary sightings. The most recent accounts of dragon encounters took place in the American hinterlands. In the late nineteenth century, the dragons made their final stand in the badlands of Arizona and the dense forests of California in a world almost completely stripped of its secrets by the inexorable advance of human knowledge.

STRANGE, YET NOW A NEIGHBOUR TO US[1]

Pamphlets and broadsides featuring lurid stories about strange creatures and monstrous births were common in early modern England. One such pamphlet about a young yet dangerous dragon living in a forest in Sussex attracted considerable attention in the seventeenth century. Published in 1614 by John Trundle (1575–1629), "arguably the most enterprising—and unprincipled—publisher of the early Stuart age," this short story thrilled urban readers with its report of a serpentine horror that left a trail of "glutinous and slimy matter" in its wake and spit venom at unwary humans and dogs that approached it.[2] Although it was more of a threat to a local rabbit warren than to the residents of the village of Horsham, the narrators of the story feared that the monster would soon grow wings and become truly dangerous to the neighboring communities. Needless to say, it was difficult for Trundle's London audience to refute the veracity of this tall tale because it took place far from human habitation in the remote woodlands of Sussex.

In Sussex, there is a pretty market-town called Horsham, near unto it a forest, called St. Leonards forest, and there, in a vast and unfrequented place, heathy, vaulty, full of unwholesome shades, and overgrown hollows, where this serpent is thought to be bred; but wheresoever bred, certain and too true it is that there it yet lives. Within three or four miles compass are its usual haunts, oftentimes at a place called Faygate, and it hath been seen within half a mile of Horsham, a wonder, no doubt,

most terrible and noisome to the inhabitants thereabouts.
There is always in his track or path left a glutinous and slimy
matter (as by a small similitude we may perceive in a snail's)
which is very corrupt and offensive to the scent, insomuch that
they perceive the air to be putrified withal, which must needs
be very dangerous. For though the corruption of it cannot
strike the outward part of a man, unless heated into his blood,
yet by receiving it in at any of our breathing organs (the mouth
or nose) it is by authority of all authors, writing in that kind,
mortal and deadly, as one thus saith: *The poison of serpents is
deadly only when mixed with the blood* (Lucan).[3]

The serpent, or dragon, as some call it, is reputed to be nine
feet, or rather more, in length, and shaped almost in the form
of an axletree of a cart, a quantity of thickness in the midst,
and somewhat smaller at both ends. The former part, which
he shoots forth as a neck, is supposed to be an ell long, with
a white ring, as it were, of scales about it. The scales along
his back seem to be blackish, and so much as is discovered
under his belly appeareth to be red; for I speak of no nearer
description than of a reasonable occular distance. For coming too near it hath already been too dearly paid for, as you
shall hear hereafter.

It is likewise discovered to have large feet, but the eye may
be there deceived; for some suppose that serpents have no
feet, but glide upon certain ribs and scales, which both defend them from the upper part of their throat unto the lower
part of their belly, and also cause them to move much the
faster. For so this doth, and rids way, as we call it as fast as a
man can run. He is of countenance very proud, and, at the
sight or hearing of men or cattle, will raise his neck upright,
and seem to listen and look about, with arrogancy. There are
likewise on either side of him discovered two great bunches
so big as a large foot-ball, and, as some think, will in time
grow to wings; but God, I hope, will defend the poor people in the neighbourhood, that he shall be destroyed before
he grow so fledged.

He will cast his venom about four rod from him, as by
woeful experience it was proved on the bodies of a man and

woman coming that way, who afterwards were found dead, being poisoned and very much swelled, but not preyed upon. Likewise a man going to chase it and, as he imagined, to destroy it, with two mastiff dogs, as yet not knowing the great danger of it, his dogs were both killed, and he himself glad to return with haste to preserve his own life. Yet this is to be noted, that the dogs were not preyed upon, but slain and left whole; for his food is thought to be, for the most part, in a cony-warren, which he much frequents and it is found much scanted and impaired in the increase it had wont to afford.

These persons, whose names are hereunder printed, have seen this serpent, beside divers others, as the carrier of Horsham, who lieth at the White Horse, in Southwark, and who can certify the truth of all that has been here related.

JOHN STEELE.
CHRISTOPHER HOLDER.
And a Widow Woman dwelling near Faygate.

A WORLD FULL OF
DRAGONS[1]

*No early modern commentator on dragons could rival the
energy and enthusiasm of Edward Topsell (ca. 1572–
1625), an English priest with a lively interest in natural
history and zoology. A diligent student of ancient and medieval history, Topsell compiled two massive illustrated
compendiums of animal lore:* The History of Four-Footed
Beasts *(1607) and* The History of Serpents *(1608). The
popularity of these two books kept them in print throughout the seventeenth century. Topsell's approach to his
subjects was exhaustive and he did not shy away from descriptions of mythological creatures, including Gorgons
and manticores. It is no surprise that he devoted many
pages of his book on serpents to their larger cousins, the
dragons. With a giddiness that betrayed his excitement
about these monstrous creatures, Topsell collected all
manner of information about the physical characteristics
and habitats of dragons and shared stories about their in-
teraction with human beings and other animals, both as
allies and as adversaries. The result was without contest
the longest treatment of the history of dragons in the western tradition before the modern era.*

OF THE DRAGON

Among all kindes of serpents, there is none comparable to
the dragon, or that affordeth and yeeldeth so much plentiful
matter in history for the ample discovery of the nature
thereof; and therefore herein I must borrow more time from

the residue, then peradventure the reader would be willing to spare from reading the particular stories of many other. But such is the necessity hereof, that I can omit nothing making to the purpose, either for the nature or morality of this serpent, therefore I will strive to make the description pleasant, with variable history, seeing I may not avoid the length hereof, that so the sweetnesse of the one, (if my pen could so expresse it) may countervail the tediousnesse of the other.

There are divers sorts of dragons, distinguished partly by their countries, partly by their quantity and magnitude, and partly by the different form of their external parts . . . It was wont to be said, because dragons are the greatest serpents, that except a serpent eat a serpent, he shall never be a dragon: for their opinion was, that they grew so great by devouring others of their kinde; and indeed in Ethiopia they grow to be thirty yards long, neither have they any other name for those dragons but elephant-killers, and they live very long.

Onesicritus writeth, that one Aposisares, an Indian, did nourish two serpents dragons, whereof one was six and forty cubits long, and the other fourscore; and for the more famous verification of the fact, he was a very earnest tuter to Alexander the Great, when he was in India, to come and see them, but the king being afraid, refused.[2]

The chroniclers of the affairs of Chios do write, that in a certain valley neer to the foot of the Mountain Pellenaeus, was a valley full of straight tall trees, wherein was bred a dragon of wonderful magnitude or greatnesse, whose only voice or hissing, did terrifie all the inhabitants of Chios, and therefore there was no man that durst come nigh unto him, to consider or to take a perfect view of his quantity, suspecting only his greatnesse by the loudnesse of his voyce, until at length they knew him better by a singular accident worthy of eternal memory.[3] For it hapned on a time that such a violent winde did arise, as did beat together all the trees in the wood, by which violent collision the branches fell to be on fire, and so all the wood was burned suddenly, compassing in the dragon, whereby he had no means to escape alive, & so the trees fel down upon him and burned him. Afterward, when the fire had made the place bare of wood, the inhabitants might see the quantity of the dragon, for they found divers of his bones and his head, which were of such unusual greatnesse, as did sufficiently confirm them in their former opinion: and thus by divine miracle was this monster consumed, whom never any man durst behold being alive, & the inhabitants of the countrey safely delivered from their just conceived fear.

It is also reported, that Alexander among many other Beasts which he saw in India, did there finde in a certain den a dragon of seaventy cubits long, which the Indians accounted a sacred beast, and therefore intreated Alexander to do it no harm.[4] When it uttered the voice with full breath, it terrified his whole army; they could never see the proportion of his body, but only the head, and by that they guessed the quantity of the whole body, for one of his eyes in their appearance seemed as great as a Macedonian buckler.[5] Maximus Tyrius writeth that in the days of Alexander, there was likewise seen a dragon in India, as long as five roods of lands are broad, which is incredible.[6] For he likewise saith that the Indians did feed him every day with many several oxen and sheep. It may be that it was the same spoken of before, which some ignorant men, and such as were given to set forth fables, amplyfied beyond measure and credit.

Whereas dragons are bred in India and Africa, the greatest of all are in India, for in Ethiopia, Nubia, and Hesperia, the dragons are confined within the length of five cubits and twenty cubits; for in the time of Euergetes, there were three brought into Egypt, one was nine cubits long, which with great care was nourished in the Temple of Esculapius, the other two were seaven cubits long.[7] About the place where once the Tower of Babel was builded, are dragons of great quantity, and under the equinoctial, as Nicephorus Callistus writeth, there are serpents as thick as beams, in testimony whereof their skins have been brought to Rome.[8] And therefore it is no marvail, although S. Augustine writing upon the 148. Psalm, doth say, *Dragons are certain great beasts, and there are none greater upon the earth.*[9] Neither is it to be thought incredible, that the souldiers of Attilius Regulus did kill a dragon which was a hundred and twenty foot long, or that the dragons in the dens of the Mountain Atlas, should grow so great that they can scarse move their fore-parts of their body.[10] I am yet therefore to speak of the dragons in the Mountains Emodii or of Arigia, or of Dachinabades, or the regions of the east, or of that which Augustus shewed publiquely to the people of Rome, being fifty cubits long; or of those which be in the Alpes, which are found in certain caves of the south-sides of the hills, so that this which hath been said, shall suffice for the quantity and countries of dragons. Besides, there are other kindes of dragons which I must speak of in order; and first of all of the Epidaurian dragons, which is bred no where but in that countrey, being tame, and of yellow golden colour, wherefore they were dedicated to Aesculapius . . .[11]

There are likewise other kinde of tame dragons in Macedonia, where they are so meek, that women feed them, and suffer them to suck their breasts like little children. Their infants also play with them, riding upon them and pinching them, as they would do with dogs, without any harm, and sleeping with them in their beds . . . Of the Indian dragons there are also said to be two kindes, one of them fenny, and living in the marishes, which are slow of pace and without combes on their heads like females; the other in the mountains, which are more sharp and great, and have combes upon their head, their backs being somewhat brown, and all their bodies lesse scaly then the other. When they come down from the mountains into the plain to hunt, they are neither afraid of marishes nor violent waters, but thrust themselves greedily into all hazards and dangers; and because they are of longer and stronger bodies then the dragons of the fens, they beguile them of their meat, and take away from them their prepared booties. Some of them are of a yellowish fiery colour, having also sharp backs like saws; these also have beards, and when they set up their scales they shine like silver. The apples of their eyes are precious stones, and as bright as fire, in which there is affirmed to be much vertue against many diseases, and therefore they bring unto the hunters and killers of dragons no small gain, besides the profit of their skin, and their teeth; and they are taken when they descend from the mountains into the valleys to hunt the elephants, so as both of them are kill'd together by the hunters.

Their members are very great, like unto the members of the greatest swine, but their bodies are leaner, flexibly turning to ever side, according to the necessity of motion. Their snouts are very strong, resembling the greatest ravening fishes; they have beards of a yellow golden color, being full of bristles; and the mountain-dragons commonly have more deep eye-lids then the dragons of the Fens. Their aspect is very fierce and grim, and whensoever they move upon the earth, their eyes give a sound from their eye-lids, much like unto the tinckling of brasse, and sometimes they boldly venture into the sea and take fishes.

OF THE WINGED DRAGON

There be some dragons which have wings and no feet, some again have both feet and wings, and some neither feet nor wings, but are only distinguished from the common sort of serpents by the combe growing upon their heads, and the beard under their cheeks.

Saint Augustine saith, that dragons abide in deep caves and hollow places of the earth, and that sometimes when they perceive moistnes in the air, they come out of their holes, & beating the air with their wings, as it were with the strokes of oars, they forsake the earth and flie aloft; which wings of theirs are of a skinny substance, and very voluble, and spreading themselves wide, according to the quantity and largenesse of the dragons body[12] . . . [Learned authors in accordance with ancient poets] do affirm that a dragon is of a black colour, the belly somewhat green, and very beautiful to behold, having a treble row of teeth in their mouths upon every jaw, and with most bright and cleer seeing eyes, which caused the poets to faign in their writings, that these dragons are the watchfull keepers of treasures. They have also two dewlaps growing under their chin, and hanging down like a beard, which are of a red colour; their bodies are set all over with very sharp scales, and over their eyes stand certain flexible eye-lids. When they gape wide with their mouth, and thrust forth their tongue, their teeth seem very much to resemble the teeth of wilde Swine. And their necks have many times grosse thick hair growing upon them, much like the bristles of a wilde boar.

Their mouth, (especially of the most tameable dragons) is but little, not much bigger then a pipe, through which they draw in their breath, for they wound not with their mouth, but with their tails only beating with them when they are angry. But the Indian, Ethiopian, and Phrygian dragons, have very wide mouths, through which they often swallow in whole fowls and beasts. Their tongue is cloven as if it were double, and the investigators of nature do say, that they have fifteen teeth of a side. The males have combes on their heads, but the females have none, and they are likewise distinguished by their beards.

They have most excellent senses both of seeing and hearing, and for this cause their name *Drakon* cometh of *Derkein*, and this was one cause why Jupiter the heathens great god, is said to be metamorphosed into a dragon, whereof their flyeth this tale.[13] When he fell in love with Proserpina, he ravished her in the likenesse of a dragon, for he came unto her and covered her with the spires of his body; and for this cause the people of Sabazii did observe in their mysteries or sacrifices the shape of a dragon rowled up within the compasse of his spires; so that as he begot Ceres with childe in the likenesse of a bull, he likewise deluded her daughter Proserpina in the likenesse of a dragon; but of these transmutations we shall speak more afterwards, and I think the vanity of these took first ground from the Africans, who believe that the original of dragons took beginning from the unnatural conjunction of an eagle and a she wolf. And so they say that the wolf growing great by this conception, doth not bring forth as at other times, but her belly breaketh and the dragon cometh out, who in his beak and wings resembleth the eagle his father, and in his feet and tail, the wolf his mother, but in the skin neither of them both; but this kinde of fabulous generation is already sufficiently confuted. Their meats are fruits and herbs, or any venomous creature, therefore they live long without food, and when they eat, they are not easily filled. They grow most fat by eating of egges, in devouring whereof they use this art, if it be a great dragon, he swalloweth it up whole, and then rowleth himself, whereby he crusheth the egges to pieces in his belly, and so nature casteth out the shells, and keepth the meat. But if it were a young dragon, as if it be a dragons whelp, he taketh the egge within the spire of his tail, and so crushed it hard and holdeth it fast, until his scales open the shell like a knife then sucketh he out of the place opened all the meat of the egg. In like sort do the young ones pull off the feathers from the fowls which they eat, and the old ones swallow them whole, casting the feathers out of their bellies again.

The dragons of Phrygia when they are hungry, turn themselves towards the west, and gaping wide, with the force of their breath do draw the birds that flie over their heads into their throats, which some have thought is but a voluntary lapse of the fowls, to be drawn by the breath of the dragon, as by a thing they love, but it is more probable, that some vaporous and venomous breath is sent up from the dragon to them, that poysoneth and infecteth the air about them, whereby their senses are taken from them, and they astonished fall down into its mouth.[14] But if it fortune the dragons finde not food enough to satisfie their hunger, then they hide themselves until the people be returned from the market, or the heard-men bring home their flocks, and upon a sudden they devour either men or beasts, which come first to their mouths;

then they go again and hide themselves in their dens and hollow caves of the earth, for their bodies being exceeding hot, they very seldom come out of the cold earth, except to seek meat and nourishment. And because they live only in the hottest countries, therefore they commonly make their lodgings neer unto the waters, or else in the coldest places among the rocks and stones.

They greatly preserve their health (as Aristotle affirmeth) by eating of wilde lettice, for that they make them to vomit, and cast forth of their stomach whatsoever meat offendeth them, and they are most specially offended by eating of apples, for their bodies are much subject to be filled with winde, and therefore they never eat apples, but first they eat wilde lettice.[15] Their sight also (as Plutarch saith) doth many times grow weak and feeble, and therefore they renew and recover the same again by rubbing their eyes against fennel, or else by eating of it.[16]

Their age could never yet be certainly known, but it is conjectured that they live long, and in great health, like to all other serpents, and therefore they grow so great. They do not only live on the land, as we have said already, but also swim in the water, for many times they take the sea in Ethiopia, four or five of them together, folding their tails like hurdles, and holding up their heads, so swim they over to seek better food in Arabia.

We have said already, that when they set upon elephants, they are taken and killed of men. Now the manner how the Indians kill the mountain dragons is thus. They take a garment of scarlet, and picture upon it a charm in golden letters, this they lay upon the mouth of the dragons den, for with the red colour and the gold, the eyes of the dragon are overcome, and he falleth asleep, the Indians in the mean season watching, and muttering secretly words of incantation. When they perceive he is fast asleep, suddenly they strike off his neck with an ax, and so take out the balls of his eyes, wherein are lodged those rare and precious stones which contain in them vertues unutterable, as hath been evidently proved by one of them, that was included in the Ring of Gyges.[17] Many times it falleth out, that the dragon draweth in the Indian both with his ax and instruments into his den, and there devoureth him, in the rage whereof, he so beateth the mountain that it shaketh. When the dragon is killed, they make use of the skin, eyes, teeth, and flesh; as for the flesh, it is of a vitrail or glassie colour, and the Ethiopians do eat it very greedily, for they say it hath in it a refrigerative power. And there be some which by certain inchanting verses do tame dragons, and rideth upon their necks, as a man would ride upon a horse, guiding and governing them with a bridle.

Now because we have already shewed, that some dragons have wings, lest it should seem uncredible, as the foolish world is apt to believe no more than they see, I have therefore thought good to add in this place, a particular relation of the testimonies of sundry learned men, concerning these winged serpents or dragons. First of all Megasthenes writeth, that in India there be certain flying serpents which hunt not in the day, but in the night time, and these do render or make a kinde of urine, by the touching whereof, all the parts of mortal creatures do rot away.[18] And there is a mountain which divideth asunder the Kingdom of Narsinga from Alabaris, wherein be many winged Serpents sitting upon trees, which they say poyson men with their breath. There be many pestilent winged Serpents which come out of Arabia every year by troups into Egypt, these are destroyed by a certain black bird called Ibis, who fighteth with them in defence of that countrey where she liveth, so that there lie great heaps of them many times destroyed upon the earth by these birds, whose bodies may be there visibily seen to have both wings and legs, and their bones being of great quantity and stature, remain unconsumed for many years after. These kinde of serpents or dragons, covet to keep about trees of frankincense which grow in Arabia, and when they are driven away from thence with the fume or smoak of stirax, then they flie (as is aforesaid) into Egypt, and this is to be considered, that if it were not for this stirax, all that countrey would be consumed with dragons.[19]

Neither have we in Europe only heard of dragons and never

seen them, but also even in our own country, there have (by the testimony of sundry writers) divers been discovered and killed. And first of all, there was a dragon or winged serpent brought unto Francis the French king, when he lay at Sancton, by a certain countreyman, who had slain the same serpent himself with a spade, when it set upon him in the fields to kill him.[20] And this thing was witnessed by many learned and credible men which saw the same; and they thought it was not bred in that countrey, but rather driven by the winde thither from some forain nation. For France was never know to breed any such monsters. Among the Pyrenes also, there is a cruel kinde of serpent, not past four foot long, and as thick as a mans arm, out of whose sides grow wings much like unto gristles.

Gessner also saith, that in the year of our Lord 1543, there came many serpents both with wings and legs into the parts of Germany neer Stiria, who did bite and wound many men incurably.[21] Cardan also describeth certain serpents with wings, which he saw at Paris, whose dead bodies were in the hands of Gulielmus Musicus. He saith that they had two legs and small wings, so that they could scarce flie, the head was little, and like to the head of a serpent, their colour bright, and without hair or feathers, the quantity of which was greatest, did not exceed the bignesse of a cony, and it is said they were brought out of India.[22] Besides, a further confirmation of these beasts, there have been noted in all ages; for it is written in the Roman Chronicles, the times of their apparition and manifestation.

When the river of Tiber over-flowed above the banks, then were many serpents discovered, and many dragons, as in the time of Mauritius the Emperor, at what time a dragon came along by the city of Rome, upon the waters in sight of all men, and so passed into the sea, after which prodigy there followed a great mortal pestilence.[23] In the year 1499, the 26 day of May, there came a dragon to the city of Lucerne, which came out of the lake through Rusa, down along the river, many people of all sorts beholding the same.

There have been also dragons many times seen in Germany,

flying in the air at mid-day, and signifying great and fearful fires to follow, as it happened neer to the city called Niderburge, neer to the shore of the Rhene, in a marvellous clear sun-shine day, there came a dragon three times successively together in one day, and did hang in the air over a town called Sanctagoarin, shaking his tail over that town every time. It appeared visibly in the sight of many of the inhabitants, and afterwards it came to passe, that the said town was three times burned with fire, to the great harm and undoing of all the people dwelling in the same; for they were not able to make any resistance to quench the fire, with all the might, art, and power that they could raise. And it was further observed, that about that time there were many dragons seen washing themselves in a certain fountain or well neer the town, and if any of the people did chance to drink of the water of that well, their bellies did instantly begin to swell, and they dyed as if they had been poysoned. Whereupon it was publiquely decreed, that the said well should be filled up with stones, to the intent that never any man should afterwards be poysoned with that water; and so a memory thereof was continued, and these things are written by Justinus Goblerus, in an epistle to Gesner, affirming that he did not write feigned things, but such things as were true, and as he head learned from men of great honesty and credit, whose eyes did see and behold both the dragons, and the mishaps that followed by fire.[24]

When the body of Cleomenes was crucified, and hung upon the Crosse, it is reported by them that were the watchmen about it, that there came a Dragon and did winde it self about his body, and with his head covered the face of the dead King, oftentimes licking the same, and not suffering any Bird to come neer and touch the carkasse.[25] For which cause there began to be a reverent opinion of divinity attributed to the king, until such time as wise and prudent men, studious of the truth, found out the true cause hereof. For they say that as bees are generated out of the body of oxen, and drones of horses, and hornets of asses, so do the bodies of men ingender out of their marrow a serpent, and for this cause the ancients were moved to consecrate the dragon to noble-spirited men, and therefore there was a monument kept of the first Africanus, because that under an olive planted with his own hand, a dragon was said to preserve his ghost.[26]

But I will not mingle fables and truths together, and therefore I will reserve the moral discourse of this beast unto another place; and this which I have written, may be sufficient to satisfie any reasonable man, that there are winged serpents and dragons in the world. And I pray God that we never have better arguments to satisfie us, by his corporal and lively presence in our countrey, lest some great calamity follow thereupon. Now therefore we will proceed to the love and hatred of this Beast, that is observed with man and other creatures.

And first of all, although dragons be natural enemies to men, like unto all other serpents, yet many times (if there be any truth in the story) they have been possessed with extraordinary love, both to men, women and children, as may appear by these particulars following. There was one Aleva a Thessalian Neatherd, which did keep oxen in Ossa, hard by the Fountain Hemonius, there was a Dragon fell in love with this man, for his hair was as yellow as any gold, unto him for his hair did this dragon often come, creeping closely as a lover to his love: and when he came unto him, he would lick his hair and face so gently, and in so sweet a manner, as the man professed he never felt the like, so as without all fear he conversed with him, and as he came, so would he go away again, never returning to him empty, but bringing him some one gift or other, such as his nature and kinde could lay hold on.

There was a dragon also which loved Pindus the son of Macedo, king of Emathia. This Pindus having many Brothers most wicked and lewd persons, and he only being a valiant man of honest disposition, having likewise a comely and goodly personage, understanding the treachery of his brethren against him, bethought himself how to avoid their hands and tyranny. Now forasmuch as he knew that the kingdom which he possessed, was the only mark they all shot at, he thought it better to leave that to them, and so to rid himself from envy, fear, and peril, then to embrew his hand in their bloud, or to lose his life and kingdom both together. Wherefore he renounced and gave over the government, and betook himself to the exercise of hunting, for he was a strong man, fit to combate with wilde beasts, by destruction of whom, he made more room for many men upon the earth, so that he passed all his days in that exercise. It hapned on a day that he was hunting of a kind-calf, and spurring his horse with all his might and main in the eager persuit thereof, he rode out of the sight of all his company, and suddenly the hind-calf leaped into a very deep cave, out of the sight of Pindus the hunter, and so saved himself. Then he alighted from his horse, and tyed him to the next tree, seeking out as diligently as he could for a way into the cave, whereinto the hind-calf had leaped: and when he had looked a good while about him, and could finde none, he heard a voice speaking unto him, and forbidding him to touch the hind-calf, which made him look about again, to see if he cold perceive the person from whom the voice proceeded, but espying none, he grew to be afraid, and thought that the voice proceeded from some other greater cause, and so leaped upon his horse hastily, and departed again to his fellows. The day after he returned to the same place, and when he came thither, being terrified with the remembrance of the former voice, he durst not enter into the place, but stood there doubting and wondering with hiself, what shepheards or hunters, or other men might be in that place to diswarn him from his game, and therefore he went round about to seek for some, or to learn from whence the voice proceeded. While he was thus seeking, there appeared unto him a dragon of a great stature, creeping upon the greatest part of his body, except his neck and head lifted up a little, and that little was as high as the stature of any man can reach, and in this fashion he made toward Pindus, who at the first sight was not a little afraid of him, but yet did not run

away, but rather gathering his wits together, remembred that
he had about him birds, and divers parts of sacrifices, which
instantly he gave unto the dragon, and so mitigated his fury
by these gifts, and as it were with a royal feast, changed the
cruel nature of the dragon into kinde usage. For the dragon
being smoothed over with these gifts, & as it were overtaken
with the liberality of Pindus, was contented to forsake the
old place of his habitation, and to go away with him. Pindus
also being no less glad of the company of the dragon, did
daily give unto him the greatest part of his hunting, as a deserved price and ransome of his life, and conquest of such a
beast. Neither was he unrequited for it, for Fortune so fa-
voured his game, that whether he hunted fowls of the air, or
beasts of the earth, he still obtained and never missed. So
that his fame for hunting procured him more love and honor,
then ever could the imperial crown of his countrey. For all
young men desired to follow him, admiring his goodly personage and strength, the virgins and maids falling in love,
contended among themselves who should marry him; the
wives forsaking their husbands, contrary to all womanly
modesty, rather desired his company then the society of their
husbands, or to be preferred among the number of the god-
desses. Only his brethren inraged against him, sought all
means to kill and destroy him. Therefore they watched all
opportunities, lying in continual ambush where he hunted to
accomplish their accursed enterprise, which at last they obtained; for as he followed the game, they enclosed him in a
narrow straight neer to a rivers side, where he had no means
to avoid their hands, they and their company being many,
and he alone, wherefore they drew out their swords and slew
him. When he saw no remedy but death, he cryed out aloud
for help, whose voice soon came to the ears of the watchful
dragon, (for no beast heareth or seeth better) out he cometh
from his den, and finding the murtherers standing about the
dead body, he presently surprised and killed them, so revenging the quarrel of Pindus, and then fell upon the dead body
of his friend, never forsaking the custody thereof, until the

neighbours adjoining to the place, taking knowledge of the fact, came to bury the bodies. But when they came and saw the dragon among them, they were afraid, and durst not come neer, but stood afar off, consulting what to do; till at last they perceived that the Dragon began to take knowledge of their fear, who with an admirable curtesie of nature, perceiving their mourning and lamentation for their dead friend, and withal, their abstinence from approaching to execute his exequies, or funerals, began to think that he might be the cause of this their terror, and far standing off from the dead bodies, wherefore he departed, taking his farewell of the body which he loved, and so gave them leave by his absence, to bestow upon him an honorable burial, which they performed accordingly, and the river adjoyning, was named by the name of Pindus-death.

By which story may appear, that these savage dragons are made loving and tame to men, by good turns and benefits bestowed upon them, for there is no nature which may not be overcome by kindenesse. And yet I may not leave this matter thus, nor from these two examples alone, conclude the practice and possibility of love betwixt men and dragons: I will therefore add some three or four examples more.

There was a dragon the lover of Aetholis (as Plutarch writeth) who came unto her every night, and did her body no harm, but gently sliding over her, played with her till morning, then also would he depart asson as light appeared, that he might not be espied. The maidens friends came to the knowledge hereof, and so removed her far away, to the intent the dragon might come no more at her, and thus they remained asunder a great while, the dragon earnestly seeking for the maiden, wandered far and neer to finde her out. At last he met with her, and not saluting her gently as he was wont, flew upon her, binding her hands down with the spire of his body, hissing softly in her face, and beating gently with his tail her backparts, as it were taking a moderate revenge upon her for the neglect of his love by her long absence.

Another like story unto this is reported by Aelianus, of a

great dragon which loved a fair woman, beloved also of a fair man, the woman oftentimes did sleep with this dragon, but not so willingly as with the man, wherefore she forsook the habitation of her place for a month, and went away where the dragon could not find her, thinking that her absence might quench his desire.[27] But he came often to the place where he was wont to meet with the woman, and not finding her, returned quietly back again, and came again another time: at last he grew suspicious, and like a lover failing in his expectation, grew very sorrowful, and so continued till the month was exspired, every night visiting the accustomed place. At last the woman returned, and the dragon presently met with her, and in an amorous fashion, full of suspicion and jealousie, winding about her body, did beat her as you have heard in the former story: and this (saith Aelianus) happened in Judea, in the days of Herod the King.

There was a little dragon-whelp bred in Arcadia, and brought up familiarly with a little boy from his infancy, until the boy became a young man, and the dragon also became of great stature, so that one of them loved another so well as man and beast could love together, or rather two play-fellows from the cradle. At last the friends of the boy seeing the dragon grow so great in so short a space, began to be suspicious of him; whereupon they took the bed wherein the boy and the dragon were lodged, and carryed the same into a far remote place of woods and wildernesse, and there set down the bed with the boy and the dragon together. The boy after a little while returned, and came home again to his friends; the dragon wandered up and down in the woods, feeding upon herbs and poison, according to its nature, and never more cared for the habitation of men, but rested contented with a solitary life. In the length of time it came to passe that the boy grew to be a perfect man, and the dragon also remained in the wood, and although absent one from the other, yet mutually loving as well as ever. It hapned that this young man travelled through that place where the dragon was lodged, and fell among theeves, when the young man saw their swords about his ears, he cryed out, and the dragons den being not far off, his cry came to the dragons ears, who instantly knowing the voice of his play-fellow, answered the same with another, at whose hissing the theeves grew afraid, and began to run away, but their legs could not carry them so fast, as to escape the dragons teeth and claws; for he came speedily to release his friend, and all the theeves that he could find, he put to cruel death, then did he accompany his friend out of the place of peril, and returned back again to his den, neither remembering wrath, for that he was exposed to the wildernesse, and there left by his play-fellow, nor yet like perverse men, forsaking their old friend in danger.

The examples before expressed being all extraordinary and beside nature, do not conclude, but that there is an ordinary hatred betwixt men and dragons, and therefore in the discourse of their enemies, men must have the first place, as their most worthy adversary, for both dragons have perished by men, and men by dragons, as may appear by these stories following.

When the region of Helvetia [Switzerland] began first to be purged from noisome beasts, there was a horrible dragon found neer a countrey town called Wilser, who did destroy all men and beasts that came within his danger in the time of his hunger, insomuch that that town and the fields there to adjoyning, was called Dedwiler, that is, a village of the wildernesse, for all the people and inhabitants had forsaken the same, and fled to other places. There was a man of that town whose name was Winckelreidt, who was banished for manslaughter. This man promised if he might have his pardon, and be restored again to his former inheritance, that he would combate with that Dragon, and by Gods help destroy him, which thing was granted unto him with great joyfulnesse. Wherefore he was recalled home, and in the presence of many people went forth to fight with the dragon, whom he slew and overcame, whereat for joy he lifted up his sword imbrued in the dragons bloud, in token of victory, but the bloud distilled down from his sword upon his body, and caused him instantly to fall down dead. And thus this noble conqueror, a man worthy to be remembred in all ages and nations, who had strength to kill the dragon being alive, yet had no power to resist the venom of his bloud, he being dead. But had it not been that his hand had been before imbrewed in the bloud of a man, I do not believe that the bloud of a dragon could have fallen so heavy upon him. But this is the judgment of God, either to punish murder in the same kinde, or else to teach us, that we should not rejoice in our own merits, lest God see it and be angry. For our Saviour Christ forbade his disciples that they should rejoice that the Devils were subject to them; and therefore much lesse may we poor creatures rejoice for overcoming men or beasts.

There be also certain little dragons called in Arabia, Vesga, and in Catalonia, dragons of houses, these when they bite leave their teeth behind them, so as the wound never ceaseth swelling as long as the teeth remain therein, and therefore for the better cure thereof, the teeth are drawn forth and so the wound will soon be healed. And thus much for the hatred betwixt men and dragons, now we will proceed to other creatures.

The greatest discord is betwixt the eagle and the dragon, for the vultures, eagles, swans and dragons are enemies one to another. The eagles, when they shake their wings, make the dragons afraid with their ratling noise, then the dragon hideth himself within his den, so that he never fighteth but in the air, either when the eagle hath taken away his young ones and he to recover them flyeth aloft after her, or else when the eagle meeteth him in her nest, destroying her egges and young ones; for the eagle devoureth the dragons and little serpents upon earth, and the dragons again and serpents do the like against the eagles in the air. Yea many times the dragon attempteth to take away the prey out of the eagles talons, both on the ground and in the air, so that there ariseth betwixt them a very hard and dangerous fight . . .

In the next place we are to consider the enmity that is betwixt dragons and elephants, for so great is their hatred one to the other, that in Ethiopia the greatest dragons have no other name but elephant-killers.[28] Among the Indians also the same hatred remaineth, against whom the dragons have many subtile inventions. For besides the great length of their bodies, wherewithal they claspe and begirt the body of the elephant, continually biting of him until he fall down dead, and in the which fall they are also bruised to pieces, for the safeguard of themselves they have this device: they get and hide themselves in trees, covering their head and letting the other part hang down like a rope. In those trees they watch until the elephant come to eat and crop of the branches, then suddenly before he be aware, they leap into his face and dig out his eyes, then do they clasp themselves about his neck and with their tails or hinder-parts beat and vex the elephant until they have made him breathlesse, for they strangle him with their fore-parts, as they beat them with the hinder, so that in this combat they both perish. And this is the disposition of the dragon that he never setteth upon the elephant, but with the advantage of the place and namely from some high tree or rock.

Sometimes again a multitude of dragons do together observe the paths of the elephants & cross those paths they tie together their tails as it were in knots, so that when the elephant cometh along in them, they insnare his legs and suddenly leap up to his eyes, for that is the part they aim at above all other, which they speedily pull out, and so not being able to do him any harm, the poor beast delivereth himself from present death by his own strength, and yet through his blindenesse received in that combat, he perisheth by hunger, because he cannot choose his meat by smelling, but by his eye-sight.

There is no man living that is able to give a sufficient reason for this contrariety in nature betwixt the elephant and the dragon, although many men have labored their wits and strained their inventions to finde out the true causes thereof, but all in vain, except this be one that followeth. The elephants bloud is said to be the coldest of all other beasts, and for this cause it is thought by most writers that the dragons in the summer time do hide themselves in great plenty in the waters where the elephant cometh to drink, and then suddenly they leap up upon his ears, because those places cannot be defended with his trunck, and there they hang fast and suck out all the bloud of his body, until such a time as the poor beast through faintnesse fall down and die, and they being drunk with his bloud do likewise perish in the fall.

The Gryffins are likewise said to fight with the dragons and overcome them. The panther also is an enemy unto the dragons and driveth them many times into their dens. There is a little bird called captilus, by eating of which the dragon refresheth himself when he is wearied in hunting of other beasts . . .

In the next place I will passe unto the poyson and venom of dragons, omitting all poetical discourses about the worshipping and transmutation of dragons from one kinde to another, such as are the hairs of Orpheus, or the teeth of the dragon which Cadmus slew, into armed men, and such like fables, which have no shew nor appearance of truth, but are only the inventions of men to utter those things in obscure terms, which they were afraid to do in plain speeches.

It is a question whether dragons have any venom or poison in them, for it is thought that he hurteth more by the wound of his teeth, then by his poison. Yet in Deuteronomy, Moses speaketh of them as if they had poyson, saying: *Their wine is as the poison of dragons, and the cruel venom of asps.*[29] So also Heliodorus speaketh of certain weapons dipped in the poison of dragons.[30] For which cause we are to consider that they wanting poison in themselves become venomous two manner of ways: first, by the place wherein they live, for in the hotter countries they are more apt to do harm then in the colder and more temperate . . . A second cause why poison is supposed to be in dragons is for that they often feed upon many venomous roots and therefore their poison sticketh in their teeth, whereupon many times the party bitten by them seemeth to be poisoned, but this falleth out accidentlly, not from the nature of the dragon, but from the nature of the meat which the dragon eateth. And this is it which Homer knew and affirmed in his verses, when he described a dragon making his den neer unto the place where many venomous roots and herbs grew and by eating whereof he greatly annoyeth mankinde when he biteth them . . . And therefore Aelianus saith well that when the dragon meaneth to do most harm to men, he eateth deadly poysonful herbs, so that if he bite after them, many not knowing the cause of the poyson, and seeing or feeling venom by it, do attribute that to his nature which doth proceed from his meat. Besides his teeth which bite deep, he also killeth with his tail, for he will so begirt and pinch in the body that he doth gripe it to death and also the strokes of it are so strong that either they kill thereby forthwith or else wound greatly with the same, so that the strokes of his tail are more deadly than the biting of his teeth . . .

Their mouth is small, and by reason thereof they cannot open it wide to bite deep, so as their biting maketh no great pain; and those kinde of dragons which do principally fight with eagles are defended more with their tails then with their teeth, but yet there are some other kinde of dragons, whose teeth are like the teeth of bears, biting deep and opening their mouth wide, wherewith all they break bones and make many bruises in the body and the males of this kinde bite deeper then the females, yet there followeth no great pain upon the wound.

The cure thereof is like to the cure for the biting of any other beast wherein there is no venom and for this cause there must be nothing applied thereunto which cureth venomous bitings, but rather such things as are ordinary in the cure of every ulcer.

The seed of grasse, commonly called hay-dust, is prescribed against the biting of dragons. The barble being rubbed upon the place where a scorpian of the earth, a spider, a sea or land-dragon biteth doth perfectly cure the same. Also the head of a dog or dragon which hath bitten any one, being cut off and flayed, and applied to the wound with a little *Euphorbium* is said to cure the wound speedily . . .[31]

In the next place, for the conclusion of the history of the dragon, we will take our farewell of him in the recital of his medicinal vertues, which are briefly these that follow:

First, the fat of a dragon dryed in the sun is good against creeping ulcers and the same mingled with honey and oyl helpeth the dimnesse of the eyes at the beginning. The head of a dragon keepeth one from looking asquint and if it be set up at the gates and dores, it hath been thougth in ancient time to be very fortunate to the sincere worshippers of God. The eyes being kept till they be stale, and afterwards beat into an oyl with honey made into ointment, keep any one that useth it from the terrour of night-visions and apparitions . . .

And thus will I conclude the history of the dragon with this story following out of Porphyrius concerning the good successe which hath been signified unto men and women, either by the dreams or sight of Dragons. Mammea, the mother of Alexander Severus the Emperor, the night before his birth, dreamed that she brought forth a little dragon, so also did Olympia, the mother of Alexander the Great, and Pomponia, the mother of Scipio Africanus. The like prodigy gave Augustus hope that he should be emperor. For when his Mother Aetia came in the night time unto the temple of Apollo, and had set down her bed or couch in the temple among other matrons, suddenly she fell asleep, and in her sleep she dreamed that a dragon came to her and clasped about her body and so departed without doing her any harm. Afterwards the print of a dragon remained perpetually upon her belly, so as she never durst any more be seen in any bath. The Emperor Tiberius Caesar had a dragon which he daily fed with his own hands and nourished like good fortune. At the last it happened that this Dragon was defaced with the biting of emmets, and the former beauty of his body much obscured.[32] Wherefore the emperor grew greatly amazed thereat, and demanding a reason thereof of the wisemen, he was by them admonished to beware the insurrection of the common people. And thus with these stories representing good and evil by the dragon, I will take my leave of this good and evil serpent.

DWELLERS BELOW[1]

While Edward Topsell was a quintessential armchair explorer, his near contemporary the German Jesuit and polymath Athanasius Kircher (1602–80) was a daring adventurer. Throughout his life, Kircher nursed a gnawing obsession with the idea that there were habitable lands beneath the surface of the earth. In 1638, he was so intrigued by the possibility that volcanoes provided gateways to these lightless realms that he had himself lowered into the active crater of Mount Vesuvius at the Gulf of Naples! A few decades later, Kircher published his lavishly illustrated, two-volume Subterranean World (Mundus subterraneus), *a sprawling potpourri of scientific knowledge and folkloric accretion about the geography and ecology of subterranean places, with long digressions on the existence of underworld megafauna, most notably dragons. Gathering his information from ancient and medieval authorities as well as the testimonies of early modern scholars, Kircher affirmed the existence of dragons not only in the distant past but also in contemporary Europe. His work was a veritable treasure trove of early modern dragon lore. Whether nesting in subterranean caverns or in flight between remote aeries in the Swiss Alps, dragons persisted in the early modern period as a carnivorous menace haunting the fringes of human civilization.*

There is a great deal of debate among writers with regards to dragons: do animals of this sort actually exist in nature, or, as is often the case in many other things, can they only be found in fables? For I was also stubbornly undecided for a

long time as to whether these animals have ever in fact ex-
isted. At last, however, it was necessary for me to set aside
my doubts, which I did easily, in light of having not only read
excerpts from a variety of established authors, but also having heard the accounts of trustworthy eyewitnesses. Because
monstrous animals of this kind quite often make their nests
and rear their young in underground caverns, we assert with
a solid basis that they are a verifiable kind of subterranean
species, in accordance with the worthy topic of this book.

We know for a fact from recent writers that this kind of
animal is of two types: one with wings, the other without. As
to whether the first is in fact a living creature, no one can
doubt this, nor should he, unless he dared to contradict Holy
Scripture (itself an unspeakable act), where in the Book of
Daniel mention is quite plainly made of the dragon Bel, whose
cult was maintained by the Babylonians.[2] Dragons are also
mentioned in various other places in Scripture, and it is quite
plainly stated that animals of this sort make their lairs in
the hidden depths of the earth; and that, when any means of
egress is found, they emerge to cause great harm both to animals and to humans . . .

So let us go forward to those accounts which describe not
only bipedal dragons, but the four-footed variety as well . . .
All say that the remote fastnesses and inaccessible caves of the
Swiss Alps sustain a population of dragons, which delight in
such places. Even now, according to the memories of men of
recent generations, these creatures can be found there. Thus it
is impossible to doubt the truth of these amazing monsters.
But I shall also here treat of flying dragons, which witnesses
describe as visible in the air by the great flapping of their
wings. The lesser kind of this variety, with which I shall
begin, are the notorious flying snakes known to inhabit the
land of the Egyptians. They are depicted in the hieroglyphic
inscriptions of that nation. Pliny, Aelian, and Solinus confirm
that to this very day it invariably happens that winged snakes
come from Arabia to Egypt after the flooding of the Nile has

occurred. Once there, their offspring are born as insects in the decaying matter of the muddy slime left behind by the flood.

In 1660, in the month of November, a Roman named Lanio was in the coastal marshes trapping birds. Instead of finding birds, he ran into a dragon about the size of a very large vulture. He judged it to be a bird and unloaded his shotgun into the creature. Wounding its wing in this way, he succeeded in enraging the beast. Then, in counterattack, the dragon charged the hunter, propelling itself headlong with a semi-flying run. When the hunter realized that he had used up his supply of ammunition, he cut its throat, and it died. After he had returned home on that same evening, he died himself, either from the toxicity of the creature's blood or from the virulence of its breath. His entire body was suffused with poison. Since this was a matter of concern to the entire city, it occurred to a certain very curious person, who had been informed of the incident by a relative of the deceased hunter, to go to the location where the struggle had taken place. There he found the rotting body of the dragon. So that he could in all truthfulness bear witness to the matter, he brought back the dragon's head to the city. This was conveyed to me even as I wrote this treatise by the most expert Lord Jerome Lancta, curate of Cardinal Baberini's museum. This head was very carefully examined and I received the report that it was indeed a true dragon, with a double row of teeth just as one can find in a snake's mouth. The dragon itself was bipedal; and it had the bizarre feature of webbed feet, like those of a duck. It is on display for all to see in my own museum. It is an example of the bipedal type of winged dragon.

In the year of Our Lord 1345, when Clement VI was pope and while Elion of Villanova, Grand Master of the Order, still lived, a memorable incident occurred which has awed the succeeding generations.[3] There was on the Isle of Rhodes, not far from the Church of Saint Stephen, a large cliff in which there was an extensive underground cavern with a stream trickling forth. In this cavern a dragon had made its nest; it was a horrid monster indeed, huge and terrifying to look upon. Not only had it preyed upon men and beast in great numbers alike all over the eastern part of the island with unspeakable savagery and rapaciousness, but it was corrupting the very air with its virulent breath. For this reason, no one was able without obvious danger to his life to approach the entrance to the dragon's lair. The Grand Master instituted by public proclamation a ban on the attempt of anyone, whatever their condition or status, to go near the place. The prohibition applied even to knights, who risked death or the revocation of their knightly status should they defy it. From this a well-deserved name had remained for the place: Malpasso.[4] There was at that time a knight living in Rhodes, who was a most noble youth endowed with great strength both of spirit and body. His name was Francisco Deodato of Gozon, for he had been born at Gascony. He deemed it a disgrace that no one, even from so many courageous soldiers and knights which lived nearby, had dared to oppose the monster. Prompted not only by a desire to do a great deed, but also by an infatuation with acquiring an immortal name for himself, the young knight perceived that there never had been a more suitable occasion to rid his homeland of the reputation for cowardice that it was acquiring by reason of its submission to the monstrous beast. And so, he set out to provoke a heretofore unheard-of battle with this horrifying, raging monster, from whose multitude of oppressive evils he would liberate the island. He considered this undertaking with such single-mindedness that he seemed unable to sleep either day or night; until, at last, he figured out how to put his plan into action. What concerned him most was how he could achieve his intentions without anyone noticing or guessing what was in his thoughts, for he greatly feared the capital punishment of the Grand Master's edict. And so, he went about it in this way: first, from the vantage point of a hidden spot, he observed the form and nature of the monster's body, and the colors of its hide.

And this was the form of the dragon. It had a head shaped like that of a large horse, but it was wide like a cow's head.

The head was scaled like a snake's and it was situated at the end of a long neck. It was known to have elongated ears like those of a mule. Its horrific gaping mouth was outfitted with massive teeth; it had oversized eyes, breath which burned like fire, and four feet with claws like those of a bear. Its tail and other hind parts were similar to those of a crocodile. The entire body was well-protected by an extremely tough hide of overlapping scales; it had two membranous wings; and its long sides were in color similar to that of dolphin fins: it was blue on its back, and its underside was a golden-yellow, while the remainder of the body was tinted with a mixture of these two colors. It behaved in a frenzied and excited manner, so much so that no horse could equal its speed, however fast it went in its attempt to outrun it. The monster seemed partly to fly and partly to go about on its feet. As it went about in search of food, its scaly hide gave off a rattling noise and the monster itself emitted an awful hiss that could be heard for miles around. By this alone, it could cause one to faint or even to die outright from sheer terror.

Once he had observed the dragon, the young knight immediately sought permission from the Grand Master to go out into the countryside, using the excuse of the necessity of taking care of household affairs. Without delay, he began to construct a model of the dragon from paper and hemp-cloth, equal in size and form to the real dragon and having the same variety and arrangement of pigmentation. He also bought a horse bred specifically for battle and likewise two very powerful mastiffs. He then ordered his servants to put on the model of the dragon and to move its limbs from the inside. Thus the dragon model was able to move forward, open its horrid mouth by the use of ropes, and flick its tail this way and that. This marvelous spectacle in the likeness of the living dragon was complete, moreover, with flapping wings. Deodato goaded both his horse and his dogs against the dragon with a simulated attack. And after he had engaged in this exercise for six months, the horse and the dogs were prepared for any effort and gripped by such a fierce desire for combat that they were scarcely able to be restrained, once they had caught sight of the dragon model. Now certain of a successful outcome to his dragon-battle, Deodato ended the shadow-fighting and without further delay made haste to Rhodes with his horse, servants, and dogs.

As soon as he had arrived at Rhodes, Deodato, recognizing that he must put his designs into effect as soon as possible, arrayed himself in a suit of armor of the better kind and armed himself with a stout lance and a sword most suitable for battle. He commended himself to God, to Saint Stephen, and to John the Baptist at the Church of Saint Stephen's, not far from the dragon's lair. Having done so, he went forward to the cave of the deadly monster. He made sure that his servants were armed and admonished them to climb a cliff nearby in order to observe the fight. This was so that, should the outcome be that he lived and the dragon was killed, they could run to his aid with the medicines he had already prepared for them; or, if he was killed and the dragon was still alive, they could flee for their lives by a pre-appointed route. Once he had given them these instructions, Deodato went before the dragon's cave with courageous resolve. And just as it seemed that nothing might happen, the ferocious monster came at him from the depths of its lair, its wild shrieking, horrid hissing, and the rattling of its scales all unnerving the horse. Deodato went forward to a level spot suitable for fighting to await the monster's charge. The dragon, thinking that it had espied easy prey, at last charged, half-flying, half-running. The dogs and the horse, not at all fearing the sight of their opponent, attacked in the manner in which they had been for so long accustomed and trained. The knight, brandishing his lance, charged and with great strength impaled the tough, scaly hide of the dragon. He then withdrew his weapon from where he had lodged it and the dragon was thus deprived of the sense of safety imparted by its hard outer armor. It was marvelous to behold! The dogs tormented the beast by chewing off its genitals, and because the dragon was occupied with defending itself against the dogs, it was forced to desist from fighting the knight. The knight was still armed with his sword and shield, and believed it to be easier at this point to fight on foot. The monster turned toward him and stood on its hind feet. While standing up, it attacked with its forepaws, using its right paw to assail the knight with its fearsome claws, and its left his shield. The knight then discerned the softer part of the dragon's neck and drove his sword into it. An enormous outpouring of blood flowed forth. With the dragon thus vexed by pain and driven into a blind rage, the knight moved himself close enough to his opponent to drive his sword all the way through its entrails, until the thrashing motions of the dragon caused the hard blade to open its underside up all the way to its throat. Once this had happened, the monster, weakened by the huge loss of blood, threw its entire mass upon the knight as it fell. The knight, now exhausted by his labors in the terrible struggle and poisoned, moreover, by a massive dose of the hellish toxin that the beast had exhaled from its open body, was now rendered nearly lifeless. The servants saw this and recalled the orders he had given. They came down from the cliff at once and flew to his aid. Dragging Deodato away from the beast, they discerned some faint signs of life in him. They then brought cold water from a nearby stream in buckets and poured it continually over his entire body until he began to revive and his heart began to beat once more.

When Deodato felt that his powers had returned to him, he straightaway mounted his horse and returned to the city. He told the story of the deed and how he had accomplished his glorious victory exactly as it had happened to the Grand Master. And while he was hoping for great glory and payment for a deed which was of such goodly benefit to the public, however illegal it may have been, he instead was forced to endure the opposite kind of reward. The Grand Master convened a council and by public censure had the knight cast into the most miserable prison for his insolence and presumptuous audacity in violating the inalterable edict. This, the Grand Master reasoned, would make a public example to knights in general. But when the news of the dragon's demise spread throughout the island, the stout-hearted determination of the knight elicited nothing but applause. And from an island now liberated from the dire calamity with which the unvanquished monster had afflicted it, great gratitude now arose. The island resounded with praises for the knight, which at last induced a consideration of his merits and led to his freedom and the restoration of his title. Not only that, he was subsequently promoted to the highest grades of the worthy Order of the Masters. Since he had been promoted to that level by virtue of his own prudence, he published accounts of his undertaking, showing the excellence of his judgment. As a result, he was eventually chosen as the successor of the Grand Master by a unanimous election, once Elion of Villanova had retired. Even today these laudatory inscriptions can be publicly seen, which were written by Jerome of Meggisero, whose pictorial rendering bore witness to the event: "Sir Deodato of Gozon, Slayer of the Dragon, Master of Province III. The Dragon was slain before He acted as Magistrate." The other, also inscribed under the same depiction, reads: "Sir Francisco Deodato of Gozon: here he valiantly slew a dreadful serpent of great size, which was devouring the inhabitants of Rhodes. Thereafter, he was elected Master in the year of Our Lord 1349."

And because those who scoff will require more than one factual account to be convinced, I shall here add others no less worthy of amazement . . . We corresponded with the worthy gentleman Christopher Schorer, prefect of Lucerne, in order to confirm the veracity of these accounts. He affirmed that not only were these things entirely true according to reports that he had received, but he had seen with his own eyes the truth of the matter: "During the year 1619, as I was contemplating the serenity of the night sky, to my great astonishment I saw a brightly glowing dragon fly from a large mountain cliff (which is commonly called Mount Pilatus) to another cave on the opposite cliffside (commonly called the Flue Cave) with a swift flapping of its wings.[5] Its body was quite large; it had a long tail and an extended neck, while its head displayed the toothsome mouth of a snake. As the creature was in the midst of flight, it spewed out sparks from its body, not unlike the embers which fly when smiths beat glowing iron. It was after I had observed all of the details that I knew it rightly to be a dragon from its bodily motions, by which I could discern the arrangement of its limbs. I write this to Your Reverence, lest you doubt that dragons truly exist in Nature." This same gentleman also wrote to us as we were still writing this work and his letters stated that he had found "something similar concerning a certain local hunter by the name of Paul Schumperlin. In 1654, around the time of the Feast of Saint James, Paul Schumperlin was hunting around the base of Mount Flue, where he ran into a dragon next to the mouth of a cave in which it was making its lair. It had a snake-like head, a neck and tail of equal length, and it walked on all fours about a foot or more off of the ground. Its entire body was covered with scales, and it was mottled with both grey and whitish-yellow spots. The formation of its head was not dissimilar to that of a horse. When it caught sight of the hunter, it retreated into its cave with a great rattling of its scales. In 1602, a skeleton of a dragon was found in another mountain cave, commonly called Mountain Staffelwand, near Mount Flue. It had been killed when the cave collapsed during an earthquake." These things were related to us by correspondence with the aforementioned gentleman Christopher Schorer.

Here I shall now add another account . . . I would hardly have believed it, had I not been persuaded of its truth by so many personal testimonies and indeed by the surviving public devotion in the Church of Saint Leodegar at Lucerne, which serves as a witness to the affair. The events occurred as follows. There was a man named Victor living in the Swiss city of Lucerne. One day, while he was looking for material to make traps in remote areas of the Alpine forests and hills, he became hopelessly lost in the labyrinthine pathways of the trackless wilderness. He did not know how he might find his way back and he wandered in all directions for the greater part of

the night. He made his way in the semi-somnolent state induced by pure exhaustion. Because of the lack of light, he did
not see the mouth of a pit gaping before him and so he fell
right into it. But because of the soft mud which had accumulated at the bottom of the pit, he suffered no injury. His mind,
however, was torn by anxiety born of the certainty of his imminent destruction. For when he looked up, he saw that the
depth of the pit was such that it would be impossible for him
to climb out of it (the pit was circular in shape, and its walls
were sheer all the way around). Despairing of ever being rescued, Victor turned his entire mind toward seeking divine assistance, soliciting both God and His mother with continual
prayers and petitions, that they might free him from so miserable a situation. Yet it pleased His Divine Majesty to afflict
him further, in order that he could accumulate merits. In the
sides of the pit were passageways of substantial length and
width. Victor entered one, hoping to find a comfortable resting place, when to his horror he found his way blocked by
two hideous dragons. Frightened half out of his wits, he attempted to retreat to the muddy pit, pleading all the while in
the midst of a great outpouring of tears that God and His
mother defend him against such terrifying monsters. But the
dragons, wrapping their tails and long necks around him, did
him neither harm nor violence. It would be easier to imagine
just what despair this man experienced, being in the company
of such frightful and bizarre creatures, than it would be to describe it. You would have seen the prophet Daniel all over
again, except that he was in a pit of dragons rather than
lions.[6] But Victor remained there, not for one day or even for
a week, but for six whole months, from the sixth of November all the way to the tenth of April. And how do you suppose
that he was able to eat during this time? Listen, and be astounded. He observed that the dragons ate no other food
throughout the winter season except a salty liquid dripping
from the walls of the pit. And so, inasmuch as he was bereft
of everything necessary to survive, he followed the example
of the dragons. He set about licking and lapping up the liquid himself, and thus revived by this sort of food, he was able

to live for half a year. At the equinox, when he felt the air to grow a little warmer, the monsters also seemed to feel that the time was at hand for them to come out of their underground lairs to look for food.[7] One of them swiftly flew upward from the muddy pit ahead of the other with a great flapping of his wings; and when the second dragon began the same ascent, Victor, seeing that this was his best chance for freedom, seized the tail of the beast and was carried away from the pit. Never was there a more marvelous sight! And once the dragons had set him down, he found, by the providence of God, a path back to Lucerne. When he came to his family, who had believed him long dead, they were utterly speechless at the account he gave of what had happened to him. It was, they decided, the most frightening experience imaginable. And because he had obtained his liberation from so horrendous a situation by the intercession of the Great Mother of God, Victor wished there to be a testament to his ordeal. And so he ordered that, as a witness to the matter for the wonder of future generations, the story of his experience be depicted by the art of needlework on a newly sewn article of priestly garb called a chasuble. It survives to this day in the Church of Saint Leodegar at Lucerne, where it is shown to foreigners. Victor himself was taken into the bosom of God for he was no longer able to take ordinary food because of the damage done to his stomach and two months after he had escaped from the pit of the dragons, he died piously in the Lord.

Many things contained in this history far exceed the powers of nature, for which reason it must be admitted that Victor's life was maintained supernaturally in so horrific an abyss. Anyone can easily surmise from this account and from others like it that the descriptions of winged dragons among various writers are accurate. And now, so that the reader's curiosity does not go unsatisfied, we shall explain the origin of dragons, and how they come into being.

How and in what kind of environment dragons come into being is a matter of no small wonder. And since no written account has yet been found that provides a treatment of this subject, we have set about here to explain the means of dragon reproduction to the extent that our relative ignorance permits.

All doctors and physiologists know that hybrid species of animals are engendered by a mixture of more than one kind of sperm. This is the case in animal species, whose representatives are complete organisms in and of themselves, such as mules, mountain antelopes, cameleopards, and other hybrid species. This also occurs in human fetuses formed from more than one kind of sperm in the womb of either a wild beast or a human female. Many examples of these monsters, such as the anthropomorphs in the accounts of Lycostenis, have been documented.[8] This process most especially occurs among insects, whose remarkable metamorphoses have been sufficiently described. A good example is the bee, which is born from cattle manure. It is undeniable upon close examination that the bee's head replicates exactly that of a cow. This is also the case for the horned head of the scarab beetle, whose head is not at all dissimilar to that of the horse from whose manure they are born. And then there is the stag beetle, which is sometimes called a goat-deer (*Tragelaphus*) because of its resemblance to the horned stag, whose manure engenders it. In fact, the feces of animals invariably generate some kind of insect showing a resemblance to the very animal in whose excrement they have been born. If the insect does not resemble the animal in its entirety, it at least resembles it in some anatomical detail. We have described this in greater detail elsewhere. And now that we have given this preliminary explanation, we shall say in a few words how dragons can come into being in remote mountain caves and in desert places.

It is a known fact that those places in which dragons are generally observed are also the haunt of eagles, vultures, and other birds of prey. Large vultures are known to nest in remote cliffs and escarpments in the Alps, so there is no need to describe their habits in detail here . . . The Isle of Rhodes abounds in formidable eagles. These birds customarily make off with all kinds of prey, such as snakes, birds, rabbits, and lambs. They even seize children and take them to their mountain fastnesses to serve as food. Many have borne witness to the fact that in the eagles' nests the prey are gradually accumulated into a heap from the continual hunting by which the eagles ensure that their food supply remains inexhaustible. The heap inevitably becomes a mass of decaying matter suitable for generating other forms of life. Inasmuch as some portion of the sperm stays in the corpse after death, it so happens that an animal can come into being in the deposited mass of fermenting matter. This occurs as a result of the confluence of various kinds of sperm. From the sperm that remains in the corpse of a quadruped, a worm is generated that resembles a quadruped. If the quadruped is a rabbit, the worm acquires elongated ears from the co-radiating force of the rabbit sperm. When the sperm of a flying animal is also present in a mass of decaying matter, it joins with the other sperm to produce a worm which, if it is not altogether winged, has at least membranes made of cartilage suitable for wings. In this way also, if snake corpses are present, their sperm imparts the head, tail, and neck of a snake to the nascent worm. The resulting serpent-hybrid embryo, once it has been formed from the variety of spermatozoa, increases in mass over time until it grows into a dragon of considerable size. If many dragons of both sexes come into being through generation in a mass of decaying matter, they are also able to reproduce sexually, as are insects which come into being in this way. And should the fecundity of such a noxious animal result in too much damage to the environment, Nature provides an excellent law by which only one dragon at a time can be generated by the mixture of spermatozoa in an underground cavern.

Another question is why dragons seem to breathe fire. The answer is that because of a certain viscous matter, they have an inborn glowing light, such as some fish, rotting wood and glow-worms have, which shines forth most brightly in darkness. And so when people see dragons glittering with light, they think that they have fiery bodies. You might ask how they acquire their extremely tough armor of scales. This is because of the same arrangement of matter by which shelled animals are covered, as well as by the moisture of a viscous and adhesive mucous that covers their outer surface all the way around and gradually degenerates into a durable, horn-like substance.

THE LAST AMERICAN DRAGONS

In the premodern world, dragons were a global phenomenon. Attested in every environment from the frigid north to the sweltering south, these monsters inspired epic stories of heroism and strange tales of peril throughout Europe, Scandinavia, and North Africa, and across the vast expanses of Asia. They were, however, a late arrival in the Americas. To be sure, the ancient cultures of Mesoamerica worshipped a supernatural feathered serpent known to the Aztecs as Quetzalcoatl, who combined the physical characteristics of a bird and a rattlesnake. Central to the pantheon of Mesoamerican religions, Quetzalcoatl was the god of rain and winds who created the world and humankind, but this deity bore only a superficial resemblance to the dragons of the ancient cultures of Europe and Asia. Even so, for a small window of time at the dawn of modernity, the Americas boasted their very own dragons. Toward the end of the nineteenth century, people living and working in remote corners of the western United States reported harrowing encounters with these large winged reptiles. Local newspapers printed breathless accounts of these episodes for a few short decades before the encroachment of human settlements and the development of modern technologies drove the American dragon into the realm of myth and fantasy.

(A) A MONSTER OF THE AIR [1]

Thomas Campbell and Joseph Howard, two wood-choppers working in the timber five miles northeast of Hurleton,

California, inform us by letter of a singular creature they saw flying through the air last Friday afternoon. They write: "About four o'clock Friday afternoon last, while at work, we were startled by the sound of many wings flapping in the air. Looking up, we perceived passing over our heads, not more than forty feet above the tree-tops, a creature that looked something like a crocodile. It was, to the best of our judgment, not less than eighteen feet in length, and would measure two feet across the body, from the head to the tail a distance of probably twelve feet. The tail was about twelve feet long and tapered from the body to a point probably eight inches wide. The head was in the neighborhood of two feet in length and the jaws (for its mouth was open) could not have been less than sixteen inches long. On each side of the body, between the head and the tail, were six wings, each projecting between eighteen inches and two feet from the body. As near as we could see, these wings were about fifteen inches broad, and appeared to be formed similar to a duck's foot. On the under side of the body we counted twelve feet, six on a side." Mr. Howard fired one barrel of a shotgun at the monster, and writes: "It uttered a cry similar to that of a calf and bear combined, but gave no sign of being inconvenienced or injured. In fact, when the shot struck, we heard the bullets rattle as though striking against a thin piece of sheet iron. The object was also seen by a number of Chinamen working near us, who were badly frightened and fled to their cabins." This is the first time we have ever heard of such a creature as this; but our informants are reliable men, hence we cannot doubt their statements.—*Gridley (Cal.) Herald*.

(B) AN ENCOUNTER IN THE DESERT[2]

A Strange Winged Monster Discovered and Killed on the Huachuca Desert

A winged monster, resembling a huge alligator with an extremely elongated tail and an immense pair of wings, was found in the desert between the Whetstone and Huachuca mountains last Sunday by two ranchers who were returning home from the Huachucas. The creature was evidently greatly exhausted by a long flight and when discovered was able to fly but a short distance at a time. After the first shock of wild amazement had passed, the two men, who were on horseback and armed with Winchester rifles, regained sufficient courage to pursue the monster and after an exciting chase of several miles succeeded in getting near enough to open fire with their rifles and wounding it. The creature then turned on the men, but owing to its exhausted condition they were able to keep out of its way and after a few well directed shots the monster partly rolled over and remained motionless. The men cautiously approached, their horses snorting with terror, and found that the creature was dead. They then proceeded to make an examination and found that it measured about ninety-two feet in length and the greatest diameter was about fifty inches. The monster had only two feet, these being situated a short distance in front of where the wings were joined to the body. The head, as near as they could judge, was eight feet long, the jaws being thickly set with strong, sharp teeth. Its eyes were as large as a dinner plate and protruded about half way from the head. They had some difficulty in measuring the wings as they were partly folded under the body, but finally got one straightened out sufficiently to get a measurement of seventy-eight feet, making the total length from tip to tip about 160 feet. The wings were composed of a thick and nearly transparent membrane and were devoid of feathers or hair, as was the entire body. The skin of the body was comparatively smooth and easily penetrated by a bullet. The men cut off a small portion of the tip of one wing and took it home with them. Late last night one of them arrived in this city for supplies and to make the necessary preparations to skin the creature, when the hide will be sent east for examination by the eminent scientists of the day. The finder returned early this morning accompanied by several prominent men who will endeavor to bring the strange creature to this city before it is mutilated.

TERROR TAMED

Domesticated Drakes in
Children's Literature

The nineteenth century witnessed a revival of interest in the European Middle Ages and with it a renewed enthusiasm for dragons. This appeal found expression in children's stories about saints and heroes that depicted dragons with time-honored attributes like great wings, lashing tails, and fiery breath. At the turn of the twentieth century, however, two authors of stories for young readers—Kenneth Grahame and Edith Nesbit—subverted the traditional depiction of medieval dragons by presenting them as misunderstood creatures unhappy with their lot as villains and eager to befriend human beings. By providing a model for the representation of dragons as allies rather than enemies, their short stories paved the way for many classic works featuring a productive partnership and mutual understanding between humans and dragons in modern fantasy literature, including Ruth Stiles Gannett's My Father's Dragon *(1948), Anne McCaffrey's Dragonriders of Pern novels (1967–present), the twelve books of Cressida Cowell's* How to Train Your Dragon *series (2003–15), and Christopher Paolini's* The Inheritance Cycle *(2003–11), among many others. Pete Yarrow's popular song "Puff the Magic Dragon" (1963), about a young boy who leaves behind a friendly dragon when he loses his innocence, is another expression of this motif. Even the deployment of dragons as weapons of warfare in George R. R. Martin's* A Song of Ice and Fire *series (1996–present) owes no small debt to the gentle giants of these path-breaking stories.*

A LIZARDY
SORT OF BEAST[1]

In 1898, a decade before he achieved fame for his book The Wind in the Willows, *British author Kenneth Grahame (1859–1932) overturned a centuries-old tradition about the depiction of dragons in western literature in a short story for children called "The Reluctant Dragon." In this charming tale, two children in pursuit of an imaginary monster hear a story about a young boy in the distant past who encountered a dragon near his home on the Berkshire Downs in Oxfordshire. Despite its intimidating appearance, this creature did not behave like an ordinary dragon, for it had no interest in hoarding treasure or terrorizing the local communities. Instead, this contemplative creature was "a happy Bohemian [who] lolled on the turf, enjoyed the sunsets [and] told antediluvian anecdotes." Even so, as the boy warned, although it had done no harm, the local townsfolk judged the dragon by his appearance and summoned St. George to vanquish it. The dragon and his boy soon convinced the saint that the monster posed no threat. After defeating his scaly opponent in staged combat, St. George declared that it intended no harm to anyone and the dragon lived ever afterward in peace with its human neighbors.*

Footprints in the snow have been unfailing provokers of sentiment ever since snow was first a white wonder in this drab-coloured world of ours. In a poetry-book presented to one of us by an aunt, there was a poem by one Wordsworth in which they stood out strongly with a picture all to themselves, too—but we didn't think very highly either of the poem or the sentiment. Footprints in the sand, now, were quite another matter, and we grasped Crusoe's attitude of mind much more easily than Wordsworth's. Excitement and mystery, curiosity and suspense—these were the only sentiments that tracks, whether in sand or in snow, were able to arouse in us.

We had awakened early that winter morning, puzzled at first by the added light that filled the room. Then, when the truth at last fully dawned on us and we knew that snowballing was no longer a wistful dream, but a solid certainty waiting for us outside, it was a mere brute fight for the necessary clothes, and the lacing of boots seemed a clumsy invention, and the buttoning of coats an unduly tedious form of fastening, with all that snow going to waste at our very door.

When dinner-time came we had to be dragged in by the scruff of our necks. The short armistice over, the combat was resumed; but presently Charlotte and I, a little weary of contests and of missiles that ran shudderingly down inside one's clothes, forsook the trampled battle-field of the lawn and went exploring the blank virgin spaces of the white world that lay beyond. It stretched away unbroken on every side of us, this mysterious soft garment under which our familiar world had so suddenly hidden itself. Faint imprints showed where a casual bird had alighted, but of other traffic there was next to no sign; which made these strange tracks all the more puzzling.

We came across them first at the corner of the shrubbery, and pored over them long, our hands on our knees. Experienced trappers that we knew ourselves to be, it was annoying to be brought up suddenly by a beast we could not at once identify.

"Don't you know?" said Charlotte, rather scornfully. "Thought you knew all the beasts that ever was."

This put me on my mettle, and I hastily rattled off a string of animal names embracing both the arctic and the tropic zones, but without much real confidence.

"No," said Charlotte, on consideration; "they won't any of 'em quite do. Seems like something lizardy. Did you say an iguanodon? Might be that, p'raps. But that's not British, and we want a real British beast. I think it's a dragon!"

"'T isn't half big enough," I objected.

"Well, all dragons must be small to begin with," said Charlotte, "like everything else. P'raps this is a little dragon wh's got lost. A little dragon would be rather nice to have. He might scratch and spit, but he couldn't do anything really. Let's track him down!"

So we set off into the wide snow-clad world, hand in hand, our hearts big with expectation—complacently confident that by a few smudgy traces in the snow we were in a fair way to capture a half-grown specimen of a fabulous beast.

We ran the monster across the paddock and along the hedge of the next field, and then he took to the road like any tame civilized tax-payer. Here his tracks became blended with and lost among more ordinary footprints, but imagination and a fixed idea will do a great deal, and we were sure we knew the direction a dragon would naturally take. The traces, too, kept reappearing at intervals—at least Charlotte maintained they did, and as it was her dragon I left the following of the slot to her and trotted along peacefully, feeling that it was an expedition anyhow and something was sure to come out of it.

Charlotte took me across another field or two, and through a copse, and into a fresh road; and I began to feel sure it was only her confounded pride that made her go on pretending to see dragon-tracks instead of owning she was entirely at fault, like a reasonable person. At last she dragged me excitedly through a gap in a hedge of an obviously private character; the waste, open world of field and hedge row disappeared, and we found ourselves in a garden, well-kept, secluded, most undragon-haunted in appearance. Once inside, I knew where we were.

This was the garden of my friend the circus-man, though I had never approached it before by a lawless gap, from this unfamiliar side. And here was the circus-man himself, placidly smoking a pipe as he strolled up and down the walks. I stepped up to him and asked him politely if he had lately seen a Beast.

"May I inquire," he said, with all civility, "what particular sort of a Beast you may happen to be looking for?"

"It's a lizardy sort of Beast," I explained. "Charlotte says it's a dragon, but she doesn't really know much about beasts."

The circus-man looked round about him slowly. "I don't think," he said, "that I've seen a dragon in these parts recently. But if I come across one I'll know it belongs to you, and I'll have him taken round to you at once."

"Thank you very much," said Charlotte, "but don't trouble about it, please, 'cos p'raps it isn't a dragon after all. Only I thought I saw his little footprints in the snow, and we followed 'em up, and they seemed to lead right in here, but maybe it's all a mistake, and thank you all the same."

"Oh, no trouble at all," said the circus-man, cheerfully. "I should be only too pleased. But of course, as you say, it may be a mistake. And it's getting dark, and he seems to have got away for the present, whatever he is. You'd better come in and have some tea. I'm quite alone, and we'll make a roaring fire, and I've got the biggest Book of Beasts you ever saw. It's got every beast in the world, and all of 'em coloured; and we'll try and find your beast in it!"

We were always ready for tea at any time, and especially when combined with beasts. There was marmalade, too, and apricot-jam, brought in expressly for us; and afterwards the beast-book was spread out, and, as the man had truly said, it contained every sort of beast that had ever been in the world.

The striking of six o'clock set the more prudent Charlotte nudging me, and we recalled ourselves with an effort from Beastland, and reluctantly stood up to go.

"Here, I'm coming along with you," said the circus-man. "I want another pipe, and a walk'll do me good. You needn't talk to me unless you like."

Our spirits rose to their wonted level again. The way had seemed so long, the outside world so dark and eerie, after the bright warm room and the highly-coloured beast-book. But a walk with a real Man—why, that was a treat in itself! We set off briskly, the Man in the middle. I looked up at him and wondered whether I should ever live to smoke a big pipe with that careless sort of majesty! But Charlotte, whose young mind was not set on tobacco as a possible goal, made herself heard from the other side.

"Now, then," she said, "tell us a story, please, won't you?"

The Man sighed heavily and looked about him. "I knew it," he groaned. "I knew I should have to tell a story. Oh, why did I leave my pleasant fireside? Well, I will tell you a story. Only let me think a minute."

So he thought a minute, and then he told us this story.

Long ago—might have been hundreds of years ago—in a cottage half-way between this village and yonder shoulder of the Downs up there, a shepherd lived with his wife and their little son. Now the shepherd spent his days—and at certain times of the year his nights too—up on the wide ocean-bosom of the Downs, with only the sun and the stars and the sheep for company, and the friendly chattering world of men and women far out of sight and hearing. But his little son, when he wasn't helping his father, and often when he was as well, spent much of his time buried in big volumes that he borrowed from the affable gentry and interested parsons of the country round about. And his parents were very fond of him, and rather proud of him too, though they didn't let on in his hearing, so he was left to go his own way and read as much as he liked; and instead of frequently getting a cuff on the side of the head, as might very well have happened to him, he was treated more or less as an equal by his parents, who sensibly thought it a very fair division of labour that they should supply the practical knowledge, and he the book-learning. They knew that book-learning often came in useful at a pinch, in spite of what their neighbours said. What the Boy chiefly dabbled in was natural history and fairy-tales, and he just took them as they came, in a sandwichy sort of way, without making any distinctions; and really his course of reading strikes one as rather sensible.

One evening the shepherd, who for some nights past had been disturbed and preoccupied, and off his usual mental balance, came home all of a tremble, and, sitting down at the table where his wife and son were peacefully employed, she with her seam, he in following out the adventures of the Giant with no Heart in his Body, exclaimed with much agitation:

"It's all up with me, Maria! Never no more can I go up on them there Downs, was it ever so!"

"Now don't you take on like that," said his wife, who was a very sensible woman, "but tell us all about it first, whatever it is as has given you this shake-up, and then me and you and the son here, between us, we ought to be able to get to the bottom of it!"

"It began some nights ago," said the shepherd. "You know that cave up there—I never liked it, somehow, and the sheep never liked it neither, and when sheep don't like a thing there's generally some reason for it. Well, for some time past there's been faint noises coming from that Cave—noises like heavy sighings, with grunts mixed up in them; and sometimes a snoring, far away down—real snoring, yet somehow not honest snoring, like you and me o'nights, you know!"

"I know," remarked the Boy, quietly.

"Of course I was terrible frightened," the shepherd went on, "yet somehow I couldn't keep away. So this very evening, before I come down, I took a cast round by the cave, quietly. And there—O Lord! There I saw him at last, as plain as I see you!"

"Saw who?" said his wife, beginning to share in her husband's nervous terror.

"Why him, I'm a telling you!" said the shepherd. "He was sticking half-way out of the cave, and seemed to be enjoying of the cool of the evening in a poetical sort of way. He was as big as four cart-horses, and all covered with shiny scales—deep-blue scales at the top of him, shading off to a tender sort o' green below. As he breathed, there was that sort of flicker over his nostrils that you see over our chalk roads on a baking windless day in summer. He had his chin on his paws, and I should say he was meditating about things. Oh, yes, a peaceable sort o' beast enough, and not ramping or carrying on or doing anything but what was quite right and proper. I admit all that. And yet, what am I to do? Scales, you know, and claws, and a tail for certain, though I didn't see that end of him—I ain't used to 'em, and I don't hold with 'em, and that's a fact!"

The Boy, who had apparently been absorbed in his book during his father's recital, now closed the volume, yawned, clasped his hands behind his head, and said sleepily: "It's all right, father. Don't you worry. It's only a dragon."

"Only a dragon?" cried his father. "What do you mean, sitting there, you and your dragons? Only a dragon indeed! And what do you know about it?"

"'Cos it is, and 'cos I do know," replied the Boy, quietly. "Look here, father, you know we've each of us got our line. You know about sheep, and weather, and things; I know about dragons. I always said, you know, that that cave up there was a dragon-cave. I always said it must have belonged to a dragon some time, and ought to belong to a dragon now, if rules count for anything. Well, now you tell me it has got a dragon, and so that's all right. I'm not half as much surprised as when you told me it hadn't got a dragon. Rules always come right if you wait quietly. Now, please, just leave this all to me. And I'll stroll up to-morrow morning—no, in the morning I can't, I've got a whole heap of things to do—well, perhaps in the evening, if I'm quite free, I'll go up and have a talk to him, and you'll find it'll be all right. Only, please, don't you go worrying round there without me. You don't understand 'em a bit, and they're very sensitive, you know!"

"He's quite right, father," said the sensible mother. "As he says, dragons is his line and not ours. He's wonderful knowing about book-beasts, as every one allows. And to tell the truth, I'm not half happy in my own mind, thinking of that poor animal lying alone up there, without a bit o' hot supper or anyone to change the news with; and maybe we'll be able to do something for him; and if he ain't quite respectable our Boy'll find it out quick enough. He's got a pleasant sort o' way with him that makes everybody tell him everything."

Next day, after he'd had his tea, the Boy strolled up the

chalky track that led to the summit of the Downs; and there, sure enough, he found the dragon, stretched lazily on the sward in front of his cave. The view from that point was a magnificent one. To the right and left, the bare and billowy leagues of Downs; in front, the vale, with its clustered homesteads, its threads of white roads running through orchards and well-tilled acreage, and, far away, a hint of grey old cities on the horizon. A cool breeze played over the surface of the grass and the silver shoulder of a large moon was showing above distant junipers. No wonder the dragon seemed in a peaceful and contented mood; indeed, as the Boy approached he could hear the beast purring with a happy regularity. "Well, we live and learn!" he said to himself. "None of my books ever told me that dragons purred!"

"Hullo, dragon!" said the Boy, quietly, when he had got up to him.

The dragon, on hearing the approaching footsteps, made the beginning of a courteous effort to rise. But when he saw it was a Boy, he set his eyebrows severely.

"Now don't you hit me," he said; "or bung stones, or squirt water, or anything. I won't have it, I tell you!"

"Not goin' to hit you," said the Boy wearily, dropping on the grass beside the beast, "and don't, for goodness' sake, keep on saying 'Don't'; I hear so much of it, and it's monotonous, and makes me tired. I've simply looked in to ask you how you were and all that sort of thing; but if I'm in the way I can easily clear out. I've lots of friends, and no one can say I'm in the habit of shoving myself in where I'm not wanted!"

"No, no, don't go off in a huff," said the dragon, hastily, "fact is—I'm as happy up here as the day's long; never without an occupation, dear fellow, never without an occupation! And yet, between ourselves, it is a trifle dull at times."

The Boy bit off a stalk of grass and chewed it. "Going to make a long stay here?" he asked, politely.

"Can't hardly say at present," replied the dragon. "It seems a nice place enough—but I've only been here a short time, and one must look about and reflect and consider before settling down. It's rather a serious thing, settling down. Besides—now

I'm going to tell you something! You'd never guess it if you tried ever so!—fact is, I'm such a confoundedly lazy beggar!"

"You surprise me," said the Boy, civilly.

"It's the sad truth," the dragon went on, settling down between his paws and evidently delighted to have found a listener at last, "and I fancy that's really how I came to be here. You see all the other fellows were so active and earnest and all that sort of thing—always rampaging, and skirmishing, and scouring the desert sands, and pacing the margin of the sea, and chasing knights all over the place, and devouring damsels, and going on generally—whereas I liked to get my meals regular and then to prop my back against a bit of rock and snooze a bit, and wake up and think of things going on and how they kept going on just the same, you know! So when it happened I got fairly caught."

"When what happened, please?" asked the Boy.

"That's just what I don't precisely know," said the dragon. "I suppose the earth sneezed, or shook itself, or the bottom dropped out of something. Anyhow there was a shake and a roar and a general stramash, and I found myself miles away underground and wedged in as tight as tight. Well, thank goodness, my wants are few, and at any rate I had peace and quietness and wasn't always being asked to come along and do something. And I've got such an active mind—always occupied, I assure you! But time went on, and there was a certain sameness about the life, and at last I began to think it would be fun to work my way upstairs and see what you other fellows were doing. So I scratched and burrowed, and worked this way and that way and at last I came out through this cave here. And I like the country, and the view, and the people—what I've seen of 'em—and on the whole I feel inclined to settle down here."

"What's your mind always occupied about?" asked the Boy. "That's what I want to know."

The dragon coloured slightly and looked away. Presently he said bashfully: "Did you ever—just for fun—try to make up poetry—verses, you know?"

"'Course I have," said the Boy. "Heaps of it. And some of

it's quite good, I feel sure, only there's no one here cares about it. Mother's very kind and all that, when I read it to her, and so's father for that matter. But somehow they don't seem to—"

"Exactly," cried the dragon, "my own case exactly. They don't seem to, and you can't argue with 'em about it. Now you've got culture, you have, I could tell it on you at once, and I should just like your candid opinion about some little things I threw off lightly, when I was down there. I'm awfully pleased to have met you, and I'm hoping the other neighbours will be equally agreeable. There was a very nice old gentleman up here only last night, but he didn't seem to want to intrude."

"That was my father," said the boy, "and he is a nice old gentleman, and I'll introduce you some day if you like."

"Can't you two come up here and dine or something to-morrow?" asked the dragon eagerly. "Only, of course, if you've got nothing better to do," he added politely.

"Thanks awfully," said the Boy, "but we don't go out anywhere without my mother, and, to tell you the truth, I'm afraid she mightn't quite approve of you. You see there's no getting over the hard fact that you're a dragon, is there? And when you talk of settling down, and the neighbours, and so on, I can't help feeling that you don't quite realize your position. You're an enemy of the human race, you see!"

"Haven't got an enemy in the world," said the dragon, cheerfully. "Too lazy to make 'em, to begin with. And if I do read other fellows my poetry, I'm always ready to listen to theirs!"

"Oh, dear!" cried the boy, "I wish you'd try and grasp the situation properly. When the other people find you out, they'll come after you with spears and swords and all sorts of things. You'll have to be exterminated, according to their way of looking at it! You're a scourge, and a pest, and a baneful monster!"

"Not a word of truth in it," said the dragon, wagging his head solemnly. "Character'll bear the strictest investigation. And now, there's a little sonnet-thing I was working on when you appeared on the scene—"

"Oh, if you won't be sensible," cried the Boy, getting up, "I'm going off home. No, I can't stop for sonnets; my mother's sitting up. I'll look you up to-morrow, sometime or other, and do for goodness' sake try and realize that you're a pestilential scourge, or you'll find yourself in a most awful fix. Good-night!"

The Boy found it an easy matter to set the mind of his parents at ease about his new friend. They had always left that branch to him, and they took his word without a murmur. The shepherd was formally introduced and many compliments and kind inquiries were exchanged. His wife, however, though expressing her willingness to do anything she could— to mend things, or set the cave to rights, or cook a little something when the dragon had been poring over sonnets and forgotten his meals, as male things will do, could not be brought to recognize him formally. The fact that he was a dragon and "they didn't know who he was" seemed to count for everything with her. She made no objection, however, to her little son spending his evenings with the dragon quietly, so long as he was home by nine o'clock, and many a pleasant night they had, sitting on the sward, while the dragon told stories of old, old times, when dragons were quite plentiful and the world was a livelier place than it is now, and life was full of thrills and jumps and surprises.

What the Boy had feared, however, soon came to pass. The most modest and retiring dragon in the world, if he's as big as four cart-horses and covered with blue scales, cannot keep altogether out of the public view. And so in the village tavern of nights the fact that a real live dragon sat brooding in the cave on the Downs was naturally a subject for talk. Though the villagers were extremely frightened, they were rather proud, as well. It was a distinction to have a dragon of your own, and it was felt to be a feather in the cap of the village. Still, all were agreed that this sort of thing couldn't be allowed to go on. The dreadful beast must be exterminated, the country-side must be freed from this pest, this terror, this destroying scourge. The fact that not even a hen-roost was the worse for the dragon's arrival wasn't allowed to have anything to do with it. He was a dragon, and he couldn't deny it, and if he didn't choose to behave as such that was his own lookout. But in spite of much valiant talk no hero was found willing to take sword and spear and free the suffering village and win deathless fame; and each night's heated discussion always ended in nothing. Meanwhile the dragon, a happy Bohemian, lolled on the turf, enjoyed the sunsets, told antediluvian anecdotes to the Boy, and polished his old verses while meditating on fresh ones.

One day the Boy, on walking in to the village, found everything wearing a festal appearance which was not to be accounted for in the calendar. Carpets and gay-coloured stuffs were hung out of the windows, the church-bells clamoured noisily, the little street was flower-strewn, and the whole population jostled each other along either side of it, chattering, shoving, and ordering each other to stand back. The Boy saw a friend of his own age in the crowd and hailed.

"What's up?" he cried. "Is it the players, or bears, or a circus, or what?"

"It's all right," his friend hailed back. "He's a-coming."

"Who's a-coming?" demanded the Boy, thrusting into the throng.

"Why, St. George, of course," replied his friend. "He's heard tell of our dragon, and he's comin' on purpose to slay the deadly beast, and free us from his horrid yoke. O my! Won't there be a jolly fight!"

Here was news indeed! The Boy felt that he ought to make quite sure for himself, and he wriggled himself in between the legs of his good-natured elders, abusing them all the time for their unmannerly habit of shoving. Once in the front rank, he breathlessly awaited the arrival.

Presently from the far-away end of the line came the sound of cheering. Next, the measured tramp of a great war-horse made his heart beat quicker, and then he found himself cheering with the rest, as, amidst welcoming shouts, shrill cries of women, uplifting of babies and waving of handkerchiefs, St. George paced slowly up the street. The Boy's heart stood still and he breathed with sobs, the beauty and the grace of the hero were so far beyond anything he had yet seen. His fluted armour was inlaid with gold, his plumed helmet hung at his saddle-bow, and his thick fair hair framed a face gracious and gentle beyond expression till you caught the sternness in his eyes. He drew rein in front of the little inn, and the villagers crowded round with greetings and thanks and voluble statements of their wrongs and grievances and oppressions. The Boy heard the grave gentle voice of the Saint, assuring them that all would be well now, and that he would stand by them and see them righted and free them from their foe; then he dismounted and passed through the doorway and the crowd poured in after him. But the Boy made off up the hill as fast as he could lay his legs to the ground.

"It's all up, dragon!" he shouted as soon as he was within sight of the beast. "He's coming! He's here now! You'll have to pull yourself together and do something at last!"

The dragon was licking his scales and rubbing them with a bit of house-flannel the Boy's mother had lent him, till he shone like a great turquoise.

"Don't be violent, Boy," he said without looking round. "Sit down and get your breath, and try and remember that the noun governs the verb, and then perhaps you'll be good enough to tell me who's coming?"

"That's right, take it coolly," said the Boy. "Hope you'll be half as cool when I've got through with my news. It's only St. George who's coming, that's all; he rode into the village half-an-hour ago. Of course you can lick him—a great big fellow like you! But I thought I'd warn you, 'cos he's sure to be round early, and he's got the longest, wickedest-looking spear you ever did see!" And the Boy got up and began to jump round in sheer delight at the prospect of the battle.

"O deary, deary me," moaned the dragon, "this is too awful. I won't see him, and that's flat. I don't want to know the fellow at all. I'm sure he's not nice. You must tell him to go away at once, please. Say he can write if he likes, but I can't give him an interview. I'm not seeing anybody at present."

"Now dragon, dragon," said the Boy imploringly, "don't be perverse and wrongheaded. You've got to fight him some time or other, you know, 'cos he's St. George and you're the dragon. Better get it over, and then we can go on with the sonnets. And you ought to consider other people a little, too. If it's been dull up here for you, think how dull it's been for me!"

"My dear little man," said the dragon solemnly, "just understand, once for all, that I can't fight and I won't fight. I've never fought in my life, and I'm not going to begin now, just to give you a Roman holiday. In old days I always let the other fellows—the earnest fellows—do all the fighting, and no doubt that's why I have the pleasure of being here now."

"But if you don't fight he'll cut your head off!" gasped the Boy, miserable at the prospect of losing both his fight and his friend.

"Oh, I think not," said the dragon in his lazy way. "You'll be able to arrange something. I've every confidence in you, you're such a manager. Just run down, there's a dear chap, and make it all right. I leave it entirely to you."

The Boy made his way back to the village in a state of great despondency. First of all, there wasn't going to be any fight; next, his dear and honoured friend the dragon hadn't shown up in quite such a heroic light as he would have liked; and lastly, whether the dragon was a hero at heart or not, it made no difference, for St. George would most undoubtedly cut his head off.

"Arrange things indeed!" he said bitterly to himself. "The dragon treats the whole affair as if it was an invitation to tea and croquet."

The villagers were straggling homewards as he passed up the street, all of them in the highest spirits, and gleefully discussing the splendid fight that was in store. The Boy pursued his way to the inn, and passed into the principal chamber, where St. George now sat alone, musing over the chances of the fight, and the sad stories of rapine and of wrong that had so lately been poured into his sympathetic ear.

"May I come in, St. George?" said the Boy politely, as he paused at the door. "I want to talk to you about this little matter of the dragon, if you're not tired of it by this time."

"Yes, come in, Boy," said the Saint kindly. "Another tale of misery and wrong, I fear me. Is it a kind parent, then, of whom the tyrant has bereft you? Or some tender sister or brother? Well, it shall soon be avenged."

"Nothing of the sort," said the Boy. "There's a misunderstanding somewhere, and I want to put it right. The fact is, this is a good dragon."

"Exactly," said St. George, smiling pleasantly, "I quite understand. A good dragon. Believe me, I do not in the least regret that he is an adversary worthy of my steel, and no feeble specimen of his noxious tribe."

"But he's not a noxious tribe," cried the Boy distressedly. "Oh dear, oh dear, how stupid men are when they get an idea into their heads! I tell you he's a good dragon, and a friend of mine, and tells me the most beautiful stories you ever heard, all about old times and when he was little. And he's been so kind to mother, and mother'd do anything for him. And father likes him too, though father doesn't hold with art and poetry much, and always falls asleep when the dragon starts talking about style. But the fact is, nobody can help liking him when once they know him. He's so engaging and so trustful, and as simple as a child!"

"Sit down, and draw your chair up," said St. George. "I like a fellow who sticks up for his friends, and I'm sure the dragon has his good points, if he's got a friend like you. But that's not the question. All this evening I've been listening, with grief and anguish unspeakable, to tales of murder, theft, and wrong; rather too highly coloured, perhaps, not always quite convincing, but forming in the main a most serious roll of crime. History teaches us that the greatest rascals often possess all the domestic virtues; and I fear that your cultivated friend, in spite of the qualities which have won (and rightly) your regard, has got to be speedily exterminated."

"Oh, you've been taking in all the yarns those fellows have been telling you," said the Boy impatiently. "Why, our villagers are the biggest story-tellers in all the country round. It's a known fact. You're a stranger in these parts, or else you'd have heard it already. All they want is a fight. They're the most awful beggars for getting up fights—it's meat and drink to them. Dogs, bulls, dragons—anything so long as it's a fight. Why, they've got a poor innocent badger in the stable behind here, at this moment. They were going to have some fun with him to-day, but they're saving him up now till your little affair's over. And I've no doubt they've been telling you what a hero you were, and how you were bound to win, in the cause of right and justice, and so on; but let me tell you, I came down the street just now, and they were betting six to four on the dragon freely!"

"Six to four on the dragon!" murmured St. George sadly, resting his cheek on his hand. "This is an evil world, and sometimes I begin to think that all the wickedness in it is not entirely bottled up inside the dragons. And yet—may not this wily beast have misled you as to his real character, in order that your good report of him may serve as a cloak for his evil deeds? Nay, may there not be, at this very moment, some hapless Princess immured within yonder gloomy cavern?"

The moment he had spoken, St. George was sorry for what he had said, the Boy looked so genuinely distressed.

"I assure you, St. George," he said earnestly, "there's nothing of the sort in the cave at all. The dragon's a real gentleman, every inch of him, and I may say that no one would be more shocked and grieved than he would, at hearing you talk in that—that loose way about matters on which he has very strong views!"

"Well, perhaps I've been over-credulous," said St. George. "Perhaps I've misjudged the animal. But what are we to do? Here are the dragon and I, almost face to face, each supposed to be thirsting for each other's blood. I don't see any way out of it, exactly. What do you suggest? Can't you arrange things, somehow?"

"That's just what the dragon said," replied the Boy, rather nettled. "Really, the way you two seem to leave everything to me—I suppose you couldn't be persuaded to go away quietly, could you?"

"Impossible, I fear," said the Saint. "Quite against the rules. You know that as well as I do."

"Well, then, look here," said the Boy, "it's early yet—would you mind strolling up with me and seeing the dragon and talking it over? It's not far, and any friend of mine will be most welcome."

"Well, it's irregular," said St. George, rising, "but really it seems about the most sensible thing to do. You're taking a lot of trouble on your friend's account," he added, good-naturedly, as they passed out through the door together. "But cheer up! Perhaps there won't have to be any fight after all."

"Oh, but I hope there will, though!" replied the little fellow, wistfully.

"I've brought a friend to see you, dragon," said the Boy, rather loud. The dragon woke up with a start. "I was just—er—thinking about things," he said in his simple way. "Very pleased to make your acquaintance, sir. Charming weather we're having!"

"This is St. George," said the Boy, shortly. "St. George, let me introduce you to the dragon. We've come up to talk things over quietly, dragon, and now for goodness' sake do let us have a little straight common-sense, and come to some practical business-like arrangement, for I'm sick of views and theories of life and personal tendencies, and all that sort of thing. I may perhaps add that my mother's sitting up."

"So glad to meet you, St. George," began the dragon rather nervously, "because you've been a great traveller, I hear, and I've always been rather a stay-at-home. But I can show you many antiquities, many interesting features of our countryside, if you're stopping here any time—"

"I think," said St. George, in his frank, pleasant way, "that we'd really better take the advice of our young friend here, and try to come to some understanding, on a business footing, about this little affair of ours. Now don't you think that after all the simplest plan would be just to fight it out, according to the rules, and let the best man win? They're betting on you, I may tell you, down in the village, but I don't mind that!"

"Oh, yes, do, dragon," said the Boy, delightedly; "it'll save such a lot of bother!"

"My young friend, you shut up," said the dragon severely. "Believe me, St. George," he went on, "there's nobody in the world I'd sooner oblige than you and this young gentleman here. But the whole thing's nonsense, and conventionality, and popular thick-headedness. There's absolutely nothing to fight about, from beginning to end. And anyhow I'm not going to, so that settles it!"

"But supposing I make you?" said St. George, rather nettled.

"You can't," said the dragon, triumphantly. "I should only go into my cave and retire for a time down the hole I came up. You'd soon get heartily sick of sitting outside and waiting for me to come out and fight you. And as soon as you'd really gone away, why, I'd come up again gaily, for I tell you frankly, I like this place, and I'm going to stay here!"

St. George gazed for a while on the fair landscape around them. "But this would be a beautiful place for a fight," he began again persuasively. "These great bare rolling Downs for the arena,—and me in my golden armour showing up against your big blue scaly coils! Think what a picture it would make!"

"Now you're trying to get at me through my artistic sensibilities," said the dragon. "But it won't work. Not but what it would make a very pretty picture, as you say," he added, wavering a little.

"We seem to be getting rather nearer to business," put in the Boy. "You must see, dragon, that there's got to be a fight of some sort, 'cos you can't want to have to go down that dirty old hole again and stop there till goodness knows when."

"It might be arranged," said St. George, thoughtfully. "I must spear you somewhere, of course, but I'm not bound to hurt you very much. There's such a lot of you that there must be a few spare places somewhere. Here, for instance, just behind your foreleg. It couldn't hurt you much, just here!"

"Now you're tickling, George," said the dragon, coyly.

"No, that place won't do at all. Even if it didn't hurt,—and I'm sure it would, awfully,—it would make me laugh, and that would spoil everything."

"Let's try somewhere else, then," said St. George, patiently. "Under your neck, for instance,—all these folds of thick skin,—if I speared you here you'd never even know I'd done it!"

"Yes, but are you sure you can hit off the right place?" asked the dragon, anxiously.

"Of course I am," said St. George, with confidence. "You leave that to me!"

"It's just because I've got to leave it to you that I'm asking," replied the dragon, rather testily. "No doubt you would deeply regret any error you might make in the hurry of the moment; but you wouldn't regret it half as much as I should! However, I suppose we've got to trust somebody, as we go through life, and your plan seems, on the whole, as good a one as any."

"Look here, dragon," interrupted the Boy, a little jealous on behalf of his friend, who seemed to be getting all the worst of the bargain: "I don't quite see where you come in! There's to be a fight, apparently, and you're to be licked; and what I want to know is, what are you going to get out of it?"

"St. George," said the dragon, "just tell him, please,—what will happen after I'm vanquished in the deadly combat?"

"Well, according to the rules I suppose I shall lead you in triumph down to the market-place or whatever answers to it," said St. George.

"Precisely," said the dragon. "And then—"

"And then there'll be shoutings and speeches and things," continued St. George. "And I shall explain that you're converted, and see the error of your ways, and so on."

"Quite so," said the dragon. "And then—?"

"Oh, and then—" said St. George, "why, and then there will be the usual banquet, I suppose."

"Exactly," said the dragon; "and that's where I come in. Look here," he continued, addressing the Boy, "I'm bored to death up here, and no one really appreciates me. I'm going into Society, I am, through the kindly aid of our friend here, who's taking such a lot of trouble on my account; and you'll find I've got all the qualities to endear me to people who entertain! So now that's all settled, and if you don't mind—I'm an old-fashioned fellow—don't want to turn you out, but—"

"Remember, you'll have to do your proper share of the fighting, dragon!" said St. George, as he took the hint and rose to go; "I mean ramping, and breathing fire, and so on!"

"I can ramp all right," replied the dragon, confidently; "as to breathing fire, it's surprising how easily one gets out of practice, but I'll do the best I can. Good-night!"

They had descended the hill and were almost back in the village again, when St. George stopped short. "Knew I had forgotten something," he said. "There ought to be a Princess. Terror-stricken and chained to a rock, and all that sort of thing. Boy, can't you arrange a Princess?"

The Boy was in the middle of a tremendous yawn. "I'm tired to death," he wailed, "and I can't arrange a Princess, or anything more, at this time of night. And my mother's sitting up, and do stop asking me to arrange more things till to-morrow!"

Next morning the people began streaming up to the Downs at quite an early hour, in their Sunday clothes and carrying baskets with bottle-necks sticking out of them, every one intent on securing good places for the combat. This was not exactly a simple matter, for of course it was quite possible that the dragon might win, and in that case even those who had put their money on him felt they could hardly expect him to deal with his backers on a different footing to the rest. Places were chosen, therefore, with circumspection and with a view to a speedy retreat in case of emergency; and the front rank was mostly composed of boys who had escaped from parental control and now sprawled and rolled about on the grass, regardless of the shrill threats and warnings discharged at them by their anxious mothers behind.

The Boy had secured a good front place, well up towards

the cave, and was feeling as anxious as a stage-manager on a first night. Could the dragon be depended upon? He might change his mind and vote the whole performance rot; or else, seeing that the affair had been so hastily planned, without even a rehearsal, he might be too nervous to show up. The Boy looked narrowly at the cave, but it showed no sign of life or occupation. Could the dragon have made a moon-light flitting?

The higher portions of the ground were now black with sightseers, and presently a sound of cheering and a waving of handkerchiefs told that something was visible to them which the Boy, far up towards the dragon-end of the line as he was, could not yet see. A minute more and St. George's red plumes topped the hill, as the Saint rode slowly forth on the great level space which stretched up to the grim mouth of the cave. Very gallant and beautiful he looked, on his tall war-horse, his golden armour glancing in the sun, his great spear held erect, the little white pennon, crimson-crossed, fluttering at its point. He drew rein and remained motionless. The lines of spectators began to give back a little, nervously; and even the boys in front stopped pulling hair and cuffing each other, and leaned forward expectant.

"Now then, dragon!" muttered the Boy impatiently, fidgeting where he sat. He need not have distressed himself, had he only known. The dramatic possibilities of the thing had tickled the dragon immensely, and he had been up from an early hour, preparing for his first public appearance with as much heartiness as if the years had run backwards, and he had been again a little dragonlet, playing with his sisters on the floor of their mother's cave, at the game of saints-and-dragons, in which the dragon was bound to win.

A low muttering, mingled with snorts, now made itself heard; rising to a bellowing roar that seemed to fill the plain. Then a cloud of smoke obscured the mouth of the cave, and out of the midst of it the dragon himself, shining, sea-blue, magnificent, pranced splendidly forth; and everybody said, "Oo-oo-oo!" as if he had been a mighty rocket! His scales were glittering, his long spiky tail lashed his sides, his claws tore up the turf and sent it flying high over his back, and smoke and fire incessantly jetted from his angry nostrils. "Oh, well done, dragon!" cried the Boy, excitedly. "Didn't think he had it in him!" he added to himself.

St. George lowered his spear, bent his head, dug his heels into his horse's sides, and came thundering over the turf. The dragon charged with a roar and a squeal,—a great blue whirling combination of coils and snorts and clashing jaws and spikes and fire.

"Missed!" yelled the crowd. There was a moment's entanglement of golden armour and blue-green coils, and spiky tail, and then the great horse, tearing at his bit, carried the Saint, his spear swung high in the air, almost up to the mouth of the cave.

The dragon sat down and barked viciously, while St. George with difficulty pulled his horse round into position.

"End of Round One!" thought the Boy. "How well they managed it! But I hope the Saint won't get excited. I can trust the dragon all right. What a regular play-actor the fellow is!"

St. George had at last prevailed on his horse to stand steady, and was looking round him as he wiped his brow. Catching sight of the Boy, he smiled and nodded, and held up three fingers for an instant.

"It seems to be all planned out," said the Boy to himself. "Round Three is to be the finishing one, evidently. Wish it could have lasted a bit longer. Whatever's that old fool of a dragon up to now?"

The dragon was employing the interval in giving a ramping-performance for the benefit of the crowd. Ramping, it should be explained, consists in running round and round in a wide circle, and sending waves and ripples of movement along the whole length of your spine, from your pointed ears right down to the spike at the end of your long tail. When you are covered with blue scales, the effect is particularly pleasing; and the Boy recollected the dragon's recently expressed wish to become a social success.

St. George now gathered up his reins and began to move

forward, dropping the point of his spear and settling himself firmly in the saddle.

"Time!" yelled everybody excitedly; and the dragon, leaving off his ramping, sat up on end, and began to leap from one side to the other with huge ungainly bounds, whooping like a Red Indian. This naturally disconcerted the horse, who swerved violently, the Saint only just saving himself by the mane; and as they shot past the dragon delivered a vicious snap at the horse's tail which sent the poor beast careering madly far over the Downs, so that the language of the Saint, who had lost a stirrup, was fortunately inaudible to the general assemblage.

Round Two evoked audible evidence of friendly feeling towards the dragon. The spectators were not slow to appreciate a combatant who could hold his own so well and clearly wanted to show good sport; and many encouraging remarks reached the ears of our friend as he strutted to and fro, his chest thrust out and his tail in the air, hugely enjoying his new popularity.

St. George had dismounted and was tightening his girths, and telling his horse, with quite an Oriental flow of imagery, exactly what he thought of him, and his relations, and his conduct on the present occasion; so the Boy made his way down to the Saint's end of the line, and held his spear for him.

"It's been a jolly fight, St. George!" he said with a sigh. "Can't you let it last a bit longer?"

"Well, I think I'd better not," replied the Saint. "The fact is, your simple-minded old friend's getting conceited, now they've begun cheering him, and he'll forget all about the arrangement and take to playing the fool, and there's no telling where he would stop. I'll just finish him off this round."

He swung himself into the saddle and took his spear from the Boy. "Now don't you be afraid," he added kindly. "I've marked my spot exactly, and he's sure to give me all the assistance in his power, because he knows it's his only chance of being asked to the banquet!"

St. George now shortened his spear, bringing the butt well

up under his arm; and, instead of galloping as before, trotted smartly towards the dragon, who crouched at his approach, flicking his tail till it cracked in the air like a great cart-whip. The Saint wheeled as he neared his opponent and circled warily round him, keeping his eye on the spare place; while the dragon, adopting similar tactics, paced with caution round the same circle, occasionally feinting with his head. So the two sparred for an opening, while the spectators maintained a breathless silence.

Though the round lasted for some minutes, the end was so swift that all the Boy saw was a lightning movement of the Saint's arm, and then a whirl and a confusion of spines, claws, tail, and flying bits of turf. The dust cleared away, the spectators whooped and ran in cheering, and the Boy made out that the dragon was down, pinned to the earth by the spear, while St. George had dismounted, and stood astride of him.

It all seemed so genuine that the Boy ran in breathlessly, hoping the dear old dragon wasn't really hurt. As he approached, the dragon lifted one large eyelid, winked solemnly, and collapsed again. He was held fast to earth by the neck, but the Saint had hit him in the spare place agreed upon, and it didn't even seem to tickle.

"Bain't you goin' to cut 'is 'ed orf, master?" asked one of the applauding crowd. He had backed the dragon, and naturally felt a trifle sore.

"Well, not to-day, I think," replied St. George, pleasantly. "You see, that can be done at any time. There's no hurry at all. I think we'll all go down to the village first, and have some refreshment, and then I'll give him a good talking-to, and you'll find he'll be a very different dragon!"

At that magic word *refreshment* the whole crowd formed up in procession and silently awaited the signal to start. The time for talking and cheering and betting was past, the hour for action had arrived. St. George, hauling on his spear with both hands, released the dragon, who rose and shook himself and ran his eye over his spikes and scales and things, to see that they were all in order. Then the Saint mounted and led off the procession, the dragon following meekly in the company of the Boy, while the thirsty spectators kept at a respectful interval behind.

There were great doings when they got down to the village again, and had formed up in front of the inn. After refreshment St. George made a speech, in which he informed his audience that he had removed their direful scourge, at a great deal of trouble and inconvenience to himself, and now they weren't to go about grumbling and fancying they'd got grievances, because they hadn't. And they shouldn't be so fond of fights, because next time they might have to do the fighting themselves, which would not be the same thing at all. And there was a certain badger in the inn stables which had got to be released at once, and he'd come and see it done himself. Then he told them that the dragon had been thinking over things, and saw that there were two sides to every question, and he wasn't going to do it any more, and if they were good perhaps he'd stay and settle down there. So they must make friends, and not be prejudiced; and go about fancying they knew everything there was to be known, because they didn't, not by a long way. And he warned them against the sin of romancing, and making up stories and fancying other people would believe them just because they were plausible and highly-coloured. Then he sat down, amidst much repentant cheering, and the dragon nudged the Boy in the ribs and whispered that he couldn't have done it better himself. Then every one went off to get ready for the banquet.

Banquets are always pleasant things, consisting mostly, as they do, of eating and drinking; but the specially nice thing about a banquet is, that it comes when something's over, and there's nothing more to worry about, and to-morrow seems a long way off. St. George was happy because there had been a fight and he hadn't had to kill anybody; for he didn't really like killing, though he generally had to do it. The dragon was happy because there had been a fight, and so far from being hurt in it he had won popularity and a sure footing in society. The Boy was happy because there had been a fight, and in spite of it all his two friends were on the best of terms. And all the others were happy because there had been a fight, and—well, they didn't require any other reasons for their happiness. The dragon exerted himself to say the right thing to everybody, and proved the life and soul of the evening; while the Saint and the Boy, as they looked on, felt that they were only assisting at a feast of which the honour and the glory were entirely the dragon's. But they didn't mind that, being good fellows, and the dragon was not in the least proud or forgetful. On the contrary, every ten minutes or so he leant over towards the Boy and said impressively: "Look here! you will see me home afterwards, won't you?" And the Boy always nodded, though he had promised his mother not to be out late.

At last the banquet was over, the guests had dropped away with many good-nights and congratulations and invitations, and the dragon, who had seen the last of them off the premises, emerged into the street followed by the Boy, wiped his brow, sighed, sat down in the road and gazed at the stars. "Jolly night it's been!" he murmured. "Jolly stars! Jolly little place this! Think I shall just stop here. Don't feel like climbing up any beastly hill. Boy's promised to see me home. Boy had better do it then! No responsibility on my part. Responsibility all Boy's!" And his chin sank on his broad chest and he slumbered peacefully.

"Oh, get up, dragon," cried the Boy, piteously. "You know my mother's sitting up, and I'm so tired, and you made me promise to see you home, and I never knew what it meant or I wouldn't have done it!" And the Boy sat down in the road by the side of the sleeping dragon, and cried.

The door behind them opened, a stream of light illumined the road, and St. George, who had come out for a stroll in the cool night-air, caught sight of the two figures sitting there—the great motionless dragon and the tearful little Boy.

"What's the matter, Boy?" he inquired kindly, stepping to his side.

"Oh, it's this great lumbering pig of a dragon!" sobbed the Boy. "First he makes me promise to see him home, and then he says I'd better do it, and goes to sleep! Might as well try to see a haystack home! And I'm so tired, and mother's—" here he broke down again.

"Now don't take on," said St. George. "I'll stand by you, and we'll both see him home. Wake up, dragon!" he said sharply, shaking the beast by the elbow.

The dragon looked up sleepily. "What a night, George!" he murmured; "what a—"

"Now look here, dragon," said the Saint, firmly. "Here's this little fellow waiting to see you home, and you know he ought to have been in bed these two hours, and what his mother'll say I don't know, and anybody but a selfish pig would have made him go to bed long ago—"

"And he shall go to bed!" cried the dragon, starting up. "Poor little chap, only fancy his being up at this hour! It's a shame, that's what it is, and I don't think, St. George, you've been very considerate—but come along at once, and don't let us have any more arguing or shilly-shallying. You give me hold of your hand, Boy—thank you, George, an arm up the hill is just what I wanted!"

So they set off up the hill arm-in-arm, the Saint, the Dragon, and the Boy. The lights in the little village began to go out; but there were stars, and a late moon, as they climbed to the Downs together. And, as they turned the last corner and disappeared from view, snatches of an old song were borne back on the night-breeze. I can't be certain which of them was singing, but I think it was the Dragon!

"Here we are at your gate," said the man, abruptly, laying his hand on it. "Good-night. Cut along in sharp, or you'll catch it!"

Could it really be our own gate? Yes, there it was, sure enough, with the familiar marks on its bottom bar made by our feet when we swung on it.

"Oh, but wait a minute!" cried Charlotte. "I want to know a heap of things. Did the dragon really settle down? And did—"

"There isn't any more of that story," said the man, kindly but firmly. "At least, not to-night. Now be off! Good-bye!"

"Wonder if it's all true?" said Charlotte, as we hurried up the path. "Sounded dreadfully like nonsense, in parts!"

"P'raps its true for all that," I replied encouragingly.

Charlotte bolted in like a rabbit, out of the cold and the dark; but I lingered a moment in the still, frosty air, for a backward glance at the silent white world without, ere I changed it for the land of firelight and cushions and laughter. It was the day for choir-practice, and carol-time was at hand, and a belated member was passing homewards down the road, singing as he went:—

> Then St. George: ee made rev'rence: in the stable so dim,
> Oo vanquished the dragon: so fearful and grim.
> So-o grim: and so-o fierce: that now may we say
> All peaceful is our wakin': on Chri-istmas Day!

The singer receded, the carol died away. But I wondered, with my hand on the door-latch, whether that was the song, or something like it, that the dragon sang as he toddled contentedly up the hill.

YOUR KINDNESS QUITE UNDRAGONS ME[1]

No author of children's literature rivalled the industry of the English writer Edith Nesbit (1858–1924), who wrote dozens of stories for young people at the turn of the twentieth century. While Nesbit is best known for her influential fantasy novel The Five Children and It *(1902) and its sequels, she also wrote playful short stories featuring dragons as farcical villains. Many of these appeared in* The Strand Magazine *in the 1890s and were published as a collection called* The Book of Dragons *in 1901. Later in her career, Nesbit composed a story about a princess and a dragon who rebelled against the roles of victim and villain imposed upon them by the literary tradition and chose instead to become friends. This tale, "The Last of the Dragons," was published posthumously in 1925.*

Of course you know that dragons were once as common as motor-omnibuses are now, and almost as dangerous. But as every well-brought-up prince was expected to kill a dragon, and rescue a princess, the dragons grew fewer and fewer till it was often quite hard for a princess to find a dragon to be rescued from. And at last there were no more dragons in France and no more dragons in Germany, or Spain, or Italy, or Russia. There were some left in China, and are still, but they are cold and bronzy, and there were never any, of course, in America. But the last real live dragon left was in England, and of course that was a very long time ago, before what you call English History began. This dragon lived in Cornwall in the big caves amidst the rocks, and a very fine dragon it was,

quite seventy feet long from the tip of its fearful snout to the
end of its terrible tail. It breathed fire and smoke, and rattled
when it walked, because its scales were made of iron. Its
wings were like half-umbrellas—or like bat's wings, only
several thousand times bigger. Everyone was very frightened
of it, and well they might be.

Now the King of Cornwall had one daughter, and when
she was sixteen, of course she would have to go and face the
dragon: such tales are always told in royal nurseries at twilight, so the Princess knew what she had to expect. The
dragon would not eat her, of course—because the prince
would come and rescue her. But the Princess could not help
thinking it would be much pleasanter to have nothing to do
with the dragon at all—not even to be rescued from him.

"All the princes I know are such very silly little boys," she
told her father. "Why must I be rescued by a prince?"

"It's always done, my dear," said the King, taking his
crown off and putting it on the grass, for they were alone in
the garden, and even kings must unbend sometimes.

"Father, darling," said the Princess presently, when she had
made a daisy chain and put it on the King's head, where the
crown ought to have been. "Father, darling, couldn't we tie
up one of the silly little princes for the dragon to look at—and
then I could go and kill the dragon and rescue the prince? I
fence much better than any of the princes we know."

"What an unladylike idea!" said the King, and put his
crown on again, for he saw the Prime Minister coming with
a basket of new-laid Bills for him to sign. "Dismiss the
thought, my child. I rescued your mother from a dragon, and
you don't want to set yourself up above her, I should hope?"

"But this is the *last* dragon. It is different from all other
dragons."

"How?" asked the King.

"Because he *is* the last," said the Princess, and went off to
her fencing lessons, with which she took great pains. She
took great pains with all her lessons—for she could not give
up the idea of fighting the dragon. She took such pains that
she became the strongest and boldest and most skilful and

most sensible princess in Europe. She had always been the prettiest and nicest.

And the days and years went on, till at last the day came which was the day before the Princess was to be rescued from the dragon. The Prince who was to do this deed of valour was a pale prince, with large eyes and a head full of mathematics and philosophy, but he had unfortunately neglected his fencing lessons. He was to stay the night at the palace, and there was a banquet.

After supper the Princess sent her pet parrot to the Prince with a note. It said:

"Please, Prince, come on to the terrace. I want to talk to you without anybody else hearing. —The Princess."

So, of course, he went—and he saw her gown of silver a long way off shining among the shadows of the trees like water in starlight. And when he came quite close to her he said: "Princess, at your service," and bent his cloth-of-gold-covered knee and put his hand on his cloth-of-gold-covered heart.

"Do you think," said the Princess earnestly, "that you will be able to kill the dragon?"

"I will kill the dragon," said the Prince firmly, "or perish in the attempt."

"It's no use your perishing," said the Princess.

"It's the least I can do," said the Prince.

"What I'm afraid of is that it'll be the most you can do," said the Princess.

"It's the only thing I can do," said he, "unless I kill the dragon."

"Why you should do anything for me is what I can't see," said she.

"But I want to," he said. "You must know that I love you better than anything in the world."

When he said that he looked so kind that the Princess began to like him a little.

"Look here," she said, "no one else will go out tomorrow. You know they tie me to a rock and leave me—and then everybody scurries home and puts up the shutters and keeps them shut till you ride through the town in triumph shouting that you've killed the dragon, and I ride on the horse behind you weeping for joy."

"I've heard that that is how it is done," said he.

"Well, do you love me well enough to come very quickly and set me free—and we'll fight the dragon together?"

"It wouldn't be safe for you."

"Much safer for both of us for me to be free, with a sword in my hand, than tied up and helpless. *Do* agree."

He could refuse her nothing. So he agreed. And next day everything happened as she had said.

When he had cut the cords that tied her to the rock they stood on the lonely mountain-side looking at each other.

"It seems to me," said the Prince, "that this ceremony could have been arranged without the dragon."

"Yes," said the Princess, "but since it has been arranged with the dragon —"

"It seems such a pity to kill the dragon—the last in the world," said the Prince.

"Well then, don't let's," said the Princess; "let's tame it not to eat princesses but to eat out of their hands. They say everything can be tamed by kindness."

"Taming by kindness means giving them things to eat," said the Prince. "Have you got anything to eat?"

She hadn't, but the Prince owned that he had a few biscuits. "Breakfast was so very early," said he, "and I thought you might have felt faint after the fight."

"How clever," said the Princess, and they took a biscuit in each hand. And they looked here, and they looked there, but never a dragon could they see.

"But here's its trail," said the Prince, and pointed to where the rock was scarred and scratched so as to make a track leading to a dark cave. It was like cart-ruts in a Sussex road, mixed with the marks of sea-gull's feet on the sea-sand. "Look, that's where it's dragged its brass tail and planted its steel claws."

"Don't let's think how hard its tail and claws are," said the Princess, "or I shall begin to be frightened—and I know you can't tame anything, even by kindness, if you're frightened of it. Come on. Now or never."

She caught the Prince's hand in hers and they ran along the path towards the dark mouth of the cave. But they did not run into it. It really was so very *dark*.

So they stood outside, and the Prince shouted: "What ho! Dragon there! What ho within!" And from the cave they heard an answering voice and great clattering and creaking. It sounded as though a rather large cotton-mill were stretching itself and waking up out of its sleep.

The Prince and the Princess trembled, but they stood firm.

"Dragon—I say, dragon!" said the Princess, "do come out and talk to us. We've brought you a present."

"Oh yes—I know your presents," growled the dragon in a huge rumbling voice. "One of those precious princesses, I suppose? And I've got to come out and fight for her. Well, I tell you straight, I'm not going to do it. A fair fight I wouldn't say no to—a fair fight and no favour—but one of those put-up fights where you've got to lose—no! So I tell you. If I wanted a princess I'd come and take her, in my own time—but I don't. What do you suppose I'd do with her, if I'd got her?"

"Eat her, wouldn't you?" said the Princess, in a voice that trembled a little.

"Eat a fiddle-stick end," said the dragon very rudely. "I wouldn't touch the horrid thing."

The Princess's voice grew firmer.

"Do you like biscuits?" she said.

"No," growled the dragon.

"Not the nice little expensive ones with sugar on the top?"

"No," growled the dragon.

"Then what do you like?" asked the Prince.

"You go away and don't bother me," growled the dragon, and they could hear it turn over, and the clang and clatter of its turning echoed in the cave like the sound of the steam-hammers in the Arsenal at Woolwich.

The Prince and Princess looked at each other. What were they to do? Of course it was no use going home and telling the King that the dragon didn't want princesses—because

His Majesty was very old-fashioned and would never have believed that a new-fashioned dragon could ever be at all different from an old-fashioned dragon. They could not go into the cave and kill the dragon. Indeed, unless he attacked the Princess it did not seem fair to kill him at all.

"He must like something," whispered the Princess, and she called out in a voice as sweet as honey and sugar-cane:

"Dragon! Dragon dear!"

"WHAT?" shouted the dragon. "Say that again!" and they could hear the dragon coming towards them through the darkness of the cave. The Princess shivered, and said in a very small voice:

"Dragon—Dragon dear!"

And then the dragon came out. The Prince drew his sword, and the Princess drew hers—the beautiful silver-handled one that the Prince had brought in his motor-car. But they did not attack; they moved slowly back as the dragon came out, all the vast scaly length of him, and lay along the rock—his great wings halfspread and his silvery sheen gleaming like diamonds in the sun. At last they could retreat no further—the dark rock behind them stopped their way—and with their backs to the rock they stood swords in hand and waited.

The dragon grew nearer and nearer—and now they could see that he was not breathing fire and smoke as they had expected—he came crawling slowly towards them wriggling a little as a puppy does when it wants to play and isn't quite sure whether you're not cross with it.

And then they saw that great tears were coursing down its brazen cheek.

"Whatever's the matter?" said the Prince.

"Nobody," sobbed the dragon, "ever called me 'dear' before!"

"Don't cry, dragon dear," said the Princess. "We'll call you 'dear' as often as you like. We want to tame you."

"I am tame," said the dragon—"that's just it. That's what nobody but you has ever found out. I'm so tame that I'd eat out of your hands."

"Eat what, dragon dear?" said the Princess. "Not biscuits?" The dragon slowly shook his heavy head.

"Not biscuits?" said the Princess tenderly. "What, then, dragon dear?"

"Your kindness quite undragons me," it said. "No one has ever asked any of us what we like to eat—always offering us princesses, and then rescuing them—and never once, 'What'll you take to drink the King's health in?' Cruel hard I call it," and it wept again.

"But what would you like to drink our health in?" said the Prince. "We're going to be married today, aren't we, Princess?"

She said that she supposed so.

"What'll I take to drink your health in?" asked the dragon. "Ah, you're something like a gentleman, you are, sir. I don't mind if I do, sir. I'll be proud to drink you and your good lady's health in a tiny drop of"—its voice faltered—"to think of you asking me so friendly like," it said. "Yes, sir, just a tiny drop of puppuppuppuppupetrol—tha—that's what does a dragon good, sir—"

"I've lots in the car," said the Prince, and was off down the mountain in a flash. He was a good judge of character and knew that with this dragon the Princess would be safe.

"If I might make so bold," said the dragon, "while the gentleman's away—p'raps just to pass the time you'd be so kind as to call me Dear again, and if you'd shake claws with a poor old dragon that's never been anybody's enemy but his own—well, the last of the dragons'll be the proudest dragon that's ever been since the first of them."

It held out an enormous paw, and the great steel hooks that were its claws closed over the Princess's hand as softly as the claws of the Himalayan bear will close over the bit of bun you hand it through the bars at the Zoo.

———

And so the Prince and Princess went back to the palace in triumph, the dragon following them like a pet dog. And all through the wedding festivities no one drank more earnestly to the happiness of the bride and bridegroom than the Princess's pet dragon—whom she had at once named Fido.

And when the happy pair were settled in their own kingdom, Fido came to them and begged to be allowed to make himself useful.

"There must be some little thing I can do," he said, rattling his wings and stretching his claws. "My wings and claws and so on ought to be turned to some account—to say nothing of my grateful heart."

So the Prince had a special saddle or howdah made for him—very long it was—like the tops of many tramcars fitted together. One hundred and fifty seats were fitted to this, and the dragon, whose greatest pleasure was now to give pleasure to others, delighted in taking parties of children to the seaside. It flew through the air quite easily with its hundred and fifty little passengers—and would lie on the sand patiently waiting till they were ready to return. The children were very fond of it, and used to call it Dear, a word which never failed to bring tears of affection and gratitude to its eyes. So it lived, useful and respected, till quite the other day—when someone happened to say, in his hearing, that dragons were out-of-date, now so much new machinery had come in. This so distressed him that he asked the King to change him into something less old-fashioned, and the kindly monarch at once changed him into a mechanical contrivance. The dragon, indeed, became the first aeroplane.

Notes

THE HYDRA OF LERNA

1. Apollodorus, *The Library* 2.5.2, trans. Sir James George Frazer (Cambridge, MA: Harvard University Press, 1921), pp. 187–89 (slightly modified).
2. Located on the eastern shore of the Peloponnese in Greece, Lerna was famed for its many springs.
3. Amymone was the daughter of Danaus and Europe. After Poseidon rescued her from a satyr, he wooed her by showing her the sacred springs of Lerna, which later authors associated with her name.

MEDUSA, MOTHER OF MONSTERS

1. Lucan, *Civil War* 9.777–924, trans. Matthew Fox (New York: Penguin Books, 2012), pp. 273–77.

CADMUS AND THE DRAGON OF ARES

1. Ovid, *Metamorphoses* 3, trans. Mary M. Innes (New York: Penguin Books, 1955), pp. 74–77.

THE DEATH OF LAOCOÖN

1. Virgil, *The Aeneid* 2.256–88, trans. Robert Fagles (New York: Viking, 2006), pp. 81–82.

THE DRAGON OF BAGRADA RIVER

1. Silius Italicus, *Punica* 6.140–286, trans. J. D. Duff, 2 vols. (Cambridge, MA: Harvard University Press, 1934), vol. 1, pp. 293, 295, 297, 299, 301, and 303.

DRAGONS AGAINST ELEPHANTS

1. Pliny, *Historia Naturalis* 8.11–13 and 37.57, trans. J. Bostock and H. T. Riley, 6 vols. (London: Henry J. Bohn, 1890), vol. 2, pp. 259–62; and vol. 6, p. 447 (updated and modified).

BIBLICAL BEASTS

1. Translated by Scott G. Bruce from the Latin Vulgate version of Genesis 3:1–15.
2. Translated by Scott G. Bruce from the Latin Vulgate version of Job 40:20–21 and 41:4–25.
3. Translated by Scott G. Bruce from the Latin Vulgate version of Daniel 14:22–27.
4. Translated by Scott G. Bruce from the Latin Vulgate version of Revelation 12:1–17 and 20:1–3.

THE GUARDIAN OF HEAVEN'S LADDER

1. "The Martyrdom of Perpetua and Felicity" 3–4, trans. Carolinne White, in *Lives of Roman Christian Women* (New York: Penguin Books, 2010), pp. 6–8.

DESCENDANTS OF DARKNESS

1. *The Acts of Philip* 8–9, trans. M. R. James in *The Apocryphal New Testament* (Oxford: Oxford University Press, 1924), pp. 446–48 (slightly modified).

2. A cubit was a unit of measurement based on the distance between a grown man's fingertips and elbow (about eighteen inches).

3. *The Acts of Philip* 11, trans. François Bovon and Christopher R. Matthews, in *The Acts of Philip: A New Translation* (Waco, TX: Baylor University Press, 2012), pp. 81–84.

4. Genesis 3:1–15.

5. Genesis 4:1–18.

6. The Watchers are known from the apocalyptic Book of Enoch, which was written around 300–200 BCE.

7. Exodus 7:8–13.

8. *The Acts of Philip* 13, trans. Bovon and Matthews, in *The Acts of Philip*, pp. 87–88.

9. The term "Monad" refers to the "oneness" of God.

THE DRAGON BECAME HER TOMB

1. Translated by Scott G. Bruce from Venantius Fortunatus, *Vita sancti Marcelli* 10, ed. Bruno Krusch, in *Monumenta Germaniae Historica: Auctores antiquissimi* 4.2 (Berlin: Apud Weidmannos, 1885), pp. 53–54.

2. For a later medieval account of Pope Sylvester's encounter with a dragon in Rome, see pp. 157–58, below.

COILED COURIERS OF THE DAMNED

1. Translated by Scott G. Bruce from Gregory the Great, *Dialogorum libri quattuor* 2.25 and 4.38, ed. J. P. Migne, in *Patrologiae Cursus Completus: Series Latina* 66 (Paris: Apud editorem, 1859), col. 182; and ed. J. P. Migne, in *Patrologiae*

Cursus Completus: Series Latina 77 (Paris: Apud editorem, 1896), cols. 389 and 392–93.
2. Modern Konya in south-central Turkey.

THE MONSTER OF THE RIVER NESS

1. Adomnán of Iona, *Life of St. Columba* 2.27, trans. Richard Sharpe (New York: Penguin Books, 1995), pp. 175–76.

GUARDIANS OF THE HOARD

1. Jacob Grimm, *Teutonic Mythology*, trans. James Steven Stallybrass, 4 vols. (London: George Bell & Sons, 1883), vol. 2, p. 689.

THE TERROR OF NATIONS

1. Translated by Paul Acker from *Beowulf*, lines 874–97, 2208–31, 2270–354, 2397–427, 2508–610, 2661–846, 2900–2913, 3028–57, and 3129–82, ed. Fred C. Robinson and Bruce Mitchell, in *Beowulf: An Edition* (Oxford: Blackwells, 1998), pp. 77–78, 125–26, 127–31, 133–34, 137–50, 155–56, and 159–61.
2. J. R. R. Tolkien, *The Hobbit, or There and Back Again* (London: George Allen & Unwin, 1937), p. 33.
3. The hero Sigmund corresponds in Old Norse to Sigmundr and his son Sigurðr, descendants of Völsungr. Sigurðr was famous for slaying the dragon Fáfnir (see pp. 74–77, below).
4. A byrnie is a tunic made out of chain mail.
5. Beowulf's sword Naegling takes its name from the Old English word for "nail" (*nægl*).

SIGURD, THE SLAYER OF FÁFNIR

1. Translated by Paul Acker from *Völsunga saga* 18, ed. R. G. Finch (London: Nelson, 1965), pp. 31–32.

WINGED DRAGONS OF THE NORTH

1. J. R. R. Tolkien, "*Beowulf*: The Monsters and the Critics," *Proceedings of the British Academy* 2 (1936): 245–95, at p. 253.

2. Translated by Paul Acker from *Ketils saga hængs* 1, ed. Guðni Jónsson, in *Fornaldar sögur Norðurlanda*, 4 vols. (Reykjavík: Íslendingasagnaútgáfan, 1950), vol. 2, p. 153.

3. Translated by Paul Acker from *Þiðreks saga af Bern* 105, ed. Guðni Jónsson, in *Fornaldar sögur Norðurlanda*, 4 vols. (Reykjavík: Íslendingasagnaútgáfan, 1950), vol. 1, pp. 156–58.

A TREASURY OF ANCIENT DRAGON LORE

1. Isidore of Seville, *Etymologies*, 12.4.4–5 and 16.16.7, trans. Ernest Brehaut, in *An Encyclopedist of the Dark Ages: Isidore of Seville* (New York: Columbia University Press, 1912), pp. 227–28 and 255 (modified).

DARK AGE CREATURE CATALOGUES

1. Translated by Scott G. Bruce from *De rebus in Oriente mirabilibus* 15–16; and *Liber monstrorum* 1.49 and 3.13, ed. Andy Orchard, in *Pride and Prodigies: Studies in the Monsters of the Beowulf-Manuscript*, 2nd ed. (Toronto: University of Toronto Press, 2003), pp. 178, 284, and 312.

2. The Brixonte is a fictional river that appears only in the *Wonders of the East*. The headless creatures described here are known as Blemmyes. Roman authors identified them as natives of Libya, Ethiopia, or India.

YOU CRUSHED THEIR HEADS UPON THE WATERS

1. Translated by Benjamin Bertrand and Scott G. Bruce from Hrabanus Maurus, *De universo* 8.3, ed. J. P. Migne, in

Patrologiae Cursus Completus: Series Latina III (Paris: Garnier Fratres, 1844), cols. 229–30.

2. Up to this point, Hrabanus has quoted verbatim the chapter on dragons from Isidore's *Etymologies* (see pp. 85–86, above).
3. Psalms 74:13.
4. Psalms 74:14.

REMEMBERING A PANNONIAN DRAGON

1. Translated by Benjamin Bertrand and Scott G. Bruce from Arnold of St. Emmeram, *De miraculis sancti Emmerammi libri duo* 2, ed. J. P. Migne, in *Patrologiae Cursus Completus: Series Latina* 141 (Paris: Apud editorem, 1880), cols. 1039–41.
2. Cf. 2 Peter 3:5–7.
3. Cf. 2 Peter 3:12–13.
4. Cf. Jude 6.
5. Job 41:6. For the description of Leviathan in the Book of Job, see pp. 32–33, above.
6. The specificity of Arnold's recollection of the date does not help us to isolate the day in late spring or early summer on which he saw the dragon, because Pentecost is a moveable feast day that falls on the seventh Sunday after Easter, the exact date of which changes from year to year.
7. Revelation 12:12. Further on the dragon in the Book of Revelation, see pp. 34–35, above.
8. Here Arnold quotes verbatim the chapter on dragons from Isidore's *Etymologies* (see pp. 85–86, above). As Patrick Geary has noted, the monk "presumably copied from the manuscript of Isidore we know to have been in St. Emmeram's at the end of the tenth century." See Patrick J. Geary, *Phantoms of Remembrance: Memory and Oblivion at the End of the First Millenium* (Princeton: Princeton University Press, 1994), pp. 158–76, at p. 161.

GOD'S FIERY VENGEANCE

1. Translated by Scott G. Bruce and W. Tanner Smoot from Herman of Tournai, *De miraculis beatae Mariae Laudunenis* 2.11, ed. J. P. Migne, in *Patrologiae Cursus Completus: Series Latina* 156 (Paris: Apud editorem, 1853), cols. 981–82.
2. A stade (*stadium*) is a Roman unit of measurement roughly equivalent to 125 paces.
3. During their tours, the canons processed with their relics of the Virgin (locks of her hair and threads from her chemise) on a litter.

BONE FIRES AND DRAGON SPERM

1. Translated by Benjamin Bertrand and Scott G. Bruce from John Beleth, *Summa de ecclesiasticis officiis* 137, ed. J. P. Migne, in *Patrologiae Cursus Completus: Series Latina* 202 (Paris: Apud editorem, 1855), cols. 141–42.
2. Psalms 148:7.
3. Modern Sebastia, a Palestinian village northwest of the city of Nablus, where Saint John the Baptist was thought to be buried.

THE PROPHECIES OF MERLIN

1. Geoffrey of Monmouth, *The History of the Kings of Britain* 7.3, trans. Lewis Thorpe (New York: Penguin Books, 1977), pp. 166–71.
2. The pagan philosopher and storyteller Apuleius (ca. 124–ca. 170 CE) wrote *On the God of Socrates* (*De deo Socratis*) about the nature of *daemones*, which he described as invisible intermediaries between the heavens and the earth.

THE DEVIL IS THE LARGEST SERPENT

1. Translated by Benjamin Bertrand and Scott G. Bruce from *De bestis et rebus aliis libri quatuor* 23–24 and 34, ed. J. P. Migne, in *Patrologiae Cursus Completus: Series Latina* 177 (Paris: Apud editorem, 1879), cols. 69–72 and 99–100.
2. The "naturalist" (*physiologus*) is the name given to the putative author of a second-century collection of Christian moral stories about animals from which the medieval bestiary tradition drew its inspiration.
3. Ephesians 4:8.
4. Here the author quotes verbatim the chapter on dragons from Isidore's *Etymologies* (see pp. 85–86, above).
5. Luke 1:35.
6. There are two accounts of the death of Judas in the New Testament (Matthew 27:1–10 and Acts 1:18), but neither directly implicates a demon as the agent of his demise.

HUNTING MONSTERS IN KARA-JANG

1. Marco Polo, *The Travels* 4, trans. R. E. Latham (New York: Penguin Books, 1958), pp. 178–80.

A THEOLOGIAN CONTEMPLATES THE NATURE OF DRAGONS

1. Translated by Anthony Kaldellis from Pseudo-John of Damascus, *De draconibus*, ed. J. P. Migne, in *Patrologiae Cursus Completus: Series Graeca* 94 (Paris: Apud editorem, 1864), cols. 1600–1604.
2. Here the author may be referring to legendary stories about the birth of Alexander the Great, in which his mother, Olympias, was seduced by the Egyptian sorcerer Nectanebo, who came to her bed disguised as the god Ammon of Libya in the form of a serpent or dragon. For a version of this story, see *The Greek*

Alexander Romance 1.4–14, trans. Richard Stoneman (New York: Penguin Books, 1991), pp. 37–47.

3. Genesis 2:9.

4. Cassius Dio was a Roman senator of Greek origin in the early third century CE who wrote a history of Rome, in which he repeated the story of Regulus and the dragon of Bagrada River well known from Silius Italicus's *Punica* (see pp. 18–22, above).

5. It is not clear which "tendon" the author means.

WHY DRAGONS FEAR LIGHTNING

1. Translated by Anthony Kaldellis from Michael Psellos, *De meteorologicis*, ed. J. M. Duffy and D. J. O'Meara, *Michaelis Pselli philosophical minora, vol. 1: Opuscula logica, physica, allegorica, alia* (Stuttgart and Leipzig: De Gruyter, 1992), pp. 69–76.

A DEMON IN DISGUISE

1. Translated by Anthony Kaldellis from *Acta sanctae Marinae et sancti Christophori*, ed. H. Usener, in *Festschrift zür fünften Säcularfeier der Carl-Ruprechts-Universität zu Heidelberg* (Bonn: Universitätsbuchdruckerei von C. Georgi, 1886), pp. 25–30.

THE TREASURY DRAGON OF CONSTANTINOPLE

1. Translated by Anthony Kaldellis from Βίος καὶ πολιτεία καὶ ἄθλησις τοῦ ἁγίου ἱερομάρτυρος Ὑπατίου ἐπισκόπου πόλεως Γαγγρῶν τῆς τῶν Παφλαγόνων ἐπαρχίας 8–19, ed. S. Ferri, in "Il Bios e il Martyrion di Hypatios di Gangrai," *Studi Bizantini e Neoellenici* 3 (1931): 69–103, at pp. 80–82.

2. Acts 28:3–5.

THE TERROR OF TREBIZOND

1. Translated by Anthony Kaldellis from Ἰωσὴφ τοῦ χρηματίσαντος μητροπολίτου Τραπεζοῦντος Λόγος ὡς ἐν συνόψει διαλαμβάνων τὴν γενέθλιον ἡμέραν τοῦ ἐν θαύμασι περιβοήτου καὶ μεγαλάθλου Εὐγενίου, ed. J. O. Rosenqvist, in *The Hagiographic Dossier of Saint Eugenius of Trebizond in Codex Athous Dionysiou 154* (Uppsala: Uppsala University, 1996), pp. 220–25.

THE OGRE-DRAGON'S PITILESS HEART

1. Translated by Anthony Kaldellis from Τὸ κατὰ Καλλίμαχον καὶ Χρυσορρόην ἐρωτικὸν διήγημα, verses 473–693, ed. M. Pichard, in *Le roman de Callimaque et de Chrysorrhoé* (Paris: Les Belles-Lettres, 1956), pp. 18–26.

THE DRAGON AND THE LION

1. Chrétien de Troyes, *Arthurian Romances*, trans. William W. Kibler (New York: Penguin Books, 1991), p. 337.

A DRAGON WITH THE DEVIL INSIDE

1. Translated by Douglass Hamilton from *Les Chétifs*, lines 1594–614, 2473–571, 2660–726, 2786–95, and 2799–869, ed. Geoffrey M. Myers, in *The Old French Crusade Cycle, Volume V: Les Chétifs* (Tuscaloosa: University of Alabama Press, 1981), pp. 38, 57–59, 61–63, and 64–66.
2. The story is set in the Taurus Mountains in eastern Turkey, through which the Tigris River runs.
3. The league was a flexible unit of distance measurement in the Middle Ages, varying from region to region, but averaging about three miles.
4. The name Sathanas evokes the name "Satan," who was often associated with a dragon.

5. Baldwin took vengeance for the murder of his brother Ernoul by the dragon.

6. Michael is the archangel who defeats Satan in the form of a great red dragon as described in the Book of Revelation. See pp. 34–35, above.

7. Longinus was the Roman soldier who pierced the side of Jesus Christ with his spear while he hung on the cross (John 15:34). He was not named in the New Testament, but he appeared by name in the apocryphal Gospel of Nicodemus, which was widely read throughout the Middle Ages.

8. John 11:1–44.

9. This refers to the Al-Aqsa Mosque in Jerusalem constructed under the Umayyad Dynasty (661–750). After the taking of Jerusalem during the First Crusade, crusaders referred to this building as the Temple of Solomon, after the holy temple of the same name in ancient Jerusalem that was destroyed by the Babylonians in 587 BCE.

10. The preacher Peter the Hermit was the leader of the more popular contingent of the crusading army, sometimes called the People's Crusade. This army was soundly defeated at the Battle of Civetot (1096) and those taken prisoner as a result are the eponymous *chétifs*, the captives of the Saracens.

11. Saint Denis, a legendary third-century bishop of Paris, is the patron saint of France. He appeared often in medieval vernacular French works.

12. The invocation of these particular saints was not arbitrary. They all had strong associations to the Frankish heartlands or to pilgrimage routes associated with crusading, were proven intercessors for those held in captivity, or were military saints with appeal to a noble audience. Saint George was renowned as a dragon-slayer (see pp. 155–57, below).

13. That is, Baldwin experienced a joy greater than receiving the prosperous city of Rohais (modern Edessa in southeast Turkey) as a fief. In the Middle Ages, an "honor" was a technical term which came to mean something akin to a fief.

14. In medieval stories, demons often took the form of black birds when fleeing the bodies of the possessed. See, for example, the twelfth-century account of the miracles of Saint Modwenna by

Abbot Geoffrey of Burton in *The Penguin Book of the Undead: Fifteen Hundred Years of Supernatural Encounters*, ed. Scott G. Bruce (New York: Penguin Books, 2016), p. 126.

15. Medieval Christians employed the pejorative term "Saracen" to describe all Muslims, Turks, and Arabs during the crusading period.

16. The bezant was a unit of Byzantine or Islamic currency measured in gold coins. Its value varied depending on the place of issue.

17. Jongleurs were French minstrels and entertainers who sang chansons de geste and other French songs to lords at their courts.

FOUR SAINTLY DRAGON-SLAYERS

1. Jacobus de Voragine, *The Golden Legend: Selections*, trans. Christopher Stace (New York: Penguin Books, 1998), pp. 116–18.

2. Translated by Scott G. Bruce from Jacobus de Voragine, *Legenda Aurea*, ed. T. Graesse, 3rd ed. (Breslau: Koebner, 1890), pp. 78–79.

3. Jacobus de Voragine, *The Golden Legend*, pp. 162–63.

4. The name Margaret derives from the Latin word for "pearl" (*margarita*).

5. Jacobus de Voragine, *The Golden Legend*, pp. 183–84.

THE DRAGONS OF FAIRYLAND

1. Edmund Spenser, *The Faerie Queen*, Book 1, Cantos 1 and 11, ed. Thomas J. Wise, in *Spenser's Faerie Queene* (London: George Allen, 1897), pp. 8–14 and 213–31.

2. The summaries of the topic of each stanza are modern devices intended to guide the reader.

3. Una's dwarf companion represented Common Sense.

4. Redcrosse is a "valient Elfe," that is, a knight of Fairyland.

5. These "bookes and papers" allude to the pamphlets attacking Queen Elizabeth and the reformed church by the papal see and the Jesuits.

6. Here Spenser calls upon Clio, the Muse of History, who is the daughter of Apollo (Phoebus).

7. A furlong is a medieval unit of measurement about 660 feet long, or one-eighth of a mile.

8. A longbow made from the wood of a yew tree.

9. On the labors of Hercules, see pp. 5–6, above.

10. Here Spenser compares the restorative properties of the Well of Life with other famous springs: the pool of Siloam where Jesus healed the blind man (John 9:1–11); the Jordan River where Naaman was cured of his leprosy (2 Kings 5:14); the medicinal spas at Bath in England and at Spau in Belgium; and the Cephise and Hebrus Rivers in Greece, both of which were renowned for the purity of their waters.

11. Phoebus is the sun god Apollo, whose golden chariot represents the sun.

12. Titan is the sun.

13. Here Spenser compares the risen knight to an eagle. It was once believed that eagles molted and renewed their plumage every ten years by flying high into the sky and then plunging into the ocean, from which they emerged with new feathers.

14. Cerberus was the monstrous three-headed dog that guarded the gates of the underworld in Greco-Roman mythology.

15. Mount Aetna (modern Etna) was—and still is—an active volcano in Sicily.

16. The Tree of Life was one of two trees in the Garden of Eden, the other being the Tree of the Knowledge of Good and Evil. See Genesis 2:9.

17. Aurora was the goddess of the dawn. Her lover was Tithonus, a mortal prince of Troy. Zeus granted him immortality at Aurora's request, but not eternal youth, so he aged forever.

A FARTING DRAGON BURLESQUE

1. Anonymous, "The Dragon of Wantley," in *Reliques of Ancient English Poetry*, ed. Thomas Percy, 3 vols., 3rd edition (London: John Nichols, 1794), vol. 3, pp. 297–308.

2. Like Spenser's character the Redcrosse Knight, the martial exploits of More of More-Hall surpassed those of the ancient hero Hercules. See pp. 5–6, above.

3. The description of the dragon of Wantley owes much to Spenser.

4. The modern village of Wortley is about nine miles from Rotherham in South Yorkshire.

5. Wortley lies about ten miles north of the city of Sheffield.

6. This stanza recalls the role of the Well of Life in Redcrosse's battle with the dragon in *The Faerie Queene*.

THE GREAT SERPENT RETURNS

1. John Milton, *Paradise Lost: A Poem in Twelve Books*, Book 10, lines 504–47, 2nd ed. (London: S. Simmons, 1674), pp. 266–67.

2. Milton borrowed this catalogue of exotic serpents from the description of the progeny of Medusa in Lucan's *Civil War*. See pp. 7–10, above.

3. Python was a giant serpent in Greek mythology that lived at the shrine of Delphi until it was slain by the god Apollo. In premodern Europe, Python was often depicted as a dragon with wings and limbs.

THE DRAGON OF DROUGHT

1. *The Rig Veda* 1.32, trans. Wendy Doniger (New York: Penguin Books, 2004), pp. 149–51.

A BLACK WIND FROM THE SEA

1. Al-Masudi, *Meadows of Gold and Mines of Gems*, trans. Aloys Sprenger (London: Oriental Translation Fund of Great Britain and Ireland, 1841), vol. 1, pp. 291–93.

NO ONE EVER ESCAPES MY CLAWS

1. Abolqasem Ferdowsi, *Shahnameh: The Persian Book of Kings*, trans. Dick Davis (New York: Penguin Books, 2016), pp. 154–55.

THE EIGHT-HEADED SERPENT OF KOSHI

1. Ō No Yasumaro, *Kojiki* 1.18, trans. Basil Hall Chamberlain (Tokyo: Asiatic Society of Japan, 1906), pp. 71–73 (modified). Chamberlain rendered several character names as long and sometimes awkward strings of hyphenated nouns, so for readability I have replaced three of them with the names "Rushing Raging Man," "Great Mountain Majesty," and "Heaven Shining" from the translation of *Kojiki* by Gustav Heldt (New York: Columbia University Press, 2014), pp. 25–27.

CHIEF OF THE SCALY CREATURES

1. Li Shizhen, *Bencao Gangmu*, trans. Carla Nappi, in *The Monkey and the Inkpot: Natural History and Its Transformations in Early Modern China* (Cambridge, MA: Harvard University Press, 2009), p. 56.

MY LORD BAG OF RICE

1. *The Japanese Fairy Book*, trans. Yei Theodora Ozaki (New York: P. Dutton and Company, 1908), pp. 1–11.

THE FISHERMAN AND THE DRAGON PRINCESS

1. *The Japanese Fairy Book*, trans. Yei Theodora Ozaki (New York: P. Dutton and Company, 1908), pp. 26–42.
2. In Japanese folklore, ghosts are depicted without legs or feet.

STRANGE, YET NOW A NEIGHBOUR TO US

1. Anonymous, *A Discourse Relating a Strange and Monstrous Serpent or Dragon* (London: John Trundle, 1614).
2. Alexandra Walsham, *Providence in Early Modern England* (Oxford: Oxford Univesity Press, 1999), p. 45.
3. Here the pamphlet printed the Latin text of Lucan's *Civil War* 9.771: *Noxia serpentum est admixto sanguine pestis*. See pp. 7-10, above.

A WORLD FULL OF DRAGONS

1. Edward Topsell, *The History of Four-Footed Beasts and Serpents* (London: E. Cotes, 1658), pp. 701–16.
2. Onesicritus (ca. 360–ca. 290 BCE) was a Hellenistic historian who accompanied Alexander the Great on campaign and later wrote a history about him.
3. Chios is an island in the northern Aegean Sea off the west coast of Turkey.
4. Legends about the adventures of Alexander the Great circulated widely in the Middle Ages in Latin and vernacular languages. His encounters with dragons were often illuminated in medieval manuscripts. A cubit was a unit of measurement based on the distance between a grown man's fingertips and elbow (about eighteen inches).
5. A buckler is a small round shield, usually measuring no more than eighteen inches in diameter.
6. Maximus of Tyre (fl. late second century CE) was a Greek philosopher. A rood of land is an archaic unit of land measurement equal in length to one quarter of an acre. Since an acre with equal sides has approximately 209 feet per side, Maximus is describing a serpent slightly over fifty feet in length.
7. Several Hellenistic monarchs had the name Euregetes ("Benefactor"), so it is difficult to narrow down Topsell's temporal reference. Asclepius was the god of medicine and healing often associated with snakes. The symbol of his serpent-entwined rod remains in use today as a logo for medical institutions.

8. The "equinoctial" is the equator. Nikephoros Kallistos Xanthopoulos (ca. 1256–ca. 1335) was an ecclesiastical historian active in Byzantium in the decades around 1300.

9. Here Topsell is making reference to Augustine of Hippo's *Exposition on Psalm 148:7*. For a convenient translation of this passage, see Augustine, *Expositions on the Book of Psalms*, in *The Nicene and Post-Nicene Fathers: First Series, Volume 8* (New York: Christian Literature Company, 1888), pp. 1466–67.

10. For the story of Regulus and the dragon of the river Bagrada, see pp. 18–22, above.

11. Epidaurus was a small Greek city in the western Peloponnese.

12. A paraphrase of Augustine of Hippo's *Exposition on Psalm 148:7*. See n. 9, above.

13. The word *derkein* means "to see" in Greek.

14. Phrygia was an ancient kingdom in western Anatolia, in what is now modern Turkey.

15. The Greek philosopher Aristotle (384–322 BCE) wrote about the anatomy and habits of hundreds of species of animals.

16. The Greek author Plutarch (ca. 46–ca. 119 CE) wrote about the intelligence of animals in his *Moralia*.

17. The Ring of Gyges is a legendary magical item that makes its wearer invisible. The Greek philosopher Plato (ca. 425–348 BCE) makes reference to it in his dialogue *The Republic*.

18. Megasthenes (ca. 350–ca. 290 BCE) was a Hellenistic historian who wrote a lost description of India.

19. A stirax (now commonly, storax) is a kind of large shrub or small tree native to warm regions.

20. King Francis I ruled the kingdom of France from 1515 to 1547.

21. Conrad Gessner (1515–65) was a Swiss naturalist who wrote about zoology and botany.

22. Jerome Cardan (1501–76) was an Italian scholar with an interest in natural science.

23. Mauritius Tiberius was the emperor of Byzantium from 582 to 602.

24. Justinus Gobler (1503/4–67) was a legal scholar based in Frankfurt.

25. This story was popularized in the Roman period by Plutarch in his account of the life of Cleomenes III, who was king of Sparta from 235 to 222 BCE.

26. Scipio Africanus (236/5–183 BCE) was a much-admired Roman military commander during the time of the Second Punic War.

27. Claudius Aelianus (ca. 175–ca. 235) was a Roman author who composed a treatise entitled *On the Nature of Animals* (*De natura animalium*).

28. The legend of the enmity between dragons and elephants dates back to Pliny's *Natural History*. See pp. 23–24, above.

29. Deuteronomy 32:33.

30. Here Topsell may be referring to Heliodorus of Emesa, a fourth-century Greek author.

31. Euphorbium is a resin made from the juice of the cactus plant called euphorbia.

32. "Emmet" is an archaic word for "ant."

DWELLERS BELOW

1. Translated by Darius M. Klein with slight modifications by Scott G. Bruce from Athanasius Kircher, *Mundus subterraneus in XII libros digestus*, 2 vols. (Amsterdam: Joannem Janssonium, 1665), vol. 2, pp. 89–96.

2. See pp. 33–34, above.

3. The Sovereign Military Order of Malta was a medieval Catholic lay religious order whose members were also known as the Knights of Malta. This story of Francisco Deodato of Gozon and the dragon was repeated well into the nineteenth century in histories of the Knights of Malta.

4. Literally "bad step" in Italian.

5. Mount Pilatus is the name given to a collection of several tall mountain peaks looming over Lucerne in Switzerland.

6. Daniel 6:1–28.

7. The spring or vernal equinox happens around March 21, when the night and day are equal in length.

8. Conrad Lycosthenes (1518–61) was a scholar of Greek and Latin who published several books on omens and portents.

THE LAST AMERICAN DRAGONS

1. *Cleveland Plain Dealer* (Cleveland, OH), April 22, 1882, p. 2.
2. *Tombstone Epitaph* (Tombstone, AZ), April 26, 1890.

A LIZARDY SORT OF BEAST

1. Kenneth Grahame, "The Reluctant Dragon," in *Dream Days* (New York and London: The Bodley Head, 1898), pp. 179–245.

YOUR KINDNESS QUITE UNDRAGONS ME

1. Edith Nesbit, "The Last of the Dragons," in *Five of Us and Madeline* (London: T. Fisher Unwin, 1925), pp. 171–78.

Credits

Index

THE PENGUIN BOOK OF THE UNDEAD

Fifteen Hundred Years of Supernatural Encounters
Edited by Scott G. Bruce

Since ancient times, accounts of supernatural activity have mystified us. *The Penguin Book of the Undead* charts our relationship with spirits and apparitions over fifteen hundred years, showing the evolution in our thinking about the ability of dead souls to return to the realm of the living.

THE PENGUIN BOOK OF HELL

Edited by Scott G. Bruce

From the Hebrew Bible's shadowy realm of Sheol to twenty-first-century visions of Hell on earth, *The Penguin Book of Hell* takes us through three thousand years of eternal damnation. Drawing upon religious poetry, theological treatises, and accounts of saints' lives, this fascinating volume of hellscapes illuminates how Hell has long haunted us, in both life and death.

THE PENGUIN BOOK OF EXORCISMS

Edited by Joseph P. Laycock

Levitation. Speaking in tongues. A hateful, glowing stare. The signs of spirit possession have been documented for thousands of years and across religions and cultures. *The Penguin Book of Exorcisms* brings together the most astonishing accounts. Fifty-seven percent of Americans profess to believe in demonic possession; after reading this book, you may too.

PENGUIN CLASSICS

Ready to find your next great classic? Let us help. Visit prh.com/penguinclassics

Ready to find
your next great classic?

Let us help.

Visit prh.com/penguinclassics

PENGUIN
CLASSICS